MARK GREANEY

ARMORED

SPHERE

SPHERE

First published in the United States in 2022 by Berkley,
an imprint of Penguin Random House LLC
First published in Great Britain in 2022 by Sphere
This paperback edition published by Sphere in 2023

This work is based on 'Armored,' written by Mark Greaney
as an original play for Audible in 2021

1 3 5 7 9 10 8 6 4 2

A CIP catalogue record for this book is available from the British Library.

ISBN 978-0-7515-8358-8

Printed and bound in Great Britain by Clays Ltd, Elcograf S.p.A.

Papers used by Sphere are from well-managed forests
and other responsible sources.

Sphere
An imprint of
Little, Brown Book Group
Carmelite House
50 Victoria Embankment
London EC4Y 0DZ

An Hachette UK Company
www.hachette.co.uk

www.littlebrown.co.uk

For Trey, Kristin, and Kyle Greaney

Creer es poder. Believing is power.

CHAPTER 1

A hazy sun descended over the azure waters of the Mediterranean and shone orange across the coastline of western Beirut, the early evening glow glinting off the high-end sunglasses worn by most of the fifteen American high-threat security operators spread around the outskirts of the crowd.

The entire protection detail, minus the team's three drivers, stood in a horseshoe-shaped formation around a parking lot next to a marina and across a wide boulevard from a row of high-rise waterfront apartments. Their protectee stood at a lectern on a stage before an undulating crowd of some five hundred souls who surged and receded, both energized by and contemplative of the words of the speaker, and the shifting movements of the gathering looked like the gentle waters of the Med lapping in the slips of the marina next to them.

On the western side of the horseshoe, a pair of security officers stood just feet apart on a low wall that separated the parking lot from the docks. The men were outfitted similarly to each other, and much the same as the rest of the team: long-sleeved moisture-wicking shirts, body armor, ball caps, jeans. Athletic boots and G-Shock watches, Oakley shades and Peltor headsets.

And rifles across chests festooned with body armor, pouches for ammo, pouches for medical supplies, pouches for radios, and pouches for a myriad of backup weapons and other gear, both lethal and less-than-lethal.

It was the job of these men to meet violence with superior violence, and they stood at the ready.

The pair on the low wall were distinct from each other, however, in that one of them was well into his forties, whereas the other was still in his twenties. Their sector responsibilities included watching both the gathering itself and the boats docked in the slips of the marina behind them, and while doing this, they could also feel the energy from a small group of men standing on the outskirts of the event in the parking lot of a sketchy waterfront hotel adjacent to the rally.

This was a campaign speech, so it was no surprise protesters were there to oppose the candidate, but the malevolence from this group of fifteen or twenty men was palpable.

The people in view were the main burden to the protection detail's work, but beyond the throngs there were dark apartment windows, shadowy alleyways, and a busy thoroughfare, as well as the marina full of boats and an ocean beyond.

Danger could come from any vector; the Americans knew this well.

The older security officer didn't transmit over his radio; instead he just whispered to the man next to him, "Ain't this a shit show?"

"These things are *always* a shit show, boss."

"We need another dozen Joes to secure this scene. Panther acts like he's fuckin' bulletproof."

The younger man glanced to the protectee, passionately speaking Arabic into the microphone. Then he looked back to the dark-eyed men on the periphery. "Hope none of those jokers over there try to prove him wrong."

The older security officer chuckled at this as his eyes worked the scene. He, like his teammates, expected an attack at any moment, because it had happened before.

The Americans had arrived in Lebanon three weeks earlier to replace what was left of another executive protection detail. The first team were locals, trained well enough to deal with some threats, but they'd been nowhere close to proficient when facing a well-trained unit of combatants, which was exactly what they'd come up against in the city of Sidon. Four of the candidate's bodyguards had been killed and another five were injured, but the candidate and his wife, who always traveled with him, had miraculously survived the attack unscathed.

The candidate then made the politically questionable decision to outsource his campaign's protection to an American firm, and since then, no one had tried anything.

Yet, anyway.

The bustle of the major metropolitan city seemed to grow in the lulls of the speech pounding from the speakers set up in the crowded lot, and all the bodyguards were certain that, somewhere out there in this metropolis, another gang of assholes was planning another attempt on their principal.

The older security officer again spoke softly to the younger. "You feel it, Bravo Five?"

The young man's eyes swept right and left. "I feel it, One."

Nothing else was said between the two; their heads just scanned back and forth, their grips tightened on their weapons, and they stole the occasional glance out to sea at the setting sun. It was seven p.m. now; there was less than an hour of light left, and the bodyguards looked at the onset of nightfall with trepidation. They wanted their protectee—the team had given him the code name Panther—buttoned up in his hotel before these dangerous streets turned dark, but Panther was signing their paychecks and calling the shots.

They'd go back to the hotel when he said they'd go back to the hotel, and not a minute before.

The two men on the wall overlooking the crowd did not speak fluent Arabic, but they had heard this speech enough times in the past three weeks to register that he was wrapping it up now. Soon the cheers from supporters grew into a crescendo as the silver-haired man pumped his fist into the air, his attractive, middle-aged wife shifting in her seat on the dais behind him.

She was more than ready to go; this, both men could tell.

Panther beckoned his wife forward, clasped his hand in hers, and raised it over their heads. The crowd applauded, the shadowy figures on the fringes stood and stared, and the two security men leaned a little closer to each other.

The older man said, "Hey, kid. Check Tabby out. Looks like she'd rather be anywhere else on Earth."

The younger man replied while still surveying the grim faces on the other side of the parking lot. "Six months ago that lady up there was livin' high on the hog in Paris. If her husband gets elected president of Lebanon, her whole world's gonna go bananas, and she knows it."

"Think he's got a shot?"

"My job is to make sure he doesn't *get* shot."

"Roger that. You think we're done for the day after this? Nothing else on the schedule, but—"

"But Panther likes to call audibles. There's still some daylight. Bet he makes one more stop at a hookah bar or a mini-mall before packin' it in."

"I hope you're wrong. My feet hurt."

"Ditto."

And then the candidate and his wife headed for the steps down from the dais to the parking lot. Just behind them, the agent in charge of the American security team moved in sync with the couple, and he spoke into his mic at the same time.

The pair on the wall heard his call through their headsets. "Alpha One to all call signs. We're movin'. I want double diamond on Panther all the way back to the motorcade. Drivers, fire 'em up. Look alive, boys."

The older man jumped down from the low wall, and the younger man followed him. The older man said, "We're on rear security."

"Roger that, One."

The crowd surged forward as the entourage made for the three SUVs just a few dozen yards away.

Alpha One put his hand on the principal's shoulder as he barked into his mic at his men on point. "Push 'em back, Charlie team. Push 'em back. We ain't set for no meet-and-greet."

4

Bravo Five heard a quick reply from Charlie One, at the front of the diamond-shaped formation. "Roger that. *Imshi! Imshi!*"

The candidate and his wife made it to the sidewalk, and local police held most of the crowd inside the gated parking lot so the VIP could get clear of the scene, but the candidate stopped abruptly and turned to Alpha One. Bravo Five watched from twenty yards back, still making his way through the locals, but his headset told him what was going on.

"This is Alpha Actual, all teams hold. Panther wants to talk to me a minute."

Bravo One shouldered up to his junior teammate. "You called it, kid. Panther ain't ready to go back to the hotel."

"Always another hand to shake, I guess."

Alpha One's voice came back over the net. "All call signs, listen up. Panther wants to take a ride down to the promenade for some glad-handing, but Tabby ain't feeling it. I'll take the lead in Alpha Vic. Charlie One, you're the limo, take Panther in Charlie Vic. Bravo One, take Tabby along with Bravos Five and Six in the Suburban. Trail the limo and the lead vic till we turn off on Saeb Salam, then get her back to the Phoenicia. The other three Joes on Bravo team can load up in the Yukon with Alpha to give us more eyes at the next stop."

Bravo One keyed his radio. "Bravo One copies all." Then he nodded to Bravo Five. "Duff, you're with me."

"On you, boss."

CHAPTER 2

They met the woman they'd given the call sign of Tabby at the rear passenger-side door of a white Chevy Suburban, and Bravo Five opened the door for her. "Madame, la banquette arrière, s'il vous plaît."

The woman barely looked his way as she climbed in, and then immediately Bravo One followed her into the back, but as he passed Five at the door, he whispered, "Love it when you talk all sexy."

"Just for you, boss," he replied as he shut the two of them inside the unarmored vehicle.

Bravo Five climbed into the front passenger seat and looked over to Bravo Six, a thirty-eight-year-old security driver who kept his focus on the rear of the Charlie vehicle in front of him, a black armored Range Rover and also the "limo," meaning the vehicle transporting the principal.

The driver said, "Keep your eyes open, Duff, least till we separate from the others. Nobody wants to kill Tabby, so we're good as soon as we leave the motorcade."

Duff elbowed the man in the arm, then motioned to the woman in the back seat with a jerk of his thumb.

Softly, the driver said, "Dude, she don't speak a lick of English, you know that."

6

Duff sighed as he rolled down his window and unfastened his rifle from its two-point sling, giving him more mobility to move the weapon around the front seat if threats arose.

Now Bravo One leaned up between the seats to speak to the driver. "You heard Alpha One, Larry. Trail them till they turn onto Saeb Salam, and then we'll stay on General de Gaulle all the way up the coast to the hotel."

"*Hate* these hasty movements, boss. Lot of shit that can go south if we haven't planned out the route beforehand."

"We'll be fine, Larry."

As the Suburban began following the other two vehicles on the boulevard, Alpha One's voice came over the team's headsets again. "Drivers, keep it tight. Scan oncoming and intersections in advance. All shooters, I want your windows down and weapons at the low ready. If you're riding shotgun, you've got traffic duty. Nobody gets into the motorcade."

The detail had conducted over one hundred movements in the three weeks they'd been in-country; this was nothing new for any of them.

Alpha One added, "Muscle through the reds, boys. All eyes open."

The driver, Bravo Six, did not divert his attention from the road ahead, but he spoke to the man next to him. "Hey, Five. When Tabby's buttoned up in the suite, can you cover my watch for an hour? Gotta run down to the souk, grab a souvenir for the old lady."

Duff kept his head at the window, swiveling it back and forth as he took in everyone in sight, hunting for pre-attack indicators that his brain had been trained to register almost subconsciously. But without hesitation he said, "Sure, Larry. No worries."

Bravo One sat in back with Tabby, who was now on her phone and speaking French animatedly, but he'd caught the exchange between the two men in the front seat. He leaned between the seats again and looked at the driver. "What you gonna get her? An 'I Heart Hezbollah' T-shirt?"

The men all laughed while they focused on the boulevard outside the vehicle. Larry said, "She wants a damn rug, but how the hell am I gonna get a rug in my kit bag? She thinks I'm over here traveling around with an empty steamer trunk or some shit."

Bravo One said, "I bought me a hajji carpet in Iraq. Got home and the motherfucker fell apart when I unrolled it. Straight-up turned to dust. One last kick in the dick from that shit hole."

Alpha One's clipped and professional voice entered their ears once more, interrupting the conversation. "Approaching first intersection. Got some protest signs on the corner. Stay frosty."

Bravo One said, "He's right, Duff. I saw some shitheads holding pro-government campaign banners on the way in. If they're still up here on the right, make sure they're behavin'."

Duff's scan was purposeful and methodical. Finally, he said, "Got 'em. They're minding their manners."

It was quiet on the drive for the next minute, other than Tabby's phone conversation in the back seat.

Larry finally said, "Thanks for taking my watch, Duff. You want me to grab your daughter a toy or something? They probably have dolls and shit."

Still examining his sector, he said, "Already picked up a gift for Mandy. If you see something for a baby . . . something blue, I guess, you could grab that. Pay you back."

"Whose baby?"

Duff replied without diverting his attention from the street. "Mine. Nichole's preggo. Again. Boy this time. Found out last night."

Bravo One was still between the seats and in earshot. "Kid, how the fuck did *that* happen? You haven't been home long enough to take your boots off since last Christmas."

"Kept my boots on, I guess."

Bravo Six kept the Suburban twenty yards behind the limo as they crossed an intersection. As he drove, he said, "Or else your baby's gonna look like the UPS driver."

"You're hilarious."

Bravo One slapped Duffy on the back. "Congrats, Duff. That's awesome." Quickly, however, he saw something in the traffic and turned his attention to the driver. "Larry, squeeze that dude out."

A middle-aged man on a low-end motorbike was close on their right, speeding up to get into the three-SUV motorcade's center lane.

"Roger," Larry said. "Fucker's tryin' to merge his way in."

Duff leaned out his window. "I got it." Waving his hand up and down at the motorcyclist, he shouted, *"Imshi! Imshi!"*

The biker shook a fist back at Duff, but he quickly noticed the buttstock of the rifle held by the Westerner with the headset and sunglasses, and he began slowing, giving up his attempt to change lanes.

Duffy quickly put a hand to his chest and nodded to the man. "Shukran. Shukran, sadiqi."

Inside the Suburban, Bravo Six clenched the wheel tightly. "Eat a dick, asshole."

Duff's attention had returned to the road ahead. "Just a dude tryin' to get home from work. We're the assholes around here, Larry."

The motorcycle fell in behind the white Suburban at the rear of the convoy, then made a left down a side street.

Alpha One came over the net moments later. "Bravo Actual, Alpha One. We're turning off ahead. Take this up the coast, and you'll be at the hotel in one-five mikes."

In the back seat Bravo clicked his radio. "One copies." And then, to Larry, he motioned ahead with a finger. "Watch this intersection up here at the turn, they're gonna have to slow for the left and—"

Larry squinted at something through the windshield, then shouted over his superior. "That southbound bus up ahead is *movin'*!"

As soon he said this, Alpha One's voice, amped up and agitated, came back over Bravo team's headsets. "Watch the bus! Watch the bus!"

Duff tallied a white passenger bus racing through oncoming traffic, approaching the motorcade at high speed.

"He's goin' for the limo!" Duff shouted. He hefted his rifle and began swinging to get it outside the vehicle, though he had no shot at the port-side bus from the starboard side of the SUV.

Duff saw it all through the windshield now, as if in slow motion. The bus sideswiped a tiny red two-door as it raced through oncoming traffic, then swerved into the motorcade's lane just behind Alpha team's big gray Yukon and in front of the black Range Rover with the candidate and Charlie team inside.

And then, just as Duff decided to shoot through the windshield at the advancing threat, the bus slammed head-on into the limo, not thirty-five yards in front of him.

Larry stood on his brakes because he'd been through some shit in his time in high-risk civilian contracting, and he knew what was coming next.

With a blinding flash, the entire intersection whited out, and then a massive fireball erupted over the limo and bus.

Shrapnel jetted in all directions.

Duff saw the windshield in front of him spiderweb as it was pelted by debris, but he heard nothing apart from the high-pitched squeal of eardrums under assault. He felt specks of glass tear into his face and crack his sunglasses, and the shock wave of the blast slammed him back hard against the headrest.

His retinas were flared from the flash, his hearing was temporarily nonexistent, but he felt the shaking and jolting of the vehicle as wreckage and rubble rained down onto them from the sky.

CHAPTER 3

The ringing stopped, and all was silent. Duff found himself staring down between his knee pads at the floorboard, his eyes blurry from the biting irritants of smoke and dust and grit. He shook his head to clear it, threw his damaged Oakleys on the floorboard, and looked back up. He didn't know if it had been three seconds since the blast or thirty, but eventually the haze both in his head and in the Suburban cleared enough for him to see. Larry was there behind the wheel, awake if not completely alert. Blood ran from his bearded face, and his hands were in his lap, but he, too, was looking around, fighting to get his head back into the game.

Duff glanced behind him and found Bravo One coughing up black phlegm and rubbing dust from under his shades, but he appeared to have no major injuries. Tabby had a cut at her hairline that bled down her face, and her eyes were unfixed as if she were in shock.

Only now did Duff recover from the effects of the concussion enough to remember what had just occurred, and he focused his attention out the damaged front windshield. He saw movement through the heavy smoke and dust, and immediately he shouted to the other men in the Chevy with him.

"Contact front!" He pressed his mic button. "Alpha! Contact, your right. A truckload of shooters east side! I . . . I don't have a shot from here!"

To his driver he shouted, "Move up, Larry!"

Alpha One's voice came over his headset immediately after, barely audible through the ringing in Duff's ears. Long gone was his tough-but-cool radio voice. Now the older man sounded utterly frantic. "Back! Back! Back!"

Multiple Kalashnikov rifles opened up on the street ahead; the Alpha Yukon went into reverse, then rocketed back a few feet as their driver desperately tried to get away.

"No!" Alpha One screamed, and then the net went quiet as the Yukon crashed into the front of the burning wreckage, AKs still pouring rounds into Alpha's vehicle.

To the driver, Duff shouted, "Advance so I can engage!"

Larry suddenly jolted back into action suddenly; he stomped on the gas, and the big SUV lurched forward.

Behind Duff, Bravo One shouted, both into his mic and for the two men in the front of the SUV: "Second contact, rooftop, third floor building, right side! Engaging!" Bravo One fired a few rounds out the window directly behind Duff, then shouted, "Shit! RPG! East!"

A rocket-propelled grenade streaked into the intersection ahead of a gray smoke trail and detonated against the already disabled Alpha vehicle forty yards in front of the three men and one woman in Bravo. Fresh shrapnel from the explosion ripped into the Suburban, and more windshield glass peppered Duff's face. Larry stomped on his brakes; tires squealed, more audible now as the effects of the initial explosion lessened in Duff's ears.

Both Bravo One and Duff fired at the rooftop on their right, dumping round after round towards a group of men there who were hurriedly aiming a second RPG. Hot ejected brass bounced around the inside of the SUV as the Americans' guns bucked and smoked.

Their protectee held her ears and screamed.

In the front seat, Duff ran his rifle empty. "Reloading!"

Bravo One slowed his fire but continued expending rounds. "Covering! We've got to go for Panther!"

Bravo Six screamed now from behind the wheel. "Look at the fuckin' limo!" It was just twenty yards in front of them at a 45-degree angle in the street. Fully engulfed in flames and nearly unrecognizable as an SUV, let alone a Range Rover, with the similarly deformed bus up against it. "Nobody could live through that shit! Alpha's dead, too! It's just us!"

Behind Larry, Tabby began to wail anew as she saw her husband's burning car just ahead.

Despite Bravo Six's words, One shouted again while he kept firing. "We're goin' for Panther!"

Larry protested, "We've got Tabby!"

"Tabby's not the principal!"

"Yeah, well, the principal's fuckin' *dead*!"

Duff engaged the bolt release of his rifle, chambering a round with a loud click. "I'm up!"

"Reloading!" Bravo One announced. As he reloaded his rifle, he said, "Listen up, Duffy. We keep the Suburban back here in case those disabled vics' gas tanks haven't detonated yet."

Duff fired twice out the window at a target on the other side of the burning wreckage. The target's head ducked back down, but Duff didn't think he'd hit him. "Roger."

One continued: "You and me. We bail out, I cover, you locate and assess the principal. If Panther's alive, you get him back here to Bravo Vic. Copy?"

"Copy!"

Larry screamed again. "No! Fuck that shit! There's a dozen gunners and RPGs. We gotta fuckin' *roll*, man!"

Bravo One released his bolt back onto a round from a fresh magazine. "I'm up! Larry, sit tight and watch Tabby. Duff . . . fifty feet to the limo. Run hard! You *got* this! Now!"

Simultaneously, both passenger-side doors of the Chevy opened, and the two men leapt out amid the persistent chatter of AK fire. They both fired their weapons, Duff at men in the back of a truck near the now-burning Alpha vehicle in the front of the motorcade, and One at men with rifles on the rooftop to the east.

Duff began sprinting towards the fiery wreckage as he kept shooting. He'd made it less than halfway through the thick smoke in the street to the limo when he heard his team leader bark over the net. "More RPGs on the east rooftop!"

Another streaking rocket raced ten feet over Duff's head and slammed into a storefront on the far side of the boulevard.

Duff pressed on, one man against an unknown number, only partially shielded by the burning debris of two vehicles full of his friends.

He glanced inside the limo, and he saw what he needed to see. Then he looked ahead at the gray Yukon. Dropping to a knee to hammer a fresh mag into his M4, he triggered his mic. "No survivors here or in Alpha Vic. Principal confirmed KIA. They're all gone, boss."

Bravo ceased fire only to respond. "Roger that. Get back here and watch out for—"

A single report rang out above the raging gunfire, louder than the rest.

Duff knew the sound of a powerful sniper rifle when he heard it.

When he'd charged his weapon again, he turned and began running back to his vehicle. Larry's voice cracked over Duff's headset. "Bravo One's down! He's on my fuckin' hood! His face is gone, man!"

Duff had pushed back through the smoke, and now he could see the white Suburban. Bravo One was on his back, his arms outstretched and his legs hanging off the side over the right front tire. His weapon lay in the street, and blood and tissue dripped from the hood down to the pavement.

Duff was twenty-five feet away when he went down to a knee, spun back to the rooftop, and fired his rifle one-handed while clicking the push-to-talk button on his chest. "Come to me, Larry! I'm covering."

Over his outgoing gunfire he couldn't hear if the Bravo vehicle was, indeed, heading to him, but he expended an entire magazine at targets, killing one man with a head-shot and forcing others to cover before looking over his shoulder to find out.

Larry skidded to a stop just feet away and then leaned over to open the front passenger door. The team leader's body still lay splayed and faceup on the hood, and Duff left it there as he spun around and dove inside the SUV.

Before he even reached to close the door behind him, he screamed, "Go! Go! Go!"

Larry stomped hard on the gas, jacked the wheel to the right to avoid the burning wreckage, and shot towards the truck with the armed men. Bravo One's body rocked back and forth on the hood on Duff's side of the vehicle, his legs still dangling.

The woman in the back of the Suburban continued to scream. She shouted something in French and then Arabic, but Duff was too busy reloading his weapon to pay attention. The driver pulled his Beretta sidearm and began firing through his spiderwebbed driver's-side window towards the truck with the Kalashnikov shooters as he passed it on the left. Many were dead, but a few returned ineffective fire.

When he had reloaded again, Duff shouted, "I'm up! Gotta get Ken off the hood!"

Duff raised both his boots up over the dash, then slammed them forward, knocking out the remaining windshield glass on the first attempt. He reached out, grabbed Bravo One by his right arm, and heaved him inside the vehicle as Larry made a hard right turn that would take them away from the coast and deeper into the heart of Beirut.

Duff was trained to render aid to gunshot wound victims, but Bravo One had caught a large round from a high-powered rifle right through the bridge of his nose, and there was nothing anyone could do for him. Still, Duff spoke to him. "Boss! Boss! Ken?"

Larry shouted, "Look at him, Duff! They smoked his ass! They're all dead but us! Shit! Where are we even fuckin' going?"

"Just keep driving!"

Duff turned around to check on Tabby again, but when he did so, he looked out the shot-out rear window. Four black pickup trucks were behind them and closing.

Larry saw them in his rearview at the same time. "Aw, shit, bro! Enemy vics on our ass! What are we gonna do?"

Duff was calmer than his driver. He began removing the bloody chest rig off his team leader, who now lay dead across his lap. He said, "I'll cover Tabby with Ken's armor, engage out the rear window, try to keep the pursuers back, and call this in to the ops center. You just drive and report anything you see."

Duff's calm voice helped keep Larry just on this side of the threshold of panic. Bravo Six nodded, sweat dripping from his face. "Yeah, yeah, okay."

It took Duff several seconds to get Ken's armor off, and several more to scoot out from under him and crawl into the back. Once there, he forced Tabby down to the floorboard and put the armor over and around her body as best he could. Then he reached to the front seat and retrieved his rifle.

Cracks of AK fire from the pursuing vehicles caused him to duck lower in the back seat as he yanked the M4 to him, changed channels on his radio, and clicked the transmit button.

"Ops Center! Ops Center! Bravo Five. We are taking fire, time now! Panther is KIA. Repeat, Panther KIA. BNR. Request immediate QRF and CASEVAC to the intersection of Saeb Salam and Habib Abi Chahla!"

Another burst of fire from behind, and then Larry shouted from the front. "Why the fuck they even chasin' *us*? Panther's dead!"

CHAPTER 4

A woman's urgent but professional voice came over Duff's headset a moment later. "Bravo Five, Ops Center copies all. Understand Panther KIA and body not recovered. I have you geolocated on Gregorius Haddad, moving east."

"That's affirm. We have Tabby and are en route to rally point . . . uh . . . break." He called to Larry in the front. "Can we make it to Delta?"

"Ain't no fuckin' *way* we're makin' Delta!"

Duff's voice retained its own professionalism. "Ops Center, we're shootin' for RP Echo. Be advised, hostiles remain in close pursuit at this time, over."

"Understand you are evasive, time now. Relay status of Alpha, when able."

"Alpha, Charlie, and three Bravo elements down in primary engagement zone. Say again, *all* down on the X." Duff spit some blood that had dripped into his mouth from a glass cut to his nose, then keyed his mic again. "Bravo Actual is with me and KIA. Bravo Six is with me and good to go. I think we're the last two. How copy?"

"I *ain't* good to go! I'm fucked. We're *all* fucked!" Panic again threatened to overtake the Bravo driver.

"Calm down, Larry."

The woman from the operations center came back over the radio. "Solid copy, Bravo Six. Stand by for ETA on QRF to rally point Echo."

Tabby began wailing even louder now, and after Larry made a hard left down a two-lane street in the business district, he dialed the vehicle radio to the operations center channel so he could hear the back-and-forth between Duff and Ops Center in case Duff was killed and he needed to communicate with HQ.

Then he shouted to Duff, "Shut her ass up so I can think!"

Duff leaned down to Tabby. "Calmez vous! Calmez vous, s'il vous plaît, Madame! Vous etes bien."

He popped his head back up, aimed his M4 at the closest truck behind him, and fired several shots. Return fire came immediately, and he ducked back down.

"What do you see back there, bro?" Larry shouted.

"I've got three technicals on our ass. Maybe eight . . . ten enemy, all with AKs. Thought I counted four vics in pursuit a minute ago, before we made that turn. Are we clear ahead?"

"Right now we are, but there are a shitload of intersections coming up. The missing tech could be moving parallel, trying to flank us."

"Watch out for him."

"No shit."

Soon the operations center came back over Duff's headset. "Bravo Five, Ops Center. QRF en route. ETA rally point Echo is thirteen mikes. Say again, one-three mikes."

Duff shook his head, fired another round at each of the pickups, then responded. "Negative, Ops Center, requesting expedited QRF! Mobile hostiles in pursuit. We will be at the RP in three to five mikes and seriously outgunned."

"Understood, Bravo Five. Uh . . . recommend you attempt to disengage from hostiles."

Larry shouted, not over the radio but to Duff. "Is she for real? Tell these motherfuckers to disengage from *us*!"

Duff rolled his eyes as he responded over the net. "Doin' our best here, Ops Center. It's just me and Larry." He fired another short burst, aware now that he needed to conserve ammo.

There was a brief delay before the ops center responded. "Bravo Five, be advised. Tabby is *not* your principal. At your discretion, you can separate from Tabby and continue to the RP."

For the first time since the limo blew up, Larry did not shout. Instead, he muttered, "What's she talkin' about?"

Duff was similarly confused. "Ops Center, Bravo Five. Say again your last."

There was no response, but soon Larry began shouting once again. "Tally on the missing technical! He's ahead of us! Next intersection! Get your heads down back there!"

Duff lay flat on the seat, his rifle cradled in his arm as he pushed his hand down on the armor covering Tabby. He clicked the transmit key again with his free hand. "Ops Center, Ops Center. Did not copy your last."

Gunfire crackled close, outside the Suburban, as Larry raced past the flanking pickup. Duff rolled onto his side, then his stomach, then checked Tabby under the armor and found her still hysterical but uninjured. He started to push himself up to his knees to continue firing out the rear window, but he toppled to his right, hard into the driver's-side rear door, as the Bravo vehicle swerved violently to his left.

"Fuck, Larry! Let me know when you're maneuvering like that. I can't watch the road while I'm back here—"

He felt the vehicle lurch to the right now, and he forced himself up to his knees and looked into the front seat. Larry's eyes were open but unfixed; his seat belt kept his torso up, but his bloody head hung to the side. Bits of Larry's brain matter had splattered across the dashboard and the body of Bravo One, who was crumpled in the front passenger seat next to them.

Duff realized in an instant that he and his protectee were in the back seat of a Suburban racing at sixty miles an hour down a busy street with a dead man at the wheel. He threw his entire body weight onto Tabby, pressing the canvas-covered armor down tight onto her and fixing her to the floorboard, and he covered his head with his arms.

Duff couldn't see what was happening, but he sure as hell could feel it. The big SUV dealt a glancing blow to one car, then another, then bounced up onto a curb and crashed hard, head-on, into an only partially yielding object. Duff was thrown against the rear of the front seats, then came to rest on top of Ken's armor and Tabby's body. It felt to Duff as if they'd slammed into a parked car, and when he raised his head to look around, he could see that they'd come to rest in a lot, and the crumpled hood of the Suburban was now up against the rear of a panel truck.

Steam hissed from the radiator. Broken glass jingled as Duff slowly sat back up, dazed. Dust and smoke hung thick in the air.

For the second time in less than five minutes, he fought disorientation as he wiped blood from his face. He shook his head to clear it, then looked down at Tabby, pulling off the armor. "You . . . okay? Uh, I mean, vous etes bien, Madame?"

She pushed off the armor, as well, and looked up at him. "I . . . I am fine."

His brain was still in a fog; he hadn't even checked behind him to see the disposition of the men trying to kill them. But still, he remarked, "English? You speak—"

Duff's cell phone began chirping in his pocket. He looked out the rear window and saw four black pickups parked close together on the street. There was no other traffic; the locals had all wisely cleared out. He could see armed men pouring out of the vehicles and then kneeling behind the trucks.

The phone kept chirping, and suddenly it filled him with hope. Not hope about his predicament, but hope that he'd be able to speak to his wife just one last time. He pulled it from a pouch and pressed the speaker button so he didn't have to hold it up to his ringing ear. His voice was soft. "Nikki?"

But a man's voice replied, speaking quickly and with authority. "Listen up, Duffy. This is the United Defense Operational theater controller. Our contract was with Panther, and Panther *only*. He's out of play, so we ain't gettin' paid for that shit you're in the middle of right now. We don't know why they're gunning for Tabby, but that's not our problem. If you drop her off and keep going, they won't pursue you."

Duff did not reply. He only looked at the Lebanese woman as she crawled off the floorboard and sat next to him. Her graying auburn hair was a mess.

Ops Command continued. "You hear me? Leave Tabby on the street, then you and Larry get your asses out of there! Hello? Duff? C'mon, man! Get rid of her and you'll make it out of this bullshit alive!"

Duff coughed in the growing smoke before speaking. Finally he said, "OPSCON, your signal is broken. Negative copy on your last."

"Dammit, Duffy, you heard me! Dump that bitch in the road and—"

Duff hung up the phone and stuck it back in a pouch, then clicked the transmitter on his radio again to communicate with the woman at the operations center. His voice was unsure, still shaken by the order to leave Tabby to die at the hands of terrorists. "Ops Center, this is Bravo Five. Be advised, Bravo Six is KIA. Our vic is inoperable at this time. Filling with smoke. I see . . . I see multiple armed combatants dismounted, and we've got no way to maneuver. It's just me and Tabby, and we're about to get overrun."

The woman did not hide her concern, but she remained professional. "Understood, Bravo Six is KIA. Vehicle inop. Stand by for QRF ETA, your poz."

Duff gave a tired and stressed little chuckle now. "Lot of guns comin' this way. If the QRF is more than a minute out . . . might as well tell 'em to knock off for lunch."

"Expediting as able, Bravo Five. Good luck to you."

Now the American in the broken-down Suburban looked over at Tabby. "How much . . . how much did you understand from that phone call?"

She coughed, then said, "Your people want you to leave me behind."

Duff nodded, looked through the shot-out back window. After a moment of silence, he hefted his rifle, dropped the magazine to check his ammo, then reseated it. He said, "That's not happenin'. We're in this together, ma'am."

Before Tabby could respond, a voice came from behind in the street. In English, shouted by a man behind one of the pickups. "My friends! My friends! We only want the woman! Send her out to us and you will live!"

CHAPTER 5

Tabby crouched down lower in her seat. "What are we going to do?"

"Let me think." Duff looked around him; it was getting harder to see with the steam and smoke building. "This is a good truck. I can probably get the engine to turn over. Tires might be shot to shit, but they're run-flats. Maybe I can make it a hundred yards before this thing falls apart on us." In truth, he didn't think much of his chances, but he saw no alternatives.

He reached up into the front seat, unbuckled the driver's body, and struggled to move it, along with twenty pounds of body armor and other gear, out of the seat.

Softly he said, "I'm sorry, Larry." He heaved the driver on top of Bravo One.

While he worked on this, Tabby asked, "What can I do?"

Duff coughed in the smoke. "Behind your seat is a black case. Keep your head down, but reach over and grab it."

Now Duff crawled up into the driver's seat, sat down in smeared blood from Larry's head wound, and noted that the smoke seemed to be pouring up from the floorboard now. There was no windshield in front of him, and the hood was crumpled. The hissing steam had stopped—probably, Duff decided, because the radiator had run dry.

"The case is open," Tabby said. "What now?"

"See the two green canisters that say 'M18 Smoke Red'? Pass those up."

Another shout from the man behind the pickup. "You have no other choice, my friends. We will attack if you do not give her to us."

Duff realized the terrorists had no idea how many armed men were alive in the truck. This was buying him a few seconds' time, but it wouldn't slow them down for long.

Tabby handed the two canisters up to Duff, who was in the process of clicking himself into the seat belt. He said, "Here's what we're gonna do. I'm going to pop both smokes and toss them in the rear of this vehicle. Then I'll reverse out of here, pedal to the floor. We won't be able to see shit, but neither will they when we drive past them."

Tabby was alarmed. "We're going to just drive away?"

"We're gonna try, anyway. I'll fire my pistol out both windows as we go, maybe keep some heads down as we pass."

"But you won't be able to see!"

"It's the only plan I got, lady. Get that body armor over you and get down."

She did so, but when she was covered, she said, "Monsieur. Thank you."

"Let's not get ahead of ourselves, I haven't done shit yet."

A new shout from behind now. "Ten seconds and we open fire!"

Duff pulled the pins on both smoke grenades and tossed them over his shoulder, past Tabby and into the very back of the SUV. Almost instantly the hissing devices began spewing opaque dark red smoke out all the broken windows and bullet holes in the big vehicle. He turned the key and slammed his foot on the gas, the Chevy turned over roughly, and then he yanked it into reverse.

Tires squealed and smoked for a moment as the Bravo team vehicle struggled to break free of the truck it had rear-ended, but then it jolted backwards.

AK fire erupted immediately; the sound of metal tearing through metal was almost as loud as the reports from the gunshots themselves. Duff didn't look behind him, he just floored it backwards in the general direction of the pickups, and he held the wheel steady with one hand while he drew the SIG Sauer pistol from his belt holster with the other.

He imagined he looked like a rocket trailing red smoke as he reversed up the street, gaining speed with every yard.

The Suburban slammed into the front left quarter panel of one of the pickups, spinning it and knocking the men using it as cover to the ground, and as soon as he felt the impact, Duff opened fire out the passenger-side window with his handgun. He could see nothing at all save for red smoke, but he fired and fired, desperate to suppress any return fire coming his way.

They were racing backwards up the Beirut street, and Duff had fired off half of his sixteen rounds when a fresh volley of automatic fire blasted on his left.

He swung his gun back across his body, ready to fire into the swirling red smoke and out his driver's-side window to subdue the threat there, but before he could squeeze off a round, he felt a blow below his left knee.

Sharp pain fired through his body like a lightning bolt.

Duff screamed; his left hand released the steering wheel and his right dropped the pistol, and he clutched at the source of the agony.

Hot blood oozed through his fingers, and sharp bone pressed into the meat of his hand.

He screamed again, shouted every obscenity that came to mind.

With the pain came a loss of sense of time and distance; he didn't know if he'd driven in reverse fifty yards or five hundred, but eventually the racing Suburban began crashing left and right into parked cars. Then it bounced up what felt to be steps, slamming its rear tires against concrete and crumpling the back bumper. It lost momentum in all this, so when the final crash came, it was among the gentlest of the dozen or so impacts Duff had felt in the past few minutes.

He found himself at rest finally, the sound of the smoke canisters and the death throes of the Suburban's shot-up engine still audible over his ringing ears.

The red smoke began to clear, and Duff looked out the window through eyes filled with tears of agony. The Suburban had wrecked out on the concrete steps heading up to a large shopping center. All around, passersby had run for cover, terrified of the gunfire and the squealing vehicles in this normally peaceful district.

Duff still clutched his wrecked knee. He'd caught a 7.62 round from a Kalashnikov, he was certain, and he had no idea if he could put any weight on the limb at all or if the bones were all shattered, rendering the leg useless.

And then he saw the fire. Flames began licking up from under the bent hood in front of him.

He called out to Tabby, "You okay?" Fresh panic was welling inside him now as he unfastened his seat belt.

"Yes, I am okay. Are you hurt?" She'd obviously heard him screaming and cussing.

"We're on fire. Get out of the truck. Left side."

Duff let go of his shattered leg, unfastened his seat belt, then grabbed his pistol off the floorboard with a hand slick with blood. He reached for the door latch. A moment later he fell out onto the steps at the entrance to the shopping center, and Tabby staggered over and helped him to his feet. There was no sign of the pickup trucks just now, but Duff knew he and his protectee couldn't wait around here for help.

"We've got to move."

Tabby put his left arm over her shoulders, and the two of them slowly made their way to the entrance to the building.

Men and women looked on in astonishment, many of them still crouched or prone on the ground.

Duff found himself able to walk with Tabby's help, more or less, but the pain was excruciating, and he could tell by both look and feel that blood loss was going to be a problem very soon. The round seemed to have missed the arteries and veins running behind the knee, but he knew that moving around with broken bones so close to all the fragile plumbing in his leg was a recipe for disaster. With each shuffled step, a shard of bone could pierce his femoral, and that would be that.

But he kept going, sweat and tears in his eyes making it hard to see as they moved through the shopping center.

All eyes were on them, of course, and soon a security guard began to approach, but when the man spoke in Arabic, Duff raised his pistol in his face.

Instantly Tabby pushed the gun down. "Stop it! He only asked if you need help."

Tabby then spoke with the man; the exchange lasted just a few seconds, and then the guard let them pass while he went running off in the direction of the crashed Suburban. This confused Duff, but he was in too much pain to think about it for long.

They continued on until they made it into an employees-only hallway. Here Duff stopped, pulled a tourniquet from the medical pouch on his chest rig, and cinched it hard around his upper leg, just below his groin. He screamed in pain again.

He realized quickly he couldn't make it tight enough on his own without lying down and working on it for a while, and he didn't think he could take the time to do that with armed men actively hunting for him and his protectee. As applied, the tourniquet would only slow blood loss, not stop it, and he told himself he would continue to bleed as long as he was up and mobile.

But he had to stay up and mobile until he got Tabby out of danger.

He thought of his wife, Nichole; of his daughter, Amanda; and the son who would not be born for another six months.

They had decided to call him Harry, after Duff's deceased father.

He kept moving, but only with Tabby's assistance.

A minute later he could feel the blood loss affecting his brain. His thoughts were muddy, fatigue had set in, and his movements were unsure. He pushed open a rear door to a loading area and found himself in front of several parked cars. Still holding his pistol in his bloody hand, he waved it left and right, scanning for targets in the low light of the early evening.

He couldn't decide what to do, but Tabby came to his aid yet again. "There! That bread truck. There is no door on the side, and the engine is running."

Duff didn't have to be told twice. They started heading for it, and along the way he said, "You're gonna have to drive."

"Me? Drive?"

He held his bloody pistol up to her, offering her the grip. "Shoot or drive. What are you better at?"

She thought a moment. "Oui, monsieur. I will drive."

CHAPTER 6

As they moved slowly towards the truck, Tabby said, "We have to take you to a doctor."

Duff shook his head. Sweat flew from his trim beard. "No, we're getting you somewhere safe." He turned and looked at her. "Where is safe?" He knew he couldn't take her to United Defense's HQ in Beirut; they'd just push her out the door for the terrorists.

Tabby had the answer. "Hospital Wardieh. It is not far. It's in a sector of town where my husband is . . . *was* . . . very popular, and the director of the facility is a donor to our campaign. They have good security there, and excellent doctors for you."

They reached the passenger door of the truck now. "Sold."

Tabby helped Duff into the seat, then rushed around to the other side of the delivery vehicle.

She ground the gears. It quickly became clear that the woman wasn't much of a driver and had never driven a big, unwieldy vehicle like the one she operated now. Still, she managed to get it out of the shopping center loading area and into the busy street while Duff did his best to conduct a 360-degree scan of the entire area.

His vision narrowed as he did so; he used his left hand to press down on the poorly applied tourniquet in his crotch, and he wished like hell he had a free hand to pull his cell phone out and call his wife back home in Virginia just one last time, because he didn't think he was going to make it.

Once they were on the road and heading to the northwest, Tabby looked to Duff. "How do you feel?"

"Like I look. Watch the road, s'il vous plaît."

She glanced back out the windshield but soon turned again to the young American.

"My husband. Are you certain . . . *how* can you be certain he is dead?"

Duff winced, both from pain and from the discomfort of delivering the bad news. "I'm sorry. He's gone. Maybe we should just leave it at that."

She didn't press. Instead, she looked down at his leg. "How bad is that?"

Duff shrugged. "It's bad. Blood loss is the big danger. If I fall asleep, I won't be waking up."

Tabby drove faster. "Let us talk. It will take your mind off the pain and keep you awake."

Duff didn't think there was a conversation he could have with anyone on Earth right now that would help him forget about the misery he was in, but he nodded anyway, then tried to think of something to say.

"The guard. In the shopping center. What did you say that made him back off like that?"

"I asked him to look at me. Told him I knew he knew who I was. Everyone in Beirut knows who I am."

Duff nodded distantly. "How did you know he was a fan?"

"I did not know. I knew only that he would either be a supporter of my husband or an enemy of my husband. If he was a supporter, he would let us pass. If he was an enemy . . ." She paused. "Then I wanted to watch you shoot him."

Duff nodded. He'd been around Tabby for three weeks, had always assumed she was a shrinking violet who was more or less controlled by her authoritative and charismatic husband. Now he was starting to understand why the opposition was after her, too.

She was a powerful force herself.

Duff felt his eyes getting even heavier. He spent a moment trying to tighten the tourniquet again, using both hands to crank the little metal windlass. His leg was all but numb, and he was sure he'd stopped probably seventy-five percent of the blood loss, but even so, he knew he didn't have long till he bled out.

He gave up on the tourniquet, rested his hands in his lap, and closed his eyes.

Tabby seemed to notice that he was drifting off. "Young man! What is your given name?"

"Josh."

"The men call you Duff."

"Short for Duffy." He then looked up at her. "I know your husband's name was Elias Khabbaz. But . . . but I don't know your first name."

"It's Rafka. Rafka Khabbaz. Nice to meet you."

Duff chuckled, and his eyes drooped again. "Is it really?"

"Yes, it is. You saved my life. You were very brave."

Duff didn't think he would make it to the hospital, but he said nothing, because he didn't want to panic her. Instead, he closed his eyes and let his head droop a little.

Almost immediately Tabby yelled at him. "Monsieur? You must wake up. We are minutes away."

Duff's head lurched up and his eyes opened. "Yeah. I'm good." He looked around. "Maybe keep talkin' to me so I don't nod off again."

"Oui. How is your leg?"

He glanced down at it, then back up. "Can we talk about something else?"

To his surprise, another smile flashed across her stressed and nearly panic-stricken face. "You are going to have a baby? A boy?"

"You . . . you heard that?" He sighed. "I wish I was gonna get to meet him."

"You *will* meet him. Doctors will take care of you, very soon."

Duff's head dropped, but then it lifted quickly. "Hey . . . why didn't you . . . tell us . . . you spoke English? Would have made things easier, considering my shitty French."

"I appreciated your shitty French very much, Josh." She drove in silence a moment, then said, "I did not like the fact that we hired Americans to protect us. I am sorry. Thank you, for back there. Thank you for not leaving me. You could have. You were ordered to. But you did not. Monsieur? Monsieur, please wake up. We have arrived, you must *not* sleep!"

Duff finally lost consciousness just as the bread truck turned into the entrance to Hospital Wardieh.

CHAPTER 7

Rafka Khabbaz leapt out and ran towards the ER entrance. Her off-white dress was smeared with blood—both hers and Duff's, and blood from Bravo One's body armor that had been draped on top of her in the back of the Suburban.

It took no time at all for her to find a nurse, and soon orderlies had pulled the American out of the truck and onto a gurney. They wheeled him up towards the entrance, where by now Khabbaz stood with a male doctor, a pair of security men from the hospital, and three nurses. Everyone recognized the woman, and they were astonished both to be in her presence and to see her covered with blood.

The doctor said, "Madame, it is an honor to meet you. I support your husband fully." Others echoed the sentiment.

She spoke Arabic to them all. "Thank you." She motioned to the unconscious man approaching on the rolling gurney. "He risked his life for my husband and myself; do whatever you need to do to help him."

The doctor didn't even look at the patient. "Where is your husband, Mrs. Khabbaz?"

"There is nothing you can do for my husband, so help this young man instead."

The doctor looked down at the man on the gurney. He saw the

body armor and chest rig, the young white face with the beard, the hiking boots and jeans. "He is just a . . . bodyguard?"

Khabbaz erupted at him. "Who will be given your best care!"

Quickly the doctor nodded, then shouted, "Room one!"

She followed the procession into the emergency room, and everyone there knew better than to try to stop her. Duff was semiconscious now, mumbling softly to himself and seemingly unaware of his surroundings. A nurse cut his left pants leg open all the way up to his hip, while other nurses struggled to get his armor and other gear off him. He was then hurriedly attached to all manner of machines to monitor his vital signs. An orderly began to remove his left boot, but when Duff cried out in pain, the doctor waved the man away.

Water was poured on his knee so that the injury could be seen, and while this was happening, a surgeon entered and immediately tightened the tourniquet where the leg met the man's groin. Duff made no reaction to this at all; he just kept mumbling softly.

The surgeon examined the bullet wound to the left side of his patient's left leg, just a couple of centimeters below the knee joint. He then checked the right side of the knee. "Bullet went all the way through. It's a miracle it didn't hit an artery, or his other leg, for that matter." The surgeon used a metal instrument to move the bone and flesh, looking for the artery. After a few seconds he looked up and began scanning the machines now recording the patient's blood pressure, oxygen, and heart rate. Then he spoke to his surgical team, who were just now arriving in the ER. "Too much damage here. Too much blood loss. We will need to remove the leg and give him a transfusion."

He turned to Rafka Khabbaz for her approval. She commanded such respect that even though he was the surgeon, he wanted her to agree with his decision.

After a long grave look, she nodded. "Whatever you have to do. Just save his life. He is going to have a child. I want him to meet his son."

"Very well." The surgeon spoke to his team. "Prepare for amputation."

Duff's eyes opened suddenly, and though they were glazed, they were clear enough to show that he was, at least, somewhat alert still. It was also clear he understood a little Arabic, as well.

He shouted in English, "No! No fuckin' way you're choppin' off my leg!"

The anesthesiologist had arrived, and he quickly gave the patient a sedative. While he did this, a nurse spoke to him in English. "Just relax, sir. You are in the best care."

"Not my leg. Please . . . please." The sedative took effect quickly.

Rafka stepped between a pair of nurses and took his hand.

"I will not leave your side, Josh."

He did not look at her—his eyes were closed now—but he did say a single word.

"No."

Just then, the EKG machine displaying his heartbeat fluttered, then went flat. A high-pitched warning tone blared.

The doctor said, "We're losing him! Get me the paddles."

Rafka Khabbaz was pushed back now as the surgical team pressed in, desperate to save the horribly wounded man's life.

His sweat-soaked shirt was ripped open; blood from facial lacerations had made its way onto his chest, smeared with perspiration across a tattoo over his heart that read "Nikki."

The crash cart was rushed into play while a nurse wiped the blood off his chest for a better contact.

Seconds later, the doctor placed the paddles over Duff's motionless chest and shouted, "Clear!"

CHAPTER 8

A man stood under steaming water, his hands on the tile on either side of the shower head so he could lean forward, rinsing shampoo from his short hair. Hot rivulets ran down his clean-shaven face, then down his throat, then down his tattooed chest.

The word "Nikki" was briefly covered by the cascading soap, but then it became visible again.

Josh Duffy's head didn't hang low only because of the need to rinse the shampoo from his hair. No, his low mood dictated its physiology, and while the water didn't have to hide any tears, the steam did serve to mask a mist in his eyes. Another day of regret, another day of humiliation. He would shake it off and put on a brave face; this he knew because he somehow managed to fake his way through each day, but it was beginning to seem as if holding his head high and carrying on was getting harder and harder to pull off.

Yes, he had things to live for, of course he did. But, he told himself, this life of his bore no resemblance to the life he'd envisioned for himself and his family.

He shook off his depression, turned off the water, and opened the flimsy curtain. Since his mind was somewhere else, he absentmindedly reached out onto the vanity, felt around for a moment, and then, coming back to the here and now, he knelt down carefully and performed a more thorough search of the immediate area.

When he didn't find what he was looking for, he sighed, then stood back up, using his hands on the walls for balance.

Yelling now, he said, "Nik? What did you do with my leg?"

"Hang on, Josh," his wife called from another room. "Mandy's bringing it."

He wrapped a towel around his waist as he listened to the beating of little bare feet across the cheap laminate floor of the hallway. He brought his shoulders back and fashioned a smile across his face, and then a five-year-old girl with curly brown hair came running playfully into the bathroom.

"Mornin', Daddy."

"Good morning, sweetheart."

In the little girl's hands she held a prosthetic limb, a lower left leg already dressed with a black dress shoe and a black sock. The leg began just below the knee and had a thick rubber sheath at the top that an amputee could snap up around his knee and upper leg before placing the appendage into the prosthetic. The leg itself was made of titanium and carbon fiber, and very light, so Mandy needed only one hand to pass it to her dad. With a smile, she said, "Mommy said it was stinky, so we cleaned it and changed your shoe for you."

"Thank you, baby. I'll be right out."

The little girl spun on her bare feet and ran out of the bathroom, singing all the way.

The man's smile disappeared as fast as it had appeared, and he stood there, sullen, dripping, and half-naked, his artificial leg in his hand.

Fifteen minutes later he was dressed in a blue blazer and a red tie, his hair was parted to the side, and he'd once again adopted a carefree air. He leaned into the tiny living room of his nine-hundred-square foot Falls Church home, where he found his daughter watching TV, his three-year-old son playing with blocks, and his wife hard at work on a sewing machine in the corner. She was in the process of stitching a dress for Mandy, and Duff could tell by the expression on her face that she wasn't satisfied with her work.

It was also clear she was a little annoyed with him, and this didn't come from her expression; it came from her mouth. "You've *got* to keep that thing clean, Josh, especially where it attaches at the knee."

"I went out for a run before work. I was going to clean it up before I got dressed."

"That's the good one. If it gets damaged, you'll have to switch to the cheap one."

"I know," he said, chastened.

She kept looking at her work while she asked, "What time do you get off tonight?"

"Six. Home by six thirty."

"Okay. I go in at nine."

Josh sighed. "Another all-nighter?"

She nodded, still concentrating on the dress. "A bank in Alexandria and two offices in Crystal City. We're waxing the floor at the bank, so I won't be home till late. Probably around six."

It was quiet for a moment other than the intermittent rumble of the sewing machine, until Duff forced some positivity into his voice and said, "I'm off work Tuesday. I'm taking my résumé all around."

His wife stopped what she was doing and looked up. "You're watching Mandy and Harry Tuesday. Remember? I'm cleaning Mrs. Parnell's that day. Two hundred. Split with my crew, but still. It's sixty bucks we can use."

Duff felt the shame that he'd felt for a long time, and again it crept into his posture. Despite his best efforts, his shoulders slumped a little, his head drooped, and his thirty-two-year-old face seemed to age in the blink of an eye.

He looked at the kids a moment, sitting in a living room so small it seemed almost claustrophobic, then said, "This won't go on much longer. I promise. We'll dig out."

Nichole Duffy stopped what she was doing, looked up at her husband across the cramped space, and then rose and walked over to him. Putting her arms around his neck, she kissed him.

She didn't smile. She didn't smile much these days. "I know we will. It's okay. We just have to keep at it."

Duff did smile, but only a little. It was a put-on; he was still frustrated with the life he'd built for himself and his family, but he loved his wife, she loved him, and he knew he couldn't let himself lose sight of that.

Mandy leapt up from the floor by the coffee table and ran over, squeezing her father around his good leg. "We love you, Daddy."

"I love you, too."

Harry didn't look up from his toys, but he echoed his sister. "Love you, Daddy."

Before Duff could reply, Mandy said, "Go protect everybody at the mall. And watch out for the bad guys."

He leaned over and kissed her on the head. "I will, baby."

Mandy went back to her show, and Duff looked at his wife.

Nichole said, "She asked where you went all day. I told her."

"Yep," he said with fresh sullenness. "That's what I do. I'm the sheriff of Tysons Galleria."

She kissed him again. "Stay positive, Josh. Please?"

He nodded. Pushed the corners of his mouth out a little in another feeble attempt at a smile. "You bet."

CHAPTER 9

The Tysons Galleria mall in McLean, Virginia, opened slowly and quietly most spring Mondays, and today was no different. Shopkeepers began opening their doors or lifting their gates, and the few patrons in the massive three-level space strolled lazily, many opting to make Starbucks or a French-style bakery their first stop to fuel their shopping.

Josh Duffy walked among them. He was the shift leader today, so he didn't wear the bright yellow tunic with "Security" festooned in black across the back that the rest of the staff wore, but instead he had slipped a silver badge over the breast pocket of his blue blazer. He strolled along slowly, a walkie-talkie under his coat on his hip, his eyes scanning both the morning customers and the shopkeepers.

He helped a diminutive Asian American woman lift the gate at the optician's office, then greeted a young man opening his register behind the counter at Louis Vuitton. He passed the Lebanese Taverna restaurant and found himself taken back to another time and another place with the smells already wafting through the air, pleasant smells, despite his own personal history with the country.

At eleven fifteen he strolled through Neiman Marcus, greeting employees with a nod as he passed, when an elderly woman stepped up behind him, reached out, and grabbed him by the arm.

He stopped, then turned to look at her, and it occurred to him how, just a few short years ago, someone coming up on his blind side and putting a hand on him would have gone down very differently.

You're soft, Duff, he told himself, and it depressed him.

Still, this woman was no threat. He forced a smile. "How can I help you?"

She pulled a blue dress out of a bag. "I bought this yesterday. I needed black. It's for a funeral. I got home and my housekeeper said it was blue. Is it blue?"

"Yes, ma'am. Very dark blue, but it's blue."

The expression on her face indicated to Duff she thought this to be the worst thing that had ever happened to her. She held it out to him. "I'd like to exchange it."

An earlier model of Josh Duffy would have pointed the old woman towards a sales clerk and then marched off on his way, but this new, softer, more docile version escorted the older lady to a counter in the women's dresses area, explained the situation to the clerk so she didn't have to repeat herself, then offered his condolences for whoever had died and necessitated the purchase of the black funeral dress.

A minute later he stepped out of the department store on the second floor of the placid mall. Muzak played; this felt like the most peaceful place on Earth, and Josh Duffy's depression threatened to overtake him fully now. What had he become? What was he if not a protector? There was nobody here who needed his protection. Who was he if not a provider to his family? This job didn't even pay the bills.

Why was he even on this earth?

He took the escalator down to the ground floor. It deposited him just behind a large Starbucks kiosk. He eyed the few customers, most of them employees of the mall waiting for beverages they'd already ordered. Duff himself only drank the free brew from the old Mr. Coffee in the security office, doused with generic creamer, because he wasn't about to spend five bucks he didn't have for some fancy shit at Starbucks.

But it smelled good, and he felt that that alone gave him a little needed jolt as he passed it ten times a shift on his rounds.

He saw a lone man in a business suit standing at the counter opening the lid on a large cup.

Duffy didn't pay close attention to the man, he just continued his stroll, but after a few seconds, he stopped abruptly. He turned back towards the kiosk, looking at the man more fully now.

For five seconds, for ten seconds. The man never looked up at him; he just dressed his coffee with cream and sugar.

Duff began walking over.

He was five feet away when the man's head rose up to face him.

Duff stopped and began grinning at the man.

"Help you?"

"Gordon?"

The man was African American, in his forties, fit, with short black hair and a clean-shaven face. He was good-looking, but the deep lines around his eyes indicated he lived a life much different than today's surroundings would suggest—an upscale shopping mall in Virginia.

He looked Duffy up and down and said, "You got the wrong guy."

"Mike Gordon," Duff said, more assurance in his voice now. "Mike . . . it's me. Josh."

"Josh?" The man didn't recognize the person in front of him, that much was certain.

"Duffy."

It took more time, but eventually the man's eyes widened. "Duff? Holy shit. Duff? Is that you?"

With a laugh, Duff said, "It's me, man. I guess I shaved since I saw you."

Gordon put his coffee down and the two men embraced warmly, slapping backs hard enough for others around to turn and look at the noise.

Duffy said, "It's been a while."

"No kidding, brother. Close to five years, I'd guess." Gordon looked off to the distance. "Man . . . last place I saw you was J-Bad."

"That's right. Jalalabad. We did a contract in Khost, too. Another in Gardez."

Now Mike Gordon smiled. "We got around, didn't we? All the

42

shit holes. But we had the best PMC in the region. Smoked a lot of hajis in J-Bad."

"Yeah. Lost a man there, too."

"That we did. That we did." Gordon picked up his coffee from the counter and took a slow sip. "South African. Tall dude. Hilarious. Always joking. Forgot his name."

Duff answered without hesitation. "Andy Caruth."

"Caruth. That's right. Good man." He took another sip and sighed. "Shit. That night was a clusterfuck."

Duff said nothing, and Gordon picked up on this. "Kid, you were a rock star through that whole thing. Yeah, Caruth caught a seven-six-two through the lung, but you got the rest of us out of there, even after my rifle went tits up. Shit happens, you know that better than almost anybody."

Duff nodded distractedly. He hadn't planned on reliving that night in Jalalabad when he came in to work this morning.

Gordon continued. "You saved my life. Never forgot. Never will. Still owe you for that. You pulled my ass out of a shit sandwich once in Gardez, too." He slapped Duff on the arm. "Dammit, kid. It's good to see you."

"Same here, boss." Gordon and Duff had been fellow low-pecking-order teammates for a private military corporation at first, but then Gordon had been promoted and served for a time as Duff's team leader before the end of the contract.

Gordon hefted his drink to take another sip, but then, seemingly for the first time in the conversation, he noticed the badge on Duff's jacket.

He stopped speaking. "Wait. Are you . . . Do you *work* here?"

"Yeah."

"No," he said with a doubtful laugh. "No way, man."

"What?" Duffy asked, although he knew what was coming.

With a voice rising with each word, Gordon exclaimed, "There is no fucking *way* that Duff from Jalalabad is a fucking mall cop!" Gordon said it as if the idea were completely unfathomable, and loud enough that everyone in earshot just stared at the pair.

Duff shrugged and kept a little smile, though he steamed with embarrassment. "What can I say? This gig takes a lot less incoming mortar fire than J-Bad."

"Yeah . . ." Gordon looked around. "I'd imagine it does." He shook his head in disbelief again.

Duff changed the subject. "You just out shopping?"

Gordon laughed and looked down at himself. "Yeah. Caught a new gig and I'm up for a TL position. Have a meeting with the agent in charge in forty-five minutes. Just bought this suit at Needless Mark-ups."

"Where?"

"That's what my ex-wife always called Neiman Marcus. Anyway, I had them cut the tags off." With another laugh, he said, "Changed in the bathroom."

"Stateside job?"

"Negative. If I get the gig today, then I'm wheels up tomorrow."

Duff didn't hide how impressed and envious he was. "You're a lucky man. They say security contracts are damn hard to get these days."

"Good ones are. This gig is dog shit, but it pays through the roof."

"If it pays, it can't be shit."

Gordon just took another sip of his hot coffee.

"Unless you . . ." Duff said, "I don't know . . . unless you lost your mind and took a job with Armored Saint."

Gordon made no response to this; he only flashed his eyes off to the side, then looked down at his watch.

"No. C'mon. Really?"

"You said it, kid. Times are tough."

"But *Armored Saint*? Damn." Armored Saint had a reputation as the worst PMC on the planet. Even the company Duff had worked for in Beirut had managed to keep its rep, if not untarnished, at least somewhat intact.

Duff changed gears quickly. "This gig. Is it back in the Sandbox?"

"Negative. Down in Mexico."

"That doesn't sound so bad."

"You don't know the mission."

"Tell me."

Gordon raised his eyebrows and smiled a toothy grin. "I'll tell you this: twelve hundred a day for a three-week assignment."

Now Duff was green with envy. "Holy hell, Mike. That's awesome."

"And if I make TL, that's another ten large. Thirty-five grand in all."

"Incredible. But . . . Armored Saint? Those guys are psychos."

Mike pointed a finger at his old colleague. "Watch it. I'm one of those guys now."

"Sorry." Duff looked around the mall quickly. "Hey, I've got to make my rounds. Can you join me for a few?"

Gordon chuckled again. "Foot mobile, like old times, right?"

"I'll take point."

"You always did."

CHAPTER 10

The two men strolled, but Gordon did most of the talking. This was exactly how Duff remembered him. A good guy, a decent team leader, but a motormouth and a bit of a gossip. Still, Duff hadn't run into anyone he'd worked with in the private military contracting business in three years, and he soaked up Gordon's words, making him feel like he was one of the guys again.

Gordon talked about some of the men they used to work with. Stories of alcoholism, drug addiction, failed marriages, even a suicide. It was hardly uplifting conversation, but Duff was riveted. He was also curious about Gordon. "What have you been up to since eastern Afghanistan?"

Gordon replied, "Stayed in the game, mostly. Had some good contracts, some bad ones." He shrugged. "Progressively worse, to be honest. Like you said, the industry isn't what it used to be. Lost my last gig with Triple when DOD funding ran out. Did some work for an Aussie PMC in North Africa, but the fucking UN put the kibosh on that cash cow. I even worked a shit-ass static post in Kuwait, but the Jihadi threat in the area never materialized, so I got downsized."

Duff laughed while waving to a young man folding shirts at a display at the entrance of Anthropologie. He said, "Those damn Jihadis. Never around when you need 'em."

Gordon replied, "Joke all you want, but you get it."

"Yeah, I get it. Without a real threat, nobody needs guys like us."

Gordon turned and looked at the younger man. "Like *us*? No offense, kid, but I do believe you climbed off the asskicker express when you took a job working mall security. Tell me about this gig. Catch any tier-one shoplifters lately?"

Duff fought shame. Defensively he said, "This is just for now. I've got feelers out, irons in the fire. That sorta thing."

Gordon wasn't one to hide what he was thinking. "This can't be paying the bills for a family man like you."

Duff kept walking, flashed his eyes over to Prada, just to make sure everything was okay in there. They had their own private security, so everything was *always* okay in Prada. Finally he said, "Dude, not even close."

"How's Nikki?"

"She's fine." He shrugged while he walked. "She's . . . *not* fine. I barely see her. Two little kids. I work days, and she cleans offices all night."

Gordon said, "Nikki's a maid?"

"She started her own janitorial service a couple years ago. But yeah. She's basically a maid. Still, she brings home twice what I do. We'd be crammed into some dumpy little apartment without her money. As it is, we're crammed into a dumpy little house. Barely making rent."

Gordon whistled. "Damn, Duff. Nikki was a badass. Born leader. She was captain at what, twenty-five? She could've hit major by thirty. Always figured she'd stay in the Army and get a pension."

"Yeah," Duff muttered. He thought about this fact every single day of his life, so none of this was news.

"Whip-smart female officer like that? She'd have hit bird colonel before forty, just like her dad. With her personality, she'd have made general. Talk about set for life."

Gordon was just piling on now, as far as Duff was concerned, so Duff's tone turned a little defensive. "Yeah, well, things looked a little different back then. I was earning a quarter mil a year contracting. We wanted kids. A white picket fence. All that shit. We had a plan."

"Then Beirut?"

Duff stopped right in front of Ralph Lauren. He was now wishing he hadn't run into his old friend today. He didn't feel like his psyche could handle this. "You heard about that?"

It had been kept out of the news, more or less, by his employer, who had the means to cover up many of the details of the company's involvement during the assassination of the Lebanese presidential candidate.

Still, word had gotten out in the industry, so Duff wasn't too surprised Gordon knew he was there.

Mike put his hand on Duff's shoulder. "I heard you did your job. I also heard your company fucked you over during the extract, and they dicked you on the medical bills after the fact."

"Yeah, pretty much."

Gordon put a finger in Duff's face now but gave a little smile while doing so. "And you were working for United, *not* for Armored Saint, so don't go casting stones at *my* employer."

Duffy started walking again, and Gordon followed, tossing his empty coffee cup in the trash as he did so.

Duff said, "Everybody says Armored Saint is worse. That if you die on a contract for them, your family has to pay for the body bag."

"That's just a joke, Duff."

"Yeah, but that joke didn't come out of thin air. Their reputation is bad."

"Enough, man," Gordon said, and Duff realized he'd gone too far.

"Sorry, Mike. Honestly, I'm just jealous. Life's rough right now, you know?"

"I get it. You and Nikki have been put through the wringer. But you are tough people, you'll come out on top." He looked at his watch again. "Been great seeing you, kid, but my meeting is in twenty, and I have to—"

"You know . . ." Duff put a hand on Gordon's arm now, looked at him nervously. "Maybe . . . maybe you could get me on."

The older man cocked his head. "Get you on *what*?"

"The Mexico gig."

Gordon recoiled in shock, then shook his head adamantly. "Forget it. Mexico is going to be a horror show, and everybody knows it. Armored Saint only got the contract because all the good PMCs said 'no fuckin' way.'"

"You just said Armored Saint was a good company."

"And you just said they sucked, and now you're trying to get a job with them. We're both full of shit, Duff. Either way, Mexico is not for you."

"I can handle the gig. I'm still solid."

"If you're solid, then why the fuck are you *here*?"

Duff looked away. "I *had* to take a break from high-risk work. Nikki freaked out after Beirut. The kids. You know how it is. Anyway, it's time I got back in."

"I heard Beirut fucked you up."

"Hell no! I'm good to go. I don't have to be a shooter making twelve hundred. I'd take less. I'd take *anything*, dude. Ops support, logistics, comms, whatever you need. You *owe* me, Gordo, you said it yourself."

"I owe you a *favor*. Taking you to Mexico won't be a favor." He nodded curtly now. "Say hi to Nikki." Gordon turned and began walking away.

Duff hurried back up alongside him, keeping his pace as he walked. "I had some . . . some medical bills after Beirut. Can't seem to break out from under them. I still owe over twenty grand. I *need* this Mexico run, Gordo."

Gordon kept walking for a moment, then stopped again and turned to his old friend. "Don't make me do this."

"*Please*, man. I'll get down on my knees and beg you if you want."

"Jesus, calm down." Gordon was silent for several seconds. It was clear to Duff he didn't want to put in a good word for him. Finally, however, he sighed, then said, "The AIC on the gig is Shane Remmick."

Duff was astonished by this news. "Remmick? The SEAL? I've listened to his podcast. Read his book. He's kind of a big deal."

"That's right. He's a celebrity. He's also a royal asshole."

"Yeah, I picked up on that. A little full of himself. Still, why the hell is he working for Armored Saint?"

Gordon shoved his finger back in Duff's face. "You need to shit-can that trash talk on AS right now! You want in or not?"

"Yeah . . . I really do, Gordo."

Gordon seemed to relent finally. "Remmick works for AS because he's friends with the dude who runs the company, and because they pay like nobody else. I'll be honest, I have no idea if he needs more swinging dicks anywhere in this operation; I figure he's got it pretty much locked down if we're setting off in just a few days, but I'll tell him about you. If he's interested, he'll probably want to see you ASAP. He's here at the Ritz."

"That's perfect," Duff said.

"You got a résumé?"

"Hell yeah, I can email it to you right now." Duff smiled. "Thanks, Gordo."

"Don't thank me. Best thing that can happen is Remmick tosses you out on your ass. Three weeks in Mexico is gonna suck worse than that year we did in Afghanistan."

CHAPTER 11

Josh Duffy had worked security at the mall for over a year, but he'd never set foot in the Ritz-Carlton, Tysons Corner. The hotel shared a door with the second floor of the Galleria, and shortly before three p.m. Duff stepped through the door, looking for the elevators to take him to his interview.

Before entering the Ritz, he'd removed his badge and left it in the security office, and he'd fixed himself up in the bathroom as much as possible. He was hoping for cushy operations work. Radio room, intelligence, something of the like. There were other administrative and logistics positions associated with this type of security contract, but they were normally staffed by much more experienced personnel. No, Duffy had been a security officer, a member of a team of men trained to fight and to protect.

He wasn't going to get a cushy high-paying job, but he also knew that he was not fit for a high-threat front-line security officer post.

He just wanted in on the contract somewhere, and he wanted enough money to pay off a few of his bills.

Duffy arrived at Remmick's suite right on time, just as Gordon had instructed in a text an hour earlier. He stood outside a moment, took a few deep breaths, then rapped on the partially open door with enough force to sound confident but not so much to sound as desperate as he was.

An authoritative voice responded on the other side. "It's open."

Duffy entered and found a large suite with an open dining room adjacent to the living room. A tall, lean, and weathered man in his early fifties sat behind the table there with his feet up. He wore a fitted polo that showed off his muscular arms, and his hair was in a high and tight that was uncharacteristic for active-duty Navy SEALs and, Duff imagined, even less characteristic for former Navy SEALs. He wore reading glasses and held some pages in his hand. He continued to peruse them, and Duff wondered if this was a printout of his résumé.

"Mr. Remmick, sir? I'm Josh Duffy. I believe Mike Gordon talked to you about—"

"Yeah, I'm looking at the CV he just emailed. C'mon in and grab a seat."

"Thank you, sir." Duff sat and tried a little jocularity. "Can't say I've ever interviewed in a room at the Ritz-Carlton. This is pretty nice."

But Remmick wasn't interested in small talk. "You were Army infantry. Eleven Bravo. Four years."

It was a statement, not a question, but Duff misread this. "Yes, sir. Post that, seven years in the high-threat security industry."

The big man looked over his reading glasses at Duff for the first time. "I can read."

"Yes, sir."

"You worked for Academi, Triple, United Defense. You spent time on some hot details. Fallujah, Jalalabad, Gardez. Quetta. Benghazi. Lot of moving around."

Duff said nothing, only nodded.

"You were in Mogadishu, way back when. Did some time there myself with Triple Canopy. How many times did you have to run the Garoonka Caalamiga?"

"Quite a few, sir."

"Everybody knows *exactly* how many times they drove through hell, son."

"Yes, sir, that *is* true. I made the run between the airport and the city two hundred four times, sir."

Remmick looked up over his glasses again, his eyes suddenly wide. "You're fuckin' joking."

"No, sir."

"Shit." He whistled softly. "I did fifty-one movements, and they *all* sucked. Got shot at a third of the time. How many times you get shot at, Duffy? I know you kept count. Everybody did."

"I did, sir. We took fire eighty-eight times."

"Fuck. How many times you shoot back?"

"Eighty-eight times, sir."

The ex-SEAL cracked a smile. "My kind of answer, son." He looked back down at the page, and his voice went lower. "Then . . . you got fucked in Beirut. I made a call just before you got here. An old buddy who works at your old employer's corporate office. He joined United after your time, but he knew a little about what happened. I'm told the injuries you received during the Khabbaz assassination ended your career."

Shit, Duffy thought. He had prepared himself to lie his way into this job, and this moment was the Rubicon he had to cross. "Not at all, sir. I'm one hundred percent fit. I'd be happy to work at the operations center, man the radio room, drive a support vehicle, whatever it is you might need for the mission."

Remmick sighed, laced his fingers together behind his head, and leaned back. "Do you have any fucking *clue* how many washed-up has-beens I have at my disposal to ride a desk at ops or drive a ration truck while I'm out leading my men through the shit? More than I need, I'll tell you that much. No, son. What I *do* need is a top-notch high-risk security officer. A shooter, not another asshole in the rear with the gear."

Duff had been afraid of this from the moment he told Gordon he wanted on the Mexico job. Yes, the protection detail officers would make a lot more money than the ops center staff, but Duff had no desire to be an actual operator in Mexico. He hadn't touched a rifle in three years, he was way out of shape for high-threat security work, and running and gunning would greatly increase the chances that his amputation would become evident to all.

Still . . . there was the money.

After only a moment's hesitation, he said, "I'm your man, sir."

Remmick scanned Duffy slowly, then said, "Normally there'd be a physical, but we're leaving in just a couple of days. Sure you're healed up from that shit that happened in Lebanon?"

Duff did *not* hesitate now. "Want to race me around the mall?"

"That's a negative. At this stage of my life, I run *after* things, and I run *from* things. I do *not* run otherwise."

"Understood."

Remmick shuffled the pages a moment, then put them down on the table and leaned forward. "Gordon told you the job pays twelve bills a day."

"I think he mentioned something along those lines."

Remmick's eyes narrowed slightly. "We're mercs, Duffy. He mentioned it."

"Yes, sir . . . he definitely did."

"Okay, I'll give you the sitrep, and then you tell me if you want in. No shame in walking out of here right now if this is more than you can handle.

"We'll be escorting four diplomats, two from the Mexican government and two from the UN, up into the mountains of western Mexico. They are going to meet with a man named Rafael Archuleta. You know who that is?"

Duffy was embarrassed to admit that he did not, but he wasn't about to lie about this, too. "No, sir."

"He's the head of Los Caballeros Negros, the Black Knights. They're the biggest drug cartel in the area and the fastest-growing cartel in Mexico."

"I see."

"The western Sierra Madres are on the brink of war. Thirteen K dead in the past two years is the conservative estimate. The government was content to let everybody in the mountains schwack one another to extinction, but the Black Knights have gotten too big, and the international outcry has Mexico City's attention. Anti-drug funding from the U.S. is being held, so forty thousand Mexican soldiers are amassed at the foot of the Sierras. Everybody knows if they go in, there will be fifty thou dead, minimum. My guess is two times that. Mostly civilians.

"Rafa Archuleta has agreed to talks, but he won't leave the Sierras to come to the table. He will, however, allow UN peacekeepers and government dips to come to him to open a dialogue. The UN wants to send in a peacekeeping force, but first they have to secure agreements from all the cartels, and then—"

Remmick stopped talking suddenly, and Duffy realized he'd been looking down at the table. He glanced up as the older man said, "I'm getting the impression that you don't really give a shit why we're going down there, do you, Duffy?"

Duff met Remmick's gaze. "My mission is protecting my principals. All my concentration goes into that. I find it's best to let my principals worry about *their* mission."

A smile grew on the man's otherwise severe face. "Son, you got the right idea. Their mission is bullshit. Those beaners down there are gonna keep on killin' till there's nothing left to kill. Still . . . this is business, and Armored Saint is happy to take money from a bunch of dumb-fuck do-gooders."

Duff said nothing.

"Any questions for me?" Remmick asked now.

"How many in the protection detail?"

"Twenty-two."

"Twenty-two guns in cartel country? That's rolling a little light, isn't it, sir?"

Remmick shrugged his broad shoulders. "The peace mission has to succeed or the narcos up there are gonna die, and they know it, so there's some protection in that. The real threats we face will be methed-up highway bandits, unaligned gangs, hillbillies who didn't get the message that we're welcome up there.

"We're not going to fight a war; we're going to fight off opportunistic assholes so the VIPs can move freely through the area.

"We'll be running five vehicles, all the dips in one vic. We'll have heavy armor, light machine guns, grenade launchers . . . big-boy toys."

Remmick shrugged. "So, how 'bout it? You want in?"

This was going to be a difficult and dangerous mission, Duff knew, especially for him, because he'd been out of the game for so long. Still, this felt like a dream opportunity, and he wasn't going to pass it up. "Absolutely, sir, I do."

Remmick regarded the younger man for several seconds, then smiled. "Dunno why, Duffy, but I like you."

"My wife says *exactly* the same thing, sir."

Remmick snatched up the CV again, leaned back, and put up his feet. "As the agent in charge, I get to pick my team leaders. Thought I had that all sewn up. I'm Alpha One, leading the entire mission along with the eight men and two trucks of Alpha." He looked up at Duff. "Eight, including myself.

"Your buddy Gordon is going to TL Bravo team, two trucks and eight more guys including him. Charlie team is just six, manning a single vic. I had a good Charlie One, a former Ranger captain with six years of security ops. But he got cold feet and pulled out this morning." Remmick added, "Pussy."

"Sorry to hear that, sir," Duff said.

"Anyway, Charlie One is an open slot. You ever serve as TL on a high-threat OCONUS mobile escort job?"

Panic welled inside Duff now. Was he actually being considered for the team leader position? He'd walked in here hoping to work in an office, miles from any action, and now it seemed there was a chance he'd be commanding a team of gunfighters through hostile territory. But again he fought his doubts, and he thought of the money. Thirty-five thousand dollars could, in his estimation, almost fully repair the damage done by Lebanon and change the fortune and future of his family. "Negative, sir, but I would like to be considered for the position if you feel I could—"

"Pays an extra ten grand over the course of the contract. Thirty-five K in all."

Duffy pushed away the worry and puffed up his chest. His eyes were on the money. "I'd do one hell of a good job for you."

Remmick raised a finger. "The catch is this. Every one of the five other Joes on Charlie team is some ex-hot-shit this or that. Special Forces, officers, Marines. Despite all your time rolling in high-threat security, you're still just an Eleven Bravo. Army infantry enlisted. A lowly-assed sergeant with four years of service. They won't respect you off the bat. You'll have to earn that respect every second of every day." He leaned his arms on the table and brought his head closer to Duff as he said, "It'll take balls to lead Charlie team."

Duff tried to control his breathing. He was scared, he was excited, he couldn't wait to tell Nichole. He said, "Balls I've got, sir."

Shane Remmick nodded slowly while looking at the CV, then tossed the pages on the table in front of him and looked back up at the younger man. "Okay. Let's go to Mexico, Charlie One."

"You won't regret it, Alpha One."

Remmick held up a finger. "Your *one* job, son, is to see that I don't."

CHAPTER 12

A black Mercedes Benz S-Class weaved along a narrow road up a mountain range overlooking Lago de Chapala in Mexico's Jalisco State, due south of Guadalajara. In the front seats sat two men in black suits with Scorpion Micro submachine guns folded under their coats and pistols on their belts. Two more similarly dressed and armed men sat in the back, but between them, a fifth man rode unarmed.

This man was not afforded the tranquil view of the beautiful lake from the Sierra de San Juan Cosalá, because along with a gray flannel suit and Italian wingtips, he wore a black silk hood that covered his head completely. He sat quietly, swaying with the twists and turns along with the other men in the Mercedes as they drove higher and higher, away from the view of the lake and into dense woods on the mountainside.

After a time the sedan rounded another turn, then passed through massive iron gates guarded by a group of three men in polo shirts with assault rifles on their backs who waved them onwards after confirming the identity of the driver.

The driveway rose through the hills, snaking around nearly as much as the road they had just left behind, but eventually the S-Class pulled to a stop at the stone steps in front of the double oaken doors leading into a massive colonial mansion. Armed men stood around; one opened the back door and led the way as the two gunmen in the back seat helped the man with the hood out of the vehicle, across a marble-chip-gravel roundabout, and up the steps.

The interior of the mansion was cool and smelled like furniture polish. The entourage—there were three armed men escorting the hooded individual now—passed a housekeeper in a black uniform using a feather duster on the frame of an untitled Mario Rivera oil on canvas, and she didn't even look up from her work at the new arrivals, as if hooded men passing by under guard were no special occurrence.

The men's footsteps echoed in a long tiled hallway, past more paintings, these by Rufino Tamayo and David Alfaro Siqueiros.

No one had spoken on the drive from Guadalajara, and no one had spoken once they climbed out of the car, but now as they walked, the hooded man said in Spanish, "You know, amigos, everywhere I go, every city, every organization . . . all different, but all the same. The hot black hood on my head, sweat running down my face, the long drive in circles, the delivery to whatever new safe house your jefe is using."

They continued in silence a moment, no one responding to his statement.

The hooded man kept on. "Yes, and of course, the silent treatment. All business. No conversation. You chicos know how to play your role, don't you?"

Still there was no reply. "Bueno." *Of course,* said the hooded man.

A hand was placed on his shoulder, stopping him, then turning him to the left. A door was opened and he was led through, then taken to a leather wingback chair in the center of a large study. Here he sat and crossed his legs, still with the black silk hood over his head.

A voice in front of him, an older man by the sound of it, spoke Spanish. "Take off his hood, give him a towel and a scotch. Neat or on the rocks, Señor Cardoza?"

The hooded man turned slightly, adjusting his head towards the sound of the man's voice, even though he couldn't see a thing through the black silk. "Un poco hielo, por favor."

The hood was pulled off by a guard; the man seated in the wingback chair blinked sweat from his eyes a few times, then saw a large desk in front of him with another high-backed leather chair facing the other way, towards a window looking out over lush green hills and a narrow valley. A man sat in the chair, but the new arrival couldn't see him.

The voice spoke again. "Oscar Jesus Cardoza Ortega. Your reputation precedes you. It is good that we finally meet."

"Señor," a guard said with a little bow as he offered a hand towel to the heavily perspiring man in the center of the room.

Cardoza took it and wiped the sweat away. This done, he handed back the towel, put out his left hand, and accepted a crystal highball of scotch with one round ice cube in it.

Cardoza was not a large man, but he was impeccably dressed and coiffed. There was some gray in his short curly hair, but his eyes were intense and intelligent, and his body had clearly been kept in good condition. He wore a hammered-silver wedding ring, but no other jewelry, and as he sipped the scotch, his gentle mannerisms belied the force of his gaze. He appeared calm, affable even, but extremely capable of cruel ferocity at the same time.

To the man facing the window, he said, "This is a nice one."

The man turned around in his swivel chair now. He wore a simple black mask covering the upper portion of his dark-complected face, and his gray, thin hair was parted and slicked back. He, too, wore an expensive business suit.

"A nice one?" the man said. "The scotch?"

"The scotch is good, patrón." Cardoza looked around. "But I was referring to the home. I like it. Well . . . what I see of it. I've been to many houses of many patróns throughout Mexico, and this office is truly beautiful. Old World, I think is the style."

The older man in the mask lifted his own drink off his desk. It appeared amber in color, and Cardoza took it for tequila or mezcal. He took a sip. "If you say so. It's my first time seeing it myself." The masked man looked around now. "I think. Last time I asked, I was told I had twenty-two homes. Have to keep moving. Like a refugee. It comes with the job, as you know."

"Not my job, patrón. I'm just a humble consultant." With a smile, Ortega said, "One home, and a lot of hotel rooms."

The man behind the desk considered the comment for a moment, then said, "Let me tell you what I know about you. Not your official job, not your official title. Let's talk about what you *really* do. You are unaligned, unaffiliated with any particular organization, but friendly with almost all. Many of them my clients. Others of them . . . my enemies."

"But they are not *my* enemies, patrón, and that is to your advantage, since you have hired me to consult for you."

"They tell me no one has more connections with as many different organizations as you. Sinaloa, La Familia Michoacán, the Jalisco New Generation, Cartel del Golfo, even those lunatics in Los Zetas. You have associations in the government, with the federales, with the army and the marines. All this *and* your day job? You must be quite a good dancer, Señor Cardoza."

"I work in the mutual interests of all the organizations. As long as there is no organized sociedad, no official partnership between the patróns, there will be value to a man who can walk among everyone and talk *to* everyone." He took another swig of scotch, and the ice clinked in the glass. "I've carved out a niche by being the only true middleman between all the cartels."

The man in the mask said, "All the cartels, señor? That's not what *I* hear."

Cardoza shrugged apologetically. "Sí. Es la verdad. I have not been able to establish relations with Los Caballeros Negros. Not yet. But I'm getting close."

"Those mountain men don't make friends with anyone."

"I am hopeful I will be the exception, patrón. But so far, Rafa Archuleta and his Black Knights have been elusive. They are high on the Devil's Spine of the Sierra Madres. He rules all the towns up there, staffs the governments and the police forces. He has an army of sicarios and locals who do his bidding. He does not play by the few rules the other organizations obey."

El Patrón said, "The civilized all have rules. Even Los Zetas know their turf and stay on it. Archuleta does not; he is beholden to no code, no master. Like you, in a way. Tell me, Cardoza, what is it like having no master?"

"You lead Grupo de Guadalajara. You control the ports in Acapulco. You almost single-handedly run the market on shipments of chemicals from China, India, Bangladesh. You, señor . . . *you* truly have no master."

"My customers are my masters. And my customers . . . can be exacting in their demands. All the organizations use my routes and buy the chemicals for processing methamphetamine from me. They can be difficult if I—"

"All the organizations, except for—"

Now the older man waved his glass. "Sí, sí. All the organizations except for one. Los Caballeros Negros. They are receiving their supply from somewhere else. We think it's coming from China, shipped through Europe and then the United States, driven over in fucking NAFTA trucks. But we don't know."

Cardoza replied, "You might find out soon. As I told your people, I have been speaking with my contacts in the capital. I have details of the upcoming government delegation that will be heading into the Sierra Madres to meet with the Black Knights."

"You said you were a consultant. Muy bien. Consult me."

"Very well. Two Mexican Interior Ministry and two senior UN officials along with their American-based security detail will leave from the capital in three days. They will head north through Guanajuato, Zacatecas, and Durango, then into the hills. They've been promised safe access by Los Caballeros Negros up into and then through the mountains."

El Patrón said, "Los Negros hope the UN can save them from the war that's coming." The masked man glanced to an attendant standing near his desk, and the attendant stepped over with a crystal bottle, pouring another shot of amber liquid into his glass. He took a drink, then said, "Señor Cardoza, it is important the UN initiative is met with . . . opposition."

Cardoza ran his finger around the rim of his own glass. "Your wishes have been relayed to me by your people, of course. But I admit that I'm confused. Why do you invest so much interest in the Sierra Madres? Those aren't your mountains, and you don't need them."

"If the army invades the Sierra Madres in force, the war will destroy the labs, poppy fields, marijuana, cocaine, and meth production up there. It will make my ports down in Acapulco more important to the groups in the north, and it will weed out Los Caballeros Negros, who are not my clients and who are, by purchasing from my competitors, both injuring my clients and strengthening my enemies.

"If the UN peacekeepers go up into those mountains, on the other hand, they will protect the Black Knights under the guise of protecting the population. The army, they will obliterate the Black Knights, but only after taking heavy losses themselves. The losses to *both* sides will only help my position." A low, almost guttural laugh emanated from the masked man's belly. "My enemies against my enemies, Cardoza. Is it so bad I'd like to watch that happen from down here?"

Cardoza finished his scotch. The attendant with the bottle approached unbidden, but Cardoza waved him off and turned his attention back to the man behind the big desk. "There is another issue, patrón. Something that will prevent the army from entering Black Knights territory even if the UN doesn't make a deal to set up safe havens."

Behind the desk, El Patrón nodded. "You are talking about the missiles."

"Sí. Sixty Igla-S shoulder-fired surface-to-air launchers, along with one hundred twenty missiles, were stolen from a Venezuelan military garrison five months ago. The Americans tracked the shipment from Caracas to our beautiful shores, where the trail ran cold until earlier this month, when two surface-to-air missiles were fired at Mexican marine helicopters flying over Sinaloa, killing nineteen. The International Criminal Court is considering charging Rafa Archuleta with war crimes if it can be proved that the missiles are in his possession and he ordered them to be fired."

"He will not let the ICC arrest him," said the man in the mask.

"I agree. But the army won't invade with one hundred eighteen SAMs in the enemy's hands, either. They will need helicopters and air support to prosecute the war, and the citizenry would not tolerate an aircraft full of young men being blown out of the sky every other day."

"So we need to find a way to remove the missiles from the equation."

"I have a way," Cardoza said confidently.

"Tell me."

Now the man in the chair in the middle of the Old World office just said, "I ask you to trust me. I don't reveal my methods, señor. Not even to a man like yourself, a man for whom I have the utmost respect."

"Fair. Results will be rewarded. I don't care how you do what you do."

"Bueno. Now, please tell me specifically what you want from me."

"I want you to speak with the other organizations. Do your magic. Align them with my desire to force the army into the Sierra Madres." El Patrón smiled, his eyes narrowed in the slits of his mask. "Simply put, I want you to make chaos for my enemies, the Black Knights."

Cardoza frowned at this. "Chaos is the natural order of the world, patrón. I cannot control it; that is what makes it chaos." Then his frown turned into a little smile. "But I suppose I can help it along."

El Patrón smiled, as well. "This is all I ask, amigo. Lunch?"

CHAPTER 13

J osh Duffy pulled his sixteen-year-old F-150 into his carport shortly before seven p.m., later than normal, but his wife understood the delay when she saw him come through the door with a small bouquet of flowers and a bottle of red wine.

She raised an eyebrow at his handful of goods and gave a suspicious smile when he handed the flowers over to her.

"What's the deal?" she asked.

He kissed her and smiled. "Good day at work. Beautiful wife and family at home. That's all."

She took the flowers and headed for the kitchen. "I'm putting these in water. See if you can find any wineglasses. I can't even remember the last time we used them."

The table was set for dinner; Duff took off his blazer, but not before pulling out two bags of candies he'd bought at the mall. He held them up to Mandy and Harry. "This is for after supper."

Nichole's eyebrows furrowed behind him as the kids cheered.

She put plates of spaghetti and meatballs at all the place settings, including Harry in his booster seat, because he'd not long ago transitioned out of a high chair, and then she put down a little plate of salad for each of them, using the candy Josh brought as a bargaining chip to get the kids to eat the greens. She finally sat down, and her husband poured her wine.

"Just a glass," she said. "I've got to work."

Josh laughed. "Calm down, I'm not trying to get you drunk."

"It's going to be a long night. I'm worried about getting sleepy."

"Okay, we'll compromise. If you'll only have one, then let's make it a big one." He filled her cheap wineglass almost to the rim.

She rolled her eyes. "Classy."

The four of them held hands around the little table, and Josh led his family in the blessing. When he was finished, Nichole took a sip of the wine and reached for her fork, one curious eye still on her husband.

The kids talked about their day as they ate. Duffy engaged with them constantly and energetically, but Nichole remained mostly quiet, eating her meal and drinking her wine and casting continued glances towards her husband, who didn't seem to notice.

It was ten minutes before there was a lull in the conversation, and at this point Nichole couldn't take it anymore. "Okay. Enough. You're killing me."

Duff put his fork down. "What do you mean?"

"You *know* what I mean. You came home with wine and flowers for me and candy for the kids. What did you do that you need to tell me about?"

He laughed at this. "Just want to celebrate a little. We'll talk when the kids go to bed. It's good news, babe, don't worry about—"

"Our kids don't want to hear good news?"

Mandy chimed in. "I wanna hear good news."

Nichole turned to her son now. He sat in his booster seat with spaghetti sauce all over his mouth and chin. "Harry, do you want to hear good news?"

"Yeah!"

Nichole turned slowly back to her husband, with a raised eyebrow and a satisfied grin.

Josh smiled and took another sip. "You've aligned the troops against me."

"I fight dirty. You knew that when you married me."

"Yeah."

"What's going on?"

Duffy paused. In truth, he was nervous, but he felt like he was covering himself well. Finally he said, "Landed a new job."

Nichole was astonished. "What? Today?"

"Yep. Got interviewed at three. Hired me on the spot."

"That's fantastic!" They embraced and kissed, and when Nichole pulled away, she was all smiles. "What kind of job?"

Duffy kept his own smile fixed to his face. "It's security work."

She cocked her head a little now. "*Security?* You already have a security job."

He turned back to his plate and reached for his fork again. "This is different. Much better than the mall."

"How so?" she asked. There was still excitement in her voice, but it was blunted with a little uncertainty.

Duffy cleared his throat. "It's OCONUS. Temp, but *really* good money. The Galleria has already said they'd give me time off." He smiled down at his plate and took a bite of spaghetti.

Mandy asked, "What does 'Oh cone us' mean?"

Nichole answered her daughter, her voice deepening a little; the initial thrill of a few seconds ago was gone. "It means outside the continental United States."

"What does 'outside the conny-nen'—"

"Daddy is saying he's going on a trip to another country. But we'll have to see about that first." She put her hand on Josh's shoulder, more to turn him to face her than out of gentleness. "It's another PMC? You're talking about administrative work? Right, Josh? Logistics? *Please* tell me it's admin or logistics, not operations."

He started to reach for his glass but determined the tell would be too obvious. He just said, "Well . . . technically, I guess . . . it *is* ops, but—"

"*Ops?* What do you mean, *ops?* You can't do ops."

He all but lunged for the wine now. When he didn't respond to her immediately, she said, "Static security? Manning a post somewhere? Somewhere in Europe?"

"Well . . . not exactly."

Nichole Duffy couldn't believe what she was hearing. "It's not static? It's mobile work? This is *mobile* you're talking about?"

He did his best to display comfort and nonchalance as he refilled his glass. "Yeah, baby, but a milk run."

She was almost shouting now. "In the Middle East?"

He shook his head vehemently. "No, of course not. This is just down in Mexico. I'll bring the kids back a piñata."

Mandy tried to ask a question. "What's a piñ—"

"*Mexico?*" Nichole shouted. "And that's supposed to make me feel better? Do you watch the news? Why don't you just go back to Lebanon and let Hezbollah finish you off?"

Duff glanced at the kids, whose eyes were wide as saucers now, then back to his wife, who seemed unaware her children were even in the room.

He was going to protest, but instead he put his hand on her hand on the table. "It's thirty-five grand, babe."

Nichole gaped at him in disbelief. "Wait . . . thirty-five thousand dollars? For how long?"

"A day prep in-country, and then about three weeks on the road." She just stared at him; he knew she was doing the math in her head, and he also knew the shit was about to hit the fan. He said, "Can you please pass the spaghetti?"

Nichole made no move towards the bowl. "I'm not stupid, Josh. If they're paying you thirty-five grand for three weeks, it's *not* for a milk run. This is high-threat, isn't it?"

Duff's shoulders slumped. He'd hoped he could paint this job in a way that would placate his wife, but he realized now that had been a pipe dream. She was too sharp for that.

"We need the money" was all he could say.

"We need money. We don't need *that* money. It's too dangerous."

"It's not going to be dangerous. Just protecting some dips and pols while they do some business. I made TL. Might set me up for a good admin job after if all goes well."

She cocked her head. "Team leader? You haven't worked in three years, you've *never* been a TL, and now you are hired into a leadership position with a new company? How did you even get on with your leg?"

"People in the industry still know my rep. They see me as a solid dude. I don't let my prosthetic hold me back. You know that."

Nichole glared at him now. "What I'm hearing you say is that there *was* no physical."

"I leave the day after tomorrow, so there wasn't time. Anyway, they could see that I have what it takes to—"

"What PMC doesn't make its contractors take a physical before a high-risk mobile OCONUS op?" She squeezed her eyes shut as the answer came to her. "Josh . . . *Please*, for the love of God, tell me you did *not* take a job with Armored Saint."

Mandy's voice seemed especially meek compared to her mother's. "May I please be excused?"

Nichole turned to her children suddenly, then bit her lip. She said, "Of course, sweetie." She grabbed her napkin and wiped Harry's face, then turned to her daughter. "Take your brother into the living room and watch TV."

Josh snuck a quick sip of wine, then said, "May *I* please be excused?"

She made no reaction to his joke; she only waited for the kids to leave. When they were gone and the sound of the TV in the other room filtered into the kitchen, she took another moment to try to compose herself. Finally she said, "I can't believe what I'm hearing from you right now. You almost got fragged working for the second-worst private military company on Earth, so now you take a job with the *absolute* worst. You know Armored Saint's reputation better than I do. And you aren't a gunfighter anymore. Mobile high-threat work in Mexico won't be like somebody stealing a cinnamon roll at the mall."

Duffy said, "First, it was a cheese Danish. And second, I caught that dude, didn't I?"

"Don't joke. Not now."

He sighed. "I can handle the gig. You have to trust me."

She put her hand on the side of his face. "I trust you. *Of course* I do. I don't trust the Mexican cartels, I don't trust Armored Saint, and I don't trust any loser who crews for Armored Saint, because nobody works for Armored Saint if *anyone* else on Earth will hire them."

"Face it. I'm that loser, babe."

"You are *not* a loser. In your prime, you were the best." She squeezed the back of his neck. "But you left that life behind."

Duffy waved an angry hand around the tiny kitchen in the tiny rented house. "And look where that got us."

She shook her head, still holding him. "Only because you got hurt. We've had a lot go against us, but—"

Duffy pulled away. "No. Not a lot. Just one thing. One fucking thing. This." He reached down and lifted his left leg, pulled his khakis up to reveal the carbon fiber prosthetic.

Nichole leaned back in her chair and crossed her arms. "Yeah, Josh. I've seen it. I was with you day and night at the hospital. I was with you through months and months of rehab. Remember?"

He lowered the cuff of his pants and put his foot back on the floor. "When I lost my leg, I hurt our future. Our kids' futures. It's *my* responsibility to fix that. That's all I'm trying to do now, babe."

She softened. "If you'd left that woman to die on the street in Beirut, maybe you would have come home with all your parts, but what kind of man would that have made you? What kind of father?"

He didn't reply.

Nichole leaned forward and kissed him. "We love you. We'll take you just the way you are, Daddy."

He pulled away a second time, his eyes resolute. "Look. Second chances don't happen to guys like me. When I went to work this morning, I was over. Done. I bump into an old friend, and now I've got one shot . . . *we* have one shot to dig ourselves out of this hole. We're barely making rent. I'm not moving my family into a trailer. I *can't* let that happen."

Now she was the one rendered silent.

"A month from now," he said, "everything will be different. I've *got* to do this."

She said, "Look. I can ask my dad if—"

"You *already* asked your dad for help. Two years ago. He said no. *I* asked him last year, he said no again. There is no way in hell either of us is going back to him to beg for money."

Nichole closed her eyes. "I'll pick up another day shift. We can make this work. We just aren't being efficient enough with our—"

"No. The only way to dig out of this hole is with money, and the fastest way to make money is for me to go back to doing what I did before. What I'm good at. You *know* I'm right, Nik."

The conversation went on another ten minutes. Finally Nichole put her head in her hands for several seconds; Josh attempted to console her by rubbing her shoulder, but when she revealed her face again, he realized quickly he'd misjudged. She wasn't crying; she was coming to terms with the inevitable.

She looked him hard in the eyes. "Nothing I say is going to stop you, is it?"

He shook his head. "Not this time."

She nodded, as if to herself. "So . . ." She pushed back from the table. "I guess we'd better get you ready. I'll call Marla, they can do without me tonight."

"Why?"

"I've got, what, about thirty hours to get you prepped? I was an Army officer. You weren't. This is your first leadership position. There's a lot you need to know. Plus . . . don't take this the wrong way, but you aren't exactly in the same shape you were in three years ago. I'm going to work you, hard, to make you as ready as possible for Mexico."

Josh smiled a little. "Okay."

She looked him up and down. "You're gonna want to change into workout clothes. It's going to be a long night."

He stood with a little smile now. "Yes, Captain."

CHAPTER 14

Oscar Cardoza made a very good living hopping from one point in Mexico to another, and he did this quickly and quietly. His brand of shuttle diplomacy kept the cartels focusing on profits, but there were always fires to put out, always rushed meetings and in-person jaunts to personally communicate the wishes of one leader to the jefe of another organization.

He used aircraft for the majority of his journeys, a way to save time and bypass parts of the nation where the highways weren't safe for travel.

Cardoza did not own his own plane; that would have created a physical trail as he ventured from place to place, and a physical trail was something that, in his profession, he needed to avoid. Nor did he rent the same aircraft from the same charter service for each operation, for exactly the same reason. Knowing he had to keep any trace of his movements clandestine, his strategy when he worked in his consulting business was to charter from one of over two hundred air transport services in Mexico using one of his two dozen carefully created and backstopped false identities—from very large companies in Mexico City or Guadalajara, establishments that owned fleets of jets, to very small operations at remote airfields in the countryside, businesses operating but a single aircraft and owned by the pilot alone.

This morning his mission had him traveling from Mexico City to Coahuila, a rural state in the north of the nation near the border with Texas, and while the distance was relatively far and he had a strict schedule to adhere to, he'd decided against a jet or even a speedy turboprop. The airfield he was heading to was remote; a jet couldn't land, and a twin-turbo might draw unwanted attention, so he'd chosen a small charter company in Toluca that ran a three-aircraft fleet of single-engine piston planes.

The fastest civilian single-engine piston aircraft in the world is the Mooney Acclaim, and Cardoza boarded a 2018 model at four a.m. for the four-hour flight from Mexico City to his destination. It was seven thirty now, and he sat in the right seat of the small aircraft as they raced fifteen thousand feet over the desert in northern Coahuila. He could see on the instrument panel in front of him that his pilot was making over two hundred knots, and Cardoza was satisfied with this.

The aircraft began its descent over the desert, but then a long row of green mountains appeared in front of them, and soon they had slowed to 120 and the Mooney began picking its way through the uneven terrain.

Cardoza's meeting was at nine, and he expected to be right on time. He knew the man he was heading to speak with well enough; they'd been face-to-face in Juarez and in Nuevo Laredo in the past, but they'd never met out here in the hinterlands of northern Mexico.

Today's meeting would be with members of Los Zetas. The Zetas used to be one of the largest drug cartels in Mexico, and while their numbers and geographical territory had decreased markedly over the past decade, they nevertheless commanded hundreds of well-trained foot soldiers, mostly up here near the border and in pockets to the west and even down south in Chiapas. While they still had a centralized commander, their structure had morphed over the years into independent local factions who dealt in regional organized crime instead of the international drug trafficking that used to be their stock-in-trade.

Los Zetas were smaller, leaner, and less influential globally or even nationally, but, Cardoza knew, the members of the organization still retained a strong military structure.

These men were fighters; they were killers.

Cardoza had met personally with two different commanders of Los Zetas in the past five years. He'd worked out an accord with the first man and the Gulf cartel, normally sworn enemies. And then, when this chief was killed a few months later by assassins from the Knights Templar cartel, Cardoza flew back again to Nuevo Laredo to work out a new deal with the new man at the top.

Today's meeting, however, would not be with the leadership. No, the top man of the Zetas had already agreed to the plan Cardoza had in mind, and now the consultant only had to work with the tactical commander of the operation to make sure he understood his role.

The Mooney landed in thin morning fog at the airfield outside the tiny hamlet of El Infante; a row of five mud-covered Jeeps waited on the little tarmac, and Cardoza climbed out of the aircraft with a single backpack, then walked to the first vehicle. He was quickly patted down by a pair of young men wearing brown fatigues and carrying AR-15s on their shoulders; his backpack was removed from him and searched, and then he was ushered into the back seat while the backpack remained up front with one of the heavily armed sicarios.

There were easily twenty men in the five Jeeps, and soon they were racing off, heading for the airport exit.

There was no black hood for Oscar Cardoza today. Instead, a red bandanna was tied around his eyes. He responded with a little shrug and then leaned back in his seat, preparing himself for the journey ahead.

After no more than twenty minutes of a winding drive, mostly descending, Cardoza felt his vehicle slow and then stop. His blindfold was removed, and he looked around and found that they had parked on a narrow muddy road with thick foliage on both sides. He heard the sound of gunfire, but it wasn't close, and the men around him did not seem worked up about it at all.

Everyone climbed out of the Jeeps, Cardoza included, and they stood there for just a moment, listening to the shooting, before a group of men appeared out of the wood line on Cardoza's right. They were all armed, all soaked and mud covered, carrying weapons and wearing magazine chest racks over their tiger-stripe fatigues.

Behind them, another man stepped out. About thirty, he was the oldest of the group, and while he was wearing jungle stripe and a pistol hung from his utility belt, he wasn't covered in grime like the younger men.

A light rain had begun falling, but neither he nor the dozen or so younger men around him paid any attention to it as they approached.

The man with the pistol grinned, looking the older man up and down, taking in Cardoza's obviously new REI adventure wear. "Señor Cardoza. Welcome back to the territory of Los Zetas."

Oscar Cardoza didn't think the Zetas held much of the territory around here anymore, but they *did* hold this jungle backwater.

"It's good to see you again, Lobo."

The two men embraced warmly. Lobo had a deep raised scar from his chin down his throat that disappeared into his tunic. His face was boyish but weathered. A city kid who'd joined the Mexican marines, then left for cartel work. Cardoza supposed the man had seen a lot of horror and committed a lot of horror in his thirty years on Earth.

With a smile showing tobacco-stained teeth, Lobo said, "I hope your journey north went okay."

Cardoza patted the younger man on the arm as he relaxed his embrace. "Thank you for accommodating me on such short notice."

Lobo shrugged at this. "Orders from above. I told them I thought it was crazy to show you around one of our training camps, but they told me they didn't give a shit what I thought and to do it anyway." He didn't seem upset about this; he just laughed. "I'm a good soldier. I know when to do what I'm told."

"As do I." Cardoza had become an expert at ingratiating himself to whomever he was dealing with in order to socially engineer them to do what he needed them to do. Around the head of the Guadalajara Group, he'd be urbane and genteel. Around a combat-hardened field commander of Los Zetas, he'd be a soldier.

He also knew how to pay a compliment. "I hear discipline in that gunfire. I hope your men are training hard for the operation to come."

Lobo grinned again. "Come and see."

They walked back up a snaking muddy trail for no more than a few minutes, until they found themselves on the lip of a small ravine, looking down at a group of armed militants. They were training in sections of twenty or so men, and there were four different groups.

"Your force is . . . what . . . eighty?"

"Yes. Four platoons, four squads of five sicarios in each, plus myself as mission commander."

Below them, one unit moved towards targets lined up in front of a hillside, firing in unison in groups of five, then breaking both left and right to allow the next squad an open lane. The first group quickly fell back in behind the last, changed their magazines, and waited their turn at the front of the line.

The gunfire was constant with this platoon, and farther up the little valley, another group shot at steel targets as they rode in the back of moving pickup trucks. The other pair of platoons were reloading rifle magazines and waiting their turns to train against the targets.

Cardoza said, "I know the plan at the strategic level. Tell me about the tactical level."

The two men higher on the ravine watched a while, and then Lobo said, "We will begin the journey to the Sierra Madres the day after tomorrow. My men know their jobs. Most have been in the army or marines. All have killed in Juarez or Nuevo Laredo. We are Los Zetas. We know how to fight."

"Weapons and transportation?"

"As you see, we have AKs, ARs, G3s, mostly. Hand grenades and RPG-7s. A *lot* of RPGs. As for transportation . . . the men will travel in buses to the west. We will have pickups waiting for us there to take us into enemy territory."

Cardoza nodded, then pulled an iPad out of his backpack. It was ruggedized for hard outdoor use, so the rain did not affect it. He opened up a map of western Mexico and began expanding it. "Muy bien. The federales will escort the diplomatic motorcade to Sombre-rete, the front lines of the army, down in the lowlands. Beyond this is the hills and then the mountains. Not even the army travels up there, so they'll stop at Sombrerete.

"The motorcade will go on alone into the Sierra Madres Occiden-tales."

Lobo touched a portion of the map southeast of the mountains with a callused finger. "We can engage the UN pendejos and their little security force just beyond Sombrerete. Before they reach the high Sierras."

Cardoza raised an eyebrow. "You are afraid of those mountains?"

Lobo responded defensively. "I am afraid of nothing. I just—"

Cardoza smiled, wiped rainwater off the ruggedized iPad, and put it back in his pack. "It's okay, amigo. I'm afraid of the mountains, too. I don't want to go up there any more than you do. But we *have* to do it. When you destroy the delegation, it must look like the work of the Black Knights. That means it has to be done in the mountains.

"That will end the peacekeeping mission, and that will bring the army in. Guadalajara has negotiated all this with the leadership of your organization."

Lobo lit a cigarette and offered it to Cardoza, who declined. The younger man said, "I know all this. Again, I have my orders from my masters. For now we do what we're told, amigo. Someday you and I will run everything, and no cabrón in Guadalajara will tell *either* of us what to do."

Cardoza put his hand on Lobo's shoulder. "You will run Los Zetas someday, Lobo. I see it. But me? No, I won't run anything. I am just a humble consultant."

Lobo scoffed at this. "I know there is more to you than that, amigo. My leaders have hinted . . . but they haven't told me. You are an important man."

With a relaxed air, Cardoza changed the subject. "We will give the motorcade time to find their own trouble. Crazy Indians and paranoid locals with old rifles and drugs they want to protect. And finally, when the delegation and their security are up on the Devil's Spine, *after* they meet with Rafa Archuleta, you will hit them, wipe them out. Then you can get the fuck out of those chingada mountains and never look back."

Lobo cocked his head to the side. "Why *after* the meeting?"

"I have some work to do between now and then, but I fully expect to be right there with Archuleta when the UN arrives. In the background, of course. The Black Knights have advanced antiair missiles. This will be discussed in the meeting, and I need to know where these missiles are being kept."

"Why?"

"Because if war comes, as we want it to, the army won't stand a chance if it can't fly. The Black Knights own the mountain; the army needs to own the air. We have to tip off the army about the location of the missiles."

Lobo hid neither his surprise nor his suspicion now. "Why does it sound like you are rooting for the fucking army?"

"I want a fair fight, amigo. It lasts longer. Causes more damage. If a half dozen troop transport jets are shot down over the Sierra Madres, the army will pull back, the UN will send another delegation, and sooner or later, los pinches gringos from the UN will control the mountains. This will protect the Black Knights."

Lobo took it all in. Cardoza knew the man was muscle; he wasn't a strategic thinker. He also knew that, though he'd just told the man he expected him to be in charge of the Zetas, there was no way this self-important goon would ever be running anything larger than the force he now commanded. Lobo was a cunning and vicious killer, a good henchman, even an effective military tactician, but he wasn't bright enough to ever be more than this.

The Zeta platoon commander finally said, "Muy bien. Your plan is crazy, but it's not my problem. My problem is killing the motorcade and making it through the Devil's Spine. The people up there, Cardoza. They are psychos. Locos. Los Caballeros Negros, of course, but not just them. Everybody up there is insane."

Cardoza answered with a smile. "How would you know? You've never been up there."

"And I thought I'd never go."

Both men laughed, and finally they embraced again. Lobo was taking the moment to mean these were two men cut from the same cloth about to undertake the same mission.

But Oscar Cardoza understood the moment for what it really was. He'd just convinced this hapless fool that they were a team and that their ends were the same.

Cardoza had made a career out of convincing people that he was one of them.

He said, "I will call you as soon as I speak to the Sinaloan leadership."

Lobo took a half step back as if he'd just been punched. "*Sinaloa? You're going to Culiacán? To meet with El Escopeta?*"

"Sí. I don't want to do that, either, but I have to ensure they don't get in the way of your operation." Cardoza added, "I know you and El Escopeta have had your differences."

Lobo took a drag on his cigarette and then threw it in the greenery by the side of the path. "I guess you could say that. He killed my cousin."

"I'm very sorry, amigo. I didn't know."

Lobo shrugged. "It's okay. My cousin was a pendejo. But El Escopeta is obsessed with the death cult of La Santa Muerte. He prays to shrines, skeletons wearing wedding dresses. He's out of his mind."

"One of my skills, Lobo, is not caring about such things. I'll talk to him, and I'll get approval from Sinaloa for your men to pass through the mountains."

"Sinaloa doesn't run those mountains. The Black Knights control the territory."

"Sí, but the Sinaloans are up there fighting them. Better I align everyone against Los Caballeros Negros to avoid any . . . additional conflict.

"Now, amigo, I have a plane to catch to Culiacán."

Lobo shook his head in wonderment. "Cardoza, I have met some crazies in my life. But some of the things they say you do . . . if half of them are true, you are the craziest pendejo I've ever met."

Cardoza laughed at this. "No, my friend. I am just a humble consultant."

With narrow eyes, Lobo replied, "Right."

CHAPTER 15

The drive from Falls Church, Virginia, to Dulles International Airport can take hours in rush-hour traffic, but at four a.m. it was a breeze for the Duffy family. Josh drove while Nichole whispered advice and counsel about leadership to her husband, and Harry and Mandy snored in their car seats behind them. Josh nodded often, spoke little, and silently worried that he was a total fucking fraud and was going to get himself and his men killed and never see his family again.

If Nichole was thinking the same thing, however, she hid it well. He'd found her encouraging over the past day and a half, if only a little overbearing, but that was nothing new. It had been their relationship from the beginning.

The two had met under horrific circumstances, years before, when he was a young security contractor and she was a young Army officer. At first it appeared they had little in common, and even now there was something of a disparity in the way they interacted with others. Nichole was straightforward and no-nonsense, Duff a little more easygoing and less inclined to ruffle feathers.

But their relationship with each other seemed to work from the beginning. They fell in love quickly and their love had remained a constant; they met under extraordinary adversity and they had withstood numerous difficulties, together. After seven years they both knew their love was the one true thing they could trust when it seemed as if everything else was falling apart around them.

Dulles was active at four forty a.m.; a row of cars lined up outside departures, disgorging passengers for six-a.m. flights across the country, up into Canada, and down into Central and South America. Duff pulled Nichole's beige 2006 Honda Odyssey minivan into the fray and found a tight space to park in, then climbed out and met his wife on the pavement. He reached to embrace her, but she grabbed both his arms and held him back away from her.

He could see it in her eyes; she was all business. "I put an extra tourniquet in your duffel. Added chemlights to the outside of your pack, water purification tablets and a LifeStraw in your go-bag. You've got extra batteries and three flashlights, but you've got to remember to recharge them whenever you can while you're down there."

"I will." He opened the back door of the minivan and found both his kids sound asleep. He leaned in and kissed Mandy on the forehead.

"Love you, baby doll," he whispered.

Then he unfastened Harry, hefted him into his arms, and gave him a gentle hug so he didn't rouse him. "Love you, little man."

He wondered if he'd ever see his kids again, but he fought giving off any indication of the disquiet he was feeling.

Once Harry was again buckled in his car seat, Duff made his way to the rear of the Honda. Nichole had already removed his two bags, and she shouldered the duffel. She hefted the backpack off the ground and handed it to him; he struggled to get it on his back because he'd been exercising nearly constantly the past thirty hours, and the muscles in his arms and shoulders were sore from the exertion.

But he got the pack on, then grabbed the massive duffel from his wife.

She said, "I want you hydrating every chance you get. Salt tablets are in your—"

He interrupted her, because he had to get moving. "I'm going to be fine, Nik." He dropped the duffel and kissed her. She kissed him back this time, then pulled back again, but just a few inches.

"You're going to be fine if you do everything we talked about and lead your men with authority. Don't put up with *any* back talk or dissent. You show them weakness, and they'll feed off that. They'll lose respect for you, and they'll coordinate with one another to challenge your authority. Trust me, if you show *any* insecurity, the sharks on your team will smell blood in the water."

Duff stole a glance at his G-Shock. "Be a dick, then. Got it."

"I'm serious."

"I know you are, babe. I've got to catch my flight."

"Are you sure you don't want to take your spare prosthetic? It's in the back seat between the kids. You don't know what might happen to—"

"I can't let anyone know I'm missing my leg. Carrying around a backup is gonna be a bit of a tip-off."

"You can hide it in your bag."

"Six men in a truck, Nikki. We aren't hiding *anything* from one another." He thought about this, then shrugged. "Except my leg. I keep my boots and my pants on, and they'll never know."

He leaned forward and kissed her one last time, and this time she kissed him back hard. He said, "As soon as the kids wake up, tell them I love them. I'll see you all in three weeks."

"Damn right, you will," Nichole said, tears only now forming in her eyes.

"I love you," Duff said, fighting his own tears.

She smiled, but he could see the only partially hidden fear in her eyes now. She said, "Come home safe so I can love you back."

CHAPTER 16

The Bell Jet Ranger helicopter took off from Benito Juarez International Airport just before eleven a.m., only ninety minutes after the American Airlines flight Josh Duffy had flown on from Dulles landed. Duff had been shepherded into the helo directly after clearing immigration and customs for the twenty-minute flight to the Mexico City headquarters of Armored Saint, housed in a small former military base in the northern urban suburb of Coyotepec.

The aircraft touched down on the dusty helipad, disgorging its lone occupant and his two bags before taking back to the hazy sky to return to the airport.

The sound of the rotors had not yet died away when he heard a voice behind him.

"Welcome to Mexico, Duff. Hope you're ready for this shit."

He turned to find Mike Gordon standing behind him in the midday sun, wearing a black Armored Saint polo, khaki cargo pants, and a ball cap with the company logo: a yellow cross on a blue shield.

"Hey, Gordo. When did you get down?"

Gordon said, "Just last night. Dude, how the hell did you make TL? What happened in that hotel room at the Ritz? You give Remmick a hand job?"

Gordon hefted Duffy's kit bag, and Duffy slung his big backpack over his shoulders. They began heading for the nearest building, a two-story structure that looked like it was being used as a barracks.

Duff laughed as he walked, doing his best to relax the muscles in his back, tight from five hours of flying. "He just offered it up during the interview. Said he lost his Charlie lead."

"Yeah, to a case of the chicken shits. And I lost an asshole this morning to the same affliction." Gordon shrugged. "Replaced him with a static-post Joe who looks like he'll do." He turned to Duffy. "Still, Duff . . . I can't picture you as TL. No offense."

"Why not?"

"'Cause back in J-Bad you were the nice guy. The easygoing dude who pulled more than his share and didn't ever bitch. Everybody took advantage of you. Me included." He shrugged again. "Me especially. Being TL takes a different mind-set man. You know that, right?"

"Trust me, Nikki has been shoving that mind-set down my throat. I'll be fine. Nobody's going to push me around."

They reached the door and entered a hallway. "I got your back if you need help," Gordon said.

"Thanks, but I'm solid."

"Whatever you say, Charlie Lead." They reached an open door, and inside were a pair of cots and a couple of small desks. One of the small sleeping areas was already packed with Gordon's gear. "We're bunking in here. We've got a meeting with Remmick in twenty, but throw your shit down and I'll run you by your team room so you can meet your crew. I've met all your Joes, so I can introduce you, at least." He looked at Duffy. "Running them will be *your* problem."

A minute later they entered a large team room. A half dozen bunk beds ran down the wall to their left, and to their right, three plastic picnic tables sat, all of them covered with gear, clothing, rations, and other personal items.

Music played somewhere; it was rap.

Duffy hated rap.

He counted five men in the room assembling gear, and he suddenly felt a pang of anxiety. He had always been the guy loading bullets in his magazines in the team room when the TL came in to introduce himself. It felt wrong somehow for him to be telling these men what to do.

But he hid his bout of nerves and nodded to the group.

Gordon stepped over to a big Bluetooth speaker sitting on a bunk and turned the music down. "Gents, meet your new TL, Josh Duffy."

A couple of the guys nodded in Duffy's direction; others just looked his way without expression.

Gordon approached the first contractor, a lean man in his midthirties who wore his hair a little long but carried himself like a military officer. He was wiry and incredibly fit-looking, and his face didn't give off even a hint of a smile.

"Duff, this is Wolfson, your Charlie Two." Duffy fought a fresh wave of intimidation looking into Wolfson's piercing gray eyes and tried to discount the feeling that he was being seen right through by them.

The men shook hands; Wolfson's grip was tight.

"Good to meet you, Wolfson."

As an answer, Wolfson said, "You're the Army guy?"

It was spoken like a pejorative, but Duffy didn't make a big deal out of it. "That's right."

Gordon jumped in quickly. "Wolfson here was SEAL Team Three. Afghanistan, Syria, bunch of shit he doesn't like to talk about."

Wolfson's eyes didn't leave Duffy's. "So, let's don't."

Duffy's own eyes narrowed now as he did his best to match the other man's hard stare. "Works for me, Charlie Two." Wolfson was going to be a handful; that much was instantly apparent.

Before anything else was said, another man stepped up to them. He appeared to Duffy to be nearly sixty years old, so Duffy immediately determined this wasn't, in fact, a member of his team, but instead a member of the Armored Saint operations support staff. He wore a threadbare white T-shirt around his burly chest and waist, and the crown of his headful of short gray hair came up to Duff's nose.

The man smiled and extended a hand with a formal flourish. He spoke in a thick French accent, which surprised Duffy. "A pleasure to make your acquaintance."

Gordon shouldered up to Duffy now. "This is Jean François Allard, your Charlie Three. He's a former officer in the Commandos Marine, French naval special ops. After that, a decade and a half in the Foreign Legion, then the last ten years in various PMCs, mostly around Africa. He's your medic."

Holy shit, Duffy thought. This guy was old enough to be his dad.

Allard said, "Most people here call me Frenchie."

Duff recovered from his surprise. "And . . . you let them?"

"Proudly. I am at your service, Charlie One."

The dude was old, but at least, Duffy thought, he seemed to understand his place in the pecking order. "Thanks, Frenchie. Good to have you on the team."

Gordon led Duffy farther into the room, up to a young African American in the process of climbing off a top bunk stacked with folded clothes, knee and elbow pads, and a pair of helmets. The man wore cargo pants with no shirt, displaying an impossibly muscular build. He looked like he worked out six hours a day and had never in his life met a carbohydrate.

There was a Marine Corps tattoo on the young man's left arm, and looking at his clean-shaven baby face, Duffy didn't think the man could have been more than twenty-four years old.

Gordon said, "This here's Squeeze, your Six."

Duffy nodded, extended a hand.

The young man's voice was loud, confident, and more than a little cocky. "All right, TL! I heard you were Eleven Bang Bang, back in the day."

Duffy cleared his throat. "I was Eleven Bravo, Army infantry, yeah. Third ID." He added, "Back in the day. You?"

Squeeze gave Duffy a halfhearted handshake. "Third Battalion, Fifth Marines." He then shouted, "Get some!"

It was the slogan of the famed Marine battalion, and Squeeze was obviously proud of it.

Duffy made an attempt to curry a little favor with the young man. "Right on, Devil Dog. Semper Fi."

Squeeze nodded while giving Duffy a little side-eye. "Yeah. Okay, man."

Gordon kept things moving. A dark-complected man with shoulder-length hair pulled back in a ponytail stood from a table on the right; in front of him was an iPad and a can of Monster energy drink.

"This is Tony Cruz. Charlie Four," Gordon said. "Fellow Army."

The two men shook hands. Cruz was smaller than Duffy by a couple of inches but powerfully built, probably around thirty-eight, and he had probing, not entirely trusting eyes, similar to Wolfson's though somewhat less intense.

Duffy said, "Glad to have another Army guy along."

Cruz shrugged. "Yeah, I was Army, but a different Army from the Third ID. I was in Fifth Group."

Another troublemaker, Duffy assessed. Fifth Group was U.S. Army Special Forces, Green Berets, a more elite unit than the one Duffy served in.

Duff responded with as much authority as he could muster in his voice. "Special Forces is badass, Charlie Four, but we served in the same Army."

Continuing his hard stare, the shorter man said, "Meant no disrespect."

Gordon spoke up helpfully again. "You're lucky, Duff. You've got a Spanish speaker on your team."

To this, Cruz replied, "I'm a Puerto Rican, raised in Chi-town. I'm not gonna fool nobody down here."

The last man in the room stepped into the conversation. He was in his thirties, with blond hair and blue eyes, an all-American look to his bright face. He wore shorts and a T-shirt that portrayed a cartoon of a bearded man. The man on the T-shirt wore both a turban and a Hawaiian shirt, and he stood next to a kiosk selling hot dogs. Underneath this odd image was the caption "Aloha-Snack Bar."

The man wearing the goofy shirt spoke now with a strong southern drawl. "You'll sure as shit fool more folks down here than I would."

Gordon said, "And this is Evans, Charlie Five. Your driver."

Evans, like Frenchie, seemed to have at least a modicum of respect for the team leader. He shook Duffy's hand and said, "Nice to meet you, boss. You can call me Nascar."

"Why would I do that?"

"'Cause I used to—"

Gordon interrupted. "He used to be SWAT in Atlanta, but he left that for rally racing. Did some Xfinity Series, which is like the minor leagues for NASCAR."

"Bullshit," Evans said. "I raced NASCAR Cup Series, too."

Squeeze said, "Yeah? How many races?"

Evans demurred a little. "One." He shrugged. "Well . . . most of one."

Duffy cocked his head. "And, what? You left that because you figured driving across cartel country would be more fun?"

The blond man chuckled at this. "Nah. Lost my sponsorship. Corporate bullshit. You know how it goes. Got my pilot's license, flew helos for Academi, a couple other PMCs, but there wasn't enough work, so I had to start driving for Armored Saint."

Cruz said, "There wasn't enough work for guys who crash helos. You slammed your bird into a river in Kandahar."

Evans explained defensively, "That was a mechanical failure, and a controlled crash. I autorotated that helo down into the drink like a rock star."

"Right, dude," was the reply, but it was clear to Duff that Cruz had been told another version of the story.

Squeeze entered the fray now. "And then you got yo' ass tossed out of two other PMCs for bad driving." The young African American looked at Duffy now. "We drew the short straw, TL. Nascar's gonna T-bone a taco stand before we get outta this fuckin' neighborhood."

Nascar started to get into Squeeze's face, but Cruz pushed them apart, cussing at them both. Before Duffy could say anything else, however, Gordon took him by the arm and addressed the team.

"Okay, kids, I'm taking Charlie One to Remmick for a meeting." Duffy couldn't help but feel that at this point, Gordon had more authority over Charlie team than he did.

He headed for the door, then turned back and gave the men a curt nod. "Good meeting you all."

"You, too, Eleven-B," said Squeeze, his sarcasm evident.

Outside in the hall, Duffy fumed, but Gordon slapped him on the back.

"I gotta say, it's nice to see that your dudes are just about as whack-adoodle as mine. I've got my own crew of dickheads, has-beens, and never-weres."

They headed towards the HQ building. Duffy said, "Wolfson and Cruz are wound tight and full of all that elite ops macho bullshit. Squeeze has the testosterone of a sixteen-year-old, probably because he's not much older than that. My driver, apparently, can't fucking drive, and . . . that French guy . . . Christ almighty. How old is he?"

Gordon slapped Duffy on the back. "Don't you worry about Frenchie. Dude is legit."

"How do you know?"

"Because I saw him killing Nazis on the History Channel." He changed the subject. "Hey, remember when I told you Remmick was a dick?"

"I do."

"Yeah, well, this is a perfect example. You and me get dudes like Nascar, while Remmick's team is stacked with legit tier-one mother-fuckers. Alpha team has ex-CIA green badgers, absolutely solid snake eaters, and they've all worked together before at other PMCs."

Duffy said, "Nothing wrong with that. Alpha will probably be the team assigned with internal perimeter security of the clients. Of course they are the first string. Tell you the truth, brother, I'm just glad to be here drawing a paycheck."

They walked out into the sunlight, heading for the HQ. Gordon said, "Then you must not be feeling what I'm feeling."

"What's that?"

"That a bunch of us are gonna die in those motherfucking mountains."

CHAPTER 17

Enter!"

Duffy had first heard Remmick's powerful voice in person two days earlier in Virginia, through the door of a hotel suite. Now it boomed through a thin wooden door in a run-down Mexican HQ building. Gordon opened it upon Remmick's instruction, and the two men entered a large room with a huge map on the wall. A dozen or so support personnel worked at laptops on tables around the room, and Shane Remmick stood ramrod straight by the map.

Gordon said, "Charlie Actual is in the house, boss."

Duffy filed in behind Bravo One and headed for the agent in charge of the mission. "Mr. Remmick. Good morning."

They shook hands, and Remmick said, "I'm Alpha One from here on out, Charlie One."

"Roger that, Alpha One."

"How was your flight?"

"Just fine, thanks. Slept most of the—"

"Nobody gives a fuck."

Duffy caught the gleam in Remmick's eye and laughed himself. "Right." His world had changed. He wasn't hanging around the sales team at Prada here; this was becoming more and more apparent.

"Okay, TLs," Remmick said. "We'll talk a few minutes, then have a full detail meeting out on the parade grounds. We'll spend the rest of today running combined drills to get everyone up to speed. Tomorrow at oh six hundred we pick up the four principals at the Interior Ministry and roll out. Solid copy?"

"Five by five, boss," said Gordon.

"Copy, Alpha One," replied Duffy.

Remmick used a laser pointer to illustrate the route on the large wall map. "Tomorrow, day one, we'll be traveling northwest through Durango, then we'll go higher, into the foothills of the Sierra Madres. First night will be in a town called El Salto . . . we'll stay in a hotel there our intel guys scouted for us. We haven't booked rooms, don't want anyone to know we're coming."

"Good," Duffy said.

"Day two will have us moving higher into the hills. The VIPs want to do a couple of welfare drop-ins on towns up there that have been hit hard by the narco wars."

Gordon asked, "These drop-ins . . . have they been set up in advance?"

Remmick shook his head. "Negative. I made clear to the VIPs before we agreed to the job that we'd take them wherever they needed to go, but other than the Black Knights, nobody will know we're up there until shortly before they see us rolling into their village.

"Now . . . day three. Weather and road conditions permitting, we should arrive at the top of the Sierras. The Devil's Spine. It's the absolute fuckin' badlands up there. The Sinaloa cartel and the Caballeros Negros are fighting for turf, with the Black Knights owning about eighty percent of the pueblos. The highways are one hundred percent disputed, with the additional snag being that many of the unaligned locals are armed, as well, and they don't exactly love or trust strangers."

Gordon and Duffy exchanged a look of concern.

Remmick continued. "The Sinaloans . . . they *want* the war to come to that territory. If it does, they'll just retreat back to Culiacán and wait it out while the army destroys the Black Knights. This means the Sinaloa cartel sure as shit does not want the VIPs up there trying to stop the army from coming in and kicking ass. Gotta figure they will fight us if they know what we're up to, so keeping a low profile is key."

Duffy cocked his head. "Isn't that gonna be a little hard to do with armored gun trucks and a series of public meet-and-greets?"

"It is what it is, Charlie One. We'll move fast on the highways and stealthy on the back roads. We'll roll hard with eyes open, and we'll meet and defeat any threat. Hoo-yah?"

"Hoo-yah," Duff said, but his tone was less assured. "What about QRF?"

"If we should get into heat we can't extract ourselves from, which I do not expect, then we'll call up Mexican military assets."

Duffy glanced Gordon's way again, then looked back to Remmick. "I thought the Mex mil wasn't in the Sierra Madres."

"They aren't. There's a camp outside of Durango, in the hills east of the mountains."

"How far is that to the top of the range?"

Remmick put his laser on a spot on the map that looked, to Duffy, to be a hell of a long way away from the top of the Sierra Madres. He said, "We can expect to wait up to eighteen hours before the cavalry arrives." He turned back to Duffy, and when Duffy said nothing, Remmick added, "We are a self-contained op. What you see is what you get."

Holy shit, thought Duffy. "Uh . . . roger that, boss."

Duff could tell Gordon was equally disturbed by the news that there was no quick reaction force. But the former Marine did not pursue the matter further. "Can you show us on the map where the VIPs will meet with Rafael Archuleta?"

"Negative. We don't know yet. We will be notified en route." He zapped a tiny speck on the map. "We're heading here, Boca Arriba, but it's just a speck on the satellite, so we figure it's a transitional location. I bet we'll be sitting there holding our dicks waiting on further instructions from the Black Knights. When we get them, we'll roll out, go meet up with Archuleta, and the VIPs will have their meeting. Assuming the Black Knights agree to terms, the VIPs then want to spend up to two weeks bouncing around to the major towns in the Sierra

Madres, letting the locals know about the peacekeeping initiative. When we're done on the Spine, we'll head north, to Creel, in Chihuahua. The VIPs will fly out from there, we'll fly to Mexico City, and our equipment will be trucked over the border and back to the home office in Dallas."

Gordon looked over the map. "I've done a hell of a lot of mobile ops in my day, but . . . this is a lot of ground. Really steep and shitty terrain. I bet the roads will be in bad shape, too. This reminds me of the Kush."

"Correct. It's not at all unlike the Afghan-Pak border. What's your point?"

"Well . . . why aren't we conducting this op in helos?"

Remmick answered immediately. "MANPADS."

"MANPADS?"

"Man-portable—"

Gordon said, "Man-portable air defense systems. Shoulder-fired surface-to-air missiles. I know what they are. I just didn't know the cartels had—"

Remmick spoke over him. "Earlier this month, a pair of Mexican marine helicopters flying over the western Madres in Sinaloa was targeted by surface-to-air missiles. Both helos went down, killing nineteen."

"Holy shit! On the news, they said those helos collided with each other."

Remmick nodded. "The Mexicans tried to cover it up. The helos were nearly three hundred meters apart when they were hit. There was no collision. Word got to the UN somehow."

"The Black Knights did it?" Duffy asked.

Remmick shrugged at this. "Could have been the Sinaloa cartel, but the UN thinks it was the Black Knights."

"How the hell did any of the cartels get fucking missiles?"

"CIA thinks they're out of Venezuela. Top-of-the-line Igla-S SA-7s, as the U.S. military has designated them. If you've got the money, you can buy whatever the hell you want down there. And the BKs have the money. The UN figures they were purchased by Archuleta the minute the army started talking about taking his territory back from him."

Gordon spoke softly, almost to himself. "I'll take my chances on the roads. I've been in a helo crash. They suck."

"Same here, and agreed," Remmick said, and then both men looked to Duffy.

"I've seen the aftermath of a helo crash. I'm with you guys. Let's stay on terra firma."

Remmick motioned back to the map, but before he could speak, there was a tentative knock at the door.

He said, "Good, that must be our cultural expert."

Gordon and Duffy looked at each other in confusion.

"Come on in, Gabby," Remmick said.

A Hispanic woman in her thirties entered. She had short brown hair, and she wore a black Armored Saint polo and cargo pants, both of which looked brand-new.

Remmick said, "Gabby, this is Gordon and Duffy, the other two team leaders on the operation. TLs, this is Dr. Gabriella Flores, from the National Museum of Anthropology here in Mexico City. We're bringing her on board our security force to serve as a regional analyst. She was born and raised in the Sierra Madres. She speaks some of the local dialects we might encounter, so we'll be able to communicate with the civs, if necessary. She'll help out with navigation and intel atmospherics, as well."

Duffy thought she looked tiny and meek, but she moved to him and shook his hand in a manner that conveyed a serious self-assuredness.

"Doctor," Duff said.

Shaking Gordon's hand now, she said, "Nice to meet you both."

Remmick continued the introduction. "Gabby will be the non-Spanish terp for the security force. She'll also keep us pointed in the right direction, let us know what she sees and what she thinks."

"And we'll keep you safe, ma'am," Gordon added.

She looked at Remmick, and now Duffy registered a crack in her confident façade. "Whether we stay safe does not depend on us. It will depend on your ability to avoid the forces up there that can destroy you, and the ability of the diplomats to keep Los Caballeros Negros willing to accept us."

Gordon glanced Duffy's way again.

Dr. Flores looked to the other team leaders now. "I only pray you understand how dangerous this will be for you and your men. There is no law where we are going. None. It is like the American West a hundred and fifty years ago, but with meth, cocaine, opium, fentanyl, armies of sicarios with machetes, trucks, machine guns, and rockets."

"And MANPADS," Gordon muttered softly.

Remmick put a paternal hand on Dr. Flores's shoulder and steered her back to the door. "Come with us to the parade ground for the briefing, and I'm sure I can convince you we'll be able to handle whatever comes our way."

They headed out of the room; Duffy could still hear Flores talking to Remmick, but he lagged behind with Gordon.

"Did you know there was no QRF on this run?"

Mike Gordon whispered back, "Remember when I told you coming down here was a bad idea? Well, the absence of a QRF ready to pull our asses out of the fire if we get in trouble is pretty much the kinda shit I was talking about."

"Did you know?" Duff repeated.

Gordon shook his head while he walked. "Nope. He just dropped that shit on me just like he did you. We're in this together, kid."

"What the hell," Duffy muttered, and then he followed his friend out the door to the parade ground at the center of the installation.

CHAPTER 18

Josh Duffy slipped his Oakleys over his eyes as soon as he stepped back into the sun's rays, and he met up with the five other men of Charlie team in front of a row of massive matte-black armored personnel carriers. Each one was nearly nine feet high and easily twenty feet in length; they had armored turrets on top, gun-ports on the sides, thick all-terrain tires, and wire mesh in front of bulletproof glass in the windshields and side windows.

The machines were also covered in slat armor—heavy steel grating used to cause an incoming missile to detonate just in front of the thick armor to prevent penetration.

The windshields and rear windows were covered in steel mesh, as well.

Duffy had worked in APCs numerous times in the Middle East, but these were among the nicest rigs he'd ever laid eyes on. His confidence level about the entire mission grew precipitously, until he remembered he'd actually have to get *out* of his armored truck at some point along the route to do his job.

Duff got his first look at the other two teams on the parade ground in front of the APCs. Every single man on Alpha looked intense and steel-eyed, like Alpha One himself. The men on Gordon's Bravo team, in contrast, seemed a little more like Duff's crew—something of a mixed bag of attitudes, physiques, and dress.

Remmick stepped in front of the twenty-one men and one woman gathered here in the afternoon heat and walked up to the grille of the closest gun truck, where he turned to face the small crowd.

In a booming voice, he said, "What you see before you are five of the best armored personnel carriers available on the market. International Armored Group, Guardian model. These APCs have extreme off-road capability, run-flat tires, high-grade suspension, on- and off-road gas-nitrous shocks, integrated air filtration, six-point-two-liter V8 engines that generate nearly four hundred horses and enough torque to get us up to the top of those mountains. They have gunports, a roof escape hatch with a mounted turret, side and rear hatches, and a belly escape hatch for covered egress.

"Each vic can transport up to eight fully geared Joes, so the twenty-five men and two women going on this little jaunt will have plenty of space, and we'll be able to haul all our grub, gas, and gear, as well."

Remmick slapped the side of the truck to his left.

"Military-grade armor, standing level four, will defeat fifty cals and grenades. Blast protection against IEDs and mines, as well."

A man on Gordon's team asked, "What about RPGs, boss?"

"The slat armor will help with that. An RPG won't puncture the armor, but a very lucky shot or a very skilled shooter can score a mobility kill by knocking out a tire. Not an easy shot, but we all know how Murphy's Law goes. Same thing for running over an IED. If it's big enough, it's a problem. Let's keep the RPGs off us, and let's keep ourselves off the IEDs."

The contractor said, "Hoo-yah, sir."

Remmick continued to address the issue. "That said, we'll have extra tires stored to deal with that. Changing a tire under fire is something most of you boys should have some experience with, and we're going to work on it this afternoon to make sure we're all squared away. How copy?"

Everyone, Dr. Flores excluded, shouted out agreement.

Remmick said, "Here's how we're gonna roll. Vehicle one in the motorcade is call sign War Horse. It's up front with five members of Alpha team, led by Jason Vance, Alpha Two." A muscular man with a thick red beard and mustache, wearing mirrored shades and a tropical hat, lifted an arm up while Remmick kept talking.

"Pack Horse One and Pack Horse Two will carry Bravo team, four men each, plus our extra gear, ammo, water, food, and fuel. Show Horse is the limo on this run and will roll in the middle of the motorcade between the Pack Horses, with the remainder of Alpha, including myself, the four principals, and Dr. Flores, our cultural liaison. That's eight in the limo."

"And lastly, bringing up the rear will be Crazy Horse. That's the six operators of Charlie." Addressing Duffy, he said, "Charlie One, your job is CAT."

Flores spoke up now. "Cat? What do you mean, 'cat'?"

Remmick replied, "Counterassault team, doc. In an ambush on the road, Crazy Horse will buy us time." He looked back to Duffy. "Charlie One, if the motorcade is engaged, you will attack the attackers and lay down an obscene amount of hate until the principals are safe. Then you will rejoin us. Got it?"

"Understood, sir."

Behind Duffy, he heard Squeeze speaking softly. "Fuck yeah, baby."

Remmick either didn't hear the comment or he didn't care, because now he turned back to Gabby. "Dr. Flores, you'll have to excuse my frankness when addressing my men now."

"Of course, Mr. Remmick."

Remmick nodded, then took a couple of steps closer to the contractors arrayed in a semicircle in front of him. "Listen up, assholes. While I'm new to Armored Saint, this sure as shit is *not* my first rodeo. I know why you're here. Some of you are in it for the money. Some for the action. Some of you are here so you don't have to be home with your fat-ass wife and your snot-nose kids. Nobody gives a fuck why you came, only what you do while you're on this movement through bandit country. This will be an extremely high-risk run; if you haven't figured that out already, then God have mercy on your dumb ass. But you're all grown-assed men, and you all signed on. For the duration of this op, you belong to me. Any dissent. Any hesitation"—the fit middle-aged man waved a finger in an arc across the crowd—"I will personally square you away, and that means I will *fuck you up*."

There were some nods, but no one said a word.

"All right," Remmick said, "go jock up with full battle rattle and be back here in thirty mikes to run some drills. In the meantime, if you have any questions . . . go fuck yourself."

There was laughter in the group, but Duffy noticed that Dr. Flores just looked around her as if she were in the middle of an insane asylum.

CHAPTER 19

The twenty-two men broke into their respective teams and walked towards the armory, a large concrete building a block and a half away from the parade ground, still inside the wire of the repurposed fort. Once inside, the men found themselves standing in a small warehouse in front of crates and racks, and behind them waited a shipping container full of gear, weapons, and ammunition.

The rest of Charlie team had already toured the armory and knew what was available, but this was Duffy's first look. He was impressed, to say the least, but not entirely surprised. Even with Armored Saint's horrible reputation in how they treated their employees and went cheap on their operational support staff, they were known for having some badass weaponry.

He was still taking it all in when Wolfson, the ex-SEAL, stepped up.

"How we gonna roll, Duff?"

He was asking about the duties of each member of the small unit, and Duffy knew he had to show utter confidence and authority now. Right or wrong, Nichole had told him, he had to comport himself as if he had no doubts.

"Nascar drives, obviously," he said.

Squeeze immediately muttered, "I done told you that mother-fucker can't drive for shit."

Duffy ignored Charlie Six and pointed to Nascar now. "I want you armed with a short-barreled rifle. A carbine, not a submachine gun. We might have to hit out to distances, but choose something compact enough to wield out your gunport while behind the wheel."

Nascar scanned a long rack of weapons on a rack across the room. "AR with a ten-point-five-inch barrel suits me."

"That'll work." Duffy then said, "I'll take front passenger seat with a short-barreled rifle on my chest and a pump shotgun between the seats."

Cruz, the ex–Green Beret, said, "Ridin' shotgun with a shotgun. That's original."

Duffy ignored this comment, as well, though his wife's insistence that he stomp down any back talk whatsoever rang in his mind. Still, he pushed on, keeping his voice self-assured. "Wolfson is our designated marksman, behind me on the starboard gunport. You will carry a sniper rifle as well as a subgun."

Wolfson nodded. "I saw an HK417 in the container, variable ten-power scope. I'll pull that for long distance. I'll grab a folding-stock Scorpion off the wall for an SMG."

"All right," Duffy said. "Frenchie will ride right behind Nascar on the port side. You're the team medic. I want you with a scoped carbine, as well. Not short-barreled, you need to hit at distance, but something you can manipulate while dismounted, as well."

Frenchie clicked his heels and nodded, which Duffy found to be both surreal and appreciated. "There's a FAMAS still in its case over there." The FAMAS was the current standard rifle for the French military and widely used in the Foreign Legion, as well. Duffy himself had never even held one, but if it was the weapon Frenchie felt most comfortable with, that was good enough for Duffy.

Now he turned to Charlie Six, knowing full well he wouldn't receive the same deference from the former Marine.

"Squeeze, you're the up gunner. You'll mount a light machine gun in the turret and have an M32 grenade launcher at the ready below the roof hatch. Draw a sub with a collapsible stock for when we're dismounted."

The young African American could not have been happier. "That's what I'm talkin' about, Eleven-B! I got you!"

Duffy sighed inwardly, felt tension in the pit of his stomach, and turned to the last man on the team. "And Charlie Four, you're back of the bus."

Cruz nodded. "Roger that. I'll be your trunk monkey, TL, but I want a belt-fed LMG, too."

"No argument from me on that," Duff said. "Crazy Horse is the last vehicle in the motorcade, and as the last vic, that means we have the only rearward-facing eyes. *And* the only rearward-aimed gun until all the turret gunners can turn around and face six. I want you carrying the biggest weapon you can wield."

Cruz said, "My biggest weapon is my swinging dick, but I hear you."

Nascar and Squeeze laughed at this.

Duffy snapped back, already reaching his breaking point with the back talk. "Stick your dick out your gunport, and I'll walk around and shoot it off myself."

Cruz smiled. "I feel you, bro. I'll save it for when I get the fuck outta those mountains with twenty-five grand. I'm gonna need it then."

Duffy took in a slow breath, then let it out. It was time to assert himself, and even though he didn't *like* it, he knew he had to *do* it. "Look, guys. Let's nip this shit in the bud. You can call me TL, you can call me boss, you can call me Charlie One or Charlie Actual, or you can just call me Duff. I don't give a damn. Just do *not* call me bro, dude, Eleven Bravo, Eleven Bang Bang, Eleven-B, Army, or *anything* else. We clear on that?"

Cruz said, "Shit, boss man. Chill out. It's all good."

Duffy took half a step closer to the smaller but obviously fitter man. "Are . . . we . . . clear?"

Cruz held his ground, hesitated long enough to save face, then said, "Roger that, TL."

Duffy kept the staring contest going a few moments more, then broke away and addressed the entire team. "All right. Everyone grabs a pistol, too. Nine-millimeter only, same ammo as the subguns so we don't have to stock an extra caliber. Keep it simple, Glocks, Smiths, or HKs, don't mess around with anything else." He glanced to Frenchie. "American, Austrian, or German handguns only."

Frenchie smiled. "I prefer the HK VP9, mon chef. An excellent German weapon."

"Good." To the entire team he said, "You've got twenty mikes to get kitted up and back on the parade ground in your positions in Crazy Horse."

The men broke off to collect weapons and ammo, and Duffy did the same. There was a wide array of weapons on display, even after many of the men in Alpha and Bravo had already taken their picks.

Duffy's eyes settled on one of only two short-barreled AK-47 rifles on the rack. This one, unlike the other, had an under-folding stock and an EOTech holographic optic on its top rail. He lifted the weapon, checked the action by sliding the bolt back and letting it drop forward a few times, then brought it to his eye, pointing it at the wall.

Yeah, he thought. He hadn't picked up a rifle since he'd left his M4 in the burning Chevy Suburban in Beirut, and he knew he'd be rusty, at least through the first few drills they did today. He needed to have confidence in his primary weapon, and the AK was as reliable a weapon as had ever been created. It wasn't a common choice for American security contractors who were *given* a choice, but Josh didn't care. He needed any advantage he could get to survive the next few weeks, and he had the utmost confidence in the AK-47.

Nascar had already loaded up his body armor and ammunition, and his short-barreled AR rifle hung on his chest. "Whoa," he said in surprise as he looked at his team leader. "You rockin' an AK, boss?"

Duffy shrugged. "I like the under-folder for vehicle work; it's got a bigger, meaner bullet than your AR, and I have a lot of time behind AKs in the Middle East."

"You probably have some time in *front* of them, too, eh, Charlie One?"

Duffy nodded. "Yeah, I do." He slung the weapon over his neck, then held it out. "I've had a lot of these bastards pointed in my direction. Maybe that's what gives me an appreciation for them." He'd likely had his leg shot off by one, too, but he certainly wasn't going to make mention of that at present.

When the rest of the team were fully laden with gear and weaponry, "jocked up" in the parlance of the trade, they followed Alpha and Bravo back to the parade ground. Duffy immediately noticed that the bright sunshine had given way to thick afternoon cloud cover, and he was glad for the cooling air that it brought. It was going to be an arduous several hours, he knew, especially for someone who hadn't done this shit in a hell of a long time.

He looked around at all the men with him and fought off a wave of impostor syndrome. If any of these dudes, other than Mike Gordon or Shane Remmick, knew that less than three days earlier Duffy's job had entailed helping a lady look for her cell phone that she'd misplaced while trying on clothes in J.Crew, he wouldn't just receive razzing. No, none of these men here would trust him with their lives, and his mission would fail before it even began.

He told himself now, not for the first time and certainly not for the last, that none of his men would ever know he'd been out of the game.

The rainy season had begun in Mexico; Duffy had been warned that the skies would turn gray virtually every afternoon and then open up with a deluge that might only last a few minutes but could well continue into the evening. Today the rain had held off till just before five p.m., but when it did come, it came with a vengeance.

Duff didn't mind the rain. They ran drills till after seven, so they had the opportunity to work as a team on the gun range and in and around the APC in the downpour, approximating conditions they expected to encounter during the mission.

After the drills, he and his team cleaned their gear, went back to the barracks, and put on dry clothes.

It was almost ten p.m. now, and Duff sat under a tin roof outside the barracks, surrounded on both sides by the few men still up, talking on cell phones, smoking, and drinking from cans of Modelo beer.

They'd have to muster at four a.m., so most of the men had retired to their bunks, but there were still a half dozen out there with him.

Duffy was too amped to sleep, but he'd been using the time to pore over maps and to work with Nascar on the layout of every piece of medical equipment, every emergency tool, and all the other gear in the APC. They packed tents and bedding and extra water and batteries and ammo on racks on the outside of the vehicle, as well. They'd gotten soaked to the bone doing it, but while Nascar took a shower and went to his bunk, Duffy decided to come outside and make a quick call to his wife.

As he dialed her number, in the distance, through the rain, Duffy saw Alpha team loading gear into one of their two APCs. The itinerary Remmick had handed to the TLs called for a four thirty a.m. load-up time, but Gordon had told Duff that Alpha team was made up of uniquely hard chargers, so it wasn't too much of a surprise to see them rolling crates of belt-fed ammo cans into War Horse, the lead vehicle in the motorcade.

Duffy's attention to the men out in the rain waned immediately when he heard a click on the phone that was pressed to his ear.

As the steady rain beat on the tin awning just above him, he heard his wife's voice, and it instantly soothed him.

"Hello?"

"Hey, Nik, it's me."

"Hey, babe. How was day one as the head honcho of your own team?"

"It went well. Good crew. Did Harry eat his dinner?"

"Had to negotiate for the last few bites. Carrots and apples earned him a cookie. Mandy said I was giving in too easily."

"She's gonna be even tougher than her mom. Real officer material."

"How are the men treating you?"

Duffy paused at this, then said, "We ran tight today in the drills. Felt a lot like my team back in Fallujah."

"I hope you don't meet any impressionable young women down in Mexico like you did in Fallujah."

Duff smiled at this. "You weren't *that* impressionable." He then turned serious. "You were right, Nik. This team leader gig is rough. Some of the Joes are tougher to work with than others, for sure."

Nichole's voice changed quickly. "You've got to police that bullshit out of them from the get-go, Josh."

Defensively, he replied, "I *am*. Two of the guys are being respectful. The driver and the medic. The other three are a work in progress, but I've got it under control."

She calmed a little. "I know you do. You roll out for the mountains tomorrow?"

"Oh six hundred. Gonna rack out as soon as I hang up."

"We miss you."

"Each team leader has a sat phone, so I'll be able to call in once in a while, but I don't know how often I can—"

"Don't worry about us. Just be careful, and lead those men."

"I will. And you lead those kids."

"I have a good second-in-command in Mandy."

"I love you," Josh said.

"Love you more," replied Nichole. Then she said, "Is it bad that I wish I was there instead of you?"

"You miss this shit, don't you?"

"Never did the stuff you did, but I do miss the Army."

Josh sighed. He'd convinced her to leave the military after six years of service, and it was another of his regrets. "I'm sorry about that," he said.

Nichole answered back, "Not what I was saying. Honestly, I just wish I could tear into those assholes who aren't showing you respect." She giggled a little. "*That's* the shit I miss."

A minute later, Josh Duffy walked through the rain towards his quarters.

CHAPTER 20

Oscar Cardoza didn't want to go to Culiacán, the capital of Sinaloa, but as he looked out the portal of his rented twin-engine Beechcraft Baron G58, he saw the twinkling evening lights over the capital of the western coastal state, and he psyched himself up for tonight's work.

Sinaloa state was known for general lawlessness and rampant drug cartel activity. Even though he prided himself on working with most of the organizations in Mexico, Cardoza's relationship between the different groups varied, and some of his relationships were more precarious than others.

Even though the Zetas were cutthroat killers, for example, Cardoza had worked closely with them countless times, and he knew his value to their leadership.

His relationship with the Guadalajara Group was still new, but the organization had been professional and eager to work with him.

But things were different with the men in Culiacán. They were the Sinaloa cartel, and they had proven over the years to be exceedingly difficult to work with. Cardoza's three operations on their behalf had been a decidedly mixed bag: one a semi-success, one an abject failure for which he was fortunately not held personally accountable, and one mission that he'd accomplished but that had led to disastrous consequences for the cartel in the form of reprisals from the Jalisco New Generation, an upstart cartel to the north that had exceeded the Cartel del Golfo in size in the past few years.

Despite his trepidation, coming here to Culiacán and working with the leader of the Sinaloa cartel was central to the ultimate success of his plan, and he knew he had to negotiate a deal before the motorcade of diplomats and gringo security officers made it into the mountains.

Cardoza traveled alone today, as was his way, and although this put him in unimaginable risk, considering the area and considering the organization he'd come to speak with, he felt that his low-profile approach was best. He told himself he wouldn't be able to rely on his physical skills to get him out of any real trouble here; he was well trained with weapons and in hand-to-hand fighting, but that would be no match for the numbers of enemy and firepower they would possess if this turned ugly.

But the one thing he did have going for him in this scenario was not his brawn. It was his brain. He trusted that he would be able to think himself out of or talk himself out of any problem that might arise here on the west coast of Mexico. He might do it with flattery or with bribery, but it was just as likely he would do it via name dropping or connection peddling. Cardoza knew virtually everyone here worth knowing, and he felt this would provide him more security than several dozen bodyguards.

He'd made it this far in life playing all sides against one another; he told himself he could do it again tonight.

At the same time, however, he fantasized about a time, very soon now, when he wouldn't have to live like this. When he could leave the danger behind, free himself from the daily anxiety of being arrested by the U.S. or the Mexican government, or of being kidnapped, tortured, and killed by an extremely dissatisfied client or the competitor of an extremely satisfied one.

After his mission up and into the mountains, he'd be able to declare himself the winner of his dangerous game, and then he would retire.

And then, he'd decided, he would get as far away from Mexico as he could, as far away from this hemisphere as he could, and turn his back on this land and its troubles.

But first, he had a few more days of the tough stuff ahead of him, and one of the toughest moments of all was right now.

His pilot taxied to a fixed operating base at Bachigualato Federal International Airport, and Cardoza climbed down onto the tarmac in the darkness and in a light rain.

Moving after dark around here wouldn't have been anyone's first choice, but he was well aware that he was operating under a ticking clock, and he had a lot to accomplish in just a few days.

He picked up his rented Jeep and drove east, and when he reached the little town of Tachinolpa, he found a gas station, filled his tank, and made a phone call. Waiting in the station for fifteen minutes, he measured his breathing and thought of his strategy.

Eventually, a young man on a motorcycle pulled in next to his burgundy Wrangler. Cardoza nodded at the man, who nodded back, and the forty-six-year-old from Mexico City climbed back into his vehicle and followed the biker onto the street, then up a series of hilly roads back to the east.

Twenty minutes after setting out, Oscar Cardoza drove slowly along a gravel path, still behind the motorbike, past cooking fires thick with the smell of wood smoke, surrounded by men and women who lived in nearby cinder-block huts.

He eyed the men along the road. He saw no weapons at first, but there was a hard edge to the population here.

Oscar Cardoza had the training to recognize trouble.

At first it was just the sense of formidability in the population that he noticed. Not long after, however, he saw the locals looking back at him with mistrust and even malevolence. He had expected this—it was nothing he hadn't seen many times before—but it continued to fill him with unease as he rolled higher into the hills.

The guns came next. Young men walking around lazily with poorly maintained pistol-gripped pump shotguns. They weren't manning a roadblock; rather, they were just armed locals ready at all times to be called to a fight. The scatterguns in the crowds graduated into old Uzi submachine guns as he climbed up the hills; these small but effective weapons hung from the shoulders of men who looked tougher and fitter than those lower and behind him. As he went even higher, the Uzis disappeared, as well, and he noticed Heckler & Koch G3s and Colt AR-15s on the shoulders and across the chests of men who peered overtly at Cardoza and his four-wheel-drive vehicle as he ascended past them.

Still, there were no roadblocks. He'd driven by easily 150 armed fighting-age males, but no one had made a move to impede his advance.

The motorcycle and the man on it were his ticket through this territory, he assumed.

No, that wasn't it. A dry little smile crossed his face now. These cabrones didn't want to stop anybody from coming up here. They damn well *wanted* a fight.

Locos, he said to himself.

These were not the high Sierras, they weren't even mountains. Cardoza had merely driven into the foothills of the Sierra Madres, so the Wrangler had no trouble making its way, until it was finally stopped by an armed checkpoint in the road. As Cardoza put the vehicle in park, he had visions of a couple hundred armed hombres in the area listening to the night intently, hoping like hell to hear the cracking of gunfire that told them their services would be needed, although he didn't imagine anyone would get too worked up over one man in a Jeep.

His identification was checked by a guard, calls were made over a handheld radio, and soon he was led onwards, again by the young man on the motorcycle, until he rounded a turn and came upon his destination.

Unlike the meeting with the patrón in Guadalajara, he was not taken to an expansive mansion here in Culiacán. He parked in the dark, just outside a squat cinder-block building with a canvas tarp for a main door. Outside the entrance were dozens of white candles, all lit and flickering in the damp night air. At least twenty people stood around, serious men wearing cowboy boots and jeans, western shirts and ball caps. More importantly to Cardoza, however, they were all armed with American AR-15 rifles, and body armor protected their chests. A pickup truck with a machine gun mounted on the back sat parked near the door to the building, the weapon's operator leaning against the barrel of his gun, bored. Still, the sentry's eyes were on the Jeep, and Cardoza knew the man only had to charge the weapon, aim it perfunctorily, and then press down on the butterfly trigger to blast the Wrangler and its lone occupant to hell.

Cardoza climbed out of the vehicle slowly, stretched his back a moment, then took off his light jacket, leaving him in a polo shirt, dark jeans, and alligator boots.

He affected an air of calm, trying to look as cool as the breeze on his back.

He'd just tossed his jacket in the vehicle when two men in their twenties approached. They, like everyone in sight now, had AR rifles, but they'd slung them on their backs.

"Turn around, Señor Cardoza," one said. The man from Mexico City did so, put his hands on the hood of the Wrangler, and was thoroughly frisked by both gunmen.

Cardoza chuckled. "You think I snuck a gun into Culiacán, the heart of the Sinaloan cartel? What would that get me but trouble, amigo?"

"Arms out."

"Right." Cardoza turned to face them and extended his arms, and the pat-down continued.

After a few more seconds both men stepped back, and one of the pair addressed him. "You may enter, señor."

"You are too kind, young man."

Cardoza stepped up to the entrance of the candlelit building; it didn't look like much from the outside, but with the faint glow through the windows and the brighter light sneaking between the canvas and the door frame, this structure almost had the bearing of a house of worship.

Inside, dust and smoke in the air reflected the glow of burning wicks, and there was soft, slow music playing somewhere. Trancelike, ethereal. Pungent incense added to the eerie haze from the candles lining the length of the floor of a long, narrow corridor, and Cardoza fought a bout of nerves as he began walking alone towards an open door at the end of the hall.

It was brighter in the room ahead, though still completely illuminated by candles.

He stepped in and found it to be a low-ceilinged space with a concrete floor and rolling doors on one side. It had perhaps been a small warehouse or a place to park farm equipment originally, but now it served another, and quite obvious, purpose. On the far wall of the windowless room, to the left of the garage doors, was an altar, three feet high and not unlike one found in a small Catholic church, except for the fact that it appeared to be made of cinder blocks and plywood. Flowers and candles and incense burners surrounded it. In the center of the platform, a hand-carved ornate wooden throne, painted in oxblood red, was elevated another foot, and upon the throne sat a life-sized skeleton wearing an intricately designed wedding dress.

The skeleton was positioned as if comfortable upon the throne, and in its left hand, a long wooden-handled scythe stood perpendicular to the floor, its blunt end affixed to the riser, and the business end, a long curved blade, angled away from the skeleton at eye level.

This was La Virgen de Santa Muerte; Cardoza knew all about the ritual of worshipping the virgin of death, although in the capital where he lived, and around those with whom he normally worked and socialized, the concept of praying to a fucking skeleton dressed like a bride was pure madness.

Still, he held a reverence now as if he were in the finest and most exclusive church just off the Zócalo, the main square in Mexico City. His hands were folded in front of him; he was silent and still, and he just gazed upon not only the garish altar but also the man who knelt down before it.

Cardoza waited patiently to be noticed. The man continued kneeling and did not turn around to look in Cardoza's direction. It was a full minute before he, while still facing the altar, spoke above the soft din of the ghostly music. His voice was soft, as if his own reverence for this location, unlike Cardoza's, was utterly authentic.

He said, "Señor Oscar Jesus Cardoza Ortega. It has been a long time, yes? Come in, closer, and behold the beauty of La Virgen."

Cardoza stepped forward, just behind the man kneeling, and he spoke. "Escopeta. Thank you for agreeing to see me."

The man stood up, next to Cardoza now, but he kept looking at the altar. He was in his thirties, and he wore his black hair slicked back in a small man bun and a flowing white shirt that was open all the way down to his jeans. He had a massive tattoo on his stomach and chest of crossed shotguns, smoke pouring from their barrels on his muscular pectorals. Escopeta, the man's nickname, meant "shotgun" in Spanish.

Even with all his connections and contacts, Cardoza had no idea what the man's real name was.

"Look at her, Oscar. Just *look* at her. So beautiful. So fragile. Yet . . . you see . . . she is so deadly."

Cardoza knew that success tonight required him doing his best to match the reverent tone of the other man. "Yes. I see. A very nice one."

Escopeta said, "The skeleton is real, amigo. A sixteen-year-old beauty queen who died before her time. Shot in a nightclub in Acapulco. Fortunately the bullet went through her belly below her ribs, missed her spine, and did not break any bones."

Not so fortunate for her, Cardoza thought, but he held his tongue.

"I had the best vascular surgeon in Mazatlán remove the flesh. The bones then were bleached for an entire year in the sun at one of my ranches in Chapala. The wedding dress she wears? Made in Paris, especially for her."

"It's beautiful, señor," Cardoza said, and he instantly realized he'd made a mistake.

"*She*, Oscar. Not *it.*"

"Yes, of course."

"La Santa Muerte."

"Of course."

Cardoza looked at the man, who had turned his attention back to the skeleton. Escopeta looked like a city dweller, urbane, almost metrosexual, but Cardoza knew what atrocities this man had committed with his own hands to help him rise in the ranks of the Sinaloa cartel.

The man from Culiacán said, "Tell me . . . do you pray before the saint at your home in Mexico City, or is that just what we crazy country people do?"

Cardoza was ready with an answer. "My religion is my work, sadly."

El Escopeta turned to look him in the eye. The man's own eyes were red and bloodshot, but Cardoza couldn't tell if it was from drugs, booze, lack of sleep, or even from crying.

The cartel boss said, "I see through you, Oscar. You think we are all religious zealots. We've been up in the mountains too long. That's it, isn't it?"

El Escopeta was insane, Cardoza had no doubt, and his unpredictability made him dangerous. But still, the man from Mexico City knew he had to move these proceedings along. He said, "Apologies, Escopeta, but these are the Sinaloan foothills. The mountains begin an hour to the east. You may have sicarios up there on the highways, but the Black Knights are the ones who control the—"

El Escopeta scoffed. "Sinaloa is made up of mountain men. Our bones are of the hard rock, our cold blood is of the spring-fed rivers. The Devil's Spine protects the Black Knights for now, but the true mountain men are down here, clawing our way back up."

Cardoza knew this was an opening for him to get down to business. "And I can help you with that."

The Sinaloan looked back to the altar. "Tell me how, then."

"El Patrón de Guadalajara is asking for your assistance. He will offer you consideration in—"

"Tell Guadalajara to go fuck himself."

Cardoza stifled a little sigh. "I will convey this message, if you truly wish, but I think—"

"The mountains protect us from outsiders. As does the saint."

"Neither the mountains nor La Virgen have protected you from Los Caballeros Negros, have they? The Black Knights have taken your labs, your fields, your territory. We can help you get it all back."

"I am not worried about the Black Knights. Don't you watch the news? The army is about to go in and kill them all."

Cardoza shook his head. "If the peace plan takes effect, the United Nations will be the ones going in, and they won't kill anybody. You won't get your war, and the Black Knights will get protection."

"The peace plan will never happen."

"I don't know, señor. It might, it might not. The leader of the Black Knights wants it. Rafa Archuleta *needs* it to happen, and say what you will about him, he is no fool.

"But if we wipe out the delegation, make it look like it was the work of the Black Knights, you have to admit, the army would be compelled to invade the very next day."

"What is it you are offering?"

"You need ports in Acapulco to bring in your chemicals from Asia. You need plazas in Nuevo Laredo to move product over the border. You need politicians in the capital to keep the pressure on the Gulf cartel and the Jalisco New Generation, not on Sinaloa.

"I am asking for you to let Los Zetas travel freely in the portion of the mountains you control."

Escopeta's attention had veered off to the altar, but now he spun to face Cardoza again. *"What?"*

Cardoza said, "You allow Los Zetas safe passage, and we'll end this UN peace fantasy once and for all, and we will force the army into the Sierra Madres. Then, as you said, the army will finish your enemies, and your new alliances will bring you great bounty."

"You have lost your mind, amigo. I don't need the fucking Zs in my territory to kill a couple dozen security guards. Did you see all my troops when you came in, or was your head up your ass?"

The trancelike music continued as the two men eyed each other in the candlelight.

"Apologies again. It's not *your* territory anymore. You have some men up there, enough to destroy the convoy, perhaps, but why not let the Zetas do that for you? You are Guadalajara's best customer right now, despite your . . . differences. He doesn't want Sinaloa implicated in what happens up there in the mountains. The Black Knights will be blamed, and the Zetas will be the actual culprits. Your hands stay clean, amigo."

Escopeta wiped sweat from his brow as he eyed Oscar Cardoza. "You aren't from Guadalajara."

"No, señor. I am just a consultant for them at the moment, but I encourage you to think of me as an intermediary, as much at your service as I am at theirs. You know me, we have done business before."

"I know you, but I don't *know* you. Where do you come from?"

"I am from Mexico City."

"I hear something else in your voice. Somewhere else."

"No, señor. Just the capital. Born and raised in Tepic. I live in Polanco now, near the park."

Escopeta put his hands on his hips and seemed to think for a moment. Then he said, "If the Zetas stay on the highways, my men will not interrupt their movements."

"A wise decision that you will not regret."

The younger man put a finger in Cardoza's face. "But I promise you this. They pull off the highway, even for a segundito, I'll personally skin those pinches pendejos alive."

"I will pass on this message."

El Escopeta grabbed Cardoza by his shoulders. Held him there as he stared deeply into his eyes.

"La Virgen promised me I would get my mountains back. She sent you to me. Don't fail her, or she will send *me* to *you*."

Ten minutes later Cardoza was back in his Jeep, heading west out of the hills and back towards the glowing evening lights of Culiacán in the distance. While he drove, again under escort by the young man on the motorcycle, he put his earpiece in his ear and made a call on his satellite phone.

It rang for a moment, then was picked up on the other end.

A strong voice said, "Bueno?"

"Lobo? It's Cardoza."

"Cardoza?" The man chuckled. "I thought they'd kill you in Culiacán."

"I am still among the living, *gracias a Dios*. I just spoke with El Escopeta."

"Yeah? What did that crazy cabrón have to say?"

"He said he welcomes your assistance in the Sierra Madres."

There was a pause on the line, just as Cardoza expected. Finally, Lobo said, "You're serious?"

"Absolutely. He's happy to have you and your men." Cardoza added, "Maybe you want to stay on the highway, just so you don't get lost."

Another pause, then Lobo said, "He told you he'd destroy us if we left the highway, yes?"

Cardoza shrugged to himself as he drove. "You know the man. He has a flair for the dramatic."

Lobo laughed at this, too. "Your beautiful words paint a picture that alters reality, Cardoza." He laughed again. "Bueno. We will load up and move out in the morning. You will be up there as well, yes?"

"You won't see me, but I'll be there. We will remain in contact."

"Going alone, as usual?"

"Yes."

"Then you are as crazy as they are."

Cardoza rounded a turn, and the motorcycle pulled over and waved him forward, the rider beckoning him to pull up next to him.

"Wait a moment," he told Lobo, and then he rolled down his window.

"Escopeta wants you to take this." The rider, who appeared to be a teenager, reached into his jacket and pulled out a small revolver. "It's loaded."

"I won't need a—"

"He said to keep it till you get to the highway on the Spine, and then throw it by the side of the road. We will message you a back route that will get you up there faster, but you might run into some trouble."

Cardoza took the handgun, put it in his glove compartment, and drove on. The motorcycle stayed where it was.

Breathing a small sigh of relief, he returned to his phone call. "There is not much safety in numbers on the Devil's Spine, Lobo." He chuckled into the phone. "You're about to prove that to the American contractors." Then his voice turned serious. "Anyway, I work better alone."

"Good luck, amigo," Lobo said, and then he hung up.

Cardoza focused on his driving as he pulled out the earpiece. "You're the one who needs the luck, amigo."

CHAPTER 21

At five fifty-six a.m. Duffy waited in the front passenger seat of the International Armored Group Guardian armored personnel carrier dubbed Crazy Horse as they sat parked, last in a line of five big black rigs, in front of the Secretariat of the Interior building on Calle Abraham González. Nascar had the engine off to conserve fuel, and it was quiet inside the hulking metal beast, for now.

All six men wore headsets attached to radios hooked to their body armor, which allowed them to communicate freely inside the big vehicle. Communication was key, they all knew, because each of the men had a different sight line through his own portal of thick bulletproof glass.

Squeeze inarguably had the best view on the team, because he could throw the latch on the hatch above his head, then stand in the turret on the roof. As the up gunner, when he wasn't working the turret, he was assigned a seat on the starboard-side bench next to Wolfson.

In addition to the men's intrateam radios, which could also turn into interteam radios to reach both Alpha and Bravo via a one-button frequency change, each APC had its own vehicle radio, which allowed Remmick in Show Horse, Gordon in Pack Horse One, and Duffy in

Crazy Horse to broadcast through speakers positioned throughout all the Guardians.

Remmick had been quiet on the net for the last few minutes, however, as he was coordinating their departure with the secretariat's staff.

The building they were parked in front of was a beautiful colonial mansion, and on the ride into the heart of the capital, Duff had been impressed by both the architecture of the city and the incredible mountains ringing the metropolis of nine million. The legendary smog that hung in the valley where the capital was positioned hadn't materialized yet—it was just past dawn, after all—but the city streets already bustled with private cars, trucks, scooters, motorcycles, and an incredible number of taxis.

Duff watched the passage of morning traffic out his front passenger window as they sat parked. This city looked much like any other big city he'd ever been to, and he shuddered at the thought of leaving it behind for the danger they were almost certain to encounter in the days ahead.

A short tone through the APC's speakers announced that a transmission was coming through the truck radio, and then Remmick's voice boomed in the cramped space.

"Alpha One to all call signs. Just got word that the VIPs will be coming out the front door of the secretariat in two minutes. I want my TLs and Dr. Flores dismounted in front of the vehicles with me to greet them."

Duff opened his door. Over his team radio he said, "I'll be back in a minute."

He jumped down from the side of the truck and shut the massive but perfectly balanced steel door behind him, following protocol to keep the hatches closed at all times except when entering or exiting the vehicle.

Protocol was important, Duff knew. Even here, in the heart of the safest place in Mexico.

He began walking towards Show Horse, where Remmick himself

was climbing out of his APC. Through his radio, Duff heard Squeeze say, "Yo, TL, pick me up some quesadillas while you're out."

He did not respond.

Duff met Remmick, Dr. Flores, and Mike Gordon at the base of the stairs leading up to the front door of the secretariat. He and Gordon bumped gloved fists, Flores stood with her hands on her hips and a grave look on her face, and Remmick was at parade rest, his hands behind his back. He was dressed head to toe in the same body armor and gear as the other men of Armored Saint, with an M4 rifle hanging off his chest.

Remmick wore a desert-sand-colored ball cap, and he'd shaved this morning, whereas both Duff and Gordon sported a couple days' growth on their faces.

In moments the front door of the secretariat opened, government security men stepped out and eyed the gun trucks and the men standing next to them, and then a group of four appeared, all rolling their own luggage. The three men wore suits, and the one woman was dressed in slacks and a cream-colored silk blouse.

Flores wore a black Armored Saint polo and cargo pants, with hiking boots and her short hair in a small ponytail. Upon regarding the four VIPs coming down the steps, she muttered in English, close enough for Duff to hear.

"Look at them. Dressed for a business meeting. They have no idea where they're going."

Remmick either didn't hear her or he didn't care, because he stepped up to meet the group at the bottom of the stairs, extending a hand and smiling charmingly to a silver-haired man. "Nice to see you again, Minister Herrera."

Hector Herrera was in his sixties, with an air of refinement and standing. He smiled pleasantly as the two men shook hands.

His English was excellent. "Good morning, Mr. Remmick. May I present my colleagues for this diplomatic mission?" He motioned to a strongly built man in his fifties, with thick brown hair, gray at the temples, and a square, strong jaw. Herrera said, "Reinhardt Helm, deputy director of the United Nations Department of Peacekeeping Operations."

Alpha One extended his hand. "Shane Remmick. The agent in charge. I've been following your career for some time, sir."

Remmick was all charm at the moment, Duff noted.

"And I yours, Mr. Remmick," Helm said, his German accent evident. "We are thrilled to have a celebrity along for the ride."

To this Remmick demurred. "I'm just the AIC on this operation. No more and no less. You guys are the VIPs."

Hector Herrera next said, "And please let me present Michelle LaRue, from Canada. She is the Latin American field manager for the UN High Commissioner for Refugees."

The woman appeared to Duffy to be around forty, with short blond hair and sunglasses high on her head.

"Mrs. LaRue," Remmick said as he shook her hand.

"It's Miss. Divorce was final last month, and don't say 'sorry,' because I'm sure not." While she said this to Remmick, her eyes looked past him, towards the five black armored vehicles.

"Well, we're pleased to have you along," Remmick said.

Herrera now said, "And I present Adnan Rodriguez, my assistant at the Interior Ministry."

Rodriguez was in his thirties, thin, with slicked-back hair and designer eyeglasses. He shook Remmick's hand. "Mucho gusto, señor."

"A pleasure, sir," Remmick said, and then he switched to halting Spanish. "Hablo solo un poco Español."

Rodriguez grinned, then switched to accented but strong English. "Won't be necessary. I went to undergrad at University of Texas, Austin; got my law degree from Rice, in Houston. I can speak English like a proud Texan Latino."

"Then we'll get along great. Born and raised in Dallas myself."

Remmick briefly waved at the three others with him. "Mr. Gordon here will be commanding the trucks that carry all the extra supplies, and Mr. Duffy is in command of the truck that will provide our rear security."

Nods all around, and then Remmick said, "And Dr. Gabriella Flores will provide us contractors with information on the location and people. She is fluent in some of the dialects up there."

Flores shook hands with the four principals, exchanging a few pleasantries in Spanish with Herrera and Rodriguez before retaking her spot next to Gordon and Duffy.

Herrera, deputy secretary for the Interior Ministry, spoke directly to Alpha One now. "Mr. Remmick, we extend our formal gratitude to yourself and to Armored Saint for agreeing to join us on this expedition. As I'm sure you heard, we had some staffing difficulties when it came to security. The party we plan on meeting in the Sierra Madres will not allow armed UN peacekeepers into their territory until an agreement is in place. Several other private military corporations . . . declined to provide services, citing the perceived danger in the mission."

Gabby stood shoulder to shoulder with Duff, just a few feet away, but she whispered softly, again in English, *"Perceived?"*

Remmick responded to Herrera with similar formality, impressing Duff with his ability to modulate his tone depending on the circumstance. He said, "Armored Saint is happy to step in. I assure you, Mr. Deputy Secretary, you and your mission are in good hands."

Duff glanced again at Michelle LaRue from the UN; she was still looking beyond the conversation at the Armored Saint vehicles. Now she motioned down the length of the motorcade in front of her. "Excuse me, Mr. Remmick. I have to ask. What is all this?"

Remmick cocked his head. "All what, ma'am?"

"The combat gear. And the tanks."

"These aren't tanks. They are armored personnel carriers."

"Still . . . I'm confused. I thought we were going up there to *prevent* a war, not to fight one."

Remmick's politeness was unflappable. "That's the understanding *most* of the parties share, but we need to be ready for any and all threats. It's a lawless land up high in the Sierra Madres. We need to take measures."

LaRue turned to the UN officer from Germany. "Mr. Deputy Director, surely you agree this sets a provocative tone for meetings with men who need little provocation to start trouble."

Helm was indulgent but firm. "Michelle, we've discussed this. The threat assessment has been done. We need the armored vehicles to ensure the safety of the mission."

Remmick stepped in. "My organization's intelligence team here in Mexico has also concluded that we need to take these measures. Frankly, Miss LaRue, I expect that inside of forty-eight hours, you'll be thankful we did."

Dr. Flores took a step forward and addressed the woman from the UN directly. "People will want to stop us, Miss LaRue. Kill us. I promise you this."

"I'm sorry, who are you, again?" she asked.

Remmick said, "Dr. Gabriella Flores is our cultural attaché. She knows those mountains."

Herrera said, "Michelle, I concur with Dr. Flores. My president has personally instructed me to use the highest level of private security sanctioned by Los Caballeros Negros for our mission. Armored Saint has determined that this is the best option for our safety, so the matter is decided."

"I agree," said Helm. "Let's head out without delay."

"One quick thing first," Remmick said. "We agreed to a strict security protocol to ensure your safety. Your side of the deal is that you will relinquish all forms of communication to me and my Alpha team. We will hold your phones in a secure area."

Remmick was affable but in control, and Duff respected this. He told himself he'd copy the demeanor of the agent in charge, meld it into his own, as he developed his own leadership style on the fly.

Reinhardt Helm reached into his shoulder bag and produced a Thuraya X5-Touch sat phone. "Here you are. This is the only device that Miss LaRue and I have with us."

Herrera pulled his own phone from his leather backpack. It was an Iridium Extreme, same as the one the Armored Saint team leaders carried, though Herrera's device was yellow, whereas Duff, Gordon, and Remmick carried green-and-black camo-pattern models.

Herrera said, "Adnan and I only have one satellite phone, as well. Here you are, Mr. Remmick. I would just like to have it back in the evenings to communicate our progress with the secretariat."

"Understood. We'll be as accommodating as possible, while making sure no one up there knows we're coming."

To this, Gabby Flores spoke up. "Except Los Caballeros Negros." There was a slightly sarcastic tone to her voice. Duff got the distinct impression Flores thought this whole escapade was ill-advised, but she had yet to say so directly.

Remmick gave her a look of displeasure now. "Obviously."

Just then, the sound of rumbling engines grew quickly behind them, and the group turned and looked on as four black Federal Police trucks rolled into view from the south.

Behind the trucks, motorcycles appeared. Masked federales with AR-15 rifles on their backs rolled two abreast up the street in a tight and orderly formation.

And behind the bikes, more pickup trucks. Men stood in the beds of the vehicles, behind machine guns mounted on their roofs, the men's faces covered by balaclavas, helmets on their heads.

Hector Herrera said, "Our escorts. A convoy of Federal Police will accompany us as far as the foothills of the mountains. I am told there are a dozen motorcycles along with a dozen or so trucks loaded with over sixty federales."

The vehicles stopped on the road; their engines continued to rumble, and the men behind the machine guns just looked on. Duff's right hand formed instinctively around the grip of the rifle slung across his chest; his trigger finger rested across the frame, a small fraction of a second away from accessing the trigger itself.

Next to him, he heard the familiar sound of a rifle clicking off safe as Gordon readied his weapon to fire. Both men squared their chests towards the new arrivals, instinctively positioning their body armor in the direction of all the guns.

Even though the Mexican federales were ostensibly allies to his cause today, Josh Duffy knew to keep an eye on armed men around his principals who were not part of his own team.

Reinhardt Helm asked, "Why are they all wearing face masks?"

Adnan Rodriguez answered this. "Unfortunately, in our country, serving in the Federal Police can get you and your family killed. Most officers hide their identity when in uniform, especially when their work involves the narcotraficantes."

Duff looked at Remmick. He didn't seem anxious at all about sixty new guns on the scene, but he clearly wanted to get moving. "Right. This vehicle here in the middle of the motorcade will be your limo. My men will take your luggage and put it in the cargo compartment; feel free to take any open seat on the benches inside."

Michelle LaRue said, "You call that a limo? It looks like a tank."

Remmick kept his cool, and Duff was respecting the man more and more for it. "'Limo' is just a term we security contractors use for any vehicle that holds our protectees. You, Miss LaRue, are one fourth of our precious cargo on this trip, so you ride in the limo."

The others began to move, but LaRue held her ground a moment. When Flores and the men stopped to look back at her, she addressed Helm again. "Sir, I'm not comfortable with this. We are basically asking for trouble going into those mountains with these weapons of war."

Gabby had been behind Duff, but she pushed past him now, closing on the woman. "*Asking* for trouble?" She sounded exasperated. "Miss LaRue, you have no idea where we are heading, do you? You are *all* asking for trouble by going there. Don't blame an armored car for what is about to happen to us."

"Gabby," Remmick snapped, losing his cool for the first time.

LaRue said, "Listen, miss . . ."

"Once again, señora, my name is Dr. Gabriella Flores."

LaRue pursed her lips, then said, "Listen, Dr. Flores. I understand there will be some threats on this operation. I'm not a fool. I've been doing this work a long time. I just think we are inviting a stronger reaction by going in there like we're looking for a fight."

Remmick jumped in before Flores could respond. "We will keep you safe *and* keep our discipline. We're professionals, and this isn't first time out past the wire.

"Let's get you all into Show Horse—that's our code name for the limo. Then I'll go talk with the officer in charge of the police escort and coordinate the movement. Gabby, I've got a man on my Alpha team who speaks Spanish, but why don't you come translate for me? You and I need to have a quick chat first."

But LaRue wasn't done. "Mr. Deputy Director, Mr. Deputy Secretary. We are now protected by dozens of Federal Police, and we're nowhere near the alleged danger everyone keeps speaking of. I don't want any accidents. I think our security guards should keep their weapons unloaded, at least until we get into the mountains."

Remmick's cool demeanor faltered again, but only a little. "Sorry, ma'am, but that's not going to happen. My men are pros, they won't—"

Hector Herrera interrupted. "Mr. Remmick, we are in Mexico City. Then we will be driving along extremely safe interstates to the northwest for the duration of the day. When we get to the Sierra Madres, do what you need to do. I won't interfere unless something warrants my attention. But on the way there, at least, I ask you to practice restraint."

Remmick paused a moment, then looked at his watch. Duff knew they were burning daylight and they had a long drive ahead. Remmick was probably thinking that the earlier they arrived at tonight's destination, the safer they would be.

Finally, the agent in charge said, "Will do." He turned to Gordon and Duff. "TLs, get back to your vehicles, we're moving out."

As the VIPs were led into Show Horse, and Remmick and Flores went to talk to the commander of the Federal Police contingent, Duff and Gordon began walking back to their vehicles.

Gordon said, "Did she call us 'security guards'?"

Duff chuckled. "I do believe she did."

"Jesus. Unloaded weapons? Is that bitch for real?"

Duff replied, "Remmick won't go for that. Gotta like the spunk of that lady from the museum, though. She doesn't take any shit."

"She's just a glorified terp who thinks we're all a bunch of dumb fucks from el Norte." Gordon arrived at Pack Horse One. "All right, man. Keep your ears on, and we'll try to get this clown show through the city in one formation."

"Will do. Have a good one." They bumped fists again. Duff was feeling more and more comfortable in this role that he used to know so well.

Gordon said, "Just a joyride through lovely Mexico today. Tomorrow we go up high, and that's when the real fun begins."

Engines began firing up and down the line as Duff walked back to Crazy Horse.

Once he climbed in, he unslung his AK-47 and unfolded the stock. He placed the muzzle on the floorboard with the stock jutting up between his knees.

Nascar turned to him after starting the Guardian's 6.2-liter V8. "How'd it go?"

Duff just shrugged. "Lady from the UN wants us to unload our weapons while we're under police escort."

Squeeze heard this in the back through his headset. He said, "Shiiiiit."

"Don't sweat it," Duff said. "Remmick is switched on. No way in hell he would—"

Remmick's voice blared over the truck's speakers. "Alpha One to all call signs. We're several hours from the edge of the mountains and under escort by the federales. I want all weapons green. I repeat, no rounds in chambers, all safeties on."

Squeeze muttered again. "The fuck is he talkin' about?"

Frenchie muttered a single word. "Merde."

There was a hesitation over the vehicle radio, until Mike Gordon transmitted. "Uhh . . . roger. Bravo One acknowledges 'weapons green.'"

Duff grabbed the handset on the center console and brought it to his mouth. "Charlie One . . . wilco."

Behind him, Duff heard the telltale sounds of rifles being unloaded. Magazines released from mag wells, bolts pulled back to remove rounds from chambers as the team reluctantly complied.

But that didn't mean they weren't going to bitch about it. "C'mon, Duff." Cruz spoke from the rear position. "Half these fucking federales are on the take from the cartels. Everybody knows that."

Duff just said, "Nascar, move out. Rear of the motorcade. Watch these cops." Duff didn't like it any more than the rest, but he was leadership now.

Nascar put the ten-ton rig into gear, and it began rolling forward behind Pack Horse Two.

Squeeze said, "I'm supposed to just stand up with my head sticking out of the turret with an unloaded machine gun? Are you fuckin' kidding me?"

Duff knew his men were right and Remmick was wrong. He also knew Remmick was under pressure to serve as something of a diplomat, while simultaneously fulfilling his duties as agent in charge.

But as far as Duff was concerned, he had no role as a dip on this job. This run was going to be tough enough without him disarming his team. The more he watched the sixty or so federales, all armed, surrounding his motorcade, the more certain he was that this was a bullshit order.

Josh Duffy used to abide bullshit orders all the time. He was a yes man. But Beirut had changed him somehow.

After a moment of consternation, he broadcast on the Charlie team frequency, which he knew Remmick wouldn't be monitoring. "Charlie . . . belay my last. Make your weapons ready."

Wolfson, who had been quiet, immediately spoke up. "But Remmick said we were—"

"*I'm* your TL, Wolfson. *Not* Remmick. All weps, condition red. These guys . . . the Federal Police." He paused, looking out the thick glass as they rolled through downtown Mexico City. "They . . . I don't know."

Nascar spoke up now. "I feel it, too, boss. Somethin's hinky with these jokers in their ski masks."

Duff listened to what he could hear in the truck over the rumble of the big engine. When he didn't hear anyone manipulating their weapons as ordered, he shouted, "I said rack 'em, Charlie!"

As one, all the men pulled charging handles on their weapons. Some drew their pistols and racked fresh rounds in the chambers of those, as well.

"Cocked, locked, and ready to rock!" Squeeze shouted from above.

Cruz added, "Damn good call, boss. You might be all right, after all."

The motorcade, nearly thirty vehicles in size, rolled out of central Mexico City towards the northwest as the morning sun glowed in the sky behind them.

CHAPTER 22

The massive entourage made good time, all but running civilian traffic off the road as they headed towards their destination.

They stopped for fuel at a truck stop in León, taken over in advance by more Federal Police so the dignitaries could move around freely to stretch their legs. Gordon's men of Bravo team dismounted to gas all the trucks while Duff's team got out to provide an Armored Saint security presence. The VIPs climbed out of Show Horse to buy snacks, surrounded by four of Remmick's men from Alpha.

Duff noticed that Flores was speaking to LaRue by Show Horse, but he kept his focus directed towards the passing vehicles and nearby pedestrians, and not on the conversation.

Soon they were back on the road again. Duff had spent the morning looking out a dusty bulletproof windshield with a metal grate over it, gazing upon hundreds of miles of highway, agave plantations to his left and right virtually everywhere there wasn't a town to break up the monotony. The afternoon would be more of the same, so he fought the urge to let his mind wander and kept his attention on the federales.

The armored truck had a good air-conditioning system, which was vital considering the high temperatures here in the lowlands. Duff ate a U.S. military MRE for lunch, and he realized for the first time in his life that the food was simply a sugar, salt, and carb bomb, designed to give a nineteen-year-old the calories he needed to fight all day, and not designed for the gastrointestinal system of anyone over thirty.

Duff was thirty-two; he looked back over his shoulder, saw Frenchie sitting alone on the port-side bench, and began to worry about the senior member of the detail.

But not for long. Frenchie pulled out his own lunch, and Duff saw it was a French military MRE. Everyone knew the French had the best rations, and he was pleased to see his medic starting his lunch with a pork pâté before he dug into his duck with mashed potatoes as an entrée.

As they drove along, Nascar chowed on his American MRE, using his knees to steer with while he ate his meal with no utensils, just squeezing a bag of cold chili into his mouth. As he did this, he gazed at the endless fields of agave on his side of the road. "That's a shit-ton of tequila right there, boss. I could go for a margarita right about now."

Squeeze chimed in from the turret. "What you bitchin' about down there in the AC? It's hot as fuck up here. Give me a cold cerveza."

As he sipped tea, Frenchie said, "A margarita sounds good to me, too."

"Frenchie, I thought you frogs only drank wine," Cruz said.

"I've spent more time out of France than inside France in my life. I'm a man of the world."

Squeeze said, "Yeah, the *old* world."

Duff decided to shut this shit down. "Pay attention to your sectors, not the crops. Tell me what you see. How are the cops around us acting?"

Wolfson, the former SEAL, chided his young team leader now. "You sound a little nervous there, TL. You gonna be okay?"

"Starting with you, Wolfson."

Charlie Two sighed into his mic, then said, "Starboard side, two motorcycles next to us, they're just sputtering along. These dudes look like it's just another day at the office."

"Three?" Duff asked, and Frenchie responded.

"Port side. Two men on bikes next to Crazy Horse. Nothing out of the ordinary."

"Four?"

"I've got three gun trucks and two bikes bringing up the rear," Cruz said. "The cops look alert . . . but not threatening."

"Six?"

Squeeze took a moment as he scanned 360 degrees in the turret. Finally he said, "These federale fuckers are behavin'. For now."

"Five?"

"I see what you see, boss," Nascar said. "We're at the ass end of the convoy, surrounded by heavily armed jokers in ski masks, and everybody seems to think everything's just hunky-dory."

Duff said nothing; he only grabbed a wad of napkins in the glove compartment and handed them over to Nascar as he started to put his food away.

Nascar said, "I mean, I'm a pretty optimistic, upbeat individual. But if these dudes wanted to make trouble for us, then they could do it whenever they wanted."

"Relax, chickenshit," Squeeze said from the turret. "I'll protect you."

Duff took Nascar's trash and started shoving it into a plastic bag, along with the remnants of his own leftover MRE. He was just finishing up with this when the beep came over the vehicle speakers indicating a transmission was coming through.

"Alpha One to all drivers. Full halt. Full halt."

"Guns up!" Duff shouted, unsure why the agent in charge was ordering the convoy to an immediate stop.

Duff hefted his AK, popped open the gunport below his window, and jammed the barrel outside. Behind him he heard the sounds of ports swiveling open, men moving around to orient themselves outboard.

Nascar brought the vehicle to an abrupt stop, federale motorcycles swerved to keep from hitting Pack Horse Two in front of him, and he guessed the bikes behind his rig were struggling to stop in time, as well.

Duff saw nothing outside his window that he took as an imminent threat, nor did he hear any gunfire.

Desperate for a sitrep, he spoke into his mic. "Squeeze? Whatcha got?"

"Negative contact. I've scanned 360, and I've got zip other than exactly like what we've been looking at for six hours." He added, "The cops don't look like they know what's up, either."

"Alpha One to Charlie One, over."

Remmick was broadcasting to Duff directly. He picked up the handset, his heart pounding, no idea what the hell was going on.

But he forced calm into his voice as he said, "Go for Charlie Actual, Alpha."

"I'm sending Flores back to you. She'll ride in Crazy Horse for the duration of the mission, break." There was a brief pause, then, "*You* will serve as her body man. I repeat, she is now *your* responsibility."

What the hell? Duff thought. He clicked the mic. "Roger that, Alpha Lead." But he did not understand. "Uh . . . anything I need to know?"

Remmick answered brusquely. He was pissed, clearly, but not at Duff. "Negative. If she's got actionable intel, just transmit it. If she's got opinions, complaints, suggestions, prognostications, premonitions, ghost stories . . . shit like that, I don't want to fuckin' hear them. How copy?"

"Solid copy on all, Alpha." Duff put the handset back in its cradle. To his team he said, "Relax, boys. False alarm. The lady from the museum is annoying everybody in Show Horse, so now she's going to ride with us."

Wolfson grumbled. "Lucky us."

Nascar said, "Can't say I've ever heard of an unarmed asset riding in the counterassault truck."

"Thought this was the CAT, not a cab. She must have *really* pissed off Remmick or the VIPs," Squeeze opined.

Duff could see her now through the windshield. She walked down the middle of the highway towards him, passing the parked trucks and bikes along the way. The cops just looked at her, confused.

Duff said, "Let her in on your side, Wolfson. She sits next to you."

Flores entered the vehicle. Even without her transmitting on the team frequency he could hear her talking to herself in Spanish.

"Los idiotas no entienden nada."

Duff saw Wolfson work to get her seated and harnessed in, and Cruz adjusted the frequency on the radio she wore so that she would now be broadcasting to Charlie and not to Alpha.

While this was going on, Remmick came back over the vehicle net. "Move out."

Nascar put his big truck in gear and again began following the rest of the convoy.

"Can you hear me okay back there, Dr. Flores?" Duff asked.

By way of an answer, she responded, "I didn't do anything. I was only talking to Miss LaRue about the UN's intentions. But their plan is foolish. It doesn't take into account the indigenous Tarahumara in the Sierras. The UN wants to disarm them, but they are a peaceful people who were forced to arm themselves. They *cannot* disarm as long as the narcotraficantes are up there. They must be allowed to defend themselves from the cartels. Even if the army comes and kills all Los Caballeros Negros, the Sinaloans or the Juarez cartel will still use the mountains to grow their poppy. The Tarahumara won't voluntarily—"

Duff interrupted. "Got it, ma'am. We'll take good care of you back here in Crazy Horse, I promise."

She didn't even acknowledge him. "And Helm says they will threaten to charge Archuleta with international crimes if he doesn't disarm. He *won't* disarm, which means he *won't* allow the peacekeepers in, which means the army will invade." When she received no response from anyone, she said, "Are you listening to me? This initiative will not work. It is doomed from the start."

Still, none of the contractors replied.

"What's wrong with you gringos?"

Frenchie spoke up now. "Madame, respectfully, I am no gringo."

This only infuriated her more. "You just think you can machine-gun your way through our civilization and—"

Duff had had enough. "Charlie Two?"

"—destroy anything you don't—"

"Yeah, boss?"

"—like and make the people of the Sierra Madres—"

"Reach over there and take her mic off her headset so I can talk but she can't respond. We'll let her cool off."

"—submit to the will of twenty gringos who don't even—"

"With pleasure," Wolfson replied.

Gabriella Flores's transmission went silent. Duff could still hear a little of her voice over the growl of the engines, and he imagined Wolfson could hear her a lot better than he could, but he figured once she realized she didn't have the full audience, she would take a breather.

Duff said, "Ma'am, let's try to start fresh. Firstly, we're not going to shoot anybody who doesn't need to get shot, I promise you that. I need you to just sit there next to Mr. Wolfson and enjoy the ride. You need anything, you have any problems, you talk to me, but not while I'm working."

Behind him, Gabby Flores unfastened her harness and made her way up past Wolfson. She put her head between Duff and Nascar. Without the benefit of the microphone, she spoke loudly to be heard. "You are just sitting there. You aren't working."

"Ma'am, all six of us have sectors to scan. All . . . the . . . time. We can't listen to a political science lesson right now. We keep radio discipline as best as possible so we can respond to threats."

"Trust me. Where we're going, you will have no response to the threats. You need a better plan before you just drive in there like this."

Wolfson had moved up to escort the woman back to the bench. He said, "Lady, why did you come along if you are so against this diplomatic mission?"

Flores shook her head. "I'm not against it. I'm against it *failing*. If this mission falls apart, if this convoy is destroyed or the UN can't get an agreement with Archuleta, the army will be fighting up there for years, and they'll kill a hundred thousand innocents."

When she received no response to this, she all but shouted at the men, "None of you care. Not one of you. You are all just here for the money, aren't you?"

"You're goddamned right, señorita," Wolfson said, and he snapped her harness to secure her in tightly to the bench next to him.

CHAPTER 23

At dusk the convoy had skirted to the north of the town of Sombrerete in the state of Zacatecas, traveling on the open highway towards the foothills to the west. Army units were encamped on both sides of the road here, their equipment lined up neatly, as if they were all ready to pile in, fire up engines, and head into battle.

But to Duff, the soldiers had an air of boredom about them. He wondered if that meant they were confident the peace plan would be accepted by the cartel up in the distant mountains, and they would all be returning to their base soon.

Duff wasn't as certain. Flores had made some good points, and even though Duff was no diplomat, he could imagine that the potential for charging Archuleta with war crimes just might rub the man the wrong way and make him disinclined to participate in a peace deal.

They kept driving, passing along next to Villa Insurgentes on the Durango–El Calabazal Highway, until they reached the final army checkpoint before the hills and the badlands beyond. The roads were blocked; dozens of dug-in emplacements lined the open ground on either side, the barrels of heavy machine guns facing to the west.

Remmick came over the radio now. "All call signs, be advised.

We've arrived at waypoint Delta. We are going to halt to let the federales peel off at the next intersection. We'll pass through the army checkpoint and proceed on alone."

He added, "All weapons go red at this time."

Squeeze spoke into his headset for the benefit of Charlie team. "Click, click. I'm red."

Frenchie and Cruz laughed at this.

The motorcade was soon ordered to a halt, and the Federal Police began pulling off down a road to the north.

From the turret, Squeeze said, "I guess our escort just said, 'No mas.'"

Nascar added, "And we keep going. Up to the mountains to solve their little problem for them."

In the back of the APC, former Army Special Forces soldier Tony Cruz peered through the thick bulletproof glass on the rear hatch, looking out towards the federale motorcyclists at the back of the line. The closest one, just twenty-five feet or so behind his window, made eye contact with the rear-facing security contractor, then took his right hand off his handlebar.

As Cruz looked on, and as he looked back at Cruz, the Mexican slowly made a gesture.

The biker then rolled off to the right, past Crazy Horse, and headed up the side street.

Cruz called over the team radio. "Hey, boss?"

"Yeah, Four?"

"One of these ski-masked motherfuckers on a motorcycle back here just gave me a look, then drew his finger across his throat." After a pause he said, "That's bad, right?"

Duff answered back softly. "Yeah . . . I'd say that's pretty bad."

Gabby Flores spoke up now. "These federales are likely taking their orders from the Cartel del Golfo, the Gulf cartel. They are enemies of the Black Knights, and they know what's in store for us on the Devil's Spine. I just wish the rest of you did."

Wolfson chimed in on the net, obviously directing his comment towards Duff and not Gabby. "Good job bringing Debbie Downer on board, boss. She's a real morale booster."

The five Armored Saint vehicles rolled on as the sun lowered closer to the tops of the hills in front of them.

Forty-five minutes later the motorcade was off the main highway and rolling along a two-lane road through low hills. They rumbled through the village of Nombre de Dios; the light was fading fast, a late dusk made more obscure by the dusty haze in the air.

They had passed into the state of Durango; their first night's final waypoint was still an hour away, so Duff was surprised when Remmick called a sudden halt in a wooded and hilly area.

Without waiting for an order, Squeeze opened the turret hatch and stood, got his hands on his Mk 48 machine gun, and began scanning all around. The other men in Crazy Horse slid open their gunports and shoved their barrels out, pressing their faces to the bulletproof glass to look for threats.

Duff himself tried to see out the windshield, but Pack Horse Two was just twenty feet ahead, and it was blocking his view of the front of the convoy.

Fortunately, Remmick came over the radio to give a sitrep to those in the rear of the motorcade. "Alpha One, all call signs. We've got an old bus parked across the road here blocking the way forward. No personnel visible inside it, but might be a roadblock. All top gunners watch the hills."

Nascar's southern accent filled his team's earphones. "Cool. An hour into the Sierras and we're already getting fucked with."

Wolfson replied, "These are the foothills, we won't hit the Sierras till tomorrow."

Mike Gordon's voice came through the speaker now. "Bravo Actual for Alpha Actual. I see some jokers in the trees. My three o'clock. Don't see weps on them, they're just watching, waiting to see what we do."

Remmick came over the vehicle net. "Alpha Actual for Charlie Actual."

Duff clicked his handset, his voice eager and intense. "Go for Charlie."

"These shitheads aren't moving without some encouragement. I want Crazy Horse to pull to the lead and have your turret gunner dump two rounds of HE forty mike-mike on the hillside, thirty meters off the nose of that bus. Show these pricks who owns this mother-fuckin' road now."

"Hell yeah!" Squeeze shouted.

Duff pointed forward and spoke to Nascar. "Go."

Crazy Horse moved out of the line of vehicles and accelerated past the others and up to the front, stopping just forty yards from the old school bus parked across the road.

Squeeze said, "Yo, Eleven-B. You want me to rake the trees with machine gun fire first? That'll send a real message to whoever's watchin' this show."

Duff was switched on now, and he snapped back at the young man. "I want you to fucking can it with the Eleven Bravo shit and do what you were ordered to do! Nothing more." He took a breath and said, "Everybody just stay cool."

Frenchie passed the six-shot grenade launcher up through the hatch to Squeeze, and while he did this, Gabby, whose microphone had been reattached only minutes earlier, spoke up on the intrateam.

"Mr. Duffy. Let me get out and talk to them."

"Absolutely not."

"But—"

"Just sit right there. We aren't attacking them unless they attack us. Squeeze will make it clear he's only firing warning shots."

Flores sighed loudly, but she gave up her protest.

Squeeze said, "Clear to fire on the hill, Eleven Bra— I mean . . . clear to fire, Charlie One?"

"You are cleared to fire two high-explosive rounds only."

"Roger that. Two HE outgoing."

Squeeze aimed for a single pine tree, west of the road and alongside the school bus, and then he pulled the trigger. The weapon made a hollow *pop* and then the 40-millimeter projectile hurtled towards the target on the hillside.

He fired a second grenade just as the first impacted with the base of the pine, sending pieces of the tree in all directions behind black smoke.

The second hit higher on the tree, blasting branches across the hillside.

The explosions had just died off when Alpha Two, the driver of War Horse, came over the radio. "I've got movement in the bus."

Duff saw it, too. Someone had boarded on the other side and now sat down in the driver's seat. In seconds, the figure fired up the vehicle, straightened it out on the road, and then pulled over to the side.

The driver put the vehicle in park, then disappeared out the other side of the bus, no doubt running off into the trees there.

Remmick broadcast again. "If that was some kind of show of force, then these idiots are in for a rough few days. Charlie, lag back and resume the trail vehicle. Everybody else move out."

Duff said, "Button up, Squeeze," then grabbed the handset. "Charlie copies Alpha."

Behind him, Squeeze closed and locked his turret hatch, then sat down on the bench next to Frenchie and across from Gabby and Wolfson.

Cruz turned around from his rearward-facing position and extended a hand to the former Marine, and the men exchanged a fist bump.

"Nice shooting, Squeeze."

"Brother, that was just a warm-up!"

Duff spoke up from the front seat. "All right, Six. Take a few breaths. Act like you've been here before."

"Ain't nothin' wrong with lovin' your job, boss. You oughta try it sometime."

Gabby just looked at the group of contractors, then said, "In the other truck, the men were more professional."

Wolfson sniffed, then said, "Go to hell, terp."

Duff shouted now, "Charlie Two, cut that shit out!" He turned around and found Gabby in the darkened cabin behind him. "I apologize, ma'am. Everyone's a little wound up. They'll perform when the time is right."

"You men need to kill something to calm down, is that it?"

Duff did not respond to this, but Cruz looked over his shoulder from the back of the truck. "Point me at the bad guys, mamacita, and believe me, I'll chillax."

The Hispanic woman's chin rose, her eyes narrowed. "Don't worry, Mr. Cruz. I won't have to lead you to them. They'll find you. They'll find us all."

Squeeze grumbled in frustration. "Why everybody gotta be so damn grumpy up in this bitch?"

CHAPTER 24

The motorcade pulled into the small municipality of El Salto shortly after eight p.m., circled a leafy municipal park with a raised bandstand in the center, and then Show Horse pulled up in front of an old colonial hotel, weathered by time but stunningly beautiful from an architectural standpoint.

Duff's Crazy Horse was first ordered into the alley behind the hotel to post security there, and the rest of the trucks were positioned on the streets around, within sight of the hotel.

Pedestrians eyed the black, unmarked APCs warily, and a curious police car pulled up within seconds. There was a man on Alpha who spoke Spanish, so Gabby wasn't required for the translations as Remmick climbed out of Show Horse to explain the purpose of the motorcade to the local cops.

They seemed to get it, especially when Deputy Secretary Herrera climbed out of the vehicle and introduced himself, and soon the VIPs and Alpha team were in the hotel securing rooms on two floors, while management furiously began calling in extra kitchen and housekeeping staff to accommodate the instant tripling of the sleepy establishment's occupancy this evening.

With one truckload of security contractors protecting the front of the building and one in the back, the other crews were allowed to lock up their APCs and go inside, one vehicle at a time.

After a half hour Crazy Horse got the call from Alpha team that it was their turn. Duff and his men, with Gabby Flores in tow, went to their three rooms on the third floor of the rickety but ornate building, and each man threw a ruck either on a bed or on a spot on the floor.

In Duff's room Frenchie got the lone bed, despite the Frenchman's protests, and Duff took an old chair with an ottoman. Nascar threw his gear on the small love seat.

Gabby was given her own room next door, but Duff told her he'd be checking on her from time to time because she remained his responsibility.

The rest of Charlie was next door to Gabby, and the protectees took the three other rooms on this floor. Alpha and Bravo teams all but filled the second floor, taking five of the six rooms there.

Just after eight forty-five Remmick broadcast on the interteam radio that the protectees would be dining in the ground-floor restaurant at nine thirty, and Charlie team would provide close security while Alpha would go off duty for a couple of hours before posting guards outside the VIPs' doors through the night. Bravo team would be set up outside, covering front and back. In the meantime, Charlie team was given forty-five minutes of R&R before getting back to work downstairs.

Duffy spent ninety seconds rinsing off the dust of western Mexico in the shower, then dressed in a fresh tunic and pants in the bathroom, not due to any modesty—he'd lived in team rooms and bunkhouses and barracks for much of his life—but rather to hide his prosthetic limb from his two roommates.

Once he'd dressed, tucking his pants tightly into his boots, he gave up the bathroom so the other guys could begin quickly cleaning up. While they did so, Duff ascended the staircase to the roof of the old building, then found a flat portion that overlooked the park. The air was surprisingly cool up here, especially considering the hot day it had been. They were 2,500 meters in elevation now, and that, as well as the sun having set hours earlier, made all the difference.

Duff pulled out his sat phone and dialed Nichole's cell.

He was tired; this wasn't anything like working mall security. Completely unused to this level of tension and activity, he wondered if he could hide how arduous this all felt to him from Nichole, not to mention from the men around him.

It took a moment to make the connection, but when she answered, he instantly shook off his fatigue and doubt.

"How was day one on the road?" she asked.

"Good," he said, speaking truthfully, more or less. "It was a modern highway just about the whole way. We've stopped for the night in a town in the foothills. You'd like it. We're bunking in this cool old colonial hotel in front of a park. My guys are cleaning up, and we'll escort the VIPs to dinner here at the lobby restaurant in a bit."

"You're making this sound like a vacation. Why do I feel like you're hiding something?"

"Not at all." He paused. "Listen, we're ready for things to go south. Mike Gordon's team is pulling security outside in two trucks, and right now I'm looking out the window at four municipal police cars in the park keeping an eye out for us.

"Trust me," he added, "we're all switched on."

Nichole's voice softened a little. "Okay. Sorry, I just worry."

"Don't. One of my guys blew up a tree. That's the full extent of the action we saw."

"Why did he blow up a—"

"It was looking at him funny." When she said nothing, he answered. "Just a show of force. Some local thugs wanted to see if they could scare us off. They tucked tail at the first sign of bang bang."

"Already," she muttered softly, her voice barely audible over the sat connection. Then she asked, "What does your gut tell you? Are your men good? Are the threats around you manageable?"

"The men are fine. Nascar, the driver, and Frenchie, the medic, are actually respectful. The other three are dickheads, but they're doing their jobs."

"You've earned the confidence of everyone you've ever worked with. They'll come around. What about the threat?"

"Too early to know. We aren't up in the Sierras yet. I will say . . . the federales who escorted us part of the way today acted like they'd much rather be killing us than guarding us."

To this Nichole exclaimed, "Well *shit*, Josh!"

"Don't worry, we left them behind with the army, so it's just us now. Better that way, as far as I'm concerned. We've got superior equipment and training to anybody anywhere near here."

"But you don't have superior numbers."

"That's what Gabby keeps saying."

"Who's Gabby?"

"Uh . . . she's like our cultural representative."

"Your *what*?"

"Yeah . . . it's a new one to me, too. She's riding with us, so I've had to hear all her griping about the way we're doing things up here, but she's made some good points."

"Wait . . . Your cultural representative is riding in the counter-assault truck?"

"The diplomats got sick of listening to her bitch about the mission, so we drew the short straw and she's with us."

It was clear Nichole was alarmed by this. "What's her complaint about the mission?"

Duff chuckled. "Everything. Literally, everything."

"Is she worried about the danger?"

Duff suddenly knew he needed to backtrack. He'd been too free with sharing his fears about his situation. "She . . . she just doesn't think it's wise, I guess, but she's along for the ride anyway, so she can't be too worried, can she?"

"What about your QRF?"

It was a sudden change of gears, but Duff had been waiting for this question. Virtually no other contractor's spouse would ever think to ask this, but Duffy was married to a woman with a hell of a lot of experience as well as a penchant for details.

But even though he'd expected to be asked this question, it still caught him off guard. He just said, "On standby," telling himself this was not a lie. Remmick *had* said the Mexican army would come into the mountains via ground transport to assist, a process that could take most of a day, depending on where the Armored Saint men were in the Sierras when they made the request.

But still, as far as Duff was concerned, that was their quick reaction force.

It was lying by omission; Josh was smart enough to know this, but he rationalized it by telling himself he didn't want to worry Nichole any more than necessary.

"They'll extract you in helos?" she asked.

Shit, thought Duff. He was digging himself in deeper. "Yeah . . . look, we'll be fine." Quickly he tried to change the subject. "How are the kids?"

He waited for more probing, questions he wouldn't be able to fudge the answers to, but instead Nichole let it go. "Harry drew a picture of you today. Can't wait for you to come home and see it. You are this big brave stick figure protecting little Mexican children stick figures. He's proud of you."

Duff smiled, then looked down to the G-Shock watch on his wrist. "That's cute. Hey, Nik, I've got to meet the VIPs to go down to dinner. I'll call tomorrow."

"Be safe."

"I'll be fine, babe, unless I burn my mouth on an enchilada."

"Smartass," she said, and she told her husband she loved him.

CHAPTER 25

The hotel restaurant had large windows that looked out over the park, and while the square was lined with gritty urban streets, it was still a nice view. But as soon as Duffy, Cruz, Squeeze, Nascar, Wolfson, and Frenchie arrived in the dining room, they asked for the curtains to be closed, concealing the patrons from the outside. Even though the four men of Pack Horse Two were dismounted or in the turret of their vehicle out front, Duff didn't want to take any chances that some asshole with a long gun might see an opportunity to take a shot at one of his principals.

The curtains were eventually drawn, to the mild annoyance of the few other restaurant patrons as well as the staff, and then Duff brought in the four VIPs and sat them at a table in the center of the room, where they would have quick access to both the door to the lobby and the back hallway to the kitchen. Michelle LaRue and Reinhardt Helm from the UN sat across from Hector Herrera and Adnan Rodriguez from the Mexican government, and they all immediately began discussing their plans for the days ahead as they were served cocktails.

Duff began assigning positions around the room to his crew, but he paused when he got to Wolfson.

The steely eyed former SEAL said nothing, just stared back at his team leader.

Duff said, "Listen, I was just up on the roof, and there's a perfect sight line of that park from up there."

"Okay."

"How about you get up there with a scoped rifle?"

Wolfson just shrugged. "Gordon's crew's got external security. Front and back."

Annoyed, Duff replied, "And *we've* got protection of the principals. Five of us can handle the body work. You can assist Gordon and his men with the overwatch."

Wolfson made no move to comply.

Duff got the impression Wolfson didn't want to do what Duff asked for no other reason than he didn't like being bossed around by an ex–Army sergeant with only four years of service.

Wolfson said, "Gordon and his boys are eight Joes. There's cops outside, too. We've got plenty of eyes on the perimeter. They don't need me to—"

He kept complaining about Duff's instructions, but Duff tuned him out, because he suddenly realized what the problem was. He hadn't delivered an order to Wolfson, he'd delivered a proposition. *Jesus, Nikki would kick me in the balls right now.*

"You're a sniper, right?"

"Yeah."

Duff nodded. "Well, I'm *not*, but I'm gonna guess that you can snipe better from the roof than you can from the maître d's stand. Go."

Wolfson didn't move.

A command, Josh. Command this motherfucker. He brought his shoulders back. "Two, you have your orders. Get out of my face."

Wolfson raised an eyebrow, then said, "Aye, aye." Slowly he turned and left the restaurant.

Duff had forgotten Nascar was standing at his side this whole time, waiting for his own orders. The blond man with the AR-15 on his chest said, "Fuckin' SEALs. Amiright, boss?"

Duff didn't even turn to him. "You cover the door to the lobby, but keep an eye on the kitchen, too."

"Roger that."

Duff felt like he was herding cats.

A half hour later, dinner was going smoothly; the four diplomats remained deep in conversation while eating salads and drinking wine, with the exception of Rodriguez, who sipped his mezcal and glanced at his watch from time to time.

Duff kept an eye on the hotel staff and guests, and he saw no threats whatsoever. Gordon was behind the hotel in Pack Horse One, and he stayed in comms with Duff, as did Bravo Two, in front of the hotel in Pack Horse Two.

Even Wolfson had chimed in from the roof that all was quiet outside.

And then, much to Duff's annoyance, Dr. Gabriella Flores entered the dining room, passing by Nascar, who watched her with a raised eye but made no move to stop her.

Duff began moving in her direction to cut her off. "You promised me you'd stay upstairs."

Flores was anything but consolatory. "I need to speak with Michelle and Reinhardt."

The very fact that the Mexican cultural advisor was referring to the two United Nations VIPs by their first names made Duff bristle; that wasn't how contractors worked close protection, and Flores was herself an asset of Armored Saint. He said, "They're having a meeting. Considering how things went today, maybe you should just go back upstairs and enjoy some bad TV and room service."

She shook her head. "Five minutes. I would like to talk to them about the route we will be taking into the Sierras. I think we should consider—"

Duff interrupted. "Your job, Dr. Flores, doesn't include land navigation."

She ignored him and continued talking. "The Devil's Spine runs along a gorge deeper than the Grand Canyon, but we will eventually arrive at the bridge over—"

Duff figured he was about to get a geography lesson he didn't really want, but then something grabbed his attention. Adnan Rodriguez, assistant to the Mexican deputy secretary of the interior, stood from the table, placing his napkin over his salad.

In English, he said, "Miss LaRue, gentlemen, if you will excuse me, I would like to return to my room. My stomach has been a little upset all afternoon."

He shook hands with the three at his table, then turned to leave.

Duff spoke into his intrateam to his Charlie Four, who was standing near the front window, looking out through an opening in the curtain. "Cruz, escort the assistant to the deputy secretary upstairs to his room."

Cruz pushed off from where he was leaning against a pillar. "Tuckin' in one of the veeps, on it."

Flores had used the distraction to make her way to the other three, and she sat down in Rodriguez's chair. Duff rolled his eyes, but before he could go and ask her to leave, a transmission came through from the roof.

"Charlie Two for Charlie One."

"Go for One."

"Uh . . . we might have ourselves a little situation."

"Tell me."

"Bravo has a few guys smokin' and jokin' outside their APC. I don't think they're seeing what I'm seeing from up here. Lookin' through my scope right now, there are four municipal police cars in the park."

"Yeah, I know."

"Yeah . . . but all four cars are empty. That sound right to you?"

Duff looked towards the curtains in front of the window. "*Empty?* The cops are on foot?"

"That's just it. Not a cop in sight. You think local five-oh takes mass coffee breaks on foot and leaves their radio cars just sitting there?"

Duff was fully on alert now. "No, I don't. I wonder if they got a phone call that told them something was about to kick off over here in—"

Before he could finish the sentence, a burst of gunfire boomed outside, and civilians in the restaurant screamed.

CHAPTER 26

Several automatic rifles chattered from the direction of the park in the center of the square, glass shattered in the restaurant's window, bullets ripped through the curtains, and patrons dove for cover or sat frozen in their chairs in a state of panic.

Duff, Frenchie, and Squeeze were closest to the principals, all within twenty feet, and they each tackled one to the ground.

Duff himself knocked LaRue from her chair to the floor, where he shielded her with his body. Then he reached up and grabbed Dr. Flores, yanking her down next to him by the arm of her sweater.

Wolfson came over the radio simultaneously.

"Got contact front! Four or five muzzle flashes behind the stone bandstand in the middle of the park! Engaging!"

A loud, low report boomed on the roof. Another followed a second later.

Flores lay fetal and still on the floor next to him, her eyes blinking rapidly, but Duff had to struggle to keep Michelle LaRue down. He felt like he was in a wrestling match with the woman, but he retained the presence of mind to transmit over the interteam radio frequency that went out to all Armored Saint contractors on the mission. Shouting over the still-incoming fire, he said, "Charlie One to Bravo One.

Gordon, get your turret gunner in Pack Horse Two engaging targets behind the bandstand, break. Charlie Two, leave the targets in the center of the park to the Mk 48 and search the rest of the park for more hostiles. How copy?"

Gordon answered first. "We're on it, Duff."

And Wolfson's voice came next. "Way ahead of you. Got two dudes crouched behind one of the police cruisers on the south side of the plaza. My two o'clock. When they raise back up, I'll smoke 'em if I see weps."

Booming belt-fed machine gun fire thundered out front as Pack Horse Two's up gunner opened fire on the bandstand area with his Mk 48.

Duff shouted again, "Nascar! Suppress from the window! Nobody gets inside this hotel!"

Nascar raced past the group of prone bodies, leapt over restaurant patrons crouched for cover, and moved the curtain out of the way. Using a pillar at the front of the dining room as cover, he began sending rounds from his AR-15 out towards targets in the park.

Wolfson's intense and steady voice came through Duff's ears. "Charlie Two's got AKs in sight. I'm engaging these fuckers."

Incoming rounds pounded the restaurant as Wolfson fired from the roof. A light fixture was shot free of the ceiling in the restaurant and crashed down on the table near Duff and the others.

Duff knew he had to get his principals out of here. "Squeeze! Go help Nascar suppress, but stay low! Frenchie and I'll take the principals and get them upstairs. Gabby, you're with us!"

Gabby was up on her knees now, close to Duff, and she nodded. Squeeze left the area around the table and ran to support Nascar, who was changing the magazine in his rifle near the window.

"Covering fire!" Duff shouted into his mic. A second later Nascar was back up, and he and Squeeze sprayed automatic bursts.

Duff pulled LaRue up into a crouch and began pushing her for the exit to the lobby.

"Stop shoving me!" she shouted back.

"Then fuckin' *move*, lady!" Duffy felt the sharp pangs of terror in his heart; there was PTSD in his emotions, recalling Beirut and his desperate run to keep himself and his principal alive.

Frenchie, Helm, and Herrera were up now, everyone running through the tables, past men and women on the ground, some with their hands covering their ears, others clearly wounded.

Helm shouted, grabbing Duff on the strap of his body armor to slow him. "A waitress has been shot!"

"Keep moving!" Duff demanded. "We're going to the stairs!"

Helm slowed. "But . . . she's been shot!"

"*You're* gonna get shot if you don't do what I say, sir!"

Just as Duff and his group raced through the small lobby, his weapon out in front of him in case any attackers had managed to infiltrate the building, Nascar transmitted, "I got one! Motherfucker's in the dirt!"

Duff made it to the stairs; he led the way for the others, and Frenchie trailed, and before long, they were on the third floor. Down a short and dark hall was Duff's room, and he fumbled with his key for a moment.

His hands shook; he didn't even try to hide it. This shit was more than he was ready for; he had no doubt of this now.

Finally he got the door open.

Behind him, Frenchie shouted, "Inside, everyone, s'il vous plaît."

But Duff didn't find the room secure enough for his principals. "I want the three of you in the bathroom. Frenchie, guard the bathroom door. I'll watch the hall."

Herrera and Helm did as they were told, but LaRue said, "I'm not hiding in the bathroom, I can stand right—"

Duff was about to explode on the woman, but Reinhardt Helm did it for him. In his thick German accent he shouted, "Michelle, you'll do as you're told!"

LaRue complied immediately, and all three protectees stood in the tiny bathroom by the claw-foot tub.

Gabby Flores remained in the bedroom with the two contractors, until Duff just pointed with a gloved hand for Gabby to lie down on the floor behind the bed. She wasn't a principal, but he *was* in charge of her safety.

Only then did Duff realize the gunfire outside seemed to have died off. The Mk 48 wasn't firing, and Wolfson wasn't banging his sniper rifle from the roof anymore.

"Charlie One for Two. What you got?"

"The oppo is bugging out. I count five, maybe six down in the park. Looks like bad guys are retrieving bodies, but I don't see any weps, so we're not engaging. All looks clear, but Bravo team has a man down outside. They're working on him behind the APC."

One of Gordon's men was wounded, but Duff had no idea of the extent of his injuries. "Shit. Roger. Everyone else on Charlie, sound off."

Frenchie was in the same room as Duff, just outside by the bathroom door, but he transmitted anyway. "Three is here with Charlie One and three principals in room 304."

Cruz spoke up next. "Charlie Four is in 306 with Rodriguez. I've got him in the tub and I'm holding security in the bedroom. No targets outside our window."

"Charlie Four," Duff said, "bring your principal down the hall to us. I'll cover the stairwell."

"En route."

Duff opened the door to the hall, took a knee, and aimed his weapon towards the stairs. An older man peered out of his room; Duff thumbed off his safety and put his finger on the trigger of his Kalashnikov, but one look at the American with the rifle, and the old man's head popped back inside his room.

Jesus Christ, Duff thought. Had he almost shot an innocent? His hands began trembling anew.

Nascar came over the net now. "Charlie Five to Charlie One. All targets suppressed. I've got three civilians wounded in the restaurant. One of them ain't gonna make it."

"Do what you can, but keep security up."

"Roger."

Squeeze transmitted next. "Six is good, I'm treating the waitress.

She took one in the arm. She should live, but I sure hope this town's got a hospital."

Cruz and Rodriguez came up the hall behind Duff. He glanced over his shoulder to ensure it was them, then returned all his attention to the quiet stairwell.

Just then, a new voice came over his headset. "Duff, it's Gordon."

"Go for Duffy."

His voice was strained, nearly out of breath. "I was out back in Pack Horse One when the attack kicked off. I'm around front now with Pack Horse Two, break." After a pause he said, "I've got one man KIA on the sidewalk out here. My number five."

Duff closed his eyes and gently tapped his forehead on the door-frame. *Son of a bitch. A dead contractor on the first night of the mission.*

He recovered as quickly as possible and said, "Copy. I have all four principals up in three zero four. Break. Charlie One to Alpha One."

No reply from Remmick came.

"Charlie to Alpha Actual, come in."

Still nothing.

"Gordo, you able to raise anybody on Alpha?"

Duff listened while Mike Gordon tried to get Remmick to respond. He had no more luck than Duff did at first, but on the second try, a booming voice came over the net.

"Alpha Actual, Bravo Actual. Report status."

Gordon said, "Bravo has one KIA, no wounded. We're up on ammo and the enemy has retreated."

Remmick didn't dwell on the news of a dead contractor. "Charlie One. Sitrep."

"Charlie has no KIA or wounded. Principals secure in room 304, but there's just three of us up here on them. Could use another gun here, and there are CIVCAS in the restaurant that need help."

Duffy had no idea if Remmick was going to give a shit about civilian casualties, but Duff's own man Squeeze was down there rendering medical aid, so he wanted to get him some assistance.

Remmick said, "Roger. I'm sending two men to you and the others to treat wounded and secure the front street so Bravo can retrieve their fallen, how copy?"

"Good copy," Duff said.

Then Remmick said, "I want all the actuals in the lobby in five minutes to talk about this."

Cruz took Duff's position at the door, and Duff went over to the far side of the bed. Gabby sat there, and he was happy to see that although she appeared shaken, she didn't seem to be overly panicked about what had just happened.

"You okay, Doctor?"

"Yes. Thank you."

"I want you with me when I talk to Remmick downstairs."

"Yes. Certainly." She cocked her head. "But why?"

"Because you know more about what's going on around here than I do. And I suspect you know more about what's going on around here than *he* does."

She climbed to her feet. "Of course I do."

He tried to temper her a little now. "But please try to be delicate."

"You are shooting people one minute, and the next you ask me to be delicate?"

Duff shrugged. "I didn't shoot anybody." He held tightly onto his weapon so that Flores wouldn't see the quiver in his hands.

Downstairs in the lobby, Charlie Five and Six stepped up to Duff and Gabby. Squeeze had blood on his arms and the sleeves of his tunic. He motioned to the entrance of the restaurant. Duff could hear sobbing and moaning from multiple people. "Alpha's treating the wounded now. Ambulance is on the way."

"Tell me about the injuries."

"Three people shot. One old guy sittin' at a table by the window caught a round right between the fuckin' peepers. Dude went lights out pretty quick."

Nascar added, "A bullet to the brain will do that to you."

Squeeze continued. "A waitress took one to the arm, and another lady got an in-and-out to the shoulder. They'll live if there are any halfway decent docs around here."

Nascar leaned closer, spoke softly. "Bravo dropped the ball, boss. If Wolfson hadn't been on the roof, this could have been much worse."

Duff had been thinking the same thing.

Squeeze added, "And what the fuck was Alpha doing when all this was—"

Squeeze stopped talking when Remmick and a couple of his men appeared out of the stairwell.

The agent in charge all but shouted across the lobby as he approached. "What the fuck happened, Duff?"

"Multiple shooters. Small arms. They're all either dead or they've bugged out."

Gordon appeared through the front door now. Sweat covered his dark-skinned face and dripped from his three-day growth of beard. Bloodstains were evident on the ammo rack on his chest and on his gloves, and his eyes were angry and narrow.

Remmick said, "Sitrep, Bravo."

The man was understandably rattled; Duff had known Mike Gordon for most of a decade, so he could easily tell. "My guys checked the bodies of the five attackers left behind. Two were cops, but they were engaging us, no doubt about it. The other three dead gunmen look like locals. Fat blood trails mean a couple more bodies were dragged away into a waiting vic and cleared the scene."

Remmick rubbed his gloved hand against his face. "So were these guys Black Knights?"

Gabby Flores said, "If this had been Los Caballeros Negros, there wouldn't have been five or ten of them. There would have been fifty or a hundred."

Remmick looked to Gabby; it appeared he was going to say something to her, but then he turned back to Gordon. "Get the wounded to the nearest hospital and the dead in body bags." He addressed Duff now. "What about the VIPs? They were all in the restaurant when the shooting started?"

Duff said, "Yes, sir. Wait . . . Actually, Rodriguez was on his way back up to his room with Charlie Four when it all kicked off."

"Keep them all together from here on out. Bravo had external security, Charlie had internal security. This did *not* need to go down like this! No more fuckups."

Gordon said, "Alpha One, can I ask where you guys were through all this?"

Remmick's eyes locked on Gordon now. "I, for one, was taking a shit. That okay with you, Mike?"

"Sure, boss."

Remmick said nothing else, he just headed out front to inspect Pack Horse Two, a couple of his guys moving silently behind him.

Duff turned to his men here and transmitted over the intrateam radio to the others. "I want all Charlie call signs to get their rucks out of their rooms now. We're sleeping in Crazy Horse tonight." He turned to Gabby. "You, too. Sorry."

"Don't be. I feel safer in the tank."

Squeeze turned to head for the stairs. Under his breath he said, "It's not a tank, terp."

CHAPTER 27

Two blocks away, just out of view from the hotel but still in sight of the park, Oscar Cardoza sat in his Jeep and lowered his binoculars. He hefted his phone off the passenger seat, tapped a few keys, and let the vehicle's Bluetooth audio establish a connection.

The phone began to ring on the speakers, and after a moment it was answered. "Bueno?"

In Spanish, Cardoza said, "Lobo? It's me. Where are you, my friend?"

"In the foothills in Chihuahua. We'll be in the mountains tomorrow morning, the Devil's Spine by tomorrow night. Where are you?"

"I am in the villa of El Salto, the foothills of Durango. The motorcade is here, just across the square from me. They are staying the night in a hotel."

"Must be nice."

"Not so nice. They were attacked."

Lobo chuckled. "On their first night in the hills?"

"Sí. Some local group sent some stoners and dirty cops. They shot one of the security troops. Might have killed him."

"You saw it?"

"I'm in a Jeep across the park watching the cleanup right now. It was quite a fireworks show, amigo."

"How did the security force perform?"

"They were unprepared. Not expecting trouble this soon, I guess. But I must say they rallied quickly. The attackers never got near the hotel. Most are dead. Others ran."

"We won't run."

"I know you won't. But *they* won't leave their guard down again, either. You and your men will need to be ready for a fight."

"We are Los Zetas. We are always ready for a fight." He laughed softly again. "Tell the local bangers to save some of the gringos for us, okay?"

"I'll keep you informed. Buenas noches."

"Buenas noches, Señor Cardoza."

CHAPTER 28

At three a.m. an old minivan pulled into a one-car carport next to a nine-hundred-square-foot home in Falls Church, Virginia. A light rain fell as a woman wearing yellow scrubs and a base-ball cap, her blond hair in a ponytail, climbed out of the vehicle, grabbed her purse, and then headed no more than thirty feet to the front porch of the equally tiny home next door.

The woman gently rapped on the storm door, and soon it opened. Another woman—like the blonde, she was also in her thirties—held a three-year-old boy in her arms, and she passed him to the woman in scrubs, while a five-year-old girl with impossibly curly hair shuffled out in her pajamas.

"They were good?" Nichole Duffy asked softly, not even hiding her weariness.

Dina Latham had been sleeping, so she shook off the cobwebs before replying. "They were fine." She asked, "How much longer till Josh comes back?"

"A few weeks," Nichole replied. "Why?"

Dina shrugged and smiled. "Honestly, I need the money, so don't rush him back from his work. I'm just thinking about you, hon."

"I'm fine," Nichole answered with a forced smile. "Josh will be fine, too."

"I know he will. Bringing the kids back over tomorrow?"

"Yeah. Pretty much every evening."

"As long as you need. Try and get some sleep."

Nichole thanked Dina, and soon she and her kids were walking back across the strip of grass between the driveways of the two homes to the carport door to her house.

She paid forty dollars a night for her neighbor to babysit two kids for eight hours, which was more than she could afford, but she knew Josh was making plenty of money to justify the nightly expense. She herself pulled in over one hundred a night, and she sure as hell couldn't clean offices all night long with a couple of kids in tow, so the arrangement was necessary.

She put both kids down quickly, then showered and changed into U.S. Army sweatpants and a T-shirt bearing the logo of Virginia Military Institute, her alma mater. The shirt bore the motto of the school, *Consilio et animis* —"By wisdom and courage"—and it was one of several remnants of her past life that she kept around, even though, if she was being honest with herself, sometimes those remnants depressed her.

She threw the dirty scrubs she wore to clean commercial property, a vestige of her present life, in the hamper, and then she climbed into her bed alone just before three thirty a.m. She'd have to be up in three or four hours, depending on how long Harry let her sleep, and though Josh had only been gone a few days, she longed for his presence in the bed with her.

She tossed and turned, worrying about her husband. Just when she'd convinced herself things would turn out fine, her cell phone rang on the table next to her.

She launched to a sitting position; her legs swiveled out from under the covers and her bare feet hit the floor.

Something terrible had happened; she *knew* it. There was no other reason for Josh to call in the middle of the night, especially since they'd spoken earlier in the evening. She feared the caller was someone from AS, and she was an instant away from learning that the love of her life was dead.

With unimaginable fear, she answered the phone and croaked out a near breathless "Hello?"

"Nik. It's me."

Josh's voice, though obviously grave in tone, caused her to let out a silent sigh of relief. She shut her eyes, said a quick prayer of thanks that he was alive, and then opened them again. "What's happened?"

"I just left the vic to use the latrine. Have to keep my voice down." He paused, then said, "One of Mike Gordon's men got killed tonight."

Nichole's eyes slammed shut again. A tear dripped from her right eye. "Oh my God. What happened?"

"Small-arms attack at our hotel. We were set up for it but didn't see it coming."

"Poor Mike."

"Yeah."

"Who did it?"

"We don't even know. We smoked a few cops, part of the attacking force. I never saw the shooters. I never even fired a shot."

As Nichole's heart pounded, she forced strength into her voice. "I need you to come home."

Her husband breathed into the phone for several seconds; she could sense the distress and dread he felt, and she was thankful it was as great as her own. Josh wasn't stupid; he was just desperate and driven.

But then he said, "I'm fine. We're fine. We repelled the attack well, got the principals to safety quickly."

"I don't care about the principals, Josh, and you know it."

"Well, I do," he said defensively. "Look, I've got to go; I just had a few seconds away from the guys. We're going to be fine; nobody is going to let their guard down again, I promise you that. Least of all me." He added, "I've got something to come home to, and I plan on doing just that."

Nichole wasn't going to be able to persuade him to abandon his responsibility down there, to abandon thirty-five grand that his family desperately needed, and return to her. She knew this, so she said the only thing that came to mind. "I love you. Please be careful."

"I will."

After her husband hung up, she kept the phone in her hand and opened Google Maps, desperate to look at the terrain where Josh was operating to learn something about the geography and the threats and the dangers that awaited him as he climbed into the mountains. She knew she wouldn't be sleeping tonight, but she also could not let go of the feeling that she had to do something to help him. Even though she was the owner of a tiny janitorial services company in Virginia, she was a former military officer, and she did not just sit idly by.

It wasn't her way.

But as much as she tried to think of something she could do to help, nothing came to mind.

She tossed and turned until dawn, and then she slept, but her sleep was far from restful, because the tension of the past few days had rekindled memories, and she paid the price for those memories in her dreams.

CHAPTER 29

SEVEN YEARS EARLIER

A pair of AH-64D Apache Longbow helicopters flew in trail formation, churning the night air one thousand feet over a patchwork of farmland, twenty miles northeast of the Iraqi city of Fallujah.

The pilots of the helos used the Pilot Night Vision System, a camera in the front of the aircraft, to see the way, and the copilot/gunners, six feet forward and positioned lower than their pilots, focused the bulk of their attention on the two large multipurpose displays over their knees and a screen in the center with handles covered with buttons on both the left and right side.

This was the TADS. The Target Acquisition and Designation Sights was in a housing mounted in front of the nose of the aircraft along with the PNVS, able to swivel in a 180-degree arc to identify, range, and maintain sight of any target chosen by the copilot/gunner.

The two U.S. Army helicopters, call signs Assassins 43 and Assassins 44, were members of First Battalion/Third Aviation Regiment of the Twelfth Combat Aviation Brigade, stationed at Katterbach Kaserne, southwest of Nuremberg, Germany. But the battalion had been rushed here to Iraq in an attempt to assist the Iraqi Security Forces in their fight with the Islamic State, a terrorist organization rapidly taking over huge swaths of territory across the nation.

ISIS had a steadfast zeal that the ISF couldn't come close to matching in its own members, and the American forces newly arrived here were both shocked by how quickly the insurgents had advanced and appalled by how pitiful the Iraqi army's response had been.

The pilot of the lead aircraft of this two-ship patrol was a forty-three-year-old Arizonan named Max Henderson. Henderson had flown the Apache for over ten years, after nearly a decade flying Blackhawks before that.

The woman in the front seat of his gunship was, in contrast to her pilot, only twenty-five. Captain Nichole Martin had graduated from VMI, then received a commission as a U.S. Army officer. She'd recently been promoted from first lieutenant to captain, and although she was newly tasked to Alpha Company and had only been deployed with this unit for a couple of weeks, she'd previously flown two combat tours in Afghanistan.

The Apaches flew a slow racetrack pattern, on station and ready for tasking from the tactical operations center in Baghdad. Heavy fighting between the Iraqi Security Forces and the Islamic State had been going on for over a week to the south of their current position; fighting had kicked off within the city of Fallujah, as well, but the villages and fields below the powerful American war machines twenty miles to the north had remained quiet so far.

Captain Martin looked at the clock in front of her and saw that it was just past three a.m. This was their third patrol since eight o'clock the previous morning, and she felt it in her body. "Been a long day," she said into her intercom.

Behind her, Max Henderson replied, "It's way past my bedtime."

Martin chuckled. "We've only got another half hour on station, Chief. We'll get you all tucked in, in an hour or so."

"Yeah, till we fly again tomorrow morning." He sighed. "Another month and I can sleep in all I want, I guess."

Martin had only flown with Henderson for a very short time, but she'd heard all about his plans to retire. "You're really going to leave all this behind?"

"Hell yeah, I am," he said. "In thirty days I'll be a civilian." He added, "Unless we get our asses blown up in the meantime."

"Yeah, let's not."

"How 'bout you, Captain? You gonna stay in for the full ride?"

She had a pat answer for this anytime someone asked. "My mom and dad were both Army, both went twenty-three years. Feels natural for me to stay in."

"Can be tough with kids," Henderson said as he began a slow turn to the south that was mimicked by the identical aircraft behind and slightly below them.

"Yeah. It was tough for them with me and my brother. I do want kids, eventually. I'll have to figure out how to make it work."

She scanned through her TADS, zoomed in on buildings on the northern outskirts of Fallujah. While she did this, she asked, "What are you going to do after the Army?"

"Got a solid plan, ma'am. I'm going to start my own aviation company."

"Aviation company? Seriously? Like an airline?"

"Yep. Made a business plan and everything. I'll lease a rotary wing, like a Jet Ranger, and a fixed-wing . . . there's a Citation I've been eyeing online. Have to get a bank loan, but I'll figure that out. I'll maintain my security clearance so I can pick up some tiny government contracts to start out. USAID, DHS, DEA. Whatever. In a few years I'll own a small fleet outright, I'll hire pilots, and I'll get bigger contracts."

"Like, all over the world?"

"Nah, don't want to get too big to where I can't fly myself." He added, "Home is Phoenix, so hopefully I can get work along the border."

Captain Martin said, "Sounds like a sweet gig. If I *do* leave the Army, I may come looking for a job."

"Hmmm," Henderson replied, playfully. "Dunno, Captain. An officer as an employee? That sounds like it would be a handful."

She agreed he might have a point, but before she could say more, a voice came over her radio.

"Assassins 44, this is Assassins 43."

Martin responded. "Go for 44."

"Uhh, we're getting a hydraulic pressure caution. Tried to trouble-shoot it, but no luck. Probably nothing, but we're going to have to RTB."

Shit, Martin thought. If the other aircraft had to leave station and return to base, she could either stay with Assassins 43 for the flight back or else remain out here alone for the rest of the patrol. The area had been quiet enough to justify calling it a night, but she also knew her flight had been sent down here for a reason, and trouble could pop up at any time.

Her own aircraft was operating fine, and a hydraulic caution light, nine times out of ten, meant nothing. Assassins 43 wasn't in dire straits by any means, so she made the decision quickly. "Roger, 43. You guys RTB. We'll stay on station for another"—she looked at the clock—"thirty minutes or so."

"Roger, 44. Good hunting."

She looked up at her rear mirror and saw the black hulking Apache behind them peel off and begin flying to the north.

Henderson said, "Doesn't look like they're gonna miss too much around here."

"No, it definitely doesn't," Martin replied while turning her direction back to her TADS with its up to 127 times magnification. As she'd done on all the patrols they'd performed here in Iraq, she slewed the camera system mounted on the nose back and forth, focusing now on distant buildings, structures, and roads several kilometers south of her, to the east of the city.

Just as she began to move the camera back to the west, however, she saw a flash of light, rendered black on her thermal camera and displayed on her monitor. Two other flashes followed in quick succession.

Henderson wasn't zoomed in like Martin, but still he saw the flashes.

"Looks like arty firing to the east of Fallujah."

"I see it," she said, and then she zoomed in on the location.

"That's going to be ISF," Henderson said. "Islamic State doesn't know how to work the big cannons they have."

"I bet they'll figure them out," she said softly, and she pinpointed the origin of fire in a dirt field next to what appeared to be some sort of agricultural processing facility.

"Wonder what they're shooting at," Henderson said.

Martin peered into the screen on her TADS. "I see the artillery. Definitely Iraqi army troops. A section of M198s. Three of them." The M198 was a 155-millimeter howitzer, an American weapon. The Iraqis had had over 120 of them in their arsenal, but no one knew how many were still in Army hands and how many had been captured by ISIS. She said, "With the range of those guns, their targets are going to be several klicks to the west. Just inside the city."

She continued scanning the Iraqi forces, but soon Henderson said, "Yep. Impacts about twelve klicks due west."

Martin radioed what she saw to the TOC, then sent along the grid of friendly forces and the approximate location of where the Iraqis were firing.

She swiveled her cam to the west, quickly at first, because she was planning on trying to ID enemy positions under fire. But she stopped tracking when she spotted a large group of personnel amassed next to a mosque well east of Fallujah proper.

She zoomed in on them, and instantly Martin realized she was looking at ISIS forces. A dozen or more pickup trucks were parked along a road that ran east, armed men moved around them, and a cluster of what appeared to be mortars was in the process of being erected.

Henderson didn't see any of this, but he reported what he did see. "Another salvo of arty outgoing."

Wherever the shells were impacting, it was outside Captain Martin's field of view. She knew the big guns weren't targeting this large group of fighters, because they were way too close to the artillery.

She said, "Holy shit, Chief. I've got . . . maybe . . . five zero enemy, four mortars being set up. Twelve klicks off our one o'clock. They are only about two klicks from the friendlies, and it looks like they're getting ready to attack them."

"Shit," Henderson said. "If the Iraqis don't know their enemy is just a couple klicks away, they're going to get their asses overrun."

Martin called to the TOC again. "Talon, Assassins 44. Do you have commo with ISF forces at my heading one seven zero, over?"

There was a delayed pause. Henderson had backed off on the collective, and now the aircraft basically hovered over a barley field eight miles to the north of the enemy in position highlighted in the FLIR.

Finally the tactical operations center responded. "Assassins 44, this is Talon. Negative commo on those friendlies. We have a JTAC with ISF forces about twenty klicks away. No imbeds or commo with the unit at your grid or south of it, over."

"Chief." She spoke into the intercom to Henderson only now. "That arty battery firing section is about to get hit with mortars and then overrun with troops." Martin looked at her FLIR for a moment, then at the multipurpose display to the left of her dash. "We've got the gas to engage."

"Yeah." Henderson sounded unsure. "But we're just one ship, and if ISIS has four mortars there with a platoon-sized element of troops, then there might be a hell of a lot more in the area we *don't* see. We have no idea what we're up against."

"We didn't come all this way to turn around when we see the bad guys, Chief. Those mortars are positioning to fire on friendlies; we have to do something."

Henderson wanted no part of this fight, but Martin saw the urgency of the moment. There was an artillery battery of ISF, a few dozen men at least, who seemingly had no idea the enemy had closed to within minutes of their position and were poised to attack.

"Right," Henderson muttered. "We can check with the TOC if there are any fast movers available."

"Negative." Martin was sure of herself. "No time to set up a nine-line and bring in other platforms." Before Henderson could respond, she radioed the tactical operations center again. "Talon, this is Assassins

44, we have enemy sighted in the open at this time. Approximately forty to fifty pax with four mortars visible. They are two klicks west of referenced friendlies in our grid. Requesting clearance to engage."

"Talon, Assassins 44, say again, you have weapons visible?"

"Assassins 44, affirmative. Belt-feds and mortars. Multiple technicals with dismounts."

A different voice, this one male, came over the radio. "Assassins 44, this is Talon Six, you are cleared hot to the target."

"Roger, sir. Understood cleared hot." She switched back to her intercom for Henderson. "Arming." She flipped a pair of switches over the keypad on her left. The weapons screen on her left showed her the quantity of each type of munition 44 carried.

She made a selection. "We'll do a pass with rockets, switch to guns for the follow-up."

"Roger that." Henderson sounded pissed.

Martin ignored him, then lased the center of the cluster of ISIS forces, right in the middle of the mortar emplacement. "Okay, Chief, put them on your nose and let's roll in. I'll fire at four thousand meters, then we egress to the east."

Henderson didn't like it, but he said, "Roger, egress heading zero, nine, zero. Rolling in."

The aircraft banked; all Martin's focus was directed at the small screen over her right knee. They weren't quite lined up the way she wanted at first.

"Swing right just a bit. Little more. There!"

"We're overflying buildings, ma'am. Can't see anybody on thermals but—"

"Stay on target, Chief."

As she watched through the camera under the nose of her airship, an ISIS fighter dropped a mortar into a tube, and a black flash indicated that the weapon had launched a projectile towards the Iraqi artillery position.

Calmly, Captain Nichole Martin said, "Firing."

She pressed the trigger. A salvo of five Hydra 70 rockets launched from the pod on each wing, then raced away; fingertips of black appeared on her TADS display.

"Egressing," Henderson said, and he began banking the aircraft to the left.

Even though the Apache wasn't facing the target any longer, the camera kept tracking the selected location so she could still watch the action through her TADS. Each rocket burst open as it neared the target and released 1,180 fléchettes, essentially tiny nails with stabilizer fins. The fléchettes slammed into the enemy position, ripping into and shredding men and equipment. Multiple pickups exploded into balls of fire.

"Impact," she said. "Fuck, yeah." Then, "Stand by."

Henderson flew to the east, then banked slowly back to the west so the 180-degree camera could continue tracking the enemy. After thirty seconds or so, Martin said, "I'm still tracking targets, Chief. About two dozen squirters, maybe more, climbing into vehicles. They have belt-fed weapons. Come back around hard, we'll make a gun pass."

Henderson said, "Ma'am, let's stand off, use a Hellfire. We can avoid overflight of the—"

"Thirty mike-mike is more effective."

"Roger that," Henderson admitted grudgingly. "Suggest we ingress from the east this time, not the north."

The woman seated in the cockpit, lower and in front of the pilot, said, "Let's do that, but speed it up. They get harder to track the faster they move."

She switched to the chain gun below her seat. It was slaved to her eye, so where she looked, the weapon pointed because of sensors in the cockpit behind her head that detected her gaze.

The chain gun fired a thirty-millimeter dual-purpose high-explosive round that was both armor penetrating and fragmentary. It had an effective range of three thousand meters, but in practice, Martin liked to get in as close as possible.

Captain Martin lined up her shot. "Firing."

Just as she said this, Henderson shouted into his mic, "RPGs!"

A pair of glowing streaks shot in front of the windscreen, racing upwards from almost directly below and passing just a dozen feet in front of Martin's position in the helo.

"Pulling off target!" Henderson shouted, and before Martin could direct him otherwise, he yanked the aircraft hard to the right. Just as they came around to 90 degrees, still almost on their side just three hundred feet above the streets below, both Martin and Henderson saw another glowing streak racing up to them from a rooftop.

"RPG!" Martin announced it this time, and she tracked it with her eyes, thinking the rocket would trail behind their aircraft.

But a pounding blow to the airframe told her otherwise.

"We're hit," Henderson announced, but there was little reason to do so, because warning alarms followed the impact, and both of Martin's MPDs began showing red cautions.

Henderson leveled out and began racing towards the west, in the general direction of the northern suburbs of Fallujah. Martin was just a passenger now, watching warning lights and listening to the alarms.

After a moment she said, "We flying, Chief?"

"For now. Hydraulic pressure is dropping, but slowly. Tail rotor sounds damaged, don't know how bad. We're going to limp this back to base."

He began banking back to the north now; his movements were slow and gingerly, lest he put too much strain on the damaged tail rotor.

Martin said, "That's over eighty miles. If you don't think we're going to—"

"Let me do my job, Captain!" a clearly frustrated Henderson shouted.

But Nichole Martin wasn't going to let it go. "We aren't going to make the base! We could crash in the center of ISIS forces. We have to go for the Iraqi army artillery position."

Henderson kept flying to the north. "That ISF arty section is still gonna get overrun, probably before pararescue shows up to pull our asses out of there. Those dudes can't help us, they've got their own problems. I'll take my chances that the aircraft makes it back to the base."

Martin began broadcasting her airship's location and status back to Talon.

When she was finished, she clicked back on the intercom. "Chief. QRF is scrambled."

"Good. Maybe we'll meet them halfway."

Just then, both Martin's MPDs lit up red with new warnings, alarms went off in her headset, and Henderson said, "We've got engine fire in one. Shutting it down."

Martin fought a pang of terror. This was bad. She forced self-assurance into her voice. "We need to turn back to the Iraqi lines now, Chief. We don't have the speed or the gas to make it to the QRF before we go down."

"I can do it."

"I've given you a fucking *order*, Chief!"

Henderson continued flying to the north, but he did not respond to her.

"Chief," she said. There was even more power in her voice now, as well as a hint of menace.

Slowly, Max Henderson began banking around to the southwest. With venom in his voice he said, "Yes, ma'am. By all means, let's go die with those Iraqis."

She bit her lip but turned her attention towards her radio to alert Talon of the change in their plans.

But before she could transmit, all three of the screens in front of her went black.

Behind her, Henderson said, "I've lost MPDs."

"Same," she said.

"Going to standby instruments." Analog instruments were positioned over the pilot's right knee so Henderson could navigate the aircraft in the event of a complete electrical malfunction. He began to fly with these instruments now, and Martin realized her pilot wouldn't be able to see anything with the loss of the thermal camera.

She clicked the radio. "Talon, Assassins 44. We have lost—"

A powerful vibration shook the aircraft, throwing Martin both left and right against her harness. She stopped talking to Talon to confer with Henderson, but before she could speak, a boom and a new shake behind her told her the rotor had exploded off the tail.

"Fuck!" Henderson shouted.

With the tail rotor gone, the aircraft immediately began spinning under the main rotor head. Henderson began a partially controlled descent as he reduced power, hoping to autorotate to a crash landing.

Twenty-five-year-old Captain Nichole Martin took hold of the grab handles on the fuselage, pushed her head back against the headrest, and closed her eyes. In her headset she heard her pilot make the radio call she'd hoped she'd never hear.

"Assassins 44, we're going down. Assassins 44 is going down hard!"

CHAPTER 30

Josh Duffy stood at the dirty window of a tin-roofed un-air-conditioned elementary school in the small hill town of El Rillito, Durango state, and he thought of home.

It was the kids that made him homesick, if he was being honest with himself. A group of little girls played outside the window, their high voices squeaking spiritedly as they whipped dirty little flags in the air in some sort of game Josh wasn't focused on, because his job required him to keep his eyes fixed on the adults inside the small cinder-block schoolhouse where he stood.

But he listened to the kids now, and he thought of Mandy and of Harry, and he thought of Nichole. After a moment of this, his mind drifted to the kids of Joe Bennett, the security officer on Bravo team who'd been shot to death with an AK round through his pelvis, a guy Duffy had barely even met.

Word was Bravo Five left behind an ex-wife and a pair of high schoolers, and Armored Saint would probably call Mrs. Bennett's home in Albuquerque and let her know, then ask her where to send his body and his personal effects.

Duff thought of Nikki getting the same call, and an icy chill of terror went down his spine.

He was in too deep, but there was nothing he could do about it now.

He pushed these thoughts away, kept his eyes scanning back and forth, just as the eyes of all the other Americans on scene did, both inside and outside the location. His right hand rested on the grip of his rifle, and he tuned out the kids and tuned into an incoming radio transmission in his headset.

Just a request from an Alpha driver to a Bravo driver to move his vehicle a few yards, nothing pertaining to Duffy or his team.

The weight of the detail losing a man the night before was still on everyone's shoulders; there was little talk among Charlie team other than clipped communications related to their work.

But still, the mission continued.

They'd traveled forty miles up into the hills from where Bennett had died; the high peaks of the Sierra Madres were in view outside in the warm, clear afternoon, and Duff knew they'd soon be back on the road, heading ever higher.

Around twenty or thirty local leaders had been hurriedly gathered together in this school building from nearby villages and settlements to hear a message delivered personally from senior members of the United Nations and the Mexican government. This was the biggest thing to ever happen in El Rillito, and yet the mayor knew nothing about the arrival of the armored trucks until less than three hours earlier, when she was called by the Secretariat of the Interior in Mexico City and told she would have important visitors who would be making a speech to decision makers from this part of Durango.

They were twenty minutes into the confab now. Michelle LaRue spoke to the crowd through a local translator; Duff listened now and then, mostly to get a feel for how much longer this would go on. In his head a stopwatch had begun ticking the moment they'd rolled into town, and while he didn't know how much time they had before this area would fill up with sons of bitches with guns, he guessed they probably didn't have too long.

LaRue was telling the people that they were working on a deal with the Black Knights, and it was an opportunity for all sides to find accommodation that would clear the path for peace. El Rillito would be a safe haven, and similar safe havens would dot the hills and mountains all the way across the Sierras.

Next, Reinhardt Helm discussed peacekeeping operations. Duff tuned out, glanced out the window a moment, and took in the little kids, no doubt students whose normal Friday had been interrupted by a row of black ten-ton armored trucks rolling into the schoolyard, topped with ball-capped men standing behind machine guns.

He focused in on a little girl who appeared to be about Mandy's age. Dark black hair and dark complexioned, she wore a ponytail that was a little longer and much straighter than Mandy's light brown curls. She played with her red flag, sang something in Spanish, and then a kid next to her did the same. The girl couldn't have looked less like his own daughter, but her vulnerability, her wide-eyed wonderment of childhood, was exactly the same as his own little girl's some four thousand miles away in Northern Virginia.

Duff remembered thinking similar things in Lebanon, in Iraq, in Somalia.

The world was full of people who looked so incredibly different, but all the kids he came across reminded him of one another.

It was only when the kids grew up and started acting like assholes that he had a problem with any of them.

Again he refocused his attention on his duties; Helm stepped aside and Deputy Secretary Herrera addressed the room, began speaking about his mandate to negotiate a peace deal in order to keep the army out of the area, but then Gabby Flores moved laterally along the back wall and stopped when she reached Duff's shoulder.

Here we go, Duff thought.

She spoke to him in a whisper as Herrera continued his speech. "Mr. Duffy. Look at the children around this school. All of them. You understand how difficult it is for them here? The poverty. The fighting. The drugs. Even without the army, even *without* a civil war, their lives are threatened every day."

Duff didn't answer for a moment, and then he whispered back. "Just scanning my sector, Dr. Flores."

She continued whispering like she hadn't heard him. "Their lives will not improve with the UN plan. These local officials will accept the peacekeepers because they think they can make money off the extranjeros . . . the foreigners. I can look into their eyes and see there are corrupt opportunists in the crowd. Nothing will change."

After another long pause—she was obviously waiting for some sort of response from him—Duff just muttered, "Uh-huh."

"These leaders won't help the UN, they will only look for ways to receive foreign funding directly into their own hands."

Another long pause; Duff wished the woman would just wander off and bug someone else, but when she did not, he said, "You're just a bundle of optimism, aren't you?"

"I am a realist. The UN is too naïve, the Black Knights are too powerful, the campesinos here are too weak, and the municipal governments are too corrupt for there to be lasting change."

Finally Duff let his frustration show a little. He rolled his shoulders, adjusting his body armor, and said, "Maybe the military coming in will actually do some good. If you say the governments here are shit, then maybe the army will help clean this place out?"

Flores responded as if he were an idiot, and Duff instantly regretted engaging with her.

"The *army*?" she scoffed. "You think the army is neutral? They are aligned with the cartels. The army uses an iron fist or a blind eye, depending on who is paying them. And up here it won't be the blind eye, I promise you. Truly, the paycheck you and your men seek is probably the only neutral exchange of money for services for one hundred miles in any direction. If you—"

Duffy hadn't exactly been listening, but he blocked out her voice fully when Herrera said "Gracias" and then received mild applause from the room. The speech had wrapped up, and Duff assumed Remmick would move everyone back into the armored vehicles posthaste.

"Excuse me, doc," he said, and then he spoke into his headset. "All

Charlie call signs, they're done in here. We're gonna mount up and cover Alpha's movement from the street out front."

He began walking, following Remmick and three of the Alpha men as they moved in a diamond formation around the four protectees towards the exit.

"Did you hear a word I said?" Flores asked, following Duff at his shoulder.

Still scanning the room he said, "*Every* word. But you're complaining to the wrong guy. In case you haven't noticed, I'm just one of the gun monkeys."

"But you are the only one here who will listen to me."

To himself he muttered, "So that's what I've been doing wrong."

"And you are one of the men who is in charge here."

Duff eyed a stairwell as they passed it, his weapon ready. As he continued moving, he said, "Lady, I have three responsibilities—Crazy Horse, Charlie team, and keeping you civilians alive. That's it."

"Keeping me and your men alive is *exactly* what I'm talking about. We are walking into incredible danger. I didn't sense how bad it was in Mexico City. But I see the faces of the villagers now. They are looking at us like those federales did yesterday. They are looking at us like we will all die if we continue up the Devil's Spine."

Duff stepped outside into the bright afternoon light, putting on his sunglasses as he did so. "I'm the same as all the other guys still alive on this detail. I'm just trying to protect the VIPs so they can do their jobs. I don't know why you're talking to me like I can do anything about the situation up here."

"You are different from the others. You care. I saw the way you looked at those kids back there. You are a father, aren't you?"

"I am, but—"

"I am not a mother, I haven't been blessed with a husband or children yet. But I can see a man who sees others as people, not just as foreign aliens. You have to listen to me when we get up on the Spine. I know what I'm doing."

Duff sighed. "Okay, tell you what. You keep talking, and I'll keep listening. But follow me back to Crazy Horse, and don't impede my mission. We've got two more of these drop-ins today before going up into the mountains tonight."

Flores nodded, following along quietly as they mounted up, and soon the motorcade left the village and the children behind as it headed back for the highway to go northwest into the Sierras.

CHAPTER 31

Oscar Cardoza was asking a lot of his Jeep this afternoon. The sturdy four-wheel-drive vehicle's all-terrain tires churned over rocky ground, climbing a steep gradient of a back road he'd learned about from members of the Sinaloa cartel who suggested he could shave hours off his ascent by taking this route.

The men from Sinaloa had also sent him up here with a revolver, which he kept in the glove compartment. He'd not wanted to carry a gun; the last thing he needed was to be caught at a Black Knights checkpoint with a handgun, but they'd convinced him there was a fifty percent chance some opportunistic group of thugs would come upon him along this back route and cause trouble, more than likely armed with nothing more than machetes, and the little .38 might make the difference between Cardoza's success or failure, his life or death.

So far, however, the drive had been without incident. He'd passed curious onlookers in a dozen tiny hamlets made up of impossibly ramshackle dwellings, and not only was he aware he was being eyed by locals with suspicion, he knew these men and women and kids could grab a mobile phone and notify whoever was in charge locally to get some men in trucks and chase him down.

But no one had gotten in his way during the hours he'd been climbing the rutted and gravel dirt track leading up.

He finally bounced his way off the steep and rocky road and back onto a stretch of winding blacktop heading generally northeast, surrounded by dense foliage on both sides of the vehicle. The danger of low-rent off-road bandits was mostly behind him, so he considered grabbing the .38 and tossing it out the window, but first he glanced to his Suunto watch, then decided to make a quick call on his sat phone to update the Patrón of Guadalajara on the progress of his mission.

It took a minute for the signal to find a satellite, but finally he got through, and a scratchy connection came through his speaker.

"Tell me, Oscar," an older voice answered in Spanish. "How are things up in the lovely Sierra Madres Occidentales? It's raining here in Guadalajara. Is it raining bullets up there?"

Cardoza smiled a little, getting into character. With El Patrón he was playing the role of an attentive, subservient, but exceedingly self-confident negotiator contracted for this dangerous job. "Only a slight drizzle last night, but the storm is approaching. I am traveling higher now; with a little luck, I will be up on the Spine by nightfall."

"And your friends? Los Zetas?" The old man in Guadalajara said this in a mocking tone, but Cardoza did not take the bait and breathlessly insist that those in the northern cartel were *not* his friends.

Instead he responded, "They will set up camp tomorrow night and confront the motorcade after it leaves the meeting with the Black Knights. Perhaps in two days' time, depending on how the negotiations go."

"Muy bien," El Patrón replied. "Tell me about those mountains. Does it look like a perfect place for a war?"

"It looks like a terrible place for a war."

"Then *that*, mi amigo, *is* perfect."

Cardoza said, "As soon as we destroy Archuleta's shoulder-fired missiles and the convoy itself, war is all but assured."

"I am patiently relying on you for that."

Cardoza negotiated a steep hairpin turn, then saw something in the road in front of him. A long wooden pole, four feet above the blacktop, blocked his path. It was attached to a fulcrum to swivel open and closed, and three men with rifles stood next to it.

Shit.

A small plywood guard shack had been built on the hillside, fifty feet or so from the blacktop, and both sides of the road were too hilly, too rocky, and too overgrown with brush to be negotiated, so Cardoza couldn't simply bypass the entire barricade.

Distractedly, he said, "I'm sorry, patrón. I have to go. There is a roadblock up ahead. I'd better deal with this."

A low chuckle came over the connection. "I know how a man like you deals with things, Oscar. You'll have to tell me all about it later."

Cardoza hung up the phone, then slowed as he approached the checkpoint.

The three sentries didn't appear to be anything special. Just mountain men with dirty rifles slung over their chests, threadbare civilian clothes, and lean, hungry faces.

Their expressions indicated they were much more surprised to see the nice new Jeep than Cardoza was to see them, though now he cursed himself for not tossing the revolver minutes earlier.

The sentries separated on the road, and one of the two men on the right held a hand out to halt the advancing Jeep, which was pro forma considering there was a large wooden beam in the way.

As Cardoza pulled to a stop, he eyed them more closely; he wasn't dealing with the cream of the crop, but he was dealing with dangerous men, this he understood. If they were Black Knights, which he suspected, they would be men chosen for this rural checkpoint because they'd been unable to handle anything more taxing mentally. Still, he was sure they'd be able to operate their guns and control the occupants of a civilian vehicle with force.

And although these men would be so low on the totem pole they'd probably never personally been within twenty miles of Rafael Archuleta, they were still members of the organization Cardoza wanted to ingratiate himself with, and for that reason alone, he wanted to avoid violence if at all possible.

Their weapons were old G3s, a big Heckler & Koch battle rifle that fired a massive bullet but was somewhat unwieldy and difficult to operate in close quarters. These guns had most likely been stolen by the cartel from old Mexican marine caches or else simply purchased on the black market. Each man had one spare magazine in a pocket, but they wore no armor or other military gear.

After lowering his window, Oscar Cardoza put both his hands back on the steering wheel to ease any suspicion the sentries might have had about his intentions.

"Buenos días, señores," he said. On his side of the Wrangler, one man approached the window but stayed a safe distance away, while the second moved towards the rear of the Jeep. On the passenger side, the third man stepped to the front window there, where he just looked inside, curious but unthreatening in his movements.

Cardoza found himself surprised by their modicum of competence.

"Turn off the engine," the man at his window said in Spanish. Cardoza complied, then immediately returned his hand to the wheel. He'd been through countless cartel checkpoints without incident in his career; he knew what he was doing, just as they themselves seemed to.

The man at the back of the Jeep looked at Cardoza through the driver's-side mirror. He was missing teeth; he was gaunt and had eyes puffy from drink. His voice seemed slurred, but Cardoza could not be certain. "You are from Culiacán?"

Cardoza shook his head. "No, amigo . . . ah, you noticed the car tags. It's just a rental from the airport. I flew in from Mexico City. I am on my way to visit family. Did I make a wrong turn?"

The man who had been closest to the window took a step even closer. His eyes were rimmed in red, runny. Around his neck he wore a simple medallion, probably stainless steel, of a marijuana plant. "You made a wrong turn when you came up the mountain. We are Black Knights. Culiacán is Sinaloa cartel."

Cardoza smiled indulgently. "I'm not with *any* cartel, mi amigo. I'm just on my way to Soyatita, my uncle is—"

The man with the steel pot plant around his neck said, "Get out of the car."

Cardoza turned his hands over on the steering wheel, held them up imploringly. "Amigo . . . it's getting late, and I—"

"Out of the car."

Cardoza sighed a little, but he did his best to hide his annoyance. "Bueno. I will move slowly, señor."

He complied with the sentry, and when he stood on the road, Oscar Cardoza was spun around and ordered to put his hands on the hood. This he did, and he was rewarded with a rough frisking from the man with the runny eyes.

As passive as he pretended to be, inside he was preparing himself for a fight. He would try to talk his way out of this situation, but his plan B had already begun taking shape in his mind.

He smelled alcohol on the man frisking him, and eyeballing the sentry going through items in the front passenger seat of his car now, he determined this man to be drunk. The third man was still behind the Wrangler.

A folding knife was removed from Cardoza's front pocket without comment by the guard frisking him, but it was tossed on the hood haphazardly, where it then clanked to the ground.

The man at the rear of the Jeep spoke up again; his speech was definitely slurred, confirming Cardoza's suspicion that all three of these men had been hitting the bottle out here on the hot and dusty road this afternoon.

"He's got Culiacán plates," the slurring sentry said, repeating something that had been well established thirty seconds earlier.

Cardoza stole a glance at his watch; he was burning time he did not have.

The sentry frisking him said, "Hey, amigo. That's a nice watch."

Cardoza nodded. "It *is*. A *very* nice watch. And it's yours if you just let me be on my way so I can see my uncle before I must return to—"

"*Pistole!*" the man searching the Jeep shouted, and then he rose from the vehicle, holding up the wooden-handled .38 like a prize.

Cardoza closed his eyes for an instant; this was going to be messier than he'd hoped. Then he opened them and returned to the character he was playing. "Oh, come on, man, you know about highwaymen up here in the mountains. I just brought something small to protect me from—"

Cardoza was spun around by the guy with the pot plant necklace and whisked away from the hood, and now he faced the little shack. To his surprise a fourth man stood in the entrance to the tiny building; his hands on his hips, he wore a cowboy hat and appeared to be well into his fifties, although Cardoza suspected the conditions up here were tough enough to make anybody look a lot older than they actually were.

The man had a Glock pistol jammed into the leather belt holding up his jeans, but no rifle.

He descended the steps from the shack with a swagger, reminding Cardoza of John Wayne in the old westerns his father used to watch with him as a boy.

The man in the cowboy hat said, "You look like a Sinaloan."

He was surrounded by idiots; this Cardoza told himself while keeping his visage blank.

The sentry closest to the window said, "He tells us he's from the capital."

"Even worse," the older man declared with a jagged grin. He stepped closer, onto the road now. He looked up and down at Cardoza's nice new clothes from REI, his trim beard, and his expensive-looking haircut.

Cardoza saw him note his designer eyeglasses and his silver wedding ring.

"You don't belong here, cabrón," the older man said. It was a declarative statement, an obvious fact.

This guy with a pistol and a cowboy hat was the man in charge; Cardoza easily ascertained this fact, and *he* would be the one who decided how the next sixty seconds were going to play out.

Cardoza had thought he could talk his way past this checkpoint without compromising his operation, but now he decided to appeal to authority. "Listen, jefe. I am here on a special mission, sanctioned by your superiors. I am an emissary from Grupo de Guadalajara. I assure you I have been granted access by Rafael Archuleta himself for a personal meeting between—"

The older man looked at his men and began laughing. His teeth were broken and showed the effects of a lifetime of smoking and drug use.

"You are going to see Rafa, sí?"

"Sí. In fact, I am."

"Why don't I know anything about this?"

Cardoza did have the meeting arranged with Archuleta, but he hadn't expected word of it to filter down to the bottom-feeders of the organization. He said, "I took a different route to save time. Believe me, my mission is a confidential—"

"And," the older man continued, "you were going to bring a gun to a meeting with the leader of Los Caballeros Negros? Is that it?"

"Of course not. I was going to throw the gun in a river before I got up to—"

"Lying pendejo," the older man barked.

Cardoza's face went from friendly to menacing in an instant. "Listen to me, caballero. I need to get back in that Jeep and continue my journey up to the Devil's Spine. All you need to do is—"

"You don't give me orders at my checkpoint. I am the king here."

Cardoza sniffed out a laugh. "King of the checkpoint." There was no sense in being friendly with drunken fools at this point, he told himself.

The man with the weed necklace stepped up to his right, his rifle pointed at Cardoza's head now, and the man in the back of the Wrangler approached on his left, also readying his gun to fire on the stranger. The third sentry remained on the other side of the Jeep, now rifling through Cardoza's backpack on the floorboard there.

The man in the cowboy hat said, "I have the authority to shoot you right here."

Cardoza shook his head. "No . . . you don't. You just are thinking about this nice Jeep and my nice watch and whatever cash I might have in my pocket. You are betting you and your amigos can kill some fool from the city and leave his body to be carried off by wolves."

"You accuse me of—"

Cardoza interrupted. "You don't believe I have been invited by Archuleta, otherwise you wouldn't lay a finger on me. But, amigo, I have my meeting, not with the king of the checkpoint, but with the king of the mountain. I will be there right on time, so I *will* be on my way."

Oscar Cardoza was a brilliant negotiator. Still, he evaluated the probability that these four drunk losers would let him pass without delay after that soliloquy to be no more than thirty-three percent.

The older man took one step closer, into Cardoza's face, and smiled at him with his destroyed teeth.

"How about I have my men put you on your knees in the street, and then I take out my gun and—"

The older man reached for the pistol tucked into his belt at his midsection, and just like that, the probability that Cardoza would be driving off without a fight plummeted down to zero.

"—kill you myself, you piece of—"

As the leader of the sentries drew the handgun, both Cardoza's hands fired out and locked onto the weapon as it appeared from behind the belt, while simultaneously Cardoza ducked, dropping roughly to his knees.

He yanked the Glock free of the surprised sentry leader's hands, spun the weapon upside down to where its barrel was point-blank in the man's midsection, and then Cardoza used his pinky finger to pull the trigger.

A pair of booming gunshots cracked just over his head as the sentries on either side of him fired at the location where his head had been, but now he was a foot below their aim.

The older man in the cowboy hat fell onto his back, clutching his eviscerated abdomen, and the drunk sentries standing on either side of him both dropped like trees felled by a lumberjack, having accidentally shot each other at a range of three or four feet.

Cardoza's ears rang as he pivoted, still on his knees on the blacktop road. He flipped the pistol into the air, spinning it back around, catching it with the correct grip. He aimed the weapon through the open driver's-side door of his Wrangler and put his sights on the sentry at the passenger-side door, who was now stumbling back, desperately trying to get his gun off his back and into position to use it.

Oscar Cardoza shot the man once in the chest, sending him down to the blacktop and out of view.

Then Cardoza lay flat on the ground on his chest, aimed his weapon under the vehicle, and shot the man again in the right side of his head.

The man from Mexico City rose slowly to his feet now, the Glock low, and he looked at the men around him while shaking his head and using his free hand to stick a finger in his ringing right ear. Swirling it around, trying to stop the pain and noise, he gave up after a moment when he realized the older man who'd taken the shot to the gut was still alive. The leader of the sentries stared at the sky, his two hands failing in their attempt to hold his blood inside his stomach, and he made a sick gurgling sound with his throat.

Cardoza, now shaking his head to stop the ringing, knelt down over the leader of this motley crew of losers.

"A bullet through the belly is quite painful, or so I've been told by those in a position to know better than I.

"Their position was quite similar to your position now. In the road at my feet. To be honest, I didn't get a lot of details about the pain from them. We didn't talk long, you see. It was more of an observation."

Cardoza looked up at the shack on the hill, fifty feet away. The door had opened a crack, and he saw the barrel of a rifle poking out, pointed in his direction.

He aimed the Glock and fired a half dozen rounds through the door. A fifth sentry tumbled out, down the wooden steps, and came to rest, dead on the rocky hill.

Cardoza shook his head again, fighting the pain in his ears.

He rose back up to his feet and looked again at the man on his back, his midsection covered in blood. "I'll be sure to mention your bungling incompetence to Rafa when I meet him." He shrugged. "I'd enjoy watching you suffer for a while, and I'm sorry I have no time for this. I must be heading up this mountain road you have done such a magnificent job protecting so I can get to my meeting with your leader."

He began to turn away, then looked back. "In the end, amigo, you died for nothing, which seems fair, because that's exactly what your life is worth."

The older man extended a bloody hand to the air and croaked out a soft "Ayuda." *Help.*

"Help?" Cardoza said with a chuckle. "I'll help you, king of the checkpoint."

He shot the prone man once in the forehead, then tossed the Glock onto the bloody body.

"You're welcome."

He retrieved his folding knife from the ground, moved the beam blocking his Jeep on the road, and climbed back behind the wheel. Still shaking the ringing from his ears, he continued on to the north, climbing up towards the Devil's Spine.

CHAPTER 32

Shane Remmick had ordered the Armored Saint convoy to stay off the highways, to remain as covert as possible as they reached the mountain range. To do this they took dirt roads that looked and felt centuries old, and this, along with the encroachment of mountains and flora on either side of them, made for grueling travel.

As Nascar looked out through the grimy windshield of Crazy Horse, he could make out little more than the rear of Pack Horse Two through the dust, the late-afternoon sun's glare on the thick glass only obscuring his vision even more.

They were averaging almost five miles an hour, glacial on a black-topped road, but virtually breakneck speed considering the condition of the dirt and gravel track below them. The men in back had lashed down everything in the vehicle to keep from turning gear into dangerous airborne projectiles flying around the small space, but still, on top of the buffeting and shaking everyone had to contend with, the sound of ammunition rattling in cans, of items shaking inside packs, and even the scratching of gear strapped to bodies slamming against the wall of the armored truck could be heard over the rumble of the enormous V8.

With hours more of this to go today, Duffy couldn't help but worry about the integrity of the vehicle. He turned to Nascar and spoke into his intrateam mic so that the man four feet away from him could hear without him having to raise his voice. "How's Crazy Horse doing?"

Nascar activated his windshield wipers. The spray coated the dirt on the glass and turned it into a thin sheet of mud, and then the rubber blades wicked it off. "She's a hell of a machine. As long as there's gas in the tank and four tires below us, I think we'll be just fine."

Behind Nascar, Frenchie said, "And ammo. We're going to need a lot of ammo."

To this Duff said, "There's five thousand rounds in this truck, extra stores for us in Pack Horse Two."

"Sounds almost adequate," muttered Wolfson.

All these guys, Duff knew, were preparing for the worst. Losing a man on the first night of the operation had taken a toll, of course, but also having Dr. Flores back here in the middle of his team helped to darken the mood. When she spoke, which seemed to be increasingly less often, she spoke in dire tones about the operation.

Duffy began thinking about himself. This drive was murder on his body; his right foot caught all the vibrations and jolts in the floorboard and sent them up his spine, and on his left side, his knee took a pounding from the carbon fiber prosthetic hidden under his pants and boot.

Still, he was just sitting here, scanning his sector. He hadn't done any fighting at all yet, so as tough as this was on his body, he knew this was the easy part.

The motorcade crested a rise and then began a sharp descent, with Crazy Horse still at the rear, but they'd only made it fifty feet or so down when Remmick's voice blasted over the speakers in the vehicle. "Full halt! Full halt!"

Nascar shouted, "Everybody grab something!" He slammed on the brakes; the vehicle skidded on the steep dirt track below them, then came to a stop again on relatively flat ground, just six feet from the rear of Pack Horse Two.

Without waiting for the order, Squeeze announced, "Goin' topside!" He turned the latch and pushed open the hatch door, then rose behind his Mk 48 and began rotating, peering through his sights and through the dust in all directions.

Duff got his own weapon out a gunport, as did all the men in the truck, unaware of the location or nature of any threat but determined to be ready to quickly engage.

Remmick clarified the situation before the dust around Crazy Horse settled.

"Alpha One to all call signs. We've got a group of men ringing us at the front, blocking the route. A half dozen pax minimum. No weapons visible. Break. Charlie Actual? What do you see on our six?"

Duff couldn't see shit from the six o'clock position; only Squeeze and Cruz had a view to the rear. "Cruz?"

"Got nothing. Trees on that hill we just came down. The rocky-assed road."

"Squeeze?"

"I can't see shit through all the dust."

"Roger," Duff said, and he began to depress the handset to report negative contact, but before he did, Cruz shouted over the intrateam.

"Wait up! I got pax, our six o'clock! Coming out of the trees next to the road."

"Where?" Squeeze shouted, and then he came over the net as Duff tried in vain to see in the rearview mirror. "Yeah! I got 'em. Multiple personnel."

Cruz spoke again. "Holy shit! Gotta be twenty of them, all in a wide row. Looks like a few of them are carrying something. Am I engaging these shitheads?"

"Do *not* engage. Squeeze, do they have weapons?"

"Can't tell what they have. It's too dusty, and the brush on the hill is too high."

"Then pull out your fucking binos and look!"

Remmick broadcast over the vehicle radio, annoyed that Duff hadn't responded. "Charlie Actual? How copy?"

Duff clicked the handset. "Charlie Actual to Alpha. We have twenty pax emerging from the tree line on our six; we have not ID'd firearms on the men but are assessing at this time, over."

"Roger. Ditto up here. Bravo, get your men looking for more threats. We have to ID weps before we engage."

Duff needed information from his men, and he needed it now. What he did *not* need at this moment, as far as he was concerned, was Gabby Flores's input.

Nevertheless, her voice came into his ear. "Let me look out a portal. I can't see any—"

Wolfson yelled at her. "Sit back down, lady, get out of my space."

Duff saw movement now outside his window. Figures in the distance, appearing from the trees on the right side of the road. "I got movement, three o'clock. Squeeze, you got glass on these guys?"

"Yeah. Hang on." After a pause he said, "Wait . . . they got . . . sticks or . . . no . . . are those spears?"

"What?" Duff questioned, still squinting into the distance through the grimy window as he pulled his binoculars from the pack at his feet.

Cruz said, "Some of these guys are carrying spears. Bright red shirts. They are all walking up to the road. I see some machetes, too. Am I shooting?"

"Hold fire," Duff shouted.

Flores shouted back. "That's not the cartel. If they have ceremonial spears, then they are Tarahumara. Indigenous. They aren't dangerous."

Cruz said, "They look pretty fuckin' dangerous from back here, lady! There's a lot of them, and they have weapons."

"Those weapons are to protect them from the narcos. They won't attack."

Squeeze shouted back at her. "Then why the fuck they steppin' up on us like this?"

"Because you strangers appeared in their land with tanks!"

"This ain't a tank!" Wolfson barked back at her.

As the ring of men closed around the motorcade from all directions, Remmick broadcast again. "All call signs. Director Helm wants us to roll through here slowly, do not engage. He says these guys are on our side since their survival depends on the peacekeepers moving in."

Gabby protested to Duff. "The Tarahumara don't know this! They know nothing of what is going on. We need to get out and explain who we are, what we are doing."

Duff and all the other men of Crazy Horse just ignored her, but she continued. "How would the Tarahumara possibly know that there is a truce between—"

Duff spun around now. He held the handset in his left hand and used the back of Nascar's seat to twist to face the woman. In frustration he yelled, "We heard you!"

Gabby had unfastened her harness seconds earlier to try to look out a portal, and now she lunged at the microphone in Duff's hand, catching him by surprise. She quickly wrenched the handset free, then clicked the transmit button as Frenchie tried to stop her.

"Miss LaRue. It's Dr. Flores. I speak fluent Tarahumara. I can de-escalate the situation by telling these locals what we are doing here. Just let me go talk to—"

Remmick's voice overrode Gabby's pleas. "Charlie One, get your goddamned mic back from your passenger!"

Frenchie pulled the handset away and handed it back to Duff, who simultaneously tried to reel it in by pulling on the coiled cable.

"Strap her in!" Duff demanded, and Frenchie began fastening Gabby back into the bench harness next to him, ignoring her protests.

Duff clicked the mic. "Uh . . . Alpha One, roger. Be advised, we *do* have a terp back here who can—"

"Negative. We keep rolling."

Squeeze shouted now. "I see long guns!"

"Me, too," Cruz said. "They're some old lever-action bullshit and hunting rifles, but they've definitely got a few guns in the crowd."

From the turret, Squeeze said, "I got armed tangos closing, all sides. I'm engaging these motherfuckers!"

"No!" Gabby shouted.

"Hold fire!" Duff ordered.

Wolfson barked at his team leader. "You're following *her* orders, now? Who's the damn TL here, Duff?"

"You are *not* cleared to engage, Squeeze!" Duff repeated.

Men in other vehicles began broadcasting that they saw an array of old rifles on the group, which now seemed to number more than fifty.

Nascar spoke up, as well. "I dunno, boss, I suggest we start smokin' these tangos."

Just then, Remmick called for the convoy to move out slowly, and Nascar began rolling Crazy Horse forward behind Pack Horse Two.

After just a few seconds, Cruz shouted out now. "Hey, boss, I got multiple fighting-age males stepping into the road on our six! They are aiming . . . they're aiming bows and arrows at us!"

"Say again?"

"They're aiming motherfuckin' bows and motherfuckin' arrows!"

Quickly, Duff ordered, "Squeeze, button up!"

"Fuck that shit! I've got a belt-fed and these dickheads in my sights! I'm not hidin' from some low-rent Apache mother—"

"Get your ass in here, now!"

"They're firing!" Cruz shouted.

Duff heard a loud clang on the armor of Crazy Horse, audible over the engine. It was followed an instant later by another.

"Button your hatch!" Duff ordered, and he reached back in vain, trying to grab Squeeze's legs where he stood between Frenchie and Gabby on the port side and Wolfson on the starboard side.

He didn't take hold of the younger man, but after another volley of clanking against the right side of the hull of the APC, Squeeze ducked down, then pulled and locked his hatch.

"This is bullshit, Eleven-B!" he shouted in frustration.

Duff was on the radio for Remmick. "Charlie One for Alpha Actual. We are taking accurate fire from bows and arrows at our six and nine o'clock. No gunfire at this time, over."

Remmick responded, "Helm says do not engage unless we are in danger."

Nascar said, "This ain't dangerous?"

Duff admonished his driver. "You're not gonna get shot by an arrow through armor, dude. Settle down. As long as we're in here, we're fine."

Wolfson responded from behind Duff. "They can pop a tire and immobilize us. We'll *have* to get out to repair it."

"They're run-flats and you know it. Calm the fuck down, Charlie team."

In the chaos, Gabby Flores had again unfastened her harness, and now she leapt across the cabin to the starboard-side hatch. Wolfson sat next to it, but he peered through the scope of his sniper rifle jutting from an open portal, waiting for the call to fire. He didn't see her move, but he did hear the latch open.

Frenchie saw Gabby exiting Crazy Horse, but he was too late to do much about it. "*Merde!* The woman!"

Wolfson got a hand on her shirt as she went through the door, but he wasn't able to stop her, either. She stumbled out of the slowly moving vehicle and into the road, then raised her hands.

Wolfson quickly shut the hatch behind her, following protocol for the vehicle.

"*Shit!*" Duffy exclaimed, and then he clicked his handset. "Alpha One, be advised. Flores has debussed from Crazy Horse."

Flores stood in the road and began waving her hands over her head at the men on the hill in front of her.

Remmick snapped back. "All halt! All halt! Dammit, Duff! Secure that woman and get your fucking house in order back there!"

Duff threw the handset between the front seats in fury and quickly began removing his AK-47 from around his neck. While doing this, he said, "Everybody stay put. I'm gonna disarm and go out and get her." He pulled his pistol out of the holster on his thigh and handed it over to Nascar, who took it wide-eyed.

"You're gonna do *what*?"

Cruz said, "You're batshit crazy, Eleven-B!"

"You guys cover me. I go down, you waste 'em."

"*That's* your fuckin' plan?" Wolfson muttered.

"You should cross your fingers, Charlie Two. You might be in charge of this vic in a minute."

Squeeze muttered to himself now. "TL is fuckin' nuts, yo."

Duff climbed out of the vehicle, his hands held high. He half expected to catch an arrow in the forehead before he walked two steps, but miraculously he did not. He saw Gabby twenty-five yards ahead of him, nearing the line of men on the rock-and-brush-strewn hillside in front of the wood line.

Gabby turned back and saw Duffy. "Stay there!" she ordered. "I'll talk to them."

"Get your ass back in the—"

She turned away from him and began speaking.

Wolfson came over Duff's headset. "Boss. You get engaged, just drop flat and I'll rake that hill with my subgun. Squeeze will waste everything back to the tree line." He added, "That dumb bitch is on her own."

Duff spoke into his microphone. "Keep your cool, Wolfson." Then, louder, he called to Gabby Flores. "What are they saying?"

"I told them you are in charge and we are all on a peace mission. Come up here."

Duff walked forward, his hands away from his body. Still no arrows whizzed by, and he took this as a good sign.

Once he was alongside Gabby and standing in front of the men on the southern hillside, the woman said, "Greet them."

Duff put his hand on his chest and bowed slightly.

Instantly, Gabby admonished him. "What is *that*? We aren't in the Middle East. Just shake their hands."

Chastened, Duff did so. He shook several hands, but the eye contact from the men remained suspicious and disconcerting to him. There was one thin young individual in front of him with a hunting rifle, and while it wasn't pointed Duff's way presently, the man could lift it up, point it, and shoot him dead before he could do much about it.

Flores began speaking again with the men. Duff didn't understand Spanish, but he'd heard enough of it in his life to know this *wasn't* it.

While he stood there, Remmick broadcast on the interteam frequency. "Charlie One, what the fuck is happening back there?"

"Uh . . . I'm outside the vic at this time securing Flores. She is speaking to the locals in their native tongue. We might be good here, boss. Wait one."

"We're not here to make nice with the fucking savages. We can button up and drive right over them if we have to."

Duff interrupted Gabby. "What are you telling them?"

"Everything. They know nothing about what's going on."

"Duff? You hear me?" Remmick growled through the mic.

Duff looked farther down the hillside. He saw men pointing bows at him as well as the trucks now. "Come on, Gabby. I've got fifteen arrows pointed at my head."

She stopped talking to the Tarahumara and turned to Duffy. "They want to know if you will kill the Black Knights. 'Yes' would be a good answer right now."

Duff shrugged. "We are against anyone who opposes peace."

She relayed this, and almost instantly several of the men reached out to shake his hand again.

Gabby spoke a moment more, then said, "Everything is fine. We can pass. Give them a moment to communicate to the others in front."

Duff again bowed to the men and patted his chest, while they just looked back in confusion. Fortunately for him, this time Gabby was saying her goodbyes, so she missed his cultural error.

Soon the two of them were walking back down the hill to Crazy Horse. Duff transmitted, "Charlie Actual to Alpha Actual. Dr. Flores has secured the approval of the locals to pass."

Remmick, however, was unimpressed. "Yeah, 'cause they didn't want to get turned to fuckin' dog food by our machine guns. Get your ass back in Crazy Horse. I want your hand around Flores's ponytail for the rest of this fucking mission, you read me?"

"Yes, sir."

Gabby ignored Remmick when she spoke to Duff. "See . . . the villagers aren't bad. They're just under siege. The Black Knights . . . *they* are the scary ones."

"Yeah," Duff muttered. "And tomorrow we're going to meet them for lunch."

Gabby shook her head. "Loco. Completamente loco."

She climbed back into the side hatch, and Duff climbed into the front passenger seat. As he buckled himself in, Nascar said, "That was nuts, boss. Maybe it worked this time, but I wouldn't make a habit of it."

"No plans to." Duff turned to look back in the cabin behind him. "Gabby, I want you sitting up here, right behind me, between the seats. Wolfson, get a Pelican case out for her to sit on. We'll rig a harness to some eye bolts in the flooring. She's going to be within arm's reach of me for the rest of this op."

Wolfson was dumbfounded. "You want her *closer* to you after that stunt?"

"She just saved a lot of lives and earned us some goodwill."

"So she gets a promotion? She's your number two now?"

"No, you are. But I don't want to start slaying locals who don't pose a threat. We're supporting the UN mission, and killing innocents won't help things. She's going to see what I see, and she's going to tell me what she thinks."

"Gracias, Mr. Duffy."

Remmick snapped angrily over the speakers. "Alpha One to all drivers. The road is clear. Everybody move out."

Nascar put his machine in gear and they jolted forward, leaving the large group of indigenous people to fill the road behind them.

CHAPTER 33

Oscar Cardoza pulled his mud-covered Jeep Wrangler into the small dusty mountain town of Boca Arriba just after six in the evening. It was a Friday night, the sun was low, and music played from the town square. Men and women walked around, many eating and drinking. Kids played in a dirty municipal park alongside the main drag.

Boca Arriba was a surprisingly urban place, up here at 5,600 feet and two miles from the highway that traversed the mountains across the Devil's Spine. Cinder-block, brick, and concrete buildings in all directions, signs advertising soft drinks and beer and auto parts affixed to everything, a fair amount of traffic on the streets. Virtually all of the vehicles were four-wheel-drive trucks, which didn't surprise Cardoza in the least, but he'd not expected this much activity tonight as he reached his first contact location with the men in the Black Knights who were arranging the meeting between him and Rafa Archuleta.

Cardoza had looked into the history of this town when he'd been told to come there. There used to be a large patchwork of small hillside farms that grew fruit in the mountains all around this area, but these days the cartels controlled the roads, they controlled the town, and they controlled the planting. Poppy and marijuana grew on any spit of earth that was at least the size of a basketball court and at least as flat as a negotiable slope. Young men and women moved rocks and tilled earth while older men and women planted crops, and all the while, pickup trucks loaded with armed sicarios were never far away, always ready to make sure everyone was doing what they were told.

The citizens of this town tended the land, but they weren't members of Los Caballeros Negros. They were just farmers, paid a pittance for the crops they brought in and threatened with absolute poverty, or even death, if they did not comply.

Cardoza saw it as a form of indentured servitude, the kind that had been going on all over the world since the beginning of time. There were a few places on Earth where people's freedoms could not be ground down into the dust, where men and women were not chattel for whoever had the most numbers or the biggest guns, but that was hardly the natural order of things. Cardoza didn't feel bad for those suffering here, and he didn't feel envy for those who carried the whips and the keys to the chains. Everyone was just acting their part.

It was brutal, but brutality, he reasoned, was simply human nature.

Oscar Cardoza saw himself above this fray, however. He was his own man. He would be leaving all this behind, and once he left this mountain and this country, he had no plans whatsoever to look back.

As he drove slowly through town, he caught the side-eye glances of many of the locals. His vehicle was unknown to them, he was unknown to them, and he expected that people figured either he was someone damn important or he was in a hell of a lot of trouble.

Cardoza knew he was in the center of the beast now, and as he waited at a streetlight for a group of evening strollers to pass, he took a moment to settle his nerves. He would affect nothing but self-assurance over the next few hours or days, but in truth, he saw his play here as desperation, a Hail Mary, his one last chance for a score big enough to walk away from it all before it all fell down on top of him.

He let his emotions get the better of him, but only for a short time now, in what would perhaps be his last private moment until this whole affair was over.

Thinking of this, he flashed a quick smile. There was a beach with his name on it, there was an icy drink that would soon be sweating in his hand with unlimited drinks lined up behind it, there was a view to die for that he would gaze upon for the rest of his life, and there was, with any luck, a woman in this paradise who would, herself, be paradise.

Or two women. Or three.

No more than three, Cardoza thought with another smile. He didn't see himself as a greedy man.

He liked to take a moment every day to think of his goal. To see himself where he wanted to be at the end of this. To manifest his dream into reality by picturing himself in it.

Creer es poder. *Believing is power.*

He shook his head to bring himself back into the here and now, dialed a number on his phone from a piece of paper he pulled from his pocket, and waited.

After a moment, there was a click on the other end. He could hear breathing, but no one spoke.

"It's Cardoza," he said after a moment. "I am just arriving in Boca Arriba now."

"We know," a voice said. "We've been watching."

Cardoza looked around him. Just across the street, he noticed two figures in a beat-up Toyota Tacoma. "Por supuesto que si." *Of course you have.* "What shall I—"

"Are you armed?"

"No guns."

"A knife?"

"Of course."

"Throw it out the window."

Cardoza sighed. He loved his Benchmade folding knife; it had been a gift. But he told himself, when this was over, he could buy one thousand more.

He pulled it from his pocket, lowered the window, and tossed it out.

It clanged on the pavement. "That's everything, amigo, what do you want me to—"

A burgundy-colored van raced up behind on his left and screeched to a stop right next to the Wrangler, on Cardoza's side. The back door slid open, and it was dark inside, but he saw the outline of two figures seated there. One held a phone to his ear.

Cardoza climbed out of the Jeep, stepped to the side of the van, and accepted the white blindfold when a hand reached out from the dark with it. He tied it around his eyes, in full view of men, women, and children who knew better than to stop and stare at something like this, and in seconds he was inside the van, and it rolled off.

No one spoke for a moment, so Cardoza said, "How long until—"

"No talking," a voice barked.

The man from Mexico City just sighed inwardly.

It was hard to judge the time or the distance, but Cardoza suspected they had been rolling for a half hour, climbing the hills on bumpy switchbacks for several miles. Always up, never back down. He was impressed with the van negotiating the jarring roads, and he imagined that every mechanic along the Devil's Spine was a master at repairing and maintaining suspensions, because each and every vehicle up here basically traveled paths that were more like uneven staircases than civilized roads. Ascents and descents, undercarriages slamming into hard-packed earth or unyielding rock every few yards.

The van Cardoza rode in slowed on a rare flat section of blacktop; Cardoza could hear other vehicles driving around, and he had the strong feeling he was in another town, much higher in the mountains than Boca Arriba.

This all surprised him, because on the map, it appeared Boca Arriba was the largest cluster of buildings in the area, and he could tell by the constant ascent of their travel that they had not doubled back.

He realized that even though he'd studied Google Maps intently before his trip, he suddenly had no clue where he was.

The van stopped, he stepped out, and a man behind him pulled off his blindfold. Taking a second to adjust his eyes to the electric lighting of a building in front of him, he looked around slowly and saw that he was in the center of a small but idyllic colonial village.

He couldn't imagine how he'd missed it on the map.

Is this Mexico's Shangri-la? he wondered.

They sat parked in a lot next to a massive building that looked like some sort of arena; the glow from the windows was the brightest light in the area. He could hear a sound broadcast over loudspeakers somewhere: Norteño music, polka-like rhythms played by bands with accordions, songs about wealth and power and murder and betrayal.

Nobody he knew played this music in Mexico City, but Oscar Cardoza had been to enough backwaters to recognize the exact song playing now.

Pickup trucks filled the lot, and while he didn't see any men at first, the size and style of all the vehicles here made him assume the building would be full of Black Knights. Big F-250s, Dodge Rams, Chevy Silverados. Gun racks in every back window.

These were cartel trucks, and there were a lot of them.

He was led inside, not cuffed or restrained, but three men from the van walked alongside him, and he was certain they were armed. The Toyota Tacoma that he'd first noticed in Boca Arriba had pulled into the lot, as well, and the two men climbed out and followed the small procession through the door of the building.

Cardoza had been frisked from head to toe during his ride here, but he was checked again at the door by a pair of young fit men with hair spiked with gel. Cardoza recognized the look of either current or former Federal Police officers, even if they weren't wearing their uniforms. They were lean, well groomed, not mountain men, and they possessed a dark-eyed malevolence.

Again, this was nothing Cardoza wasn't used to.

Soon he was moving again, through a small lobby and into an impossibly large room that had the size, look, and feel of a horse arena, with sawdust floors and bleachers around the sides. There were five men ringing him at this point, and they walked onto the main floor, past men and women who simply looked on.

The music wasn't coming from inside the room; it sounded as if there was a gathering of some sort going on out back behind the building.

But Cardoza wasn't heading out back. He was heading, he realized, to the large round table in the center of the arena.

There, a man in his fifties sat alone, a steak the size of a pizza hanging off the sides of a plate in front of him, juices dripping onto the white tablecloth adorning this one table in the middle of the sawdust-strewn arena.

A candle sat in front of the man, as did red and white wineglasses, both empty, and a bottle of tequila had been positioned next to a shot glass, with a lime and salt set up next to that.

There was a small mirror on the table, where two lines of perico, the local slang for cocaine, waited patiently to be snorted.

There was a faint smell of horse shit in the room, Cardoza couldn't help but notice.

He had never seen Rafael Archuleta, and he'd never seen a picture of the man, though he had all the resources to do so if an official photo existed.

But this had to be him. His look of bored confidence, the deference paid to him by all the armed men standing around, the obvious desire by the man at the table to demonstrate both an imposing show of force and a nonchalance about the entire affair.

It was gangster boss 101 stuff.

It was comforting, a little anyway, that Archuleta, considered so mysterious as to be almost mythical, was just like every other cartel head.

The man at the table wore a mustache and a short pointed beard that was almost gray, though the hair on his head was nearly all black and quite thick. He wore a bandanna around his neck as if he'd spent the day on a cattle drive, a yellow silk cowboy shirt with a red rooster embroidered onto each breast, and a gold watch on his wrist.

Somehow, to Cardoza, the man appeared to have some ethnicity that was not common to Mexico, but he was not able to pinpoint the man's origin. His face was wide, his jaw strong, and his dark eyes particularly deep set.

He did not look up when Cardoza was led to the table in front of him; he just cut into his meat with a serrated knife so big and imposing that it appeared it could also be used to saw off a shotgun.

Cardoza stood there patiently, taking the man in.

Finally, Archuleta swallowed a huge bite of meat, washed it down with a full shot of tequila, and looked up. He pointed at Cardoza with his big knife, but his words were to his people around him.

"Make a place for him at the table. Bring him a steak." To Cardoza he said, "I like mine rare. How about you?"

"Rare is the only way to cook a steak." In truth, Oscar Cardoza preferred medium, but he wasn't going to quibble about his dinner at a time like this.

Archuleta regarded him. "Do people in Guadalajara drink tequila, or is it all gin and Chablis for you guys?"

"I drink tequila, like any proud Mexican, but I do not hail from Guadalajara. I'm from the capital."

"The capital. Oh, then you must like rosé?"

Men around laughed. Cardoza smiled pleasantly. "I prefer tequila, mezcal, and scotch."

Archuleta raised his eyebrows; the men stopped laughing.

This was a dick-measuring contest, nothing more. Archuleta was questioning Cardoza's manhood, and Cardoza knew he had to establish his manhood to gain the man's respect.

Cardoza loathed Archuleta already, just like he loathed all the cartel leadership he'd met in his long career.

Two women appeared and quickly set the table next to Rafa. He'd cut himself another bite, and then he noticed something on the fresh place setting just before Cardoza sat down. "Take away his steak knife. Are you crazy? I don't trust this pinche cabrón from Mexico City. He can cut his meat with a butter knife."

CHAPTER 34

The men around began laughing again, louder this time, and Archuleta himself smiled and winked at Cardoza.

Cardoza chuckled politely as he sat down.

The leader of the Black Knights didn't extend a hand for a shake, so Cardoza simply said, "Señor Archuleta. It is an honor to finally meet the leader of Los Caballeros Negros."

Archuleta wasn't interested in an introduction. He just said, "People talk about you. The famous negotiator from Mexico City who wants to turn all the cartels into one big happy family."

A woman reached in front of him to pour a shot of tequila. Cardoza leaned to be ready for eye contact with Rafa should the man look up from his food again. He said, "I have been mediating matters between the organizations for some time, señor. If you all suddenly become one big happy family, I will be out of work."

Archuleta snorted out a laugh. Swallowed a bite of bloody steak. "Well, we can't have that. I guess we'll all keep killing one another so you can have a job." As an afterthought, he asked, "Any problems getting up here?"

Cardoza shrugged as he took hold of his tequila. "One of your roadblocks *did* try to execute me."

Rafa's eyebrows rose again, but he kept eating. With a mouthful of food, he said, "You were brave to come alone."

"You invited me."

"I invite people to their deaths all the time." He lifted his tequila glass, and Cardoza did the same. With a halfhearted toast, Rafa drank, and Cardoza followed. When their empty glasses were back on the table, the leader of the Black Knights said, "So, how many of my men did you kill?"

Here we go, Cardoza thought. He told himself the next ten seconds might be the most important ten seconds of his life. With nonchalance of his own, he said, "Four or five. Don't recall exactly."

Archuleta was utterly unfazed. He motioned to the woman to refill their glasses, then cut off another piece of steak. While focused on this, he said, "You don't seem too inconvenienced."

"It was nothing," Cardoza replied.

Archuleta's eyes flashed up now, away from his food and onto his guest. They narrowed slightly, and Cardoza realized he'd just overplayed his hand. The cartel boss didn't give a damn about five dead sentries at some dirty roadblock, but even those idiots were an extension of his own power.

Making light of dispatching them had been met with some displeasure from the man who saw himself as the ruler of all he surveyed.

Oscar Cardoza fought the urge to demur; he let the moment pass in silence, his own show of strength.

The tense moment was broken when a steak appeared in front of Cardoza, sweating and dripping, its grill marks telling him the cut had been on the fire for no more than a couple of minutes per side.

Rafa went back to his own meal; Cardoza struggled to cut into it with the plastic knife he'd been given, but he did so and took a bite. Oscar preferred filet mignon on a bed of beurre blanc with a 2015 Altura Máxima Malbec, not a sickeningly raw porterhouse with a midrange tequila, but he was playing his role, so he ate and drank as if more than pleased.

Cardoza had suffered through countless dick-measuring contests, but it occurred to him this might be the first one that threatened to leave him with *E. coli* at the end of it.

Finally, Archuleta spoke with a mouth full of his own bloody steak. "So, what is so important Guadalajara sends its man all the way up here to meet with me?"

"Apologies, Señor Archuleta. I am *not* Guadalajara's man. I am just a consultant. Hired by Guadalajara in this case to serve as an emissary to speak with the relevant parties. I am as much *your* man as I am *his*."

"Dangerous work." Archuleta seemed bored, but Cardoza expected that this was all for show. The man needed something from him, though he would pretend he did not.

"At times. But not as dangerous as your work."

Archuleta squeezed his big steak knife hard and looked up again. "Is that some kind of a threat?"

"No, señor. Nothing like that. Not from me, and not from El Patrón in Guadalajara, either. He wants better relations with you. Frankly, and this is me talking, he *needs* better relations with you. Everyone knows Los Caballeros Negros are the future power, and he would simply like you to consider the services he can provide."

The leader of the Black Knights said, "What do I need him for? I get my chemicals from other sources; I don't need to pay off Guadalajara to get access to the ports in Acapulco. My shit doesn't come through Acapulco."

"The patrón of the Guadalajara concern promises me he will undercut your current supplier by twenty percent. As I said, he knows you are taking over the market share of the supply moving into the U.S., stripping market share from Sinaloa, Cartel del Golfo, Los Zetas, Juarez, and Jalisco Nueva Generacion. His business is hurting. Again, he didn't authorize me to say this, but I will anyhow. He is nearly desperate to make you his customer."

Archuleta laughed. "If he's desperate, then he can drop the price by fifty percent."

The men standing around the table laughed, but Cardoza put down his fork and rubbed his chin thoughtfully. "I think that would be too high, but I believe thirty percent would be possible with effective negotiation."

Archuleta put his elbows on the table and leaned forward. "I want to hear more, but as I'm sure a man with your connections knows, I'm busy trying to keep the army out of my territory at the moment."

"Of course. Your sicarios up here are legendary, but truthfully they are no match for forty thousand troops."

Archuleta poured another tequila for himself and his guest. He said nothing.

"But," Cardoza continued, "Guadalajara has a way to help you, I believe, to keep the army out."

"I don't need his help. The UN is sending a delegation to broker a peace deal. I only have to agree to it, agree to stop fighting the Sinaloans up here, and the UN will move in. Forty-five hundred peacekeepers only, with strict rules of engagement that mean they will be no threat to my operation. This will keep the army out, and the fucking UN will be contained in certain areas, far away from my processing labs and warehouses."

"If only it were so simple, señor."

"What's so complicated?"

Cardoza and Archuleta made eye contact between bites. "The shoulder-fired missiles. *That* is your complication."

Archuleta affected an air of confusion. "What about them? That has nothing to do with me. I don't have that kind of weapon. Don't need it."

"The problem is, Señor Archuleta, the United Nations and the Mexican Interior Ministry think you *do* have the missiles. The peacekeepers will only come in, and the army will only stay out, if you hand them over."

"The Sinaloans shot down those helicopters."

"The authorities think otherwise, claim to have proof, and if they don't recover the SAMs, the UN is prepared to charge you with war crimes."

Archuleta stood up quickly, fury evident on his face. Cardoza was surprised by how short he was, and also surprised that the man seemed to have been genuinely stunned by what he had just learned.

"War crimes? What is this shit you are saying?"

Cardoza saw a silver belt buckle on the small man that was the size of a bread plate, an AK-47 etched into it.

He said, "They will tell you this themselves when they arrive here and speak with you face-to-face. The delegation wants the shoulder-fired missiles destroyed. The Mexican government won't agree to the terms of the peacekeeping mission until the Igla-Ss are out of your hands. This will leave you with two choices. One, give up the missiles, which will show everyone that the Black Knights were, in fact, responsible for shooting down the two marine helicopters. You might be tried for war crimes anyway, in spite of promises by the United Nations.

"Or, two, deny that the weapons are in your possession, and thereby kill the peacekeeping deal. This will bring the army up onto the Devil's Spine, and you will be fighting a long, protracted, costly, and ultimately a losing battle."

Archuleta got control of himself, sat back down, and reached again for his fork and knife. "If I had the missiles like they think I do, then I could just blow their army helicopters out of the sky, couldn't I?"

Cardoza had remained calm, and he'd remained seated. He said, "And when you do that, the Americans will get involved. They are fighting the drug war here, still. If they see a threat to their aircraft, they will send in the U.S. Air Force. Attack jets and drones will fly over the Sierra Madres, with antimissile countermeasures, and in numbers too great for you to shoot down. They will hunt for you day and night. Their rules of engagement won't be anything like those of the United Nations."

"You're crazy."

"Am I? Everyone has an interest in getting the SAMs out of the hands of the cartels, but only I have a way for it to happen without the Black Knights ever being implicated in their purchase or use."

"If I had them, which I don't, I could just destroy them, couldn't I? No one would ever know for sure who shot those helicopters down."

He said it as if the matter were solved, but Cardoza just shrugged. "That would be a mistake."

"Why is that?"

"Because I, señor, can make everybody think someone else shot those helicopters down, remove all suspicion from you, and lay suspicion at the feet of your enemy. It's a delicate proposition I have. Perhaps we should speak more privately and I can—"

Archuleta held a finger up to stop Cardoza from talking, then waved his hand in the air. The armed guards fanned out, backing up to the walls of the horse arena, and now they were all out of earshot, especially with the bleed-through of amplified accordions pumping away out back.

"You have my attention," he said softly.

Cardoza looked around, then spoke in a quiet and conspiratorial tone. "There is a man in the UN motorcade. He works for me. During the meeting, he can slip away, and your men can take him to the missiles, assuming they're close by. Once he confirms the total, then your men load the weapons onto trucks and drive them to the airfield on the lip of the canyon, just south of Babunica. You know the place?"

Archuleta stared at the man from the capital. "Of course I know the place. It's my airfield, but it's not on any map."

"I know."

"Tell me, how do *you* know the place, Señor Mexico City?"

Cardoza poured his own tequila now. He was in the driver's seat, at least for now, and he knew it. He refilled Archuleta's, as well. "There is a plane parked there. Hidden under camouflage. But in the heat of the day, it warms. At night, satellites using thermal imaging can pick up the radiant heat." He smiled. "A plane hidden next to the flattest stretch of ground for thirty miles in any direction means it's an airfield."

"And Guadalajara has thermal imaging satellites, do they?"

Cardoza smiled. "I was brought into this affair because of my contacts in our nation's government. I found the airfield through means available to me, Señor Archuleta. I am afraid that is all I am prepared to say."

Archuleta let it go. "That's *my* plane. My very first. I used it in the old days to fly black tar and hash into the States, back when I was younger and crazier. But we don't use it anymore. It hasn't flown in years. If your plan is to use it to—"

Cardoza shook his head. "We don't need that plane. An aircraft will land at that grass airfield, one large enough to accommodate all the missiles. We will then fly them to a warehouse in Badiraguato, Sinaloa. A warehouse owned by El Escopeta and the Sinaloa cartel."

Rafa dumped another shot of tequila down his throat. "That crazy pendejo."

Cardoza ignored him. "A day later, while you are still here with the UN talking about a peace deal, still professing your ignorance about the shoulder-fired missiles, we will leak the location of the weapons to the federales in Mexico City. They will dispatch marines to the warehouse, men not in the employ of the cartel, and it will be proved that the Sinaloans are the ones responsible for war crimes, not Rafa Archuleta and his Black Knights. The peacekeepers will come into the mountains, the army will stay out of the mountains, and you won't face a tribunal in The Hague."

Archuleta leaned over to the side of his plate, sniffed a line of coke off the mirror with the efficiency of a pro, and then looked back up. "Guadalajara wants to help me? Bullshit. What's in it for them? You say they want my business, but if I were destroyed by the army, their regular customers would regain the market, and Guadalajara would benefit."

"I have convinced El Patrón de Guadalajara that Los Caballeros Negros are the future. You've only been around five years, and already you produce more, you distribute more, and you sell more than almost all the other concerns. We see how much potential there is to grow the market en los Estados Unidos. El Patrón believes in you, and is willing to help you in return for good business relations."

The last bite of Rafa's steak was fat and gristle, but he ate it anyway. While chewing, he said, "I find you interesting."

After downing his shot of tequila, Cardoza replied, "I guess I'd be dead if you did not."

"Sí, es la verdad. I will think about what you said, but I am not ready to decide."

"Very well. But you will need to make your decision by tomorrow. The negotiations will take some time, but the opportunity for my contact on the inside to slip away from the others is limited."

Rafa nodded. "I'll decide by morning. In the meantime, I want you here. Close to me. Guadalajara, the Zetas, the government, and the Sinaloans might trust a consultant who changes hats for each conversation . . . but *I* don't. I will have you taken to Cinco Lagrimas, the site of the meeting. You'll be put in the hotel across the street from the municipal building where the UN meeting will take place. It's very nice, overlooking a park. You are free to move about town, but I will have a couple of my men nearby. Just to watch you. I want you here, in the background, when the delegation arrives."

"It would be an honor to serve you in any capacity, señor."

Archuleta leaned forward slowly, his steak knife in his right hand. Pointing it close to Cardoza's eye, he said, "Don't fuck me over. Don't even think about it. I am not like the other cartel leaders. I am Apache. My grandfather was full-blooded. My people came down here from los Estados Unidos, hid in these mountains, over one hundred years ago. We are fighters, mountain men. Survivors.

"If you have any other plan, any other scheme than what you have told me, it's only going to lead you to your death. Understood?"

Cardoza nodded slowly. "Understood."

Archuleta nodded, sat up straight, and looked back over his shoulder to the women standing by the kitchen. "Dessert!"

CHAPTER 35

The Armored Saint convoy spent the night camped next to a massive hillside cemetery in a reasonably flat but rocky clearing just off a gravel road that ran adjacent to the highway that led up to the Devil's Spine. Remmick posted sentries with night vision gear in the gun turrets, switching out every couple of hours to keep eyes fresh, but the rest of the men and women slept inside their vehicles or on bedding on the open ground next to them.

He had forbidden campfires to keep a low profile, and it was cooler up here in the low mountains. Duff wore an oversized black Armored Saint windbreaker over his body armor to stay warm, and others in the motorcade did the same.

And the night, while uncomfortable, passed without incident.

They broke camp just after six a.m., fired up their engines, and again began heading to the north along a road that felt to Duff as if they were constantly driving across a washboard, ascending with each mile. The cactus and tumbleweed had given way to cypress and pine, the air was noticeably crisper, and the smell of cooking fires wafted from settlements hidden within the rocks.

The IAG Guardian's 95-gallon fuel tank gave the APC an impressive five-hundred-mile range, but Pack Horses One and Two each carried a pair of palletized 275-gallon intermediate bulk fuel containers along with a hand pump, and Duff had seen that War Horse, one of the two Alpha vehicles, contained a similar-sized palletized tote of their own. This meant the motorcade was self-sustaining on fuel for over a thousand miles, but Remmick also wanted to take every opportunity he deemed safe to top off when they passed a fuel pump, so as they rolled through a small town just off the main highway, he commanded all drivers to pull up to a two-pump Pemex gas station in front of a small market.

The stunned female owner stood gobsmacked while the five massive vehicles lined up at the pumps, and men and women passing on the steeply graded street immediately stopped to stare.

Remmick, Gordon, and Duffy each directed some of their men to dismount for a show of force, while others in the motorcade, the principals included, climbed out to stretch their legs, still stiff from the previous night.

Duff followed Flores into the market, where she bought some fresh food and a bottle of Coke, and he followed her back out, his hand on the grip of his rifle and his eyes scanning all directions.

She stopped to talk to a woman making tortillas, and Duff strolled back over to Crazy Horse.

There were other businesses nearby, as well as residential dwellings, and a growing crowd of onlookers had materialized in the street while Duff was inside. Ball-capped turret gunners swiveled their weapons around, and armed men stood by their vehicles with their sunglasses on, eyeing everyone standing around.

There was no open nastiness from the locals, but suspicion and mistrust hung in the air like the smells of cooking fires on the mountainside around them.

A woman walked up to Cruz, who had himself dismounted out of the rear hatch to stand there with his MP5 submachine gun around his neck. She asked him in Spanish if he was Latino, and when he told her he was, she showed him a wrinkled photograph of her son. He'd vanished after going up into the mountains months earlier, she explained, and she was certain his disappearance was at the hands of Los Caballeros Negros.

Cruz was polite, said if he ran into her son, then he would let him know his mom asked about him, and the woman just shook her head. She said she knew her boy was dead, and she was warning Cruz not to go up higher himself.

"Did he have all this to back him up?" Cruz asked, his Puerto Rican Spanish laced with the South Side of Chicago. He waved at the motorcade, the men, the guns.

She looked at him a moment and said, "No, he did not. And they killed him just the same." She started to turn and walk away.

"Mamacita," Cruz called out to her. "Say a prayer for us, okay?"

With a rueful smile, the small woman said, "Praying for your survival is a waste of time. I will, instead, pray for your souls."

The American said nothing as the woman turned again, heading down the street.

Duff hadn't understood the exchange, but Gabby had stepped up behind him, and she relayed it to the Charlie team leader. He listened, nodded, while at the same time feeling the low hum of deep suspicion from the bystanders. It was not quite malevolent but more than a little contemptuous.

It was as if everyone in this town knew the motorcade of strangers was blindly driving somewhere to die, while accomplishing nothing in the process.

As before, he tried to focus on the $1,666 a day he was making, but he found it harder and harder to do so.

Duff stood outside next to his vehicle while Nascar operated one of the two pumps at the station. Gabby stood next to him, eating fresh corn tortillas she'd purchased from the lady by the door who, along with her two adolescent daughters, stood at a small fire pit and deftly flattened and baked the bread.

Other than relaying the old woman's warning, Gabby hadn't spoken to Duff once all morning. She looked distant or angry, Duff couldn't tell which.

Duff sipped coffee from a Yeti thermos Frenchie had brought him, purchased from the gas station, and he looked at the craggy mountains ahead of them in the morning light.

"You okay, Dr. Flores?"

She said nothing.

After the awkward silence, he said, "So . . . help me out. You're like a museum curator?"

She rolled up a tortilla and took a bite, then washed it down with her Coke. "No. I'm not a curator. I work for the Museo Nacional de Antropología in Mexico City. I have a doctorate in anthropology with concentrations in non-Hispanic citizens of Mexico and Central America. I study the peoples of this nation."

Duff shrugged. "Right . . . That sounds like a pretty cush job compared to what you are doing now. So why would you come here? Put yourself through all this?"

After wiping her mouth with a paper towel, she said, "I don't want to stand by and bear witness to the eradication of entire peoples. The Tarahumaras, the innocent Sinaloans and Chihuahuans who live on the Devil's Spine, they're not hurting anyone. They're just surviving. I thought that if there was any way at all I could help prevent a war, then I should come. I have spent my life learning about civilizations that have died. Now one is threatened, here in my own country, in my own lifetime. I couldn't just sit in my office in the capital while it happened so I could write history papers about it when I'm old."

She finished her tortillas. "Seems so naïve now. I mean, all of us are fools on this mission, aren't we?"

"Guess that's why they chose us," Duff said, still scanning for threats.

Wolfson leaned against the starboard cabin hatch of Crazy Horse, five feet away, his sniper rifle propped next to him. After putting a big wad of chewing tobacco in his mouth, he said, "Lady, you should show us some gratitude. We're down here tryin' to help fix your country's fuckups. Hell, you guys keep sending drugs up to destroy America, and still we're here to try to make peace."

Duff expected a strong retort from the woman, so it was no surprise when she said, "Nobody down here feels any sympathy for you Americans and your drug problems. Why should we? You have *everything* you want up there. Opportunity to make anything out of your lives you can imagine. And twenty percent of you throw your lives away, buying the drugs that fuel the wars that kill my people. I wish America would stop taking drugs, but you won't, so I don't care what happens to you. I just want you to stop hurting our country with your debauchery."

Duff stepped into this now. "Lay off us, Gabby. We're not your enemy. And, as I told you before, we also aren't those folks up in Show Horse who make the rules."

"Yes, I know. You are just a hired gun. Just like all the men who will try to kill us up here."

Duff wasn't having it. "I don't take money to kill. I take money to protect."

"That's what those people up there higher in the mountains are doing. They see us as a threat to their people, their way of life. They think they are protecting their families, their patróns."

Duff looked back towards the other pump and saw that the last of the vehicles, War Horse, was now topping off. "Then they're full of shit. I'm not fighting for anything, lady, except to keep you and the VIPs alive. And if I can get myself home in the process, then that would be freaking awesome."

She regarded him as she ate. "You are not like the others. You care. You aren't a mercenary."

With his eyes back on the group of onlookers, he muttered, "Not sure what I am."

Nascar finished gassing up Crazy Horse, replaced the fuel cap, and locked the door to it.

Gabby was still focused on Duff. "You are a father, you told me. *That's* what you are. How many children?"

"Boy and a girl." He glanced her way, but only an instant before returning his attention towards the crowd.

"You are a husband, too?"

"I am. Six years."

"Then the Lord has blessed you."

"Funny. Sometimes I think he's out to get me."

"He has given you no challenge you cannot rise above."

Duff smiled at this. "Even this operation?"

"It might just be that, very soon, you will get to meet God so that you will have the opportunity to thank him for all the blessings he has bestowed upon you.

"That is a blessing, too, I think."

"Yeah. Lucky me."

Remmick's voice came over their headsets. "All right. We're done here. Everybody saddle up."

Duffy led Gabby back into the truck, then climbed into his seat, where he was met by Nascar, waiting behind the wheel. The blond man from Alabama said, "Reminds me of a gig I did in Haiti a couple years back. Another five minutes and these folks start throwing rocks. Trust me, it only goes downhill from there."

"Yeah," Duff said. He'd had the same feeling.

The driver continued. "Everybody with a cell phone has already called somebody higher on the mountain."

"I know."

"We ain't surprisin' nobody up—"

"Nascar?"

"Yeah, boss?"

"Can it."

"Consider it canned." Crazy Horse was the last vehicle to roll out of the gas station, heading north.

CHAPTER 36

A mountain lion on a craggy rock face stalked a young deer on the dirt road below her. As she poised to pounce, her would-be prey lifted its head and turned to look to the south. Then the deer bolted, and the cat detected a sound herself. She turned and focused on the origin of a noise so faint only the sharpest of the animals around could hear it.

The noise grew, and grew more, and soon the mountain lion's fight-or-flight response kicked in. There would be no fight; this sound only meant trouble to the cat's trained ears, so she scrambled up the rock, disappearing into a high pine-oak forest above.

It was nearly a minute before the grille of War Horse appeared around a bend in the road below, the tires of the big truck working individually to negotiate the rugged surface. To the left of the vehicle was the rock face, with the pine-oak above that, but to the right, the earth gave way to a long low valley.

The gradient of the mountainside down the valley was steep but negotiable if taken slowly by the big, fat-tired machines, though the motorcade had every intention of going up the road, not down the mountain. Here and there smaller trails wound off and down to the rocky valley floor, then back up to the far side.

The fifth and final vehicle to pass the position the mountain lion just vacated was Crazy Horse. Duff wiped his eyes under his Oakleys, then took a sip of warm pickle juice out of a jar he kept in the driver's-side door. The pickle juice was full of salt and electrolytes, and it helped him stay hydrated when dressed head to toe in heavy gear and body armor.

He offered the jar to Nascar, who took it, keeping one hand on the wheel and both eyes on the road.

After a swig, he said, "Can you imagine the dust cloud we're kicking up? Everybody in that valley sees us like we're a freight train passing through."

Duff looked out his window, down at what appeared to be nothing but rocks and trees for miles and miles. But he knew it would be foolish not to expect danger lurking behind every stone, every tree trunk.

Duff could, at times, look through his dirty window and see for twenty miles, green and white and brown and gray and even pink in the distance, where the snowcapped mountaintops reflected the sun.

This also meant someone twenty miles away could see him, of course, so as beautiful a vista as it was, he wasn't able to enjoy it.

They passed others on the road—a few in old cars, but many of them on horses or on foot—who moved between the little hamlets in the area. Gabby softly remarked to Duff that every single man, woman, and child over the age of fourteen was surely working on behalf of Los Caballeros Negros in some capacity.

In addition to the unarmed civilians, several times pickup trucks full of narrow-eyed men passed on the road, as well; weapons were visible, but the men just stared as the twenty-foot-long black Guardian APCs raced by.

No one raised a weapon, no vehicle turned around to pursue, but any hope Duff might have retained about staying low profile on this mission was long gone now.

He spoke into his intrateam for the first time in nearly a half hour. "Squeeze? You tally anything on the other side of the valley?"

"Hey, man, I'm just up here swattin' flies bigger than Cessnas and watching out for an avalanche on our left. Didn't know I was lookin' for bad guys five hundred yards away."

"Well, you're the dude with his head sticking out of the armored truck, so I figured you'd be the first who'd *want* to know if we were being spotted by opposition."

Squeeze rotated the turret to the east, in the direction of the valley, but he did not reply.

After several seconds, Frenchie spoke up. "We've reached the elevation where I can feel it in my joints. Thin air."

Duff figured he was twenty-five years younger than Frenchie, but he also felt the altitude. On his map, he saw they'd climbed above seven thousand feet, and he sensed the lessening of oxygen up here. It took more effort to fill his lungs, he was more tired than he should be, and his joints ached even more than the continuous pounding of the drive would have caused on its own. He knew the motorcade would be traveling above nine thousand feet along their route, and by then he'd be huffing and puffing, especially if he had to run laden with body armor, weapons, and ammo.

Duff just said, "Hang in there, Frenchie. Want some pickle juice?"

"You Americans and your weird habits."

After a beep on the vehicle's speakers, Mike Gordon's voice resonated through Crazy Horse. "Bravo One for Alpha One."

As Duff listened, Remmick replied, "Alpha. Send traffic."

"Yeah, Pack Horse One's engine temp just started redlining. Sounds like the fan is turning fine; it could be a damaged water pump or a clogged fuel line. We're going to need to stop and check it out. We can probably do it in five mikes."

Remmick answered back. "In about three klicks we'll be in the forest, less exposed to the valley. Can you make it till then?"

"Uh, negative. We're overheating for some reason. That's ten minutes at this speed, and if we don't deal with this now, we could be looking at some serious damage by then."

There was a long pause. Duff knew Remmick didn't want to stop, especially here. But Alpha One soon said, "Alpha to all drivers. Full halt."

Duff immediately shifted into high gear. "Three-sixty security.

Squeeze, focus eyes to the east. Cruz, stay on six. Everybody else, pop your ports and scan sectors."

Nascar said, "Duff, if Bravo's having trouble, I should take a peek under our hood, too. Everything reads okay on the dash, but there is a ton of shit on these roads that could be damaging belts or the coolant reservoir."

Duff nodded. "Okay, I'll go with you." He unfastened his harness and turned around in his seat. To Gabby he said, "Stay in the vehicle. This isn't exactly an ideal place to break down."

Flores's small and sweaty face nodded behind a bottle of tepid water she was drinking.

Duff climbed out, dropping down onto the almost-black dust and dirt in the rutted road.

Pack Horse Two was right ahead, and then a gentle turn in the road meant he could only see the rear of Show Horse from where he stood. Pack Horse One, where they were working on the vehicle, and War Horse in front of it were both completely out of Duff's view, hidden by the steep turn in the hill of volcanic rock just off the left of the road.

From back here he couldn't see Gordon or his men working on their vehicle, but he could hear the clanging of metal along with occasional cussing as Bravo worked on their rig.

He kept his hands on his rifle and his eyes in the valley, while behind him, Nascar quickly checked all the belts and hoses under the hood of Crazy Horse.

The sun beat down on the men who had dismounted along the stretch of track overlooking the valley. While the temperature was only in the midsixties, Duff was suffering. He had been wearing his body armor nearly constantly for more than two days, and it felt heavy and uncomfortable as he stood there, his eyes scanning the low ground to his east.

After what was only five or six minutes but felt like an eternity to Duff, Gordon's voice came back over his headset. "Bravo One for Alpha Actual."

"Go for Alpha."

"It was just a clogged line. We got it open, the engine will cool while we drive."

Remmick responded, "Roger that. Everybody mount up."

Nascar shut his hood, jumped down, and turned to head back to the driver's door.

Just as Duff reached for his own door, the sudden *zip-crackle* of incoming bullets whizzed above him, followed immediately by the sound of impacts pinging off the rocky ledge next to them. As he opened the big door, he heard the clang of a round slamming against the armor of his truck.

The sound of the gunfire itself then rolled over the motorcade, indicating the shots had come from some distance.

Men began shouting up and down the line, engines turned over and revved. Duff felt the clenched-heart feeling of being under fire, his head instinctively turtled lower into his body, and he tried to pinpoint the origin of the shooting as he climbed into the vehicle, but he could not identify where it was coming from.

As out of practice as he was, Duff didn't panic. He assessed the situation as three or so guns firing from long range. He'd been in enough coordinated ambushes in his past life to know that, so far, this wasn't anything this motorcade couldn't handle.

But this didn't mean he was safe. A bullet could slam into his forehead as long as he was out in the open.

He dropped hard into his seat and shut the door behind him, and then he heard Remmick's voice over the radio.

"Who's got a target?"

Duff called out on his intrateam. "Squeeze?"

"The echoes are bouncing all around the valley. Can't get a fix on where the fire's coming from."

A screaming whine of a ricochet off a rock nearby instinctively sent Duff's head down again, though he was now protected by the heavy steel and ballistic glass of the IAG Guardian APC.

"Stay low up there!" he said.

"Ain't gotta tell me that!" Squeeze shouted in reply.

Remmick broadcast again a moment later. "Charlie Actual, that's definitely coming from behind us, back around the curve where you guys are. Alpha and Bravo do *not* have an angle to return fire. It's up to the CAT to suppress."

Duff was in command of the counterassault team, so this gunfire was his problem. He clicked his handset. "Roger that. We're scanning for the origin of fire." He lifted his binoculars and began looking. To Wolfson, the man with the sniper rifle, he said, "Charlie Two? Anything in your scope?"

A loud crack just behind Duff's seat told him a round had impacted against the thick bulletproof glass.

Wolfson responded, "I don't see them, but they sure as shit see us."

Gabby said, "It might be the indigenous who don't know that—"

Wolfson cut her off. "Nobody gives a shit now, lady! They're shooting guns at us! We're shooting back, *whoever* the fuck they are! Sit down and shut up!"

Duff scanned with his binos, higher on the opposite mountainside and slightly behind his position. He locked onto motion, and then adjusted his focus. "I got 'em! Four o'clock, 'bout three hundred fifty meters. In the copse of trees there, maybe fifty meters higher than our elevation. You tally, Wolfson?"

"Scanning."

The fire picked up a little more, Duff estimated eight to ten shooters now, using regular battle rifles and not machine guns. Crazy Horse had taken a dozen hits on its right side.

Squeeze shouted now. "I see 'em, boss! Three hundred fifty meters to the east."

Gabby pleaded with the group. "Don't shoot! They might be—"

But her voice was drowned out by Nascar.

"If the motorcade moves out, I can just drive us around the curve and they won't have line of sight."

Duff shook his head; he knew what to do. "Negative. We don't want these guys popping up later. We're eliminating this threat."

Cruz shouted from the back, "Fuck yeah, we are!"

Gabby grabbed Duff by the shoulder. "Señor Duffy. Let me at least try to identify them first."

Duff looked out the window, then back to the woman. "Everybody hold fire a sec." To Gabby he said, "Okay, get up here with me and look, but make it fast."

"I tally," Wolfson announced. "More like three sixty-five. They've got AKs."

"Hold fire," Duff said again as Gabby Flores moved closer to look out his window.

More bullets clanged against Crazy Horse. The enemy was aiming in, and the gunfire was picking up in intensity as well as accuracy.

"Are you fuckin' kidding me, Duffy?" Wolfson barked. "We gotta slay these fuckers! What if they have an RPG?"

Cruz said, "C'mon, TL, we gonna light these bitches up, or what?"

"Hold fire!" Duff ordered for the third time. His hands were shaking, but he squeezed them shut. The bulk of the anxiety he felt wasn't about being under fire, it was about making decisions. He forced authority into his voice. "Stay behind cover, Squeeze, and hold fucking fire."

Gabby took the binoculars and began crawling up between the front seats over the center console, nearly ending up in Duff's lap. Duff said, "Those low brown trees between the dry creek and the dirt road up the mountain on the other side of the valley. A couple of pickup trucks. I see men around them, think they're the ones shooting."

As she worked to get into position with the binos she said, "They could be Tarahumara or other civilians who just think you are narcos. The indigenous don't all look like Native Americans, you know."

Duff felt the pressure from the threat, the pressure from Remmick to suppress the threat, and the pressure from his own team to fight back against the attack. Angrily, to Gabby, he said, "Stop talking and start looking! You better be quick or we're gonna have to waste them all."

She focused the binoculars. "No! Wait! I see them! I see them."

Remmick's voice boomed. "Duff? What the *fuck* are you guys doing back there? Why don't I hear any outgoing?"

Gordon's voice came next. "Duff? Christ, dude, you gotta neutralize that shit!"

Josh Duffy had a half dozen people yelling at him right now, but he pushed the pressure away as best as possible. As calmly as he could, he said, "Gabby?"

She continued looking, and Wolfson barked again. "I tally a guy reloading. My crosshairs are on his brain pan! Let me split this fucker's wig right—"

"Gabby?" Duff repeated, cutting his Charlie Two off.

"Yes . . . I see them . . ." She took her eyes out of the binos and looked at Duff. "Those are *not* Tarahumara. Not civilians. The trucks, the guns, the posture. Those hombres are narcos, for sure."

Duff adjusted his boom mic. "Charlie team. Smoke 'em."

In under one half second, Wolfson fired his sniper rifle, the boom incredible inside the vehicle, even with the noise-canceling headsets worn by everyone. Squeeze opened fire with his Mk 48 above, long bursts of fifteen to twenty rounds at a time, and hot spent shell casings rained down inside the compartment.

Through the incredible noise, Duff transmitted on the truck radio. "Charlie has tally. Three pickup trucks to the east. Approximately ten dismounts. We're engaging at this time, over."

Remmick answered back, still annoyed but clearly relieved. "Roger that. We're moving out. Crazy Horse is clear to break off from the motorcade and pursue the attackers, draw their fire."

"Copy that." Gabby was rushing to get herself back behind the front seats into her harness, and Duffy now looked to Nascar. "Can you off-road it down this hill and up the other side in this battle wagon? Looks pretty damn steep."

"Boss, I could make that drive in a Tercel."

"Then let's go get these assholes!"

Frenchie, who had been on the opposite side of the action through all this, finally saw himself getting a chance at a target. "Attack!" he shouted.

The APC roared down a dirt goat track, winding back and forth as it descended, everyone inside holding on to something to keep from being thrown forward. Even strapped in and hanging on, however, the bouncing and jarring they'd been accustomed to all day became exponentially worse.

Duff tried to aim through his gunport, but the instability in his shooting position was too much to compensate for. "Squeeze, it's on you! I can't hit them on the move."

Squeeze laid down on his light machine gun, firing over one hundred rounds in controlled bursts.

As the truck bottomed out in the valley and picked up speed towards the other side, Nascar squinted through the windshield glare. "They're breaking contact! They know they're fucked!"

Duff could see it, too. The fire had stopped; a pickup spun and raced for cover, followed by another, while the others sat motionless, smoke rising from them.

By the time they arrived at the small hillside grove where the men were firing from, there was nothing left but bodies and a pickup engulfed in flames. Squeeze had had time to reload his Mk 48 as they approached, and he had the best angle on any further threats.

He also had the best view. "I count five dead. The two other trucks are buggin' out up the hillside! Chickenshits!"

"Shoot 'em," Duff ordered. Even though the enemy was running away, Duff had been at this long enough to know they would probably just regroup and try again. The enemy had made the decision to engage the motorcade, and that decision had consequences, even if the enemy had changed its mind.

Squeeze fired off just a few more rounds, and then his weapon went silent again. "No target. They went around the side of the mountain up there."

Nascar said, "I can pursue."

Duff shook his head. "Negative. They could be trying to lead us into an ambush."

Wolfson said, "You're giving these dumbasses too much credit."

Duff ignored his Charlie Two, ordered Nascar to turn to begin heading back to the motorcade, and broadcast over the handset. "Charlie One for Alpha One."

The truck rolled slower now, the chase behind them. Dark volcanic dust covered everything, and Nascar ran the wipers and sprayers to clean the windshield.

Remmick's voice crackled over the speakers. "Go for Alpha."

"Five enemy KIA. No losses our side. We ran the rest of them off. We're up on ammo, but I decided not to pursue around a blind curve."

"Copy. You made the right call. No casualties here. Gordo says we've got some chipped paint on the back of Pack Horse Two, but that's it."

"Roger that, we're rejoining the motorcade."

"Copy. Alpha out."

The men were quiet a moment over the intrateam radio, till Squeeze finally sat down, closed the hatch, and broadcast to the others in the vehicle.

"I'm just gonna say it, yo. Those dudes sucked."

Gabby Flores answered this. "They were *not* the Black Knights. There weren't enough of them. That was ten men I saw, maybe. It was a patrol from the Sinaloa cartel, I'm sure."

Wolfson said, "Whoever they were, they were stupid as shit for firing AKs across three hundred sixty-five meters at armored vehicles. No RPGs, no machine guns . . . idiots."

Cruz said, "Dead idiots. Play stupid games, win stupid prizes. If those dipshits with their bad aim are all we've got to worry about up here, then I'm suddenly liking our chances."

Duff didn't want to hear any more of this. "Don't get cocky, boys. Those men saw us from a distance, thought we were a threat, and then dumped some mags our way thinking we'd run. A coordinated attack is going to go down much differently, so stay frosty."

Squeeze said, "How frosty can we be if we gotta get the terp's thumbs-up every time we want to kill some asshole shooting at us?" Charlie Six's scathing remark made Duff bite the inside of his cheek to blunt his response. The rules of engagement were clear. If the men were fired upon, they could fire back. Still . . . Duff knew that twenty-one men weren't going to survive these mountains without being extremely careful in their use of force. Squeeze wasn't wrong, but Duff knew he wasn't wrong, either. He said, "We get engaged like that again, you are weapons free."

"But—" Flores began, and then Duff cut her off.

"If you shoot guns at us, Gabby, then you are the enemy. That's just the way the world works."

"Absolutely," Frenchie agreed from the back.

Duff looked down at his hands; the trembling was still there, but it was manageable, and no one else could possibly notice it in the bouncing and rumbling vehicle.

The adrenaline that had coursed through him during the fight would wear off soon, and he'd have to fight a wave of exhaustion, this he knew from experience.

Crazy Horse again began climbing back towards the road, hurrying to catch up with the rear of the motorcade.

CHAPTER 37

There were no students walking the halls of the Alexandria campus of Northern Virginia Community College at eight p.m., but a six-person crew mopped floors, wiped grease boards, sanitized equipment in the gym, and performed other janitorial deep-cleaning duties the daytime staff couldn't manage on their own.

Nichole Duffy didn't just organize and supervise the team; she also got her hands dirty every single night.

She disinfected the stair railings in the Center for Design, Media, and the Arts, and while she worked, her mind wasn't fully on task. Instead of the cleanliness of the college, she was mostly thinking about her husband, praying for a call from him, though she did her best to give off no outward appearance of unease to her employees.

Mercifully, the call came at eight sixteen, just as she began cleaning the windows outside the bookstore on the ground floor. She dropped her squeegee in a bucket, wiped her hands quickly on her scrubs, then tapped her finger against the earbud.

"Josh? Is that you?"

"It's me, babe."

The line was scratchy, but even so, she could hear obvious fatigue in her husband's voice.

"Are you okay?"

"Yeah, I'm fine. We've stopped in a village to refuel. The VIPs are using the bathroom, my guys are dismounted, and I'm guarding the truck in the turret."

She responded that it was good to hear his voice, and then he said, "Sorry, you're breaking up a little. We're high in the mountains now. These peaks around us might be obstructing my sat link."

She tried again. "How is everything going?"

"Fine. We'll drive a couple more hours, then rack out in our vics again. I'm sure our VIPs will love that."

"Any more contact?"

The line popped, then Josh responded. "We had a little dustup, no big deal, though."

"What do you mean, 'a little dustup'?"

"It was nothing. Dudes with rifles firing at the motorcade. We engaged them, they ran. Maybe Remmick's plan of using back roads instead of the highway is working."

Nichole took it as a given that her husband was sugarcoating the day's events. "Any casualties?"

"Just bad guys."

"How many?"

He paused. "Five, we think. Another five ran." Quickly he added, "These guys weren't Black Knights, they were probably just a patrol from Sinaloa, thought they could scare us or something."

"Two gunfights in two days, Josh. And you have two and a half weeks to go."

"We're fine, babe. I promise. Tomorrow the VIPs meet with Archuleta, the head of the cartel, assuming he shows."

Every third or fourth word was broken, but she more than got the gist. She sighed, then slid down the wall of the bookstore until she sat on the floor. "If he doesn't show, does that mean I get you back sooner?"

"Yeah, I guess so. But with a lot less money. I only get paid for the days I'm on this run, remember?"

"And do *you* remember the money isn't as important to me as you are, or don't you?"

The connection faltered a moment; she called her husband's name a couple of times, until finally she heard him respond.

"Half of me hopes the UN decides to turn back before going to the Black Knights. The other half wants to keep going so I get paid."

Nichole's frustration began to boil over. "Then one half of you is sensible, and the other half is becoming a mercenary."

He only replied, "We are fine, Nik. Everything is fine."

"Josh, I love you, but I don't exactly believe you."

Josh did not reply for several seconds. Finally, he said, "I love you, Nik. I love the kids." A sigh was audible over the bad connection. "I've got to go."

The line went dead. She put her head in her hands and began rubbing her forehead.

Something about Josh's tone, something about the way he worked so damn hard to hide the fact that he was scared, weighed on her. She saw through him, and more than anything else, she could feel his desperation, his guilt for what had happened in the past and how that affected the present and his family.

Josh was throwing himself into unimaginable risk to earn thirty-five thousand dollars for his family.

And something else was eating at her. Josh wouldn't just risk his life for his family. He'd shown her time and time again that, no matter the potential consequences, he would *always* be the hero.

Nichole knew her husband had the heart of ten men, and his sense of right and wrong sometimes overshadowed his abilities. Even when he was in the prime of his work life as a security contractor, long ago now, he'd thrown himself into impossible danger to help others.

Not just in Beirut. Not just with his teammates in Afghanistan and Somalia and other nations.

No, not just then. Nichole Duffy had known from the minute she met Josh the danger he was willing to put himself in to protect others, and this both terrified her and made her love him even more.

CHAPTER 38

SEVEN YEARS EARLIER

Nichole Martin woke with a jolt. A pang of terror, source unknown, shot through her fuzzy brain. She tried to look around to see where she was, but something was holding her head in place; she was unable to turn it much at all.

Dust or smoke filled the air around her, and she couldn't see. She knew she was in the crew compartment of her helicopter; the pressure of the helmet on her head and the pulling of the harness keeping her in her seat told her that. But it was silent; the machine's rotors were not turning, nor was the engine running, and there was no light around.

She wasn't on level ground; this became clear when she noticed the uneven strain on her harness. She was leaning forward against the chest straps; she estimated she was hanging at roughly a 45-degree angle, pitch down, and she couldn't imagine why.

She fought through the fog in her head now, trying to remember her last clear thought. *What the hell is going on?* Then she remembered, but only barely. *Shot down? We've been shot down?*

She couldn't believe it.

Blinking away debris from her eyes, she took in what she could from her obstructed view.

The dust cleared a little, but the cockpit was black, no electricity operating anything around her, and it was at this point she also realized the canopy was gone. The warm night air blew against the portion of her face not covered by her helmet. Either the cockpit canopy jettison handle had been pulled or accidentally tripped somehow, or perhaps the canopy had been sheared away in the impact.

There were lights around, but distant. As the dust cleared further, she realized her airship had come down in a dirt-, trash-, and sand-strewn vacant lot next to an edgy-looking street. Amber streetlights at an intersection ahead of her, one hundred meters away or so, were the closest light sources she could see from her vantage point.

And then she thought of Henderson. He was six feet behind her and, if she was right about the awkward position of the aircraft, several feet above her.

"Chief? Chief?" she called out to her pilot, but the chief warrant officer did not reply. She had an emergency radio in her vest, but as she tried to reach for it with her left hand, she realized the right side of her body was completely pinned against the side of the crew compartment, which had caved in slightly.

She couldn't turn to look in that direction, because there was a spaghetti-like matrix of wires and hoses and twisted metal wrapped around her head, cinching her helmet more or less straight forward.

Looking down with just her eyes now, she saw that the entire crew compartment, along with her flight suit, was covered in dirt, and she couldn't imagine how that had happened.

Then it occurred to her. For the helicopter to be in such a bad state with her somehow still alive inside it, she decided they must have crashed somewhere else, onto a nearby rooftop, perhaps, and then rolled, multiple times, into the lot, coming to rest awkwardly, and covered in whatever the violent rolls had picked up off the ground.

"Max!" She yelled it this time. There was no one out in the street, at least not yet, and this surprised her. ISIS was close by, that much was obvious by the little she remembered from tonight's flight. Surely they'd seen the Apache go down, but they hadn't made it to her yet.

She used her left hand to unfasten the harness across her chest and another across her waist, but she found she had no more mobility after doing this. The crushing of the damaged helo on the right side of her body had all but welded her into position, and she couldn't reach the other buckles holding her in place.

Suddenly a new sound startled her. A vehicle, running without lights, apparently, raced up on her left and skidded to a stop next to her wrecked Apache.

A car door opened but did not shut.

"Chief? Can you get to your weapon?"

Henderson didn't answer, and Nichole continued trying in vain to get her left hand down the right side of her body to her pistol. She was so wedged into the wall of the airframe, however, that she found it impossible to do so.

She detected the sound of metal bending, straining, and she realized quickly that someone was climbing up to her position. Her left hand pushed harder against her own right hip, trying to reverse-cross-draw a pistol that she still could not even touch because of the way she was wedged in.

A man appeared over her instruments, having climbed up from the ground. He was young, bearded, local. He looked at her in the low light with malevolence she had never before witnessed, and she knew she was dead.

He called out to someone below him, and suddenly a Kalashnikov rifle appeared, tossed up from the ground, and the young man caught it with one hand while holding on to the instrument panel with the other.

He lowered the rifle towards her.

Martin stared right into his eyes.

A rifle cracked; the man lurched forward a little, almost falling on her, and then he dropped his weapon and tumbled off the crumpled nose of the helicopter, out of Captain Martin's field of view.

She heard him hit the dirt several feet below.

Another burst of gunfire came, and then all was silent.

Martin had an M9 on her right hip that she couldn't reach and an M4 rifle in a cradle over her right shoulder that was equally inaccessible. She rocked side to side, trying to loosen herself, but she barely budged.

"Max?" She said it again, more softly this time. "Max, can you get to your M4?"

There was no reply, but almost immediately she heard a new noise. She squinted her eyes shut again.

It took her a moment to fix on the sound and identify it, but when she realized what she was hearing, terror all but overtook her. Someone else was making their way through the wreckage, climbing up the side of the aircraft to her.

She closed her eyes a moment, to blot out the fear, and then she opened them again, ready to meet whatever danger was approaching.

But before she saw anyone, a voice called out. "Friendly! Friendly!"

A bearded man wearing a backwards-facing baseball cap pulled himself up to her level, some ten feet or so above the damaged street. He held on to the instrument panel, his bare hands over the MPDs and the TADS, just as the first man had done.

He looked her over in the dim light, his eyebrows furrowed with worry, and she just stared back at him.

He said, "Sir? Sir? Can you hear me?"

He was American, that was clear, but he wore no uniform. He didn't have a rifle, and she couldn't see if he wore a pistol from his position. Still, considering they were in the middle of Iraq, she assumed him to be a member of some U.S. special operations force, either a Green Beret or a Navy SEAL, or perhaps even something more covert. She saw the men around the base with their relaxed grooming standards and civilian clothing, though she had no interactions with them herself.

She didn't correct him as to her gender. "Yeah, I'm okay. Help Henderson."

He didn't miss a beat. "Sorry, ma'am. I'll check out your backseater in just a sec." He flipped on a small flashlight with a red lens and shined it down around the cockpit, looking her over. "Are you hurt?"

"I don't . . . think so, but I'm wedged in."

"I'll get you out. I'm gonna check out your pilot and be right back."

Martin looked around at the street, her helmet still caught in wires. "Where is . . . where is everybody with you?"

"It's just me. Sit tight," he said as he began climbing the wreckage like a ladder the six feet up to Henderson.

"Sit tight?" she mumbled to herself. *Is that a joke?* She fought again against the crumpled metal and miles of wiring and yards of hoses and pounds of dirt holding her in place.

"Shit," she mumbled, giving up again, and she slammed her helmet back against the headrest in frustration, somehow causing the first jolt of pain in her right leg.

Twenty-five-year-old Josh Duffy made his way to the pilot's seat to find a large man whom he initially took for dead. But when he reached out and checked the man's pulse on an artery on his exposed neck, he was surprised to find it strong.

"Sir?" He held the man's face up, and his eyelids flickered. The monocle over the man's right eye was broken away, just as it had been on the helmet of the woman in the front seat, but this man had blood smeared on his face and forehead.

He started to reach for his medical kit on the right side of his body armor; he had smelling salts in there that could rouse an unconscious man, but the man lifted his head slowly.

"What happened?" he mumbled.

"Can you move?"

He nodded.

"Okay. Get your harness off. I'm going to work on freeing your front-seater, then I'll be back to help you down."

Duffy slid back down to the copilot's crew station.

The woman was trying her best to free herself, but she'd achieved little more than pulling some hoses loose.

She looked him in the eyes from a foot away. "How is he?"

"He's alive, conscious, sort of. Breathing seems fine. No idea about internal injuries, but it looks like I'll be able to move him."

Martin said, "Negative. If you don't know about internal injuries, you can't move him."

Duff looked back over his shoulder quickly, then back to the woman. "Ma'am, bad guys saw your bird go down. Two have already shown up, and more are on the way. I don't want to, but I'm going to have to get both of you out of here before we draw a bigger crowd."

He started feeling for the harnesses that still had her restrained.

She tried to push him away with her left hand. "I . . . I can do it. I think my right foot is broken. You touch me and I'll kick your ass."

Duff moved her hand out of his way and began prying twisted metal. As he did this, he said, "With your other foot? What will you stand on while you do that, ma'am?"

She cocked her head at the man. "You think you're funny?"

"One shot of that morphine I'm going to hit you with as soon as we find cover, and you'll think I'm funny, too, Lieutenant."

"It's Captain."

Duff didn't stop working. "Got it, sorry. I've almost got you loose, I'm gonna have to pull." Duff kept working, but he looked over his shoulder, down the dusty street. A crackle of gunfire told him fresh fighting was not far away, but he didn't see anyone with eyes on him.

The woman protested, "I told you, I've got it."

"And I told you, we've got to move our asses!"

"Do you always speak to superior officers like this?"

"You aren't my superior officer. I'm a civ."

"Civilian?"

"Yep. Contractor with Triple Canopy." When she just looked at him, he added, "Security company."

"What are you doing here?"

"I was about three klicks east, heading to our HQ for supplies. I saw the arty firing to the south, then saw your tracer fire from the north. Were those rockets?"

She didn't answer his question, because she had one of her own. "You were traveling alone?"

As he pried on the metal around the woman's right side, he said, "I'm working with a team guarding a radio station south of here. We ran out of water. We're short-staffed, so I volunteered to go back to HQ and pick up some cases. It had been pretty quiet around here, though we knew it was just a matter of time before it all went to shit."

He looked around quickly. "It's official. It's all gone to shit."

He was pulling away wires now, trying to push the last of the twisted metal to free the Army copilot. As he did this, he said, "Then I saw you go down. I thought I might get to you before your CASEVAC."

"And you came alone?"

"Sometimes one dude in a keffiyeh in a pickup is safer than forty jocked-up shooters in Humvees."

"Sometimes, yeah," the woman said. "But not right now."

Duff smiled a little. "No kidding. Okay, I think you're free; we're going to have to get you to cover."

"What's cover around here?"

"Good question. I'll get you in my truck and we'll haul ass. You aren't going to be so difficult, but your warrant officer looks like a handful."

He pulled on the woman, and she screamed out in pain.

"Your foot?"

"Yeah. It's still wedged, and it's definitely broken."

"Sorry, but I'm going to have to yank again."

"Christ."

More headlights washed over them. Duff ignored them and said, "Here we go, ma'am."

He pulled again, and she cried out but broke free, using her left leg to help the man doing his best to rescue her.

Her right arm hurt when she was able to move it, but still she reached for something. Duff saw that she was trying to get her hand on her rifle.

Duff said, "Leave it."

She continued reaching for it, but he yanked her hard enough to pull her out of her seat completely. Together the two of them started to fall from the crumpled Apache.

"Shit!" she screamed as they slid and then tumbled; Duff wrapped his body around her, taking the impact on the hard earth with his back and right shoulder.

The wind knocked out of him, the woman groaning in agony on top of him, he looked up the street and saw figures fanning out a hundred yards or so away.

The captain rolled off him and pulled her helmet off with her left hand. Still showing the agony on her face, she coughed out an admonition. "No offense, dude, but you suck as a rescuer."

He rolled onto his stomach, then up onto his knees. Hefting the M4 now, he said, "No offense, ma'am, but you suck as a helicopter pilot."

She rolled into a sitting position now. "We got shot down, dick."

At this moment she saw the silhouettes of men in the street ahead, as well. "Henderson?" she said.

"I'll get him, take the carbine."

She reached to take the rifle, but a noise above them made them both look up.

The chief warrant officer had regained consciousness and was climbing down the wreckage.

He'd only made it a few feet when gunfire kicked off from the men one hundred yards away. Duffy pulled the carbine back and returned fire, and the captain drew her pistol and began suppressing, as well.

Henderson came falling down to the ground next to them. Quickly he climbed back to his feet, ran in the opposite direction, and scrambled behind the port-side wing.

He didn't have his rifle with him and, Duff noticed, he'd not drawn his handgun.

Duff dropped the now-empty carbine and grabbed his own rifle, an AK-47 he'd left here on the ground next to the wreckage. As he aimed in on a target, he yelled, "Chief! Your captain's injured. You're going to have to carry her to my truck. It's only about thirty feet, but I've got to keep up suppressive fire."

There was no response from the man behind him.

The captain shouted, as well, just as she ran out of ammo. "Max?" She reloaded her pistol awkwardly. To Duff, it looked like she might have an injured wrist or hand, as well as her broken ankle, but soon she got the gun back into battery and back into the fight.

"Chief?" she called again. "I'm ordering you to come to me. I'll cover."

"Fuck that!" the chief said from behind the wing.

Duff stood now as rounds whizzed by him; there might have been no more than four or five attackers, but they were rocking AKs at full auto. He grabbed the injured woman and pulled her by the shoulder strap of her body armor. She screamed as he dragged her towards the truck, but she kept shooting her pistol, emptying a second magazine.

He pulled her up to the passenger door and started to put her inside, but she turned to him. "Give me your rifle. You go for Henderson, I'll cover."

"He seems happy right there," Duff said, willing to leave the man behind if he wasn't even going to help with his own rescue.

But the captain just glared at him.

"Yes, ma'am."

Standing on her good leg, she took the AK, leaned over the hood of the truck, and fired individual rounds, desperate to keep the enemy's head down while the Triple Canopy contractor ran back to save her pilot.

Duff sprinted across open ground again, back to the wing shielding the Apache flier. He didn't know if Henderson was badly injured or not, but more headlights were approaching, so he didn't really care about the man's condition. If they weren't out of here in seconds, his injuries would be a moot point, because all three of them would be dead.

He found the pilot cowering; he hadn't even drawn his weapon. He hefted the man without even speaking to him, and when the pilot seemed to stand on his own, Duff shoved him out from behind the wing. Together they ran for the pickup, getting there just as the captain ran out of ammunition.

"Get in!" Duff shouted to the woman, and he helped Henderson into the bed of the vehicle.

Still under fire, he made it around to the driver's door, jumped in, and threw the vehicle into reverse.

As he raced backwards as fast as he could go, the windshield shattered just before he performed a reverse one-eighty maneuver, throwing the transmission into drive, and then flooring it.

He accelerated from the scene with his foot to the floor.

The woman was blond; he only noticed this now. Her hair was short, sweat-covered, and mashed from her helmet. She looked back over her shoulder at Henderson, who was in the little bed of the truck, looking back towards the area where they had just crashed.

Duff said, "Your pilot didn't exactly bathe himself in glory back there." She didn't say anything, so he added, "I guess that's what you get for flying with your dad."

She chuckled a little bit now, but he could tell her pain was getting worse. "He's a good pilot, but I guess he's never been put through stress like this. He defied a direct order tonight, twice. I could have his ass court-martialed."

"Will you?" Duff asked.

She shrugged. "I'll worry about him later. His military record is pretty low on my priority list right now."

Duff saw the pain she was in, and he saw that it was increasing by the minute as the adrenaline rushing through her began to subside. He reached into the medical kit on the right side of his body armor now; it took him a moment, but he eventually fished out a morphine autoinject, a spring-loaded syringe with ten milligrams of the heavy narcotic pain reliever.

"You need this. The sooner, the better."

"No," she said authoritatively. "I'm going to wait till we're secure. Might need to fight again."

"I've got you. We're going to the Triple Canopy compound; you need to treat that pain before it gets worse." He started to hold it over her leg, but she pushed it away.

"I said no! I need to be clearheaded till this shit is over."

He let it go for a second as he looked at her. "No offense, but aren't you a little young to be a captain?"

"No, I'm not, but I guess I should be flattered, especially given how I look right now."

"I bet you clean up."

"You're ex-military?"

Duff nodded. "Army."

"Aren't you a little young to be a veteran running around as a gun for hire?"

Duff shrugged. "Yeah, but I'm still working for the good guys."

She smiled weakly. "I'm in no position to argue with that."

"You aren't going to argue? That must hurt worse than your broken foot."

She groaned in pain before saying, "Not even close. Why'd you leave the service?"

"I left active duty because I wanted more action." He looked around at their predicament now. "Nailed it."

"Nailed it," Martin repeated, and then she moaned in agony again.

"Ma'am, I *have* to give you something for that pain."

"Fuck that. You don't get to fight ISIS on your own."

Duff nodded back behind him to the pilot. He was lying on his side in the fetal position. "Don't worry about me. If the shit hits the fan, I've always got Henderson."

She laughed again, grimacing along with it. "It would have been better if you brought other guys."

"And it would have been better if you didn't get your ass shot out of the sky."

He looked into her eyes. They were going glassy. "You're no good to me if you go into shock." He quickly jabbed the autoinject past her shielding hand and slammed it into her leg. She cried out in surprise.

He said, "I know you're pissed, but I promise you'll thank me later."

He tossed the spent syringe on the floorboard.

"You son of a bitch!" she shouted.

Duff shrugged; he didn't argue the point.

They drove in silence for a minute, Duff's eyes in his rearview every few seconds.

Then the woman spoke again; her angry tone had mellowed considerably. "Our intel sucked. We didn't even know there were any Triple Canopy guys in the AO."

Duff rolled his eyes. "Well, that's par for the course. Us poor forgotten security contractors always get the shaft."

"What's your name?"

"Duffy."

The injured captain turned to him in the low light. "Is that a first name or a last name?"

"Josh Duffy. Guys on my team call me Duff."

Her words were becoming more slurred now. "Duffy . . . Duff . . . That doesn't really save very much time, does it?"

"Guess not."

"How about I call . . . you . . . Josh?"

Duff had noticed the officer's name tape. "And I'll call you Captain Martin."

"Nikki."

"Yes, ma'am." He nodded as he drove. "I think the morphine is kicking in a little. You're going to be okay."

She watched the road a moment, then said, "Sorry about before. Sometimes when I get stressed, I can be a bitch."

The bearded man grinned at this. "Same here. You're fine, ma'am. You kicked some serious ass back there."

She smiled now; her eyes fluttered a little. "Thanks, Josh." In seconds she was asleep.

Josh smiled himself now, then looked back over at her for an instant. "Anytime."

CHAPTER 39

PRESENT DAY

In the mountain town of Cinco Lagrimas, Chihuahua state, Oscar Cardoza sat in the tiny hotel restaurant at a table by himself, finishing a pedestrian meal of steak in chimichurri along with tequila and beer, all brought to him by a kind, matronly woman in her sixties who seemed wholly unaware that she lived and worked in a city where virtually everyone else above the age of fourteen was employed in the brutal drug trade. This had been a lawless land for a very long time, Cardoza knew, inhabited by those who wanted to stay away from the eyes and guns of the federal government, from any outsiders, and the locals up here did what they could to survive.

He had changed into a business suit for dinner, a habit of his picked up in Mexico City, though here he realized there was no need to make a good impression. Guards watched him, and mountain people who didn't give a shit about some suit from the capital looked his way and then looked away.

He had not seen Archuleta again since the night before; instead, he'd remained in the hotel alone, waiting. He made a few inconsequential calls with his satellite phone while sitting in the lobby or on the tiny patio out front, but he knew the guards were listening to everything he was saying, so he had not been able to get any real work done.

He finished his second steak of the day just before nine p.m., adjusted his tie, then rose. He passed on effusive compliments to the smiling and blushing woman and headed up to his room.

Three armed sicarios stood in the hotel lobby off the restaurant, and they pushed off from the wall when he exited. An open archway that led to the hotel cantina was opposite the restaurant hallway entrance, and a group of hard men sitting at the bar in there looked his way. He nodded to them politely, then turned for the stairs.

His room was on the third floor; it was small but clean and efficient, and there was a little balcony that looked out over the plaza, giving him a view of the municipal building where the meeting with the UN and government officials was to take place the following day. After bidding his guards a good evening and shutting the door, he slipped off his suit coat, loosened his tie, and stood out on the balcony, taking in the cool mountain air, listening for a moment to Bandera music coming out of the windows of a passing Chevy Silverado.

The street was mostly empty, which would hardly be the case in most small towns in Mexico on a weekend evening at this time, but Cardoza knew all the citizens were under the brutal authority of Archuleta and the Black Knights, so any revelry was kept to a minimum.

Cardoza knew cartel towns. There was a dark, taut energy. A desperate character, an implacable atmosphere encompassing every facet of life.

He sighed and didn't waste any more energy contemplating the plight of the locals. He instead began thinking about the day ahead and all that was at stake.

Tomorrow and the next day would be the most important of his life, of this he had no doubt. His plan would either work flawlessly, giving him riches and freedom and everything he wanted, or else he was a fucking dead man.

Only time would tell.

He thought about his future now, which was easy to do, because he had it all planned out. When this was over, he'd fly to Bogotá, then, a couple days later, catch a flight to Buenos Aires. From there he'd fly again, thirteen and a half hours over the Pacific to Papeete, Tahiti. Once there, he would board a tiny puddle jumper that would take him to the atoll of Rangiroa, and there he'd board a boat for a ninety-minute open-water journey to the tiny island of Motu Teta.

It was the most beautiful place on Earth, this he knew without question. He'd never been there himself, but his research over the past few months had led him to this conclusion.

It was utterly remote, but for a man with means, Motu Teta had all the creature comforts he needed.

He'd live the rest of his days, perhaps half a lifetime, far away from the insanity, the danger, the politics, and the stress of the narco wars.

It was so far away from here, but it was so fucking close he could taste it.

Just then, his sat phone buzzed in the pocket of his suit coat back on his bed. He went to it, looked down at the incoming number, and immediately sensed something was wrong.

He didn't want to take a call from El Lobo here while surrounded by Los Caballeros Negros, but he knew that whatever was going on, he couldn't trust the Zeta war commander to make the right decisions on his own.

He stepped out onto the balcony, far enough away from the doors, he hoped, to hide his conversation. Quickly he covered the mouth-piece of the phone, and he began to whisper.

"Bueno?"

"It's Lobo."

"Make it quick. I'm with Los Caballeros Negros. They have me in a hotel in Cinco Lagrimas, but there are men outside in the hall."

"I am calling with good news."

"Tell me."

"We have the motorcade in sight. They are moving up a narrow mountain road and will be up to us in five minutes. This is a perfect opportunity for an ambush. They have no escape. We can finish this right now."

Cardoza was confused. "What? They're off the highway?"

"Yes."

"And *you're* off the highway?" The Zetas were told to remain on or near the flat-top road that went along the Spine to avoid Sinaloan or Black Knight patrols.

"Sí. It is unbelievable luck. We see them winding around the mouth of the valley. They are coming right at our encampment. I've set an ambush, and I have vehicles moving to trail them so they can't turn around. We will destroy them!"

Cardoza, in contrast to Lobo, was not happy about any of this. "No, you must not do that, amigo. You must get out of the area, wait until *after* they meet with Los Caballeros Negros."

"This opportunity is too good. Why does it matter where and when we kill them, anyway?"

"The missiles! We have to find out where Archuleta is hiding the missiles, or the entire scheme falls apart. Look, you need to remain out of sight. Wait for my call before you attack. Might be tomorrow. Might be the day after."

"You don't understand. We can't pack up and run, we have to block the road and take them now. Los Caballeros Negros are everywhere. We were almost discovered three times today."

Cardoza fought to keep his voice low. "You *have* to wait!"

Lobo's excited tone turned darker. "You don't tell me how to do my job."

"Never, amigo. I'd never do that. But the attack must come *after* the UN motorcade has left their meeting."

"I am in command of this operation. My leadership wants me to come up here and destroy those five vehicles and the people inside, and to protect my men. I am going to do both of these things. Now. You'll have to find your missiles some other way. I'm *not* giving up this tactical advantage."

"Listen to me!" Cardoza implored, but Lobo ended the call.

"Hijo de puta," the man on the hotel balcony said, and this he did not whisper.

The door to his room opened behind him, and a man in a ball cap with a G3 hanging from his chest looked at him curiously. He was one of the guards who had been with him all day long.

"Señor?" the young man said. "Everything okay?"

"Sí. Sí." Cardoza recovered quickly. "Just talking to my brother-in-law, el pinche pendejo."

The man nodded. "I have a brother-in-law like that, too. Buenas noches."

He turned and pulled the door shut, and Cardoza looked up the road to the south. It was black in the mountains, but he knew that just a few hours' drive in that direction, a battle was about to begin.

He also realized that he was, at this point in time, rooting for his enemy to prevail.

Josh Duffy rubbed his eyes under his clear ballistic glasses and looked through the windshield at the motorcade in front of him as it twisted slowly on a winding road, rolling its way along the Devil's Spine, passing deep ravines, steep gorges, and canyons and in view of many of the 10,395 named peaks in the impossibly rugged range.

Squeeze said, "Not even a moon out tonight. I can't see shit past the lights of the APC."

"Nascar? How's your viz?"

"I've got Pack Horse Two's running lights to follow, although this dust is making it—"

Tony Cruz interrupted the intrateam radio transmission. "Charlie One, Charlie Four. Vehicle on our six, one hundred fifty meters back, running without lights!"

"Rotating!" Squeeze said, and he turned around in the turret to face the rear.

Duffy spoke back over the radio. "Roger that, Cruz. Can you ID?"

"Wait one, let me break out my FLIR."

Squeeze shouted, "I can't see shit up here with all the dust from the vics in front of us!"

Duffy snatched up the radio handset now. "Charlie One for Alpha

One. Be advised. We've got some sort of victor running dark, our six o'clock."

Remmick replied, "Copy that. Our turret gunner says he can't see through all the damn dust. You've got command of the encounter. How copy?"

"Understood. You want us to lag back from the motorcade?"

"Negative. Might be more trouble ahead. Let's keep it tight."

"Wilco." Duff took the handset from his mouth and spoke through his boom mic for the men in his truck. "All call signs scan sectors for contact."

Cruz shouted now. "Two vehicles now! Both pickups, no lights. One hundred fifty yards. They're matching our speed, not closing. I've got . . . one subject standing in the back of the lead vehicle. Not sure what he's doing."

"He armed?"

Squeeze interrupted the transmission. "I tally the victors. I see the dude in back of the one on the right. He's . . . he's got a . . ."

Squeeze said nothing for a moment; Duff desperately tried to look through his rearview behind them, but since the unknown vehicles were running without lights, he couldn't see them at all.

Then, as one, Squeeze and Cruz shouted into their mics. "RPG!"

A rocket-propelled grenade slammed into the cliff side between Crazy Horse and Pack Horse Two, forcing Nascar to swerve to avoid debris that tumbled from the rock face to the dirt road.

He slammed his foot on the gas pedal, closing the distance to the rear of the APC in front of him, as automatic rifle fire from behind ricocheted off the armored hull of Crazy Horse.

Shit, Duff thought, *here we go again.*

"Light 'em up, Four. Squeeze, drop some forty mike-mike!"

Duff triggered his handset again. "Contact rear! Taking accurate RPG fire from multiple hostile technicals on the road."

Frenchie lunged for the grenade launcher and passed it up to the young African American, who took it while feeding the Mk 48 down through the turret. Frenchie took the machine gun and held on to it, ready to make the switch again.

But as soon as Squeeze took the weapon, he looked out of the turret and dropped back down into the cab. "RPG!" he shouted again.

A powerful jolt slammed into the rear of the vehicle, raising it off its two rear tires for an instant before it slammed back down hard on its chassis.

Next to Duff, Nascar said, "That's a hit, but we're okay." He patted the dashboard. "Good job, baby."

Cruz called from the rear, "Took it in the armor back here. That bitch hit close to my gunport."

Wolfson turned to Gabby in the back now. He had no target, and his frustration was evident. "If your sweet injun friends have RPGs, then they're dead meat."

She did not respond; she only looked into Duff's eyes as he tried to get a glimpse of the action behind by looking back between the seats.

Squeeze popped several grenades in the direction of the trailing vehicles. Explosions buffeted the hillside, but the pickups drove through the smoke and kept coming.

Cruz stopped firing to transmit. "No effect, Squeeze. Lower your aim."

"Roger."

Gordon's voice came over the radio now. "Bravo One to all call signs. Pack Horse One has contact left! Multiple pickup trucks off road on the mountainside. Looks like they're dug in and set up for us!"

The commander of War Horse came over the net now. "Alpha Two to all signs. Something in the road ahead, might be a roadblock. Everybody lay down some fuckin' hate on these guys!"

Back in Crazy Horse, Duff announced what all the men in the vehicle were thinking: "L-shaped ambush!"

CHAPTER 40

Squeeze fired more grenades, their outgoing *thunk*s and their high-explosive impacts behind the motorcade evident to Duff's trained ears.

Soon Cruz shouted into his mic. "Yes!"

"Nailed the rear vic!" Squeeze proclaimed proudly.

Cruz said, "I took out the RPG gunner in the lead vic, but it's still coming."

A pair of new RPGs lit up the sky now, launched from higher on the hillside on their left and down towards them. They both went right over the motorcade and disappeared into a valley on their right, but a third rocket slammed into the deeply rutted road right in front of Show Horse, pelting the entire motorcade with dirt and rock.

Remmick immediately transmitted. "Charlie, maneuver to cover the limo!"

"Roger that," Duff responded, then said, "Pack Horse Two, you've got the fight at the rear." He turned to Nascar. "Pass on the left, put us between the ambush and the limo."

Nascar floored it, jacked the wheel left, and rolled up off the road onto even rougher ground. Everyone inside the APC bounced around, harnesses strained to keep them in their seats. Meanwhile, Duff kept his instructions coming for his team. "Squeeze, you've got nine o'clock, look for that ambush. Frenchie, give him some support through the port-side hatch."

"Already on it, boss," the former Commandos Marine officer said as he peered through his ballistic glass with his rifle out the gunport.

Nascar expertly placed his truck to the left of Show Horse and rolled abreast with it as it picked its way along the narrow trail under withering small-arms fire. Squeeze fired off a few grenades, and machine guns from other trucks belted staccato bursts of lead up towards a tree line higher on the mountain.

But just a few seconds later, a new message confirmed their fears.

"This is Alpha Two in the lead vic. Be advised, we've got felled trees blocking the road ahead."

Remmick shot back, "I don't give a shit. Roll over or go around them."

"Ah . . . negative, Alpha Actual. These logs are two feet thick, and there's no lane to pass them. Even in the APC we can't—"

"Can you chew them up with forty mike-mike HE?" Gordon asked.

"It's gonna take a lot of time and ammo. We need to get the chain saws up here and dismount to cut through the obstruction and then push through. We do that or else we need to turn around."

Remmick again. "We can't turn on this road! We'd go over the cliff side. We're pushing through! Alpha One to Bravo One!"

"Go for Bravo One."

"Your guys have got the chain saws in Pack Horse Two. Send them up past War Horse and deal with that obstacle."

Gordon said, "Roger. Duff, get your driver to push ahead of Show Horse so my Two can pass on your left."

Nascar began moving forward immediately; incoming small-arms fire pinged against the left side of Crazy Horse, and a round slammed into Nascar's driver's-side window. Soon Pack Horse Two, driven by Bravo Two, rumbled across the hill on the left, driving along at nearly a 45-degree angle, and then it rolled back onto the narrow road, passing Gordon in Pack Horse One and pulling to a stop next to War Horse in the front of the convoy.

Behind Duff, Cruz said, "Boss? That pickup hasn't shown around the bend of that last turn. Either I killed the driver or—"

Duff finished the thought. "Or they are hanging back to get out of the way of the others."

Frenchie asked now, "Are these Black Knights? Why would they be trying to kill us if they invited us—"

But Gordon came over the speakers, interrupting Frenchie. "Pack Horse Two is in position. They're deploying two men with chain saws out the belly hatch. They're gonna need a lot of cover."

Remmick answered back over the persistent gunfire, both incoming and outgoing. "Roger that, we'll ratchet up the return fire to keep oppo heads down. Charlie, push forward again fifty meters to give some armored cover to the left of the dismounts. Can't fit another vehicle on the right, so those two on the chain saws will have to duck any fire coming from the other ridge line."

"Floor it, Nascar," Duff ordered.

As he drove, Nascar said, "Hey, boss, I'm not sayin', I'm just sayin'. This was an ambush set up by somebody who was expecting us."

The Alabama native slammed on his brakes just in front of Pack Horse Two. In front of him, Duff could easily make out a large obstruction of felled pine trees lying across the mountain road.

Duff could also see two Bravo contractors with chain saws as they ran out in front of their vehicle, making it through sporadic incoming fire, then dropping down to begin cutting through the roadblock.

He shouted into his mic. "Shoot up the hill or across the valley to keep enemy heads down. Make some fucking noise!"

Squeeze popped rounds from the grenade launcher; Frenchie, Nascar, and Cruz fired up the hillside towards the trees there.

Wolfson scanned for targets on the opposite side of the valley.

The battle continued for a couple of minutes before Gordon said, "Alpha Actual, Bravo Actual. My guys are halfway through the logs. Once they're cut, they'll use Pack Horse Two to push them apart, but it's gonna take a minute."

"Speed it up, Bravo!" Remmick ordered.

New enemy gunfire kicked up; the men on the port side of Crazy

Horse fired at muzzle flashes in the trees above them, but it was clear incoming rounds were zinging in from all compass points now.

After an AK round rang the steel turret next to him, Squeeze ducked down. "We're up against fifty enemy, minimum, and these ain't fuckin' druggies or locals with old bolt guns. These dudes are fuckin' soldiers! They got actual marksmanship and shit!"

Frenchie passed him his machine gun, and the young former Marine rose back up to use it.

Duff had no targets in sight on the starboard side of the vehicle, so he could only watch in horror in front of him as bullet strikes kicked dirt and stones up in the road between Crazy Horse and the two exposed men on the chain saws.

Letting his frustration get the better of him, Duff opened his heavy door, then leaned out, standing on the running board as he aimed over the roof, just a few feet in front of Squeeze in the turret. He opened fire with his Kalashnikov into the trees above them, desperate to force the incoming fire to slacken.

He was looking up the hillside when Nascar's voice rang through the intrateam comms.

"Aw, shit! One of the Bravo dismounts went down hard. Looked like a fuckin' head-shot!"

Duff dropped back in his truck to reload, and as he did this, he heard Gordon over the speakers. "Pack Horse Two has a man down!" He looked out the windscreen and saw the fallen contractor through the headlights now. He was crumpled in a ball, his chain saw next to him, and his partner was scrambling for cover between the logs.

Frenchie called out, "Boss, I can go treat him."

Duff snatched the handset. "Bravo One, our medic will attend. We're on the left, just twenty meters back. We'll maneuver forward and—"

Remmick broke in. "Negative. Crazy Horse stays where it is. I want you close enough to protect the limo. You can deploy your medic on foot, but I want that gun truck drawing fire and engaging enemy. You are *not* authorized to move!"

Cruz shouted his disapproval from the back. "We're gonna draw fire wherever the fuck we are! That's bullshit!"

Frenchie said, "I'll still go. I can debus through the floor hatch, run to the barricade, and find cover with the wounded man."

Josh Duffy's chest pounded so hard now he was worried about a heart attack. He swallowed and said, "Frenchie . . . negative."

"*Negative?* I'm the closest medic, and they have an injured man."

"And you aren't running across twenty meters of open ground under direct fire to get him."

Now the other Bravo operator out of his vehicle with a chain saw came over the net. "Bravo Eight to all signs. The limbs are cut! You can push through! Be advised, Bravo Four is KIA. I'll drag his body back to Pack Horse Two and—"

Remmick shouted back, "Leave the body and get back in your vic!"

"I'm not leaving—"

"Leave him or we run you down. We are getting the fuck out of here!"

Men in Crazy Horse shouted to one another as they fired, either at muzzle flashes or blindly to keep heads down. Frenchie, however, slammed the buttstock of his rifle on the floor in frustration.

"Nothing you could have done for him, Frenchie," Duff said. "Get your gun back in your gunport and shoot some bad guys."

Remmick's voice came over the speakers again. "Bravo, order your other vehicle to push through those obstacles and make us a hole."

"Roger." Gordon's voice was unsure. Duff imagined that the fact he'd lost a second man had left him stupefied, but he was still in the fight.

Pack Horse Two rumbled forward; their dismount with the chain saw was trying to pull the body of his fallen comrade towards the machine as it began moving the logs, all cut down the middle and therefore relatively easy to push to the side. Once done, the man with the body and two chain saws to deal with rolled under the vehicle, passed a saw up, then returned to expose himself to the still-raging gunfire to pull the dead man forward.

"Boss," Cruz shouted out now through the headset. "I see additional vics approaching our six o'clock! Fifty meters back down the road."

"We must be doing some damage to them if they're bringing in reinforcements," Duff replied.

Squeeze had ducked down into the cabin next to Frenchie and Wolfson and just behind Gabby to grab a fresh 200 box of ammo for his Mk 48, but into his mic he said, "Reinforcements? I thought we were comin' up here to fight cowboys and dopeheads. Cowboys and dopeheads don't have no goddamned reinforce—"

He stopped talking for an instant, and then he screamed, "RPG, incoming! Southeast!"

Duff pulled his door all the way shut quickly, and just as it clicked closed, a crash and a flash overtook his vehicle. Duff's window and door were slammed with shrapnel and fire.

First he thought he'd taken an RPG to his door, but quickly he realized Crazy Horse hadn't been hit by a rocket at all. Pack Horse Two, just ahead on the other side of the logs, was burning now; flames shot out from under the vehicle.

"Oh my God," he said softly.

And then, to Duff's horror, Pack Horse Two underwent a high-order detonation. Fuel and ammo discharged, set off by the warhead, and the vehicle blew into pieces. The windshield on Crazy Horse cracked, and Duff's ears, even while protected by his noise-canceling headset, rang while his head pounded.

As soon as the smoke and dust cleared enough to see out the windows, Duff knew there would be no survivors in that vehicle. Additionally, Bravo Eight, who had been dragging the dead operator towards the belly hatch, was nowhere to be seen, probably, Duff thought, because the explosion had flung him and his dead comrade off the side of the mountain.

It was quiet on the radio for several seconds while the rest of the motorcade sat in stunned silence.

And then Gordon shouted over the net. "Willie? Chris?"

Gabby unfastened her harness and leaned forward, looked out

past Duff through the cracked ballistic glass, and made the sign of the cross. "Madre de Dios," she said softly.

Gunfire continued to rage, and the vehicle's speakers blared new orders and shouts from the other APCs, and Wolfson called into the intrateam from his position just behind Duffy.

"Charlie Actual, I'm debussing to check for survivors."

"Negative," Duff barked back. "They're all dead."

"Duff, I *am* leaving Crazy Horse to assess!"

Accurate machine gun fire raked the port side of Crazy Horse now.

"No, you're fucking *not*! They're all dead! Stay inside the armor."

"Come on, man, we can't leave—"

"Keep scanning the valley! That RPG gunner is still out there."

Pack Horse Two burned uncontrollably in front of them, lighting up the entire area above and beyond the headlight beams of the four large trucks. Duff shook away the panic and shouted into his mic, "Nascar, move up behind the burning vic." To the rest of the men on board, he said, "Stay on your guns! I'll ask for the okay to recover the bodies."

Duff clicked his handset, "Alpha One, if you let us stop just to the left of Pack Horse Two, we can dismount and retrieve the fallen."

"Negative!" Remmick shouted. "Nobody leaves the vehicles!"

"There are four men dead out there!"

"Who we can do nothing for! I am not risking lives and this mission to return bodies to loved ones! Push through the barricade and get off my net! We are under fire!"

"But we—"

"Off the net!"

Squeeze spoke into the intrateam. "Fuck Remmick, Army. Let's get the bodies. Shit, I'll do it myself."

"I'll go with him!" Wolfson said. "Come on, Duff!"

"Negative! Everybody stand fast. We keep moving through the ambush."

"We can't just leave them burning in the fuckin' truck!"

"Remmick's right! We can't lose more men to retrieve bodies, and leaving the APC here is walking into a buzz saw."

Squeeze fired a burst at a target on the mountainside, then said, "So, you just gonna leave my ass up here in this shit hole if I die? Huh?"

"Everybody shut up!" Duff screamed, overtaken by the moment.

The motorcade pushed through the felled logs and rounded a turn, and instantly the fire died down. Crazy Horse went back to the rear of the four vehicles, and Cruz confirmed that the pickups that had been behind them had disappeared. Remmick speculated that the majority of the enemy had been firing from dug-in positions; they had no way to quickly maneuver to pursue, and the truckloads of men knew they would be overmatched if they went after the Americans alone.

Cruz said what everyone else was thinking. "If those were the Black Knights, then I don't think we are as welcome as the UN says we are."

Gabby spoke up now for the first time since the engagement began. "Who else could it be other than Los Caballeros Negros? The Sinaloans are in the Sierra Madres, yes, but they are not this far up on the Spine, and they wouldn't leave the highway."

Wolfson snapped at her. "Nobody cares."

But she continued, "If there are this many, they are definitely Black Knights, unless some other cartel managed to sneak through the Sinaloans and the BKs. I've not heard of any other group up here in over two years."

The men in Crazy Horse continued to complain angrily, and Duff realized a lot of it was misplaced fear. He was feeling the same thing; he'd never seen that many contractors die at one time, and the prospect of continuing on with this mission seemed utterly insane to him.

But he held his opinions to himself, admonished his men for the chatter, and told them to reload and to stay vigilant, and soon they drove on in silence.

Finally, Nascar spoke softly into his mic. "Poor Gordon. The detail has lost five men, all from Bravo. It's just him and two Joes left in Pack Horse One."

"Yeah," Duff said, mostly to himself. "Poor Gordon."

Finally, Cruz said, "If we don't turn around and go home, we're all gonna die. I mean, Flores says there isn't anybody else up here in numbers except the fucking Black Knights. And they were the only ones who knew we were coming, right?"

Duff had all the misgivings of Cruz, but he had to lead these men forward, at least until Remmick pulled the plug on the operation. He said, "We've driven through a dozen little towns in the last two days. Anybody with a phone could have told someone in any organization up here on the Spine to be on the lookout for us." Before Cruz could say anything else, Duff said, "Remmick is assessing the situation. He'll figure out if we're going home or going forward."

Squeeze said, "We go home now, we don't get paid for the next two weeks."

"I'm here to get paid," Nascar said.

"Fuckin' A," Wolfson chimed in.

But to this Cruz just said, "Know what? Those five poor sons of bitches on Bravo team were here to get paid, too. And look where that got them."

There was no more conversation on the drive along the mountain road.

CHAPTER 41

Oscar Cardoza sat out on the tiny balcony of his hotel, a bottle of Buchanan's DeLuxe scotch whisky on the table next to him. The glass in his hand was his fourth of the evening, which was saying something, because Cardoza thought the whisky was shit. He preferred eighteen-year-old Macallan or Jura, but the only scotch whisky available up here was twelve-year-old Buchanan's, and it was that or tequila or fucking Jack Daniel's.

As he sat, he looked out across the tiny town square, over the municipal building to the mountains to the southwest. He couldn't hear gunfire, but he assumed a battle was raging. Seventy-five entrenched sicarios against twenty-one civilian contractors in heavy armor, and while he assumed the Americans would make it through, he didn't know how costly an encounter it would be for them. If it was bad enough that the security detail decided to turn the motorcade around and head home, everything Cardoza had worked so hard to create would amount to nothing.

He knew what that meant for him personally, and the lack of control he was feeling right now was almost too much to bear.

And he couldn't even afford the luxury of emoting about it now. If he broke furniture, cursed the gods, stomped around his room, then it would tip off the Black Knights that he had knowledge of what was happening with the motorcade, and that would just not do.

So instead, he sat and drank.

He figured when it was all over up there, he'd either hear first from Lobo with the Zetas, or from his informant in the motorcade. Two sides fighting against one another, neither knowing that Cardoza was pitting them against each other.

Just as he put the lid back on the bottle and drained the contents of his glass into his mouth, telling himself the way to act naturally at this hour would be to go to bed and stop staring at the mountains, his phone rang. He sat on his bed, threw his blanket over his head to muffle any sounds that could be heard by the men in the hall, and took the call.

Oscar Cardoza spoke with the caller as softly as he could, and he dispassionately acknowledged everything the other party said.

He'd only just hung up from this first call when his phone buzzed again in his hand.

Just as silently as before, he answered.

"Bueno?"

"Cardoza?" As expected, this time it was Lobo.

"Yes."

"Where are you?"

Cardoza said, "I'm where I was an hour ago when you called. I'm in Cinco Lagrimas, in my hotel room. You want to tell me what happened?"

"We engaged the motorcade."

"Go on."

"I lost eleven men, killed or wounded. The enemy lost at least that many. Maybe more."

"They lost four. A lucky strike from one of your RPG crews hit an open hatch and blew a truck up from the inside out."

"Wait . . . How do you know that?"

Cardoza's voice was cold, superior. "I know everything. And I know the security team is now going to be that much more ready for you next time. I also know the Black Knights will be out hunting for you in force. In addition, the UN is probably now wondering if this is a setup by another cartel, which was exactly what I was worried about."

Lobo answered back with confidence that Cardoza found impressive, especially because fifteen percent of his forces had been taken out of the equation tonight. He said, "We'll kill them. We'll kill them all. Los Caballeros Negros will never find us, and we'll move to a position with more time to dig in. Trust me, we *will* destroy the motorcade and the delegation."

"I have a faint recollection of you saying that before."

"Fuck you, Cardoza."

Cardoza chewed the inside of his cheek a moment. It was hot under the blanket, and he rubbed sweat from his eyes. "Would you like me to go to the Sinaloans? Cut your organization out of this plan?"

Lobo didn't miss a beat. "Would you like me to go to your house? Cut your wife's throat?"

"I am divorced, sadly." Cardoza fidgeted with the wedding band on his finger absentmindedly. "Kill her if you want, you would be doing me a favor."

"We are the fuckin' Zetas, pendejo."

Cardoza sniffed. "No, right now you are . . . how many? Sixty-four? Sixty-four men far from home, and you are just one phone call away from getting slaughtered by the Black Knights, whose sicarios number in the thousands. A phone call, I might add, that I myself will make to my new friend, Rafa Archuleta."

He let Lobo fume a moment quietly, then continued. "If you don't do exactly what I tell you to do from now on, I promise you that you will never leave the Devil's Spine, and if you should somehow manage to do so, you will only be met by your own leadership back in Juarez, who will slaughter you for breaking the agreement I have with Los Zetas."

He expected a macho, angry retort from the Zeta war chief, but when nothing came, he nodded, eager to finish the conversation and go to bed. "Find a place to hide to the north of Cinco Lagrimas, far away from the roads, and wait for my signal that the delegation is leaving. However long it takes. *Then* you can engage, and you better get the job done next time."

"I'm not afraid of you."

"Of course not. You aren't intelligent enough to be afraid of me. But you *are* afraid of your masters. Deathly afraid of them. You've seen what they do to those who defy them, and you are just barely smart enough to know you don't want to end up in an oil drum full of acid, so you *will* do what I say, now won't you?"

Lobo hesitated, then hung up the phone, but Cardoza wasn't worried. He knew the man would comply.

His life, and the lives of everyone he loved, depended on it.

CHAPTER 42

I t was well after eleven p.m. when the four vehicles remaining in the Armored Saint motorcade found a partially hidden open field of poppies that gave them a good vantage point to see the winding road around the valley and yet remain shielded from any attacks from the sheer mountain wall above them, and here they positioned their gun trucks, backs to the rock, grilles forward towards the road and valley beyond. Remmick ordered headlights and other white light sources to be kept off, and the men donned headlamps switched to the red filter so they could see one another and still preserve their night vision.

Sentries sat in all the turrets except for Show Horse, and they wore night observation devices and stayed vigilant, gloved hands resting on the buttstocks or barrels of their mounted light machine guns.

The mood was somber. The principals wandered around the poppy field, each lost in their own thoughts now, and security men erected tents and rolled out sleeping bags or dug into chow.

Duff passed a man on Bravo team sitting in the open hatch of Pack Horse One, weeping softly.

Remmick squatted in the poppy field near the road, fifty yards away from the vehicles, talking on his phone to Armored Saint's HQ. Duff had stepped over to Pack Horse One, taking the opportunity to try to talk to Gordon, but his old friend just waved him away, mumbling something about having to do some gun maintenance, so instead, Duff went back to Crazy Horse.

Squeeze manned the turret, and Wolfson, Frenchie, and Cruz broke open a case of MREs and began eating. Gabby Flores looked at a map open across her knees, struggling with the red light on her head to see the small print.

Duff was utterly exhausted; he would rather sit down in his seat and close his eyes, but Dr. Flores had been talking his ear off for most of the last half hour, and he needed a break from that, so instead of climbing back up into the vehicle, he walked around it with Nascar, examining every inch of the armor carefully, making sure the vehicle remained in good working order.

The RPG strike that Charlie team took in the rear was a dark gray scar in the black armor, a one-inch gouge in the armor slats a foot or so below the ballistic glass Cruz had been looking out of, and just to the left of the gunport, which had been open when the rocket hit. Through the glow of their red headlamps, both Nascar and Duff realized how close they'd come to catching an internal detonation, just like what happened to Pack Horse Two.

"Whoever they are, these sons of bitches can shoot," Nascar said, marveling about the accuracy.

"Yeah," Duff replied as he ran a gloved finger over the disfigurement in the steel.

But the armor had held in the rear of Crazy Horse, and the dozens of pockmarks around the truck indicated where machine gun rounds had struck, but they'd done little more than aesthetic damage, even to the windshield.

After Remmick finished his call, he passed by Crazy Horse and told Duff he was convening an immediate meeting of the principals and security team leaders in Show Horse. Duff asked if he could bring Flores along, but Remmick just shook his head and walked off to go tell the others.

Five minutes later Gordon and Duffy sat in the limo, the side and rear hatches closed so that they could use white lights inside.

While Duff waited for the conversation to begin, he looked to his old friend. Despite his dark skin, he appeared pale and drawn, dog-tired and beaten down, not quite in shock but not far from it. Duff's second attempt to console him had also fallen on deaf ears, and now the man just looked out one of the side ports, his M4 carbine pointed down between his knees.

Michelle LaRue entered the cabin, deep in quiet conversation with Reinhardt Helm, who stepped in and took a seat next to her on the bench across from the security contractors, and then the two Mexican officials, Minister Herrera and his second-in-command, Adnan Rodriguez, climbed aboard and sat down quietly on the rear bench. Rodriguez had a brown backpack in his hand, and he put it on the floor and kicked it under the bench below him.

All four of the principals expressed condolences to Duff and Gordon for the loss of more of their colleagues, but Duff tuned it out, again looking at Mike, thinking about what it must have felt like to lose five men.

Gordon, for his part, distractedly nodded his thanks at the sympathy voiced to him, but his eyes remained locked on Rodriguez. Duff noticed this, but Rodriguez didn't seem to be aware.

Soon Remmick climbed in from the outside and pulled the hatch closed again. Duff and Gordon both sat up straighter and became fully involved in the proceedings.

Another round of condolences came from the four VIPs, this time directed at the agent in charge, and then Deputy Director Helm said, "What is your assessment, Mr. Remmick, about who attacked us tonight?"

The AIC had taken his headset off, and it rested on his knee. He rubbed his tired eyes, then his short hair, smearing sweat across his forehead and through his visible scalp. "I don't think this was the work of the Black Knights."

"I agree, totally," Michelle LaRue said with an aggressive nod.

Duff hadn't planned on doing much talking, but he couldn't help himself. "How can you know that, one way or the other?"

Instead of Remmick, it was Adnan Rodriguez who spoke. "Mr. Duffy, the Black Knights want us here, and *need* us here for their own survival. There is no way they would—"

"Then who was it?"

Minister Herrera said, "It was the Sinaloa cartel. An attempt to stop the peace initiative."

Duff looked back to him. "How did the Sinaloans know about the peace initiative? How did they know about the motorcade? How did they know the route we'd take? Either this was the Black Knights, or there is an informant who's tipping off another bad actor here in the Sierras." Duff was all but parroting things Gabby had said to him since the attack, but he felt like she'd raised good questions, so he spoke up here on her behalf.

Michelle LaRue shook her head. "I disagree. The Sinaloa cartel used to run this entire mountain range; they still have forces up here vying for territory. We just ran into them and they attacked us, not knowing who we were or what we were doing. They probably thought *we* were the Black Knights."

Duff sighed, looking to both Remmick and Gordon for help, but received nothing from either. He said, "Do you think the Black Knights drive ten-ton armored personnel carriers around up here? They're in pickup trucks, exactly like the bastards we just fought. And that was a prepared ambush, hastily assembled maybe, but well executed by a force that knew exactly what they were up against. It was *not* a chance encounter."

LaRue turned to Alpha One. "Mr. Remmick, I sympathize with your losses, I truly do, but frankly it sounds like some of your men are getting cold feet. You guys came up here expecting a fight, and now that you've got one, you want to go home. Is that it?"

Remmick said, "Nobody's going home, ma'am."

But Duff persisted, turning his attention to Shane Remmick now. "Sir, this group we fought tonight was twenty-five times better than those goofballs we ran into earlier today. If *those* were Sinaloa, then *these* were something else."

Remmick said, "I am trusting the deputy secretary's assessment, and I say the mission goes forward."

"Sir, can we just bring Dr. Flores in here for her insight into—"

"Negative."

LaRue spoke up again. "That woman doesn't know a thing about diplomacy, or how peacekeeping operations work."

"But she knows these mountains, these people, the narco groups."

LaRue just waved the comment away. Duff was used to being ignored as a security officer, even when—*especially* when—it came to matters of security. Principals often felt their protectors were overly protective, and Duff got that, but considering the fact that five men had died on this mission already, LaRue's dismissive behavior seemed out of line.

But still Remmick said nothing.

Reinhardt Helm cleared his throat, and his German accent all but reverberated around the cab of the vehicle. "If the Black Knights want to destroy the motorcade, all they have to do is wait for us to come to them, when we will surely be outnumbered dozens to one, and do it then. Why would they conduct a"—he looked to Duff now—"as you yourself just said, a hasty ambush, in the mountains, in the dark?"

Duff had no answer to this.

The meeting broke up a few minutes later, the only resolution being that the mission would continue. Gordon exited the vehicle without a word to anyone and walked off in the dark in the direction of Pack Horse One, but Remmick grabbed Duff by the arm when they were both outside and out of earshot of the principals. In a soft and surprisingly conciliatory voice, he said, "Look, Charlie One. You're right. Whoever hit us tonight knew what they were doing. These were military forces, ex-military forces, something like that. Doesn't sound like the Sinaloa cartel, and it doesn't sound like what we know about the Black Knights, either. There's somebody else up here, and there's not shit we can do about it but make it to the Black Knights tomorrow."

He put his headset back on. "Like it or not, we need them to keep us alive up here."

Duff was dumbfounded. When he met Remmick in the Ritz-Carlton in McLean, Virginia, barely a week earlier, Remmick hadn't characterized the mission as the men putting their lives in the hands of a murderous drug cartel.

But that was, apparently, the way things stood at present.

Duff offered up a hoarse "Copy," because he didn't know what else to say, but he knew what he was thinking.

He was thinking this was goddamned insanity for $1,666 a day.

Remmick said, "We'll get through this, son. Have faith." With a pat on Duffy's shoulder, he said, "Go check on Gordon. Make sure he hasn't stuck a pistol in his mouth after losing three fourths of his crew."

CHAPTER 43

Duffy found Gordon behind Pack Horse One, removing his body armor to change into a clean shirt. One of his men, Bravo Six, was up in the turret, and his driver, Bravo Three, the man who had been crying, now appeared to be sound asleep behind the wheel.

Bravos Two, Four, Five, Seven, and Eight were all dead, their bodies left behind on the road, and Duffy couldn't imagine the hell Gordon was going through right now.

"Hey, man. You feel like talking?"

Gordon yanked off his sweat- and dirt-stained shirt, threw it on the ground, and pulled a long-sleeved gray Carhartt thermal over his head, careful to keep from snagging the red headlamp he wore. As he reached to heave his chest rig and armor back on, he said, "Five guys in three days, Duff. You ever hear of anything like that?"

"Not your fault, Gordo. Bad fucking luck. The important thing now is you gotta get your head back in the game."

"The *game*? The game is 'We're all gonna fuckin' die,' and my team is winning."

Duff didn't know the right thing to say, didn't know if there *was* a right thing to say, so he just slapped Gordon on the back and said, "You and me are gonna rally, and we are gonna get through this bullshit."

Gordon put his headset back on now, adjusted the microphone, then reached for his walkie-talkie inside the open hatch of the APC. "They knew we were coming. They were fucking set up for it."

"Yeah, that's what I keep thinking. A three-way ambush like that, four or five trucks in pursuit, dug-in PPK machine guns, a half dozen or more RPGs expended." He just looked at Gordon's face through the red glow of his headlamp. "That sounds like a force that was totally expecting to deal with mobile armor, doesn't it?"

"It does. And what you said back there about an informant, I think you're right, and I think he's right here in the motorcade."

Duff cocked his head. "*In* the motorcade? I don't know about that."

"You guys took an RPG, right?" Gordon asked.

"Yeah."

"Where did it strike?"

"Rear armor, almost went through an open gunport."

The man nodded, his red headlamp rising and lowering in the dark. "My vic caught one on the right side. Low, like they were going for a tire. War Horse has got a big-assed RPG scar on its right rear quarter panel. Again, just above the tire. Pack Horse Two . . ." He paused. "Well, we know they caught one up the belly hatch."

"Yeah," Duff said again.

Gordon plugged his radio back into his headset and slipped it back in a pouch in his armor. While he did this, he raised his eyes at Duff. "Good shooting, huh?"

"Damn good shooting."

"So . . ." Gordon pulled a wad of chewing tobacco out of a pouch and put it behind his lip. Wiping his mouth, he said, "So . . . I walked around the limo just now. It's got some rifle fire, but no RPG strikes. Not one."

Duff saw where Gordon was going with this, and he wasn't buying it. He shrugged. "C'mon, Mike. You know how combat is. Dude next to you dies and you don't get a scratch. A dozen trucks run down a road without incident, the thirteenth triggers an IED. Nobody said shit in this job's got to make any sense."

Gordon stepped closer, brought his voice down a little. "Let me ask you something. The other night in the hotel. You said Rodriguez went back to his room right before the shooting started, right?"

This caught Duff off guard. "That's right."

"That's pretty fucking convenient, isn't it? Also, when he climbed into Show Horse for the meeting, he had his backpack with him. The principals had just been standing around out in a dark poppy field. What the hell he need his pack for? And when he sat down, he made extra sure to secure that shit under his bench, all casual like, but I was watching, and he was looking to see if we were looking."

Duff cocked his head now. "Are you saying you think the assistant to the Mexican deputy secretary of the interior is feeding intel to the enemy?"

Gordon spit, shrugged. "I'm sayin' if we go shake that sharp-dressed motherfucker down, I bet we find a phone on him he's not supposed to have."

Duff sighed. He wasn't convinced at all, but he knew Gordon was a mess at the moment. He said, "Let's talk to Remmick about it."

Mike Gordon slung his M4 around his neck again, letting it hang behind his back with the barrel facing down. "I've got an even better idea, kid. How about we talk to Remmick when we have something to talk to him about?"

"What do you mean by—"

Gordon began stomping off in the direction of Show Horse. Duff stood there, but only for a moment.

"Son of a bitch," he muttered, and then he hurried after Bravo One.

The four principals were still inside their massive APC, eating rations now from foil bags and drinking bottled water. The door was open, so the lights were off, but a couple of red headlamps had been turned on, hanging from hooks on the interior walls of the cabin, giving an eerie view to the scene.

Gordon looked in; Duff stepped up behind him and put a hand on Bravo One's arm, trying to dissuade him from going forward. He knew if they found nothing on Rodriguez, then Remmick and the principals would be beyond furious for the intrusion.

But Gordon wasn't thinking straight, and he shook off the hand, kept staring inside the APC.

Michelle LaRue drank water from a plastic bottle, but lowered it when she saw the two contractors staring in. "Can we help you?"

Mike Gordon said, "No, ma'am, just a routine security check."

Reinhardt Helm cocked his head. "A *what*?"

Suddenly, Gordon shined a bright white flashlight into the eyes of Adnan Rodriguez. Everyone recoiled in the glare. "Sir, I'm gonna need you to step out of the vehicle. Bring your backpack along with you."

Rodriguez did not move. He just sat there, rigid, and Duff looked in and instantly recognized fear on the man's face.

Oh shit, he thought. *This dude is hiding something.*

Herrera spoke up now. "What is going on, Señor Gordon?"

The security contractor ignored the deputy secretary. Gordon said, "Rodriguez, either you come outta there, or I come in and get you."

Rodriguez looked to the other principals for help, and he got it in the form of the deputy director of peacekeeping operations.

Helm's voice boomed. "What has happened? What is it you think this man has done?"

Gordon shined the light on the man from the UN. "This doesn't involve you."

"Everything on this mission involves me!"

Gordon shifted the beam back on Rodriguez. "I know how you Mexicans like spicy food, but have you ever been pepper-sprayed, my man?"

Herrera said, "This is absolutely outrageous."

LaRue added to the chorus. "What's wrong with you? Get that damn light out of his face!"

But Gordon stood firm, and Duff stood back. Slowly Adnan Rodriguez reached down and grabbed a backpack, but it wasn't the one he'd brought into the vehicle before the meeting. Gordon missed this, said nothing, but Duff did not, and although he'd wanted to stay out of it at the beginning, Duff found himself fully caught up in the proceedings now.

He shined his own flashlight on the correct backpack. "That's the bag we need to take a peek at. Bring it with you, please, sir."

With poorly hidden reluctance, Adnan Rodriguez took hold of the pack and climbed out.

Gordon yanked the bag from his hand and passed it to Duff, then expertly turned Rodriguez around to where he was facing the vehicle next to the open hatch. "Hands on the armor."

"But—"

"Like I said, totally routine." He kicked Rodriguez's legs apart, pushed him up against the truck roughly, and began frisking him.

Now the other three principals were demanding an explanation, climbing out of the APC, but the American contractors were so assertive, so self-assured, that it seemed no one really expected to be listened to.

Duff began looking through Rodriguez's backpack with his red headlamp, while Gordon checked the man's pockets.

Gordon's frisk turned up nothing. Duff's anxiety grew by the second, thinking of the verbal beating he was in for in a matter of moments by Remmick if he didn't find anything, but he kept digging, hoping like hell he'd have something to show for this decidedly undiplomatic incident.

There were clothes, writing tablets, a bag with some prescription medication.

An outside pocket was zipped closed. Duff squeezed it and felt something inside, so he opened it and reached in.

Bingo. He instantly recognized the shape and feel of a satellite phone.

He pulled it out. "What's this look like, Mike?"

Gordon stepped back and put his hands on his hips, his rifle hanging across his chest. "That's a Thuraya Hughes. Older model, but it gets the job done. Don't it, Rodriguez?"

Rodriguez looked back over his shoulder at the phone and adopted an expression of stunned confusion that Duff didn't buy for a moment, but he said nothing.

Remmick appeared in the red glow around the APC; Herrera and LaRue and Helm were now all standing around the scene.

"What the hell is going on here?" the AIC asked.

Gordon said, "Rodriguez here had a sat phone stashed in his backpack. Probably the one he's been using to communicate to the outside."

"No," Rodriguez said. "I haven't been—"

Remmick glared at the young Mexican government official, an instant rage of fury that Duff hadn't expected. "Shut the fuck up!" He took the phone from Duff and looked it over, then turned to Herrera. "Did you know about this?"

Duff thought the deputy secretary's stunned countenance appeared utterly authentic. "I . . . I don't believe it. Adnan?"

"¡Le prometo! No communique con nadia con respecto—"

Gordon launched at the man, slamming him against the hull of Show Horse.

"Speak English, motherfucker!"

"I . . ." Rodriguez turned around and faced the group. He appeared to be on the edge of tears. "I . . ."

"You *what*?" Remmick barked.

"I brought the phone. Yes. But only to communicate with a . . . friend in Mexico City. You can check the call log."

Herrera turned to his assistant. "*What* friend?"

With a dramatic wince, the younger man said, "It's . . . a girl. She's my . . . girlfriend. She's pregnant. Nine months. Due any day. I couldn't just—"

"You're married," Herrera said flatly, clearly disbelieving his assistant.

Another wince. "It's complicated, señor. But it is the truth. I am not working against this delegation. I have only texted with her, checking on her. I've spoken with no one else."

Remmick called out for Alpha Two, his second-in-command. When the man appeared out of the dark, he tossed the phone to him. "Check it out. See who he called or texted, when the contacts were made."

"On it, boss." The man turned and headed back into the darkness towards War Horse.

"I promise you," Rodriguez repeated. "I have not imperiled this mission." Turning to Herrera, he said, "Deputy Secretary, you know I am the one who laid the groundwork for the—"

Herrera turned his back on the younger man. "Mr. Remmick. Please accept my apologies. This should not have happened. I'm certain my assistant had no intention of causing any problems, and he is no threat to this mission." He turned to Rodriguez. "Other than by his stupidity."

Remmick sighed audibly. "Herrera, he's your second-in-command. You really knew nothing about this?"

"I knew *nothing* about a satellite phone. I agreed to the terms of the security protocols in good faith. I thought we all did."

Remmick nodded, seemingly deep in thought a moment. "Minister Herrera, Deputy Director Helm, Miss LaRue. I'm going to send members of my team over here to go through all your personal belongings. If I find any other communication devices, I will have no other choice but to end this mission."

Duff, Gordon, and Remmick himself began going through the bags while the principals stood in silence. Gabby Flores appeared, clearly confused by what was going on, so Duff explained the situation.

Rodriguez sat down in the open door of the APC; he'd been admonished repeatedly by Herrera, but no one else had spoken to him.

The search of the principals' luggage took ten minutes. Three Alpha men, Duff, and Gordon all performed the check, and as they all finished going through the last bit of Michelle LaRue's rolling duffel bag, Alpha Two's voice came over the interteam radio net. The principals couldn't hear him, but the Armored Saint contractors could, as could Flores, who was wearing a headset herself.

"Alpha Two for Actual."

"Actual," Remmick said. "What you got, Vance?"

Duff listened in to the commo. "Yeah, boss, he's got some software on here to delete his messages as soon as he sends them. I can't see *what* he texted, but I can see that he sent five messages today, the most recent about two hours ago."

"To the same number?"

"Yep, all of them a 667 area code."

Gabby Flores gasped, and the three Americans standing next to her turned her way.

Softly, glancing at an unaware Rodriguez sitting fifteen feet away, she said, "Culiacán. Sinaloa."

Remmick raised an eyebrow. "That right?"

She nodded.

Now the AIC turned to Rodriguez. "Where's this baby mama of yours, Rodriguez?"

"The *what*?"

"Your girl. Where does she live?"

"I told you already. She's in Mexico City. Where I live."

"Okay. So who were you reaching out to in Sinaloa?"

Rodriguez appeared confused. He leapt to his feet and started walking up to Remmick. "*What?* No one! I have not messaged anyone in Sina—"

Mike Gordon took a single step forward and slammed his fist into Adnan Rodriguez's jaw, dropping the smaller man flat to the ground on his back.

"Mike!" Duff shouted, grabbing him from behind and pulling him away.

Gordon screamed now. "Motherfucker got my Joes killed! And it's not over! The bastards who hit us tonight know where we are, where we're goin'. They know how many are in the unit, what weapons we have, what tactics we've been using. They know every last thing because of that bag of shit lying there in the dirt! He's killed all of us!" He pointed to the principals. "You, too. We're all dead."

Remmick spun Gordon around to face him. With barely contained fury he said, "Well, Bravo One, *whoever* he was in contact with will remain a mystery for now because you've knocked him the fuck out!"

"To hell with him."

285

Remmick looked to Duff. "Don't let him do that again."

"Yeah, boss." Duff took Gordon by both shoulders, but to Remmick he said, "Sir . . . this mission is compromised. We have to end it! Now."

To Duff's astonishment, Remmick shook his head. "Negative. This wasn't the Black Knights. They already knew we were coming, how many of us there are. They would have no need for a man on the inside tipping them off. Whoever Rodriguez was talking to needed his intel. There's someone else up on this mountain who doesn't want this mission to proceed. We are just a few hours away from the Black Knights, and once we make it to them tomorrow, we'll be fine."

Flores looked to Duff, then said, "He's right. If we turn around now, we'll have to go back through the gauntlet we just went through. Our chances are not good either way, but at this point, they might be better with Los Caballeros Negros."

Remmick said, "I'm gonna zip-tie Rodriguez myself and put him in War Horse. He can ride point for the duration of this mission." He ordered a couple of Alpha men over to help carry the Mexican diplomat off.

The two from the UN were silent now, but Herrera said, "Señor Remmick, I object to—"

"I'm in charge of security. We do it *my* way. When we get you to your meeting in one piece, *then* you can make the rules about the negotiations."

Herrera conceded the argument. "Yes . . . fine. But it is very important that the Black Knights not learn about what has happened. If they find out one of the government delegation was working for their enemy, there is no way they will trust us in the negotiations."

Remmick understood. "They are expecting four of you, not three. I'll keep Rodriguez out of sight while we are with the BKs, but coming up with a story about what happened to him is your problem."

"It's no problem at all. I'll think of something."

Remmick squared up to Gordon now.

"Mike. This mission is ongoing. That means I need you to be in command of your men and your vehicle. You copy?"

Gordon nodded. "Solid copy, boss. Just had to get that out of my system. I'm good to go."

Remmick nodded, then glanced at Duffy.

"Deal with him."

"Yeah, boss." Duff began walking Bravo One away. "C'mon, Gordo, I'll take you back to your vic." Gabby Flores followed behind.

CHAPTER 44

Nichole Duffy stood in a gymnasium at Northern Virginia Community College, divvying up supplies to the three women working with her tonight. She was efficient and professional with her actions, but her mind was a couple thousand miles away, like it had been the last several evenings while working.

It was midnight now, and this was her second job since seven p.m., having first cleaned a bank in Rosslyn with her team. And after she finished here at NVCC, she and the ladies would head to their third location of the night, a penthouse apartment in Crystal City that needed a quick once-over before being photographed to go on the market the day after tomorrow.

She'd get off work at six a.m., then try to get a couple hours' sleep while the kids watched cartoons.

She was exhausted, but she wasn't thinking about herself right now. She separated from the others, hefted a janitorial cleaning caddy full of supplies, and headed to the men's locker room. She was pleasantly surprised to find it wasn't as bad as she'd feared, and she began with the mirrors, spraying glass cleaner and wiping it off.

She'd told Josh not to worry about her, to only call when he had time and to keep his focus on his mission, but she'd spent the last three hours hoping her phone would start chirping.

Just like the previous couple of nights.

She was fifteen minutes into the locker room clean—she'd just sprayed foamy grout cleanser in the showers—when the sound she'd been praying for chimed in her right ear. She touched her cheap Bluetooth earbud to accept the call and hurried out of the locker room and into the gym, hoping for a clearer signal.

"Josh?"

There was a brief pause, and Nichole's excitement turned to worry.

"Josh? That you?"

"It's me."

She could hear torment in his voice, even worse than in their previous conversations. "What is it? What's wrong?"

"We . . . we got hit hard tonight, Nik."

She sat down on the bleachers overlooking the basketball court. "Again?"

"Not like before. This was a mobile pursuit pushing us into an L-shaped ambush. Unknown number of enemy, but . . . it was . . . had to have been fifty, sixty. Military equipment. Military precision. Military competence."

"My God, Josh. Losses?"

"Me and my guys are okay. Alpha team and the principals are okay." He paused, breathed into the phone for a moment, then, "A Bravo team APC with an open hatch took an RPG. Four more of Mike's men got killed."

Tears had already begun welling in her eyes, but now they flowed. Sadness and pain. Anguish and worry. She tried to sniff away the tears. "Five KIA. Jesus, Josh, you've got to get the hell out of there."

"It gets worse. One of the Mexican dips had a clandestine sat phone. We think he was in comms with the Sinaloa cartel up here, dead set on having the army come in and rout out the Black Knights."

"You can't even trust the people you are there to protect?" She brought her shoulders back and sat up straighter. Her voice rose, all but echoing in the gym. "I want you to come home. Tell me you will turn around right now."

"I've still got people to protect. Anyway, we couldn't if we wanted to. Turning around means going back through the shit we just went through."

"And what does 'going forward' mean?"

"I don't know, to be honest."

"How long on the QRF?"

Her husband did not reply. "Josh? The QRF. Remmick called it in, right? They're still en route?"

Still nothing, but she could hear him breathing.

"You've lost nearly twenty percent of your detail. *Please*, tell me the QRF is on the—"

Josh interrupted now. "Nikki. There *is* no QRF. We're on our own."

The cinching pain in her heart fell into her stomach. She began breathing hard, staring across a gym floor but looking into the abyss. "What do you mean? You told me—"

"We can call the Mexican army, but they won't fly in. There are shoulder-fired SAMs up here somewhere."

"SAMs? In the mountains?"

"Yeah. It'll take the army a day to get here by land, and the Black Knights will sure as hell open up on them when they arrive, and wipe us out for being with them. We're better off going on ahead without any backup."

"Josh . . . you *know* this is insanity. You *have* to—"

Nichole stopped talking when she heard another voice. Quickly she realized it was coming from Josh's radio, probably over the speakers in his truck.

"Alpha Actual to all actuals. Herrera has just learned we have about a five-hour movement north in the a.m. before we meet the BKs. Rotate your security to get your Joes some sleep. Morning briefing at zero-five-thirty."

"I've got to go, babe," Josh said over the phone.

She heard Mike Gordon's voice now. He sounded distant. Distracted. "Bravo One copies."

"Josh. Talk to me. What do you want me to do?"

"Charlie One copies," Josh said, obviously to Remmick, and then he turned his attention back to his phone call. "Kiss the kids and say a prayer for us. I love you."

"Josh, wait. You can do this. I know you can."

But her husband had already hung up the phone.

Forty-five minutes later Nichole had not returned to her cleaning crew. Instead, she sat at a computer terminal in the NVCC library, Google Maps open in front of her, and she took notes on a notepad. She'd already researched the names of the top employees of Armored Saint, and read decidedly less-than-stellar accounts of the company's practices around the globe.

As she racked her brain for ways to find more information, a thought occurred to her. It was one hell of a long shot, but she knew a man who might be able to fill in her knowledge gaps on the subject of western Mexico, the cartels, and the UN.

She Googled a name, found what she was looking for, then wrote down a number on her pad.

Seconds later she made the call, and though it was after ten p.m. in the location she was calling, it was answered on the second ring.

"Henderson Aviation. Max Henderson speaking."

"Max? It's Nikki Duffy."

There was a short pause. "Nikki . . . who?"

"Oh, sorry. Nichole Duffy."

Now there was a longer pause. "I'm not sure . . . sorry, we meet in a bar or something?"

She realized her racing mind wasn't making this easy. "I'm sorry. You know me as Captain Martin."

Now the man answered quickly, his tone adjusted to comport with the person he was speaking with. "Yes, ma'am! I'm sorry about that. It's been a hell of a long time, is all. How are you?"

"I'm okay, how about you?"

"Doing great. Good to hear from you. Jeez, you still in Virginia? Must be past midnight."

She replied, "I was talking to Chief Brunetti last year, he's still in the battalion."

"Yeah, I ran into Scotty myself a few months ago."

"He mentioned you were down in El Paso. You'd started that aviation company you told me about."

"Your info is accurate, ma'am. I've got five aircraft—well, I lease them, anyway. We fly out of El Paso and Tucson. Eight pilots on the payroll, plus myself. Contracts with DHS, Commerce, DEA, State, we operate all over Central and even South America. It's not gunships in Afghanistan and Iraq like the bad old days, but it's a living." Henderson was clearly proud of his success and happy to talk about it.

"That's terrific. You are just the man I want to talk to."

"Really? About what?"

"I was wondering if you might have information about what's going on in Mexico these days. Specifically, up in the Sierra Madre mountains."

He whistled softly. "I'm not flying up *there*. That's no-man's-land. Black Knights territory. Sinaloa cartel is up there fighting them, and the army is getting ready to surge up into the range and cause real havoc."

"Yeah," she said softly. "That's what I hear. I'm just looking for some intel. What the army's plan is. Who the players are there, that kind of stuff."

"You making your summer vacation plans?" he joked.

"Not quite. You know anything about a UN peace initiative?"

Henderson thought a moment. "No. Haven't heard about that, but I'm just a pilot. I'm not read into anybody's intelligence product other than what I need to do my job. If it's something they're working on in back channels, I'm gonna learn about it on the news, same as you, probably."

Nichole drummed her fingers on the little table. "Where do they send you in Mexico?"

"Depends. I'm flying a Grand Caravan myself down to Hermosillo the day after tomorrow. Just cargo for one of the three-letter agencies." He cleared his throat. "What's this all about?"

"It's about Josh. He's doing contract work for the UN down there."

"Cool." He paused, then asked, "You . . . you don't mean in the Sierra Madres?"

"Unfortunately, yes."

"Dear God. I hope he's not alone."

"He's not alone, but he's not exactly rolling around with the Third ID. He's working for Armored Saint."

Henderson whistled softly. "The hell's he doing that for?"

Nichole closed her eyes. "Because he's desperate, Chief."

"Jesus Christ." This pause was longer. "Look, I know a guy in Dallas who works at AS's U.S. HQ. He's an exec, does a lot of hiring and firing, I guess. I'm happy to ask him about their mission down there, but I'm not going to learn anything your husband doesn't already know."

"What Josh knows and what I know are probably not the same." She sighed. "I have suspicions he isn't being exactly candid about what's going on. They had five contractors killed in the past few days. He says they are safe going forward, but . . ."

"But you're still Captain Nichole Martin, and you can't just sit home helpless while your husband is downrange."

Nichole squeezed her eyes shut. "I just need to know what's happening."

"Yes, ma'am," the older man said. "I'm happy to ask around."

Nichole Duffy hung up the phone a minute later and walked back to the locker room, unsure how she was going to concentrate on scrubbing grout right now.

CHAPTER 45

The specter of death hung in the air over the small encampment as dawn broke. Men in gun turrets fought exhaustion, their eyes on the valley breaking in front of them but their minds on the horror of the evening before. Men began breaking camp while the VIPs woke in their tents, another night on the hard ground, another night without a hot meal.

Gordon organized his vehicle with his two remaining contractors; Duff kept mostly to himself and away from Dr. Flores—her constant prognostication of doom was the last thing in the world he needed right now.

The four remaining Armored Saint trucks were packed up and ready to go by six a.m., roughly the same time the three team leaders finished their morning brief.

Duff returned to Crazy Horse to find Frenchie holding a thermos.

"Morning, boss. I made some coffee on the gas stove. It is instant, terrible, but it *is* caffeine."

"There's no such thing as bad coffee." Duff took the thermos and downed a slow sip. "I stand corrected."

"You're welcome."

Wolfson was on the turret at the moment, and Duff called him down, asked everyone to meet at the hood of Crazy Horse. When everyone congregated around Charlie One, he said, "All right, men, Gabby. I just talked to Remmick. We're leaving in ten mikes. We should arrive at our destination around eleven a.m."

"What's our destination?" Wolfson asked.

"Herrera just spoke with the Black Knights. We keep heading north along this road, then turn off to go a few klicks east to a village called Cinco Lagrimas. We are to pull in slowly, park along the square, and wait."

"Wait for what?" Cruz asked Duff, but Squeeze was the first to reply.

"Another RPG up the ass, probably."

Duff ignored him and continued. "At some point the Black Knights leadership will show up. You can figure on a sizable security contingent with Archuleta, but how big, we don't know. When they arrive, the VIPs will conduct their meetings with the Black Knights in a municipal building there off the square."

Duff turned to Gabby now. "Know anything about this town?"

She nodded. "Cinco Lagrimas is just over the border in Chihuahua State, not in Sinaloa. I was there once while I was in college, many years ago. I remember a little town with a pretty square. Colonial style. Down in a gorge but still high on the Spine. It's surrounded on all sides by rock walls. It's about ten miles from the lip of the canyon."

"What canyon?" Frenchie asked.

To this Gabby smiled. "Only the most beautiful canyon you've ever seen. Mexiquillo. Eight thousand feet deep."

Nascar whistled. "Eight thousand! That's like a mile and a half."

Cruz spoke up now. "Gabby, why is it called Cinco Lagrimas?"

"I have no idea."

Cruz turned to the others on his team. "It means 'five tears.' Kind of a weird name for a town, don't you think?"

"Sounds inviting," Nascar joked.

Duff refocused on the team's duties for the day. "It's a town, so lots of angles to defend if shit kicks off. Remmick wants us to roll in ready for anything. If shit *does* kick off, Alpha will get the principals back into the vics, and we'll unass the area. How copy?"

Gabby said, "If the Black Knights attack us, four tanks won't be enough to protect us."

Duff sighed a little. "Four tanks would be a damn fine start, Gabby. But these aren't tanks." He shook her comment off. "We'll be fine," he said, but he knew he didn't sound that convincing.

CHAPTER 46

The drive across nearly impassable roads lasted five hours, but it felt like five days on the joints of the seven personnel bouncing around in Crazy Horse. The mood remained somber and serious because of the ambush last night, the knowledge that the enemy had been getting real-time intelligence from inside the convoy, and the unknowns of going forward into the jaws of a bloodthirsty drug cartel. Seventeen men in four trucks could cause a lot of damage, but ultimately they all knew that in a real fight with the Black Knights, their guns would be pissing into the wind.

The bouncing threatened to lull Duff to sleep, but he fought it, finished Frenchie's shit coffee, and soldiered on, his eyes both scanning his sector and keeping an eye on the road itself, ready to leap into action if Nascar nodded off.

Just after eleven a.m., Nascar pointed at something in front of him. "Check it out, boss."

Duff followed his driver's eyes and saw that just up ahead, Pack Horse One bounced off the rutted dirt road they'd been traveling and up onto a paved road that appeared to be brand new.

"That's real flattop," Nascar said. "Like a regular road. Haven't seen one of these for a minute."

Gabby Flores was sitting just behind the two front-seaters. "I'll take it," she said. "We've been getting knocked around for days."

The drive smoothed out for Crazy Horse when they rolled onto the road, and soon Remmick radioed that the town was just up ahead.

Squeeze had been seated in the cabin next to Frenchie, but he instantly popped his hatch.

Simultaneously he broadcast, "Up and on the 48, ready for one of these motherfuckers to try—"

"Copy," Duff interrupted. "Just chill out. Anything we start from this point forward is gonna be finished by the other side."

"Well, I sure as shit am not gonna sit here and take fire without firing back."

"Nobody expects you to. Just keep your finger off the trigger and report what you see."

"Solid copy, Eleven-B."

Asshole, Duff thought, but as he looked out the dirty windshield into the late-morning glare, his mind wasn't on his turret gunner. It was on the other side of this equation.

A town materialized around a bend: two-, three-, and four-story colonial buildings, neat streets, trucks parked in rows in lots, bright bougainvillea covering whitewashed walls that ran along narrow but well-kept sidewalks.

There were no vehicles running on the streets at all, and no one out strolling, either.

It appeared to be a ghost town.

"Charlie team," Duff said, "keep an eye on the buildings. Rooftops, windows. Hell . . . everything."

Duff instantly noted that there was no trash, no urban decay here in Cinco Lagrimas. They'd passed two dozen towns in the past few days, and this was the first that looked like an idyllic colonial village.

Remmick's voice came from the second vehicle. "We aren't seeing anybody out here. War Horse? What you got?"

War Horse was in the front, with Alpha Two in command. "Alpha Two, Alpha Actual. We spot one armed fighting-age male, just a guy in a doorway with a rifle on his shoulder. Not posing a threat."

"Copy that," Alpha One said. "I want every armed individual called out."

Squeeze benefited from his 360-degree view in the turret of the rear vehicle. "It's weird that we don't see but one of Archuleta's men, isn't it?"

"Yeah, we do," Wolfson replied. "I tally a second gunner. Five o'clock, second story of that brown building."

"All the buildings are brown," Cruz said from the rear.

"The one with the red Coca-Cola sign."

"Got it," Cruz said. "I see him."

Frenchie added, "I have two armed men in the alley on our left."

"What are they doing?" Duff asked.

"Just . . . just watching us."

"Cruz? Your guy?"

"AK on his chest, he's just a sentry, doesn't feel like he's lookin' to start taking potshots."

Now Nascar spoke up. "Boss, I tally one tango, eleven o'clock high, in the bell tower on the left side of the church."

"I see him," Duff confirmed.

Remmick's voice broadcast again. "Alpha One to all trucks. We've got multiple armed males up here in the town square. Not an aggressive posture at this time. They're just watching us like they expected us. Everyone proceed with caution. We'll do a lap around the square and park where instructed."

Squeeze said, "I've got more gunners in the street behind us. Weapons are down. They are walking around like they own the place."

Gabby said, "Because they do. This village is the property of the Black Knights. That's why there is no decay, no dirt, no trash, no graffiti, no crime."

"No crime?" Wolfson said. "It's a fucking drug cartel."

"I mean no petty street crime," Gabby clarified.

"Awesome," Nascar quipped. "Don't have to worry about my car stereo getting boosted. I guess I can relax."

The motorcade drove a slow lap around the town square, and then they came around to the front of the three-story-tall colonial municipal building. War Horse, then Show Horse, then Pack Horse One, and finally Crazy Horse slowed even more now. As the first vehicles began to park, Duff said, "Nascar, keep us behind Pack Horse One."

Squeeze said, "Yo, TL. Can we just start calling it Pack Horse, seein' how there's only one of them left?"

Duff sighed a little. "Guess so."

Nascar stopped the truck for the first time in over five hours. "Leave the engine running, boss?"

"Hell yeah. For now, anyway."

Remmick ordered the other trucks to stand by. No one dismounted from any of the vehicles; they just sat there, rumbling alongside an empty square of green with a large empty fountain in the middle. Gunports were open, eyes scanned all around; every single armed individual in the streets, the windows, or on the rooftops was tallied and called out by a member of the detail.

There were over twenty gunmen, but they appeared utterly relaxed. Probably, Duff reasoned, because they didn't consider four armored trucks to be any real threat.

That would only be the case, he surmised, if there were a hell of a lot more than twenty guys armed with AKs out here.

After a five-minute wait, Duff was relieved to hear Remmick's voice again. "All call signs. Minister Herrera is in comms with the BKs at this time. We've been given the go-ahead to dismount, break." After a pause, he then said, "Charlie One, Alpha One. I'm sending the VIPs over to Crazy Horse. You are principal protection while me and Alpha coordinate with the Black Knights on our security posture outside. You are to take the VIPs into the municipal building; the locals will search you there. Follow our hosts' instructions, report if you have any issues. We'll trade positions after my meeting out here in the park with BK security."

Duff depressed the button on his handset. "*Search* us, sir?"

"Affirm. We can expect that this advance force of Black Knights standing around is going to want to check us over. Everybody just relax. This is all part of the agreement. They have agreed *not* to take your guns; they are just looking for cameras and recording devices."

"Copy," Duff said, but he didn't like it.

Behind him, Wolfson said, "Awesome, we're about to get a body cavity search by a bunch of armed thugs."

Nascar turned off the engine, put his hand on the door, and looked to his boss. "Not liking this part, Duff."

"As opposed to all the other parts of this mission that you found so enjoyable?"

The man with the Alabama accent shrugged. "Fair point."

Duff opened his own door. "Squeeze, you stay on that MG. Everybody else, out. Dr. Flores, you're on my shoulder at all times we're dismounted, with one exception. If any shooting starts, I want you away from me, as fast as possible. I'll be returning fire, which means I'll be *taking* fire. If you see me raise my weapon, you run. Make a beeline back to Crazy Horse on your own. Don't wait to be told. My guys will get to you and put you back in the truck."

"I understand," Gabby said.

Gabby and five men from Charlie team met the VIPs in the street, and together they began walking towards the municipal building. Armed men stood on the stairs outside, but the front door was being held open, and none of the Mexicans were adopting any sort of a threatening posture.

Still, Duff and the other armed men around the protectees kept their gloved hands on the grips of their rifles.

Gabby was right at Duff's shoulder, just as she'd been instructed. So close he leaned to her and whispered as they walked.

"What do you make of these guys we see?"

"Narcos. No doubt. They are just estacas, though, not sicarios."

"I know what a sicario is. A killer. What's an estaca?"

"It means 'fence post.' It's what they call the lower-quality soldiers working for the cartel. Not so much training, but dangerous because—"

Duff interrupted, "Because they aren't pros, they're quick on the trigger, they don't have the discipline to follow orders, and are probably stupid."

"So you *do* know about estacas, then?"

Duff sniffed out a dry laugh. "Dr. Flores, every country I've ever worked in, including my own, has idiot assholes with guns trying to prove themselves to some big shot. So yeah, I know fence posts. My world is full of them."

Gabby looked around just as they got to the sidewalk. "Rain. A lot of it."

"What's that?"

"It's going to rain. This area gets incredible showers in the afternoons this time of year."

Michelle LaRue was right behind them, and she heard this. "There's barely a cloud in the sky."

"Rain," Gabby said again.

Now they took the stairs. Wolfson and Frenchie were the first two in the building; they soon stepped back out and waved the others forward seconds later. The expressions on their faces indicated they were completely switched on.

Reinhardt Helm stepped up to Duffy as they entered. Softly, he said, "This is the difficult part. I hope your men are prepared for some unfortunate but necessary indignities so we can move along with the proceedings?"

"As long as they don't take our guns, our body armor, our vehicles, or our radios, then we'll be fine."

LaRue said, "This was all arranged above your pay grade, Mr. Duffy. You'll just have to go with the flow."

They started up a short hallway, where armed men were waiting for them outside an interior door.

"With respect, ma'am," Duff said, "I'm not gonna tell you how to set up your refugee camps. Don't tell me how to run—"

LaRue snapped now. "Refugees are people from other countries. We will be setting up camps for the internally displaced persons. The IDP population will—"

But Helm just said, "Michelle, not now."

Duff stepped in front of the rest so that he would be the first up to the group of ten or so armed men. They all wore ball caps, boots, jeans. They looked relatively fit and healthy. These weren't drugged-out fence posts; these were the interior perimeter of security.

They were young, not one of them over twenty-five, and even their weapons were obviously of higher grade. Their rifles had modern optics on them, body armor looked new, and the radios they wore were of the same quality that Duff and his men carried.

Behind him, he heard Squeeze mutter, "Well, shit. We just bumped up against the A-Team."

The Black Knights men fanned out in the hallway, their rifles still hanging down behind their backs and their pistols still in their drop leg holsters. One of their number spoke in Spanish, authoritatively.

"Manos arribas todos."

Gabby said, "He wants you all to put your hands up."

She did as instructed, and the delegation members did the same.

Duff raised his own hands. "Do it, Charlie team, but if they try to remove your weapons, push them off."

Behind him, Michelle LaRue said, "Nobody's pushing anybody."

"They don't get our guns, ma'am."

The pat-downs happened simultaneously. Duff stood compliantly as a young man checked him over carefully. Behind him, however, he heard Nascar speak, annoyance in his voice.

"Hey, buddy, take it easy."

"Chill, Nascar," Duff said.

"I'm chill, but this dude's tryna stick his hands down my pants."

Squeeze spoke up. "TL says they get to grab our junk all they want, just not our weps."

Duff rolled his eyes. "I definitely did *not* say that."

Now Wolfson started complaining. "Hands off the rifle, asshole."

"Keep your tone firm but respectful," Duff admonished.

Wolfson amended himself. "Hands off the rifle, *Señor* Asshole."

Just then, the man feeling through Duff's body armor unfastened his radio pouch and started taking the device out.

Duff said, "No, no, those are just our team radios. Tell him, Gabby, he's not getting them."

Flores said, "Señor, estos son los radios para comunicaciones entre el equipo de seguridad."

The man replied to her, and suddenly other Charlie team members began arguing with the Black Knights, because the BKs were attempting to secure all the team radios. Cruz yelled at a man in Spanish, and the man yelled back.

Reinhardt Helm had just completed being frisked, and he stepped up to Duff, looking at the man arguing with him.

"What is the problem here?"

Gabby said, "They are insisting no recording devices."

"They're fuckin' radios," Nascar said. "Do these dipshits not know what a radio looks like?"

Cruz said, "They've got the same ones on their chest rigs. They're just fucking with us, boss. Trying to remove our commo."

"Look, Gabby," Duff said, "tell them we need those so we can stay in communication with one another."

"I'll tell them again." She did so, but the men continued pulling at the equipment. All five Charlie men were resisting, and the situation felt to Duff like it could quickly get out of hand.

Michelle LaRue said, "Duffy, just give them your damn radios!"

But Helm's German-accented voice boomed in the hallway. "No! This was not part of the plan. You keep your weapons and your radios, but the Black Knights have authority over your movements."

Herrera said, "I agree, Deputy Director Helm." He turned to the gunmen, addressing them for the first time. "Los oficiales se quedan sus radios o esta reunion no se hace."

"No pueden quedárselos."

Gabby said, "He says you can't keep the radios."

Herrera turned to the UN peacekeeping official. "Look, Deputy Director, our bodyguards still get to keep their weapons. Maybe we give up the radios in the sake of diplomacy. We allow this one change to the agreement for the benefit of—"

But Reinhardt Helm wasn't having it. "Dr. Flores. Thank the gentlemen for their time today. We are leaving. Ask them to tell Señor Archuleta that since the rules have obviously changed to something we have not agreed to, we won't be able to continue our discussions at the present time."

The argument only heated up after she passed this on, and Gabby wasn't translating it at present, so Duff concentrated on keeping his men from lifting their weapons to their shoulders and escalating this even further.

Finally, after a minute more of yelling and grabbing, the Black Knights security men stopped when one of their number took a call on his radio, then held up a hand.

He looked to Gabby.

"Está bien quédense con los radios."

"Gracias, Señor," she replied. To Duff she said, "You can keep them."

They were then told they'd be taken to a conference room on the second floor, and while they ascended, Duff shouldered up to Helm.

"Deputy Director? Thanks for that back there."

"Of course. You boys don't stand a chance if the Black Knights decide to fight, but there is no reason to make the fight even more lopsided by taking away your communications."

"Thanks for the vote of confidence."

"I am German. We value facts and statistics. I'm also a soldier. I know what happens when comms break down."

"True enough."

In the conference room, the three members of the delegation found seats around a simple oak table. Charlie, Gabby, and the BK security forces stood around the sides of the room, waiting, but soon Shane Remmick entered, followed by three other Alpha contractors. He stepped up to Duff. "What's the situation?"

"All good, sir. Under control."

"Excellent. I have three more of my men on the way up. When they arrive, get your team back to Crazy Horse. Coordinate with Bravo to establish security on the east side of the municipal building. Alpha Two will take the west side, and I'll take close protection of the

VIPs inside the building. This will probably last all day, into the night."

"Roger, Alpha," Duff said.

While they were talking, Gabby made her way over to the deputy director.

Softly, she said, "Deputy Director Helm. May I sit in on the meeting? I am the only person in our entourage who knows the area, and I worry Archuleta will use your ignorance of the territory against us."

LaRue was seated on Helm's right. "I wasn't born here, Dr. Flores, but I've been doing this for a long time. I'll call for you if I have any questions."

Remmick stepped up behind Gabby now and put a guiding hand on her shoulder. "You work for me, remember? I want you outside, advising the security detail."

She sighed. "You haven't asked me for one piece of advice in four days. What expertise will you suddenly need while we're parked outside in the rain?"

Remmick grinned at her now. "It's not raining, Gabby. Maybe your expertise of the area isn't as strong as you think it is." He turned to Duff. "Charlie One, escort the asset back outside. We'll take it from here."

"Copy."

Charlie team headed for the door with Dr. Flores in tow.

CHAPTER 47

Oscar Cardoza tied a bandanna around his neck, slid the ends under his light blue western shirt, and snapped the ivory buttons closed. He adjusted his large belt buckle in the mirror and took in his entire ensemble.

If he wore a suit and tie to today's meeting, he would stand out, and Cardoza did not need to stand out. He'd planned from the very beginning to be in the room for the negotiations, so he'd brought along worn clothes, ostrich boots, even a straw hat, so that he could blend in with the sicarios and underlings certain to be present around Archuleta.

He decided the straw hat was a bit much; most of the men around here wore ball caps, and the cowboy hats he did see were of a different style than his, so he just slid a ball cap borrowed from one of his minders on his head, covering as much of his face as possible, then stepped up to the window of his third-floor hotel room.

He didn't step onto the balcony, and he didn't open the blinds except to peek out. He saw two massive armored black trucks parked on his side of the street, just opposite from el edificio de ayuntamiento, the town hall. He saw men in the turrets of both vehicles: a young black man in the front one, and a tall blond man with a beard in the rear, both behind powerful Heckler & Koch light machine guns.

Other security contractors manned positions on foot; a second black individual walked up an alleyway next to the town hall with another security officer. He saw a man positioning himself on top of a gas station; the Black Knights sentries standing in front of all the buildings just gazed on as the strangers took their positions.

Looking around at the street scene before him, Cardoza decided most of these men had, by his estimation, no more than twenty-four hours to live, and as this thought went through his mind, he realized he could not possibly care less about them.

His phone rang in the pocket of his jeans, and he answered it quickly.

"Bueno?"

"It's going to rain, amigo."

It was Archuleta, as expected, but Cardoza didn't understand the comment.

He looked up at the sky. "Really? It doesn't look like rain to me."

"What does a man from Mexico City know about the rainy season in los Sierra Madres Occidentales?"

"Admittedly nothing," Cardoza confessed.

Archuleta switched gears. "We are on the way. How does it look there to you?"

"I'm watching from the window in my hotel room. The two from the UN and the deputy secretary of the interior entered the municipal building a few minutes ago. Your men checked over the security force outside; I assume they did the same to those that went in."

"Just the deputy secretary? There are supposed to be *two* men from Mexico City."

"I only saw Herrera and the pair from the UN."

"Whatever." Archuleta chuckled. "The other pendejo probably ran away."

"By the way." Cardoza was feeling lucky. "I heard your men talking about gunfire in the mountains last night. Any more news on all that?"

"My people spoke to the deputy secretary this morning. He said they were attacked by fifty or more sicarios. Four of the motorcade security men were killed."

"But . . . it wasn't your guys doing the shooting, was it?"

"It sure as shit wasn't my boys. If it *had* been my sicarios, there wouldn't be anybody left for me to meet with. I've sent men out to protect the area so it doesn't happen again, but we aren't looking for the Sinaloans too hard. I don't want to start a fight with them while the delegation is here."

"You think it was Sinaloa?"

"Of course. Nobody else up here. Still . . . in numbers like that . . . it's never happened. Whoever they are, we'll find them and kill them all, *after* the meeting. Do some last damage to El Escopeta before the peace agreement."

Cardoza kept looking out the window. More security men appeared on his right, walking in the street in front of a cantina next to his hotel. Black Knights men stood still as stones, watching them. Everyone was wearing guns, but everyone was also minding their manners. He said, "Remember, señor, there won't be any peace agreement unless those missiles turn up somewhere else, and quickly."

"Sí, I understand. I will give them to you, but only if the UN says they will definitely come in if it's proved I don't have them."

"Muy bien. Where are the missiles now?"

"I had them moved into town last night. They are loaded onto flatbeds that are under guard. I'll give you the location when I am convinced the UN is serious about this."

"A very wise decision."

Archuleta said, "We will arrive in five minutes. When we pull into town, come out of the hotel. You and I will go into the municipal building together."

"I will see you soon."

CHAPTER 48

Duff kept his eyes out his windshield while he ate meatballs in marinara out of a foil pouch, digging in with his spoon to the lukewarm but filling concoction he'd pulled out of an MRE bag. The engine was off in Crazy Horse, so he could hear others eating around him.

Gabby dined on a fruit-and-nut mix filled with M&Ms and drank orange drink from a bag, all while looking at her map laid out over her knees.

Squeeze was up top still but was in the process of shoving the contents of a bag of cheese tortellini into his mouth between sips of Gatorade.

As Duff ate his chow, he looked through his windshield and saw a sullen-looking Gordon on a two-man foot patrol passing in front of the town hall. Bravo kept a man in the turret of Pack Horse, parked forty yards behind Duff at the other end of the park, but Remmick had told Gordon he wanted him and his last Bravo teammate to work foot mobile, a tiny show of force in front of the town hall.

So Gordon wandered aimlessly, Bravo Six on his shoulder, and to Duff, it looked like his old friend was just idly biding his time till he, too, was killed on this run.

Just as he shook these negative thoughts away, Nascar spoke up from behind the wheel.

"Anyone want the rest of my rations? Dry crackers that taste like cardboard and old-ass applesauce that tastes like baby puke?"

There was no response from the others.

"Whatever. I guess I'll save this for later." He started wrapping up his food.

Remmick's voice came over the speakers. "Alpha One, all team leaders. Alpha team is with the VIPs in the conference room on the second floor of the municipal building. Report status, Bravo."

Gordon keyed his mic. "Bravo—what's left of it, anyway—is on foot in the street outside the building with one up gunner in Pack Horse One."

"What do you see?" Remmick asked.

"I see a hell of a lot more of them than I do of us."

"No shit. Just remember, for today, anyhow, they aren't the bad guys. They're providing protection for us from the Sinaloans who hit us last night."

In Crazy Horse, Gabby heard this exchange and leaned forward to Duff.

"I don't think they were Sinaloans."

Duff hushed her, because he knew he'd be next.

"Charlie? Go with sitrep," Remmick ordered.

"Charlie Actual is in Crazy Horse with my up gunner and driver, along with Dr. Flores. Cruz, Frenchie, and Wolfson have taken up other positions around the square across the street from the town hall."

Remmick copied Duff's last, and the net went quiet again for nearly a minute, till Wolfson spoke up on the intrateam radio, meaning he could be heard only by the other Charlie contractors and Gabby.

"Charlie Two to Charlie Actual."

"Go for Actual."

"I'm in overwatch on the roof of the gas station. There's one BK dude eye-fucking me from the window of the municipal building across the street, so my presence is *not* covert. Break . . . I've got eyes on a large convoy of four-wheel-drive vics moving overland just to the northeast of the town. ETA one mike."

"These look like the guys that hit us last night?"

"Seriously, TL? Every fuckin' vehicle in the Sierras has looked the same to me since we got here. It's a row of dirty pickup trucks. Just like last night. That's all I can tell you."

"Roger that. Everybody keep sharp." He then relayed all this to Shane Remmick.

"Alpha copies. Herrera just got a call from the BKs. Archuleta is in that group of vics pulling up. They say anybody who points a gun out there is gonna get RPG'd . . . so don't."

"Roger," Duff acknowledged, as did Gordon, and then Duff broadcast on his intrateam.

"Squeeze. Come down out of the turret."

"But—"

"Don't talk back. Just button up and shut up."

Squeeze sat down, pulling the hatch closed above him. He sighed audibly into his mic, like a kid who was told he couldn't go out and play.

Gordon ordered his turret gunner to leave the vehicle, lock it up, and meet him and the other Bravo man at the front door to the municipal building.

A massive row of pickup trucks appeared from the north, heading into the town square. They began slowing and stopping in the road, in front of Duff, just on the other side of the municipal building and in front of the hotel on the opposite side of the street. Duff counted fourteen trucks in all: heavy-duty Rams, Silverados, F-250s, and others. All dirty and worn-looking, which was no surprise considering the rugged terrain of the Devil's Spine. But still, they were all quality vehicles.

They seemed to average about four men per truck, which told Duff that together with the twenty men outside the town hall and the dozen or so men he saw inside, there were now around ninety armed sicarios positioned around his force of seventeen.

The steel walls and five-inch ballistic glass he was enshrouded in was comforting, but he knew good and well he'd be dismounting for one reason or another before long, and there would be no chance in hell any of his men could survive even the slightest of skirmishes against this number of adversaries.

Next to Duff, Nascar whistled and adjusted his body armor higher on his smallish frame. "Ho-ly shit, there are a fuck-ton of them. Must be sixty dudes in those trucks. Do you know what Archuleta looks like, boss?"

"No idea. But you know how it is. Just focus on the guy everybody on the security team is focused on. That'll be the big cheese."

Nascar pointed ahead. "Like that asshole right there?"

In front of them, a group of sicarios assembled around a massive silver GMC Sierra 3500 Denali crew cab and opened the back door, and a middle-aged dark-complected man in a red shirt and jeans climbed out. He had a pointy gray beard and dark hair, but other than the fact that he appeared older than the men around him, there was nothing obviously noteworthy about him.

But as he stepped into the street, he was surrounded by bodies, so it was clear to Duff that this was, in fact, the man in charge.

Ahead of Crazy Horse and on the right, the front door to the hotel on the corner opposite the park opened, and a man in a black ball cap and a light blue western shirt exited. He wore sunglasses and seemed to shield himself from the two security trucks on the street as he walked towards Archuleta.

These men shook hands in the center of the road—the leader of the Black Knights had shaken no other hands in the group—and then together they began walking towards the building where the meeting would be held.

Duff keyed his handset. "Alpha One, this is Charlie One. Archuleta is moving to the municipal building at this time. About fifty new security around him."

"Alpha One copies. We're ready for them up here. I want Crazy Horse in front of the hotel across the street and to the north of the municipal building, Pack Horse One parked behind them in the street to the south of the building. Show Horse and War Horse will take the western two corners of the block, with a driver and a turret gunner in each. That will leave me and three men for security in the meeting itself."

Duff acknowledged; he and Bravo were already set up in compliance with the agent in charge's wishes.

Nascar spoke up softly. "That's pretty thin."

"Yeah," Duff replied. "But it doesn't matter. If we had fifty dudes covering, we couldn't stop the Black Knights from doing whatever they want with our protectees right now. There are just too many of them, and they own the territory."

Gabby leaned between the front seats. "For every man you see, there are ten waiting nearby, ready to come to the sound of guns."

The main entourage of Archuleta, his friend from the hotel, and a phalanx of a dozen security guys disappeared into the town hall, and the rest of the armed men around either went back to their trucks or fanned out in other directions. Nobody seemed in any way threatened by the Armored Saint men here; they just seemed bored.

Squeeze sat in the back behind Gabby. "What do we do now, other than smile and wave at all the dudes with guns standing around?"

"Just hang out and wait," Duff replied. "Remmick says the meeting might go for two days."

To this the young former Marine said, "I'll hang out in the turret. Nothing wrong with a little show of force."

"Hands off your MG unless directed otherwise."

"I'm not a fuckin' idiot."

Duff let the comment go, but Nascar spoke up again.

"So, boss, what are you and I gonna talk about for two days?"

"Who says we have to talk?"

Gabby leaned forward between the seats. "I can give you both a history lesson about this mountain range, a little background on the canyon nearby, and—"

Duff interrupted, "So, Nascar. What's your real name?"

"—the indigenous . . ." Gabby realized she was being actively ignored. "Oh, never mind, then," she said, and she moved around Squeeze's legs, then lay down on the bench running down the starboard side of the cabin.

Nascar replied to his boss. "It's Larry. Larry Evans."

The TL replied softly to this. "Another Larry."

"What's that?"

"Had a driver named Larry once. Another detail."

"Is the other Larry still doin' this shit?"

After a pause, Duff said, "Negative. He got out of it."

"Good for him. Where'd he go?"

"A better place."

Nascar was oblivious to Duff's melancholy moment. He said, "Yeah, I'm lookin' to retire soon myself. Just need enough money to open up a body shop. I know a thing or two about how to get dents out of vehicles."

Nascar began going into the process of repairing cosmetic damage to car bodies, but after a moment, Duff chimed in.

"How 'bout we just sit here and watch the square in silence for a bit?"

"Suits me, boss. I've got a full thermos of Frenchie's suck-ass coffee. I'm not gonna be sleepin' for a few days."

Duff realized that even with all the danger around him, he himself wanted nothing more than to go to sleep.

CHAPTER 49

Two hours into the meeting, Remmick thought everything was going about the way he would have expected. Rafa Archuleta had made his opening remarks; Remmick stood behind his protectees and listened to the translations from Hector Herrera, finding the leader of the Black Knights to be a confident if also a rambling speaker. Minister Herrera did the interpretation into Spanish for the benefit of Helm and LaRue. This would have been Rodriguez's job, but he was, according to Remmick, comfortable but under guard in War Horse, and fortunately Rafa Archuleta had not asked about the other Mexican government official they had been expecting.

Herrera himself then made a lengthy and florid speech about the need to calm the flames of war in this part of the nation, and his government's desire to partner with the Black Knights in this endeavor. Michelle LaRue next lined out her plan for internally displaced peoples, enclaves, and safe havens around the mountains should the peacekeepers meet resistance from the Sinaloa cartel, and Rafa had asked her questions, even referring to a large map he had one of his men bring in from another office here in the town hall.

Next it was Deputy Director Helm's turn. Over a twenty-minute talk, he outlined the plan for the peacekeepers, including their mandate, their rules of engagement, even the potential nations that would be called upon to provide troops should the agreement go forward.

It was well past three p.m. when Reinhardt Helm wrapped up his comments. "Therefore, Señor Archuleta, in summary, we feel a robust peacekeeping operation in the Sierra Madres, coupled with Ms. LaRue's safe havens and camps for the internally displaced, will benefit you directly, and the community at large."

Rafa thought a moment, then spoke in Spanish. Herrera gave a competent running translation in English.

"And you won't destroy my fields or factories?"

The big German smiled. "We are not fans of the Afghanistan model. The Americans tried eradication of the poppy fields, but its only result was to disenfranchise the locals that they needed on their side."

After Herrera conveyed this, Archuleta said, "Yes. And poppy production in Afghanistan increased during this time."

Helm nodded. "The Americans failed miserably. We are the United Nations. We are more reasonable. We will respect your territory and not intervene in your activities as long as you and the Sinaloans cease all hostilities."

Michelle LaRue added, "Sir, if you let us in unmolested, allow us to do our work and patrol the highways, you will retain the vast majority of your authority in the mountains, and you will save the lives of countless civilians. There is truly no downside to this at all for you."

The cartel boss stroked his beard. "I will not attack the Sinaloans, but I have to have the ability to defend myself from El Escopeta's sicarios. If I accept your plan, it would only be under the condition that my men remain armed."

"Certainly," Helm replied. "Small arms. Rifles, handguns, light machine guns." He raised an eyebrow now. "These weapons only."

The leader of the Black Knights shrugged. "That's all we have, anyway."

Michelle LaRue turned to Hector Herrera. "Minister? Should we . . ."

Herrera nodded. "Yes, Michelle," he said in English, and then he switched to Spanish. "Señor Archuleta, this leads me to the other matter we must discuss."

"I am listening."

"The surface-to-air missiles."

"Ah . . . Sí. Has Mexico City determined who fired them in Durango last month?

"We have. *You* did. Our intelligence apparatus, as well as the American CIA, informs us the missiles were stolen in Venezuela and brought over in a container ship through the port of Tijuana. We have traced the route of the trucks to the Sierra Madres."

Rafa slammed his hand on the oaken table and stood. Even in his boots, he was not five foot seven.

"Then all your so-called intelligence people are liars! What proof do you have?"

"We can provide you with some of our intelligence to assure you we take this matter very seriously, and we are certain of our conclusions. This entire peace agreement depends on this matter being resolved to our satisfaction. The army is at the base of the Sierras, Señor Archuleta. I do not want them to come up here, and neither do you."

"These missiles. These missiles that, I repeat, I do *not* have. If you don't leave with them, then the army invades?"

Helm spoke now. "That is exactly the situation we all find ourselves in, señor. If we get the missiles, Mr. Remmick, the leader of our security detail, has brought explosives that he can destroy them with. We will witness this, and once that is done, the UN will come in." He stopped himself and held up a conciliatory hand. "With your approval, of course."

Archuleta nodded and sat down. He seemed deep in thought.

Helm spoke English. "It is a difficult situation, to be certain, but we came up here in good faith to talk to you, with respect, about a solution."

Archuleta spoke quietly to one of his men for a moment. Then he said, "I will make some calls. Try to find out what I can about where these missiles are."

No one replied to this.

"There is a dining room here on the second floor, just down the hall. Please go in there, and food and drinks will be brought to you."

Herrera said, "Thank you for your hospitality. If you continue to negotiate in good faith, especially in discussions about the missiles, then we will be more than happy to stay here as long as necessary."

"Excelente." Archuleta rose again.

As the men and woman at the table stood, Remmick stepped up behind his three protectees. "Deputy Director Helm, if you all will follow me down the hall, I'll get you situated."

Herrera took Remmick by the arm and whispered. "Will Adnan Rodriguez be given a room? I haven't had a chance to talk to him since—"

"For security reasons, we are keeping him in War Horse. He is being well taken care of, I assure you."

"But I—"

"Please let me do my job, Minister, so you can do yours."

LaRue asked, "Can we at least see him so we know he's all right?"

"Of course you can. Tonight I'll take you to him."

"Why not now?"

"If we do it now, the BKs might see us, and they will wonder why one of Mexico's top government officials is under guard."

"Yes, of course, Mr. Remmick. I understand."

The entourage filed out of the conference room, with Shane Remmick and three of his men providing diamond protection as they headed up the hallway.

CHAPTER 50

With the conference room cleared of foreigners, only Archuleta and his own protection detail remained, along with the man in his forties wearing a ball cap who stood against the far wall and had said nothing for the entire meeting.

The leader of Los Caballeros Negros stood and walked over to a shelf, took a bottle of mezcal that had been placed there for him, then shooed his protective detail out the door, until there was no one else in the room except for him and Oscar Cardoza.

Archuleta opened the bottle, took a long swig, and then offered it to Cardoza. When the man from Mexico City looked like he was going to demur, Rafa said, "You might dress like one of us, but you don't smell like one of us. Go on, drink, it will help your disguise."

Cardoza smiled as he took the bottle, downed a shot, and kept his eyes placid and his expression unchanged.

Rafa was impressed. He took the bottle back, had another swig himself, and wiped his mouth with the back of his hand. "So. You've been watching us talk for hours. What are your thoughts?"

"The UN has met their match in you, señor. You are doing beautifully with the negotiations."

"I agree, but it is not hard. They want what I want. A peacekeeping force in the mountains." With another swig, he said, "There is only one little snag remaining."

Cardoza nodded. "I would suggest that now we move the surface-to-air missiles to the airstrip at the canyon's edge. As you can see from the talks, this is a deal-breaker if not handled delicately."

Archuleta rapped once on the door to the room with the bottle. Instantly it opened, and a handsome man with a ponytail stepped in. He wore a silver revolver in a shoulder holster, and his shirt was unbuttoned halfway.

"Sí, jefe?"

To Cardoza, Rafa said, "This is Diego, my lead sicario. He will take you to the missiles. The crates of Igla-Ss are already loaded on three flatbed trucks, hidden under tarps, and they will be driven to the airfield as agreed. What time will the plane land to pick them up?"

"It's in the air now, waiting on my call to land."

"Muy bien. We fly them out this afternoon, stall the negotiations tonight, and by tomorrow the weapons show up in Sinaloa, implicating El Escopeta and allowing the UN to come in instead of the army."

"Exactamente, señor," Cardoza said. "Diego, I will follow you just as soon as my contact in the entourage can get free from the others and join us."

"Sí. We will go in my truck out back. I parked it where instructed."

CHAPTER 51

The four people in Crazy Horse sat quietly, but then a crack of thunder shattered the still air with no warning, startling the three men in the truck. Squeeze ducked from the turret a moment before standing back up, Duff sat up straighter and looked around, and Nascar cussed in surprise.

Gabby Flores, in contrast, did not react.

A few seconds later the first raindrop hit the windshield, and within a minute Duff found himself watching a deluge.

"Well, you were right about the rain," he said.

Gabby replied, "It will last for an hour. Maybe seventy-five minutes. No more."

"It's not like we're going anywhere," Duff said.

Nascar turned his way. "Speak for yourself. I've gotta go."

"Go where?"

"Go. Like, find a latrine."

Duff sighed. "Piss in a water bottle. Gabby will avert her eyes. I will, too, as a matter of fact."

"Disgusting," Gabby muttered to herself.

But Nascar made no move to do this. Instead he said, "Negative, boss. Not that kind of mission. I gotta drop a deuce."

Gabby cocked her head between the seats. "A *what*?"

But Duff just rubbed his eyes under his ballistic glasses. "Really, dude? Right now?"

"Shoulda gone before the rain, but I figured the doctor was wrong." When Duff didn't reply, Nascar said, "You told us we could be here two days. I've been eating MREs and drinking Frenchie's coffee. C'mon."

Duff looked back over his shoulder and saw Squeeze's legs behind Gabby. "Squeeze, you good up top?"

Over the radio, he heard, "Me? Oh, yeah, I'm great, TL. Never better. Y'all down there all dry, and my black ass is up here gettin' rained on."

"Look on the bright side. You're the first one of us to get a shower since Wednesday."

"Yeah, right. Whatever."

"All right, Nascar, go find a john in the municipal building, just tell the guards 'baño.' I'll crawl over behind the wheel so we can move, if necessary. Make it quick."

"Quick's not gonna be a problem. Finding a shitter in the next sixty seconds might be, though."

"Oh my God," Gabby muttered.

"Then move already," Duff ordered.

"It's already movin'," Nascar joked as he opened the door and stepped out into the rain.

When he was gone, when the door was closed behind him, Squeeze said, "That's one nasty redneck."

"We're all nasty after four days in the mountains," Duff replied. "Okay. I'll take the wheel."

He unfastened his rifle from his sling, left it balanced against his seat, then climbed to his knees. He got his right leg over the center console of the big APC, then used his hands to pull himself over by the steering wheel.

He put his left boot on the console to stand on so he could reposition his body to sit in the driver's seat, but his foot slipped, the tip of his boot jamming down between the console radio and the passenger seat. He was wedged in tightly, and his first attempt to pull his foot out was unsuccessful.

His prosthetic was in that boot, and instantly a pang of worry washed over him, but he tried to remain nonchalant as he pulled again.

His prosthetic would stay in place on his leg unless he really yanked and applied a little torque, so he wasn't overly worried, but he knew he needed to back up into the passenger seat, pull his boot free, and try again to climb over.

But before he did this, Gabby Flores noticed his predicament. "I can help. It's wedged in."

"It's fine, just give me a second and I—"

"We'll pull together. Ready?" She grabbed onto his boot.

"No," Duff said, and any pretense that everything was fine disappeared in an instant. "I've got it. Let go and I—"

"But I've almost . . . got—"

"I said let go!"

Duff instinctively tried to yank his boot away, just as she pulled it hard towards her. She flew backwards into Squeeze's legs, then onto her back in the center of the cabin.

She looked down slowly and realized she was holding Duffy's boot and lower leg.

She screamed.

"Calm down," Duff said softly.

Duff went to his knees and reached back between the seats for the boot, but Flores was too far away. "Calm down!" he repeated.

Squeeze lowered down into the cabin on hearing Gabby's scream. "The fuck is goin' on down—"

He stopped talking when he saw her, saw what she held. He sat down on the port-side bench slowly, then turned to Duff.

"Yo, TL. How come the terp's got your foot in her lap, and she's six feet away from you?"

"Squeeze, just take a breath. It's okay. It's a . . . a prosthetic."

"I see what it is, Eleven-B. You got yourself a fake leg. Are you fuckin' kiddin' me right now?"

"Hand it back to me, Gabby. It's okay."

"My TL be hoppin' around on a fuckin' stump and didn't nobody tell me, and that's okay? Fuck *that* shit."

Gabby Flores had sat up on the floor, under the open hatch, and rain poured onto her as she handed it back up to Duffy. As she did so, she spoke softly. "I am so, so sorry."

Duff sat in the passenger seat, lifted his pants leg, positioned the device, and folded the thick rubber back over the stump below his left knee. He said, "Not your fault, Gabby. It's not a big deal. I'm fine."

Squeeze, however, clearly was not going to let this go. "You outta your fuckin' *mind*! Does Remmick know about this? Does Gordon know?"

Duff sighed and turned back to him. "Nobody knows. Nobody but you, and I'd appreciate it if you didn't—"

"Oh, fuck that! I'm damn well tellin' everybody! You can't fake your injured ass into a high-threat OCONUS job and score a damned TL position on top of that."

Duff felt both defiance and anger well inside him. "What's Remmick gonna do, kid? Fire me? You want to be another man down out here on this run, after all the shit we've already come up against?"

"You ain't no full man, Eleven-B."

Duff's eyes narrowed. "Why don't we step out in the road and you can find out how much of a man I really am."

"Fuckin' bring it, you gimpy-assed bitch!"

Gabby grabbed onto the young African American. "No. Please. Listen to me! Listen to—"

But Squeeze broke free of her grasp, opened the starboard hatch, and climbed out, dropping down to the ground in the torrential thunderstorm.

Duff slid down from the driver's-side door, the rain saturating him in seconds; he stepped around the front of the vehicle, ready for a fight, but Squeeze was on him before he even got his bearings, tackling him to the ground.

Fists flew, and the men grunted and jockeyed for position on one another.

And even in the rain, it didn't take long for all of this to be noticed.

Duff's headset was still in place, and while he rolled onto his back into a water-filled gully next to the road, he heard Wolfson's voice. "Hey! Charlie One, why are you guys fighting down there?"

Frenchie came over the net next. It was clear he was too far away in the park to see the action through the heavy downpour. "Who is fighting? You need me, boss?"

Squeeze was on top of him now, using one hand to hold Duff's head down, and another to block the punches thrown at his face.

Duff grunted as he spoke. "Everybody stand fast. Hold your positions. It's . . . It's fine."

Cruz spoke up next. "You're rolling in the mud with Squeeze. Well, *that's* a good look, TL."

The two men fighting by the APC in the curbside gully were making noise, but not as much as Gabriella Flores. "Stop it! Stop it!"

This drew the attention of a pair of Black Knights sentries who had been standing in front of the hotel, and they crossed the street and came over now, more curious than concerned.

"Que esta pasando?"

Duff rolled Squeeze over now, throwing a glancing blow to the side of his head as he did so, and climbed high on the man's waist. He stole a quick look at the BKs, then another at Gabby. "Tell them we're fine."

"Tranquilla, señores. No es nada. Pinches gringos locos."

The men laughed and continued standing in the downpour, watching like spectators at a prizefight.

Duff was getting the upper hand, but Squeeze wasn't done. He landed a shot to Duff's right eye, breaking his ballistic eyewear but causing little pain or damage to the man wearing them, and then Duff readied to rain down a powerful right cross, but just as he launched it, Mike Gordon grabbed Duff's arm, and yanked him all the way back up to his feet.

"What the fuck is going on here?" Gordon yelled.

Squeeze leapt to his feet, as well, slowed by his body armor, but then he came charging again for Duff.

Bravo Six appeared in the rain and grabbed him, then threw him up against the APC.

"Keep them apart!" Gordon ordered.

Still in a torrential downpour, the three Bravo men, Gabby, Squeeze, and Duff, along with two Black Knight bystanders, all stood on the sidewalk between the APC and the park.

No one spoke for a moment, and then Gordon said, "Charlie One, why the hell are you beating up your Six?"

Squeeze said, "Fuck that, I was kickin' his—"

Gordon pointed a gloved finger in Squeeze's face. "Shut it!"

"We're fine, Mike," Duff replied. "Just carry on, we'll get back in the vic and—"

"Bravo One," Squeeze said, "I wanna move over to your team. You'll have four guys, Duff will have five."

The two Mexican estacas quickly grew bored with all the conversation in English, so they turned around to go back to the hotel and get out of the rain.

Gordon eyed the younger African American a long time. "What makes you think I want you on my team?"

To this the youngest man on the detail said, "Duff ain't gotta left leg."

"He . . . he *what*?"

"He ain't gotta—"

"He heard you, Squeeze!" Duff said, "Mike, I can explain."

Gordon looked down at Duff's soaked jeans, then back up into his eyes.

"Show me."

"It doesn't really—"

"Show me."

Duff sighed. "Okay." He lifted his soaking wet pants leg out of his boot, lowered his sock, and exposed a prosthetic lower limb with a "Go Army" bumper sticker positioned vertically on it.

"Son of a bitch," Bravo One muttered as he took off his ballistic glasses to look more carefully.

Duff said, "Has it affected me at all in the past few days? I'm as solid as anybody in the detail, and you know it."

Gordon looked like he was in pain. After a moment he said, "Maybe, but what about the next few? What if you have to run?"

327

"I can run."

Squeeze said, "Unless your fuckin' peg gets caught on a radio, right? Then what happens? Oh yeah, it pops right off. Ain't no big thing."

Duff started to speak, but Gordon held a hand up. "You and me need a place out of this rain where we can talk."

"Let's get back in Crazy Horse," Duff suggested.

"Alone," Gordon demanded. "We'll go into that hotel cantina across the street."

"We can't leave our—"

"Remmick is in the municipal building; he and his men have the protectees eating in the dining room. It's fine. We put the rest of our Joes back where they belong; we don't have to report that we're taking five."

Squeeze wiped rain off his face. "What's there to talk about? Eleven Bang Bang ain't got no leg. End of fuckin' story."

Duff turned to Squeeze. "Get back in the turret." On the intrateam he said, "Wolfson, Frenchie, Cruz, hold your positions. Nascar, get your ass back here and behind the wheel. How copy?"

Nascar replied over the radio. "Be just another minute, boss."

"Where the fuck is Nascar?" Gordon asked.

"Latrine. He'll be back."

Gabby said, "What about me?"

Duff said, "Just climb back in the truck. There are some towels in a duffel in the back by Cruz's station. Dry yourself off and wait for me to return."

Squeeze and Gabby climbed back into Crazy Horse, and Duff and Gordon walked through the rain, in silence, towards the cantina.

They passed a few sentries along the way but ignored their stares. The vibe remained surprisingly nonthreatening, more so because the Black Knights out here now regarded the motorcade's security force as a group of lunatics, fighting with one another over God knows what.

CHAPTER 52

Duff and Gordon entered the cantina; it was empty other than a woman behind the counter. Beer signs lit the dark space, the sun all but blotted out of the windows because of the heavy storm outside.

The woman raised an eyebrow at the soaking-wet men, both laden down with guns and armor and magazines, headsets and radios and med pouches, and knee and elbow pads.

Gordon said, "Dos Coca-Colas, señora."

She opened two cans of Coke and slid them across the bar.

Duff fished pesos out of his pocket and handed them over, then put several more bills down. "Cinco minutes?"

She understood, turned, and disappeared behind a door, leaving the room to the two foreigners.

Gordon took a long pull from the cold can, eyeing Duff all the while. "Christ, Duff. Look at you. You're a mess."

"I can explain about the leg."

"You lost it in Beirut, didn't you?"

He nodded, sipping his Coke.

"Shit," Gordon said, "that explains a lot."

"Yeah. That's why I was working at the mall. What detail is going to hire me on like this, right?"

Gordon gave a little laugh without smiling. "Well . . . you got your answer."

"Yeah, Armored Saint. But only because they didn't know."

Gordon just stared off into space for a long moment. As distant as he'd appeared since he'd lost four men on the road the night before, he looked absolutely catatonic now.

"What is it?" Duff asked.

Gordon refocused on him. "Shit. *Shit*, Duff!"

"What is it?" he repeated.

"I'm thinkin' . . . I'm thinking maybe they *did* know."

"What do you mean?"

Gordon sat down on a bar stool, his rifle hanging down between his knees and banging against the wood. "Rodriguez said that he didn't call anybody in Sinaloa, right?"

Duff cocked his head. "*Rodriguez?* What's my leg got to do with—"

"He was like, genuinely confused right before I decked him. I saw it, but I'd already committed to the punch."

"So?"

"So maybe I fucked up. Maybe we should have heard him out."

"Why? He's full of shit, because *someone* was communicating with the guys who attacked us, and he had the only phone."

"Not the only phone. There's three more split among the Armored Saint teams." He stood back up slowly now. "What if there's someone else in this motorcade tipping off the bastards who hit us?"

"Like, who?"

"I don't know. But I *do* know one thing. Alpha, Bravo, Charlie. One of these things is not like the other."

Duff shook his head. "You've lost me."

"Duff . . . Every last man on this entire run was sought out and hand selected by Shane Remmick, Alpha One. He stacked his team and gave us the rejects. Why?"

"He didn't seek *me* out. I ran into you at the mall, asked you to help get me hired on. You tried to talk me out of it."

Gordon said nothing.

"Right?"

"That's not . . ." Gordon looked away, clearing his throat. "That's not exactly how it went down."

"What are you trying to say?"

"Man, Remmick *sent* me to where you worked, told me to bump into you and talk up the money of the Mexico run, then play hard to get when you went for the bait."

Duff was thunderstruck by this news. "Wait . . . Remmick? Remmick recruited *me*? Why the hell would he do that?"

"I don't know, Duff, but I sure as hell would like to."

CHAPTER 53

The rain continued unabated as a black Ford F-150 SuperCrew rolled to a stop in front of a low, tin-roofed warehouse three quarters of a mile up a winding road from the town square of Cinco Lagrimas. There were already four pickups parked outside, and eight armed men stood wearing AK-47s over their raincoats, their straw cowboy hats protecting their faces from the storm.

A loading dock sat on the side of the building, and more men stood in the darkness just inside, looking out, waiting.

Archuleta's chief lieutenant, Diego, was behind the wheel of the F-150, and one of his crew of gunmen sat in the front passenger seat. Behind them in the back seat were two more men. Oscar Cardoza sat behind the front passenger, and he leaned forward now to address Diego.

"This is the place?"

"Sí, Señor Cardoza. There are three flatbeds in the warehouse here. About twenty crates on each one. Fifty-nine in all. One launcher and two missiles for each crate, just as they came from the Venezuelan army." He looked in his rearview mirror at the man directly behind him. "You boys better have a big airplane."

The man seated in the back next to Cardoza replied, "Don't you worry about that. I want to see the merchandise before we move it."

"Of course. Of course. I will go in first, tell the sentries what we are doing and remove the tarps, and then I'll call you both forward."

Diego and his gunmen climbed out in the rain; they adjusted their hats to shield their eyes from the torrential rain and ran to the open dock.

Oscar Cardoza turned to the man seated next to him now. "I need to know that we understand each other. When the time comes, you and your men will escort the missiles to the airstrip, and then—"

Shane Remmick interrupted, his voice laced with an anger he'd hidden from the two Mexicans who'd just left the truck. "Me first, asshole. What the *fuck* happened on the road last night? Those were *your* sicarios!"

Cardoza held up an apologetic hand. "I told you last night. The leader of the Zeta force here in the mountains . . . He is their best fighter, but he is a loose cannon. He wasn't supposed to leave the highway. He saw your motorcade and set up a hasty ambush, against my direct instructions."

"Well, he almost got the entire diplomatic mission canceled. It was your job to manage the Zetas."

"They are Zetas, Mr. Remmick. Managing them is a . . . challenge."

"They weren't supposed to engage the motorcade at all until after I flew out with the missiles."

"If you remember, this was *my* plan. I contacted you with it all figured out. I don't need you reminding me of the details."

"Well, after what happened last night, I think a refresher is in order."

"I assume you found a way to place the blame on Rodriguez, and that's why he is not part of the delegation."

Remmick nodded, still furious. "Yeah, I figured out a way to solve for *your* fuckup. Nothing else better go wrong. The next couple of hours are crucial."

Cardoza waved to the warehouse. "Do your job, and it will all go to plan."

"You really trust these Black Knights to hand over the SAMs, Cardoza?"

"If I really trusted narcos, I wouldn't be alive, Mr. Remmick. No, I don't trust them. But I left Rafa Archuleta with no options, so I believe they want the missiles gone, just as we want the missiles to sell back to the Venezuelans."

Remmick looked out at the heavy rain. "Fifty-nine launchers, one point one million a pop. Even split between you, me, and my team, that's a lot of lifetimes on easy street for us all, but only if your Zetas don't fuck it up again."

"They aren't *my* Zetas. I am just a consultant."

"Bullshit. I know what you are."

"You know what I was. After today, I'll be a man without responsibilities, with nothing but time." His eyes glazed over, but only for a second, and then he was back on mission. "You have to take those weapons twelve miles down a mountain trail and fly them out from a bad airstrip. You and your team are the ones who have to come through now."

"I've got it handled." Remmick looked around. Heavy rivulets of muddy rainwater raced down the dirt road. "Jesus fucking Christ, I can't wait to get out of this hellhole."

"You'll be in Colombia by ten p.m., and when the buyer wires the money to our accounts, I'll give him the location of the aircraft. This time tomorrow, you and I will be in much better environs."

He added, "I presume you have your disappearing act planned?"

"Don't you worry about me," Remmick said, then he held up a finger. "And don't even think about a double cross."

"Why would I—"

"Because all you do is double-cross! Lucky for me, I've got the goods on you. You try to double-cross me, and I go straight to your employers, your *real* employers, tell them about who you really are, and *what* you really are."

"There is enough money for us both, and there is the knowledge that a betrayal from either side will create mutually assured destruction for us both."

"Right."

Diego appeared in front of the truck and waved the men into the warehouse.

Remmick started to move, but Cardoza put his hand on his arm. "Everything is ready to go with the . . . incident?"

"As far as my Bravo and Charlie teams are concerned, Alpha team will cease to exist in about ten minutes."

Cardoza smiled, and then both men stepped out into the mid-afternoon storm.

CHAPTER 54

Mike Gordon held his head in his hands as he sat on the bar stool. Duff stood over him.

"I don't understand, Gordo. You're saying you tricked me into coming here to Mexico?"

"I was just doing what I was told, man. He said I would only get the TL position if I brought you on, and he told me how to do it on the down low. I mean, I knew you needed the dough, figured Remmick had his reasons for wanting you but not asking you outright."

Duff loomed over Gordon. "You're a son of a bitch, you know that?"

Gordon shrugged, his head still hanging. "Yeah, that's me. Look, bro, I'm sorry. I didn't know how bad it was gonna be, and I sure as hell didn't know you were handicapped."

"What does any of this shit have to do with my leg?"

Gordon stood up now, went eye to eye with Duffy. "Remmick chose us all, like I said. He stacked Alpha with the tier-one dudes. But the other details? Bravo and Charlie? Every last man, we all have strikes against us. Stuff making us completely unemployable outside this gig."

Duff was confused. "What do you mean?"

"Hell, two of my guys were raging alcoholics, fired from Aegis

Security in London years ago, haven't worked since. I caught them chugging tequila in Pack Horse Two before we even left the wire." He shrugged. "They're both dead now. Two more of my guys were dumped from other PMCs for poor performance, insubordination, shit like that. The others couldn't follow orders, couldn't shoot for shit, or both. None of them could get hired on anywhere else in the world."

Duff waved away Gordon's comment. "*My* guys are solid."

"You're running them like they are, and maybe you're right, but they all have seriously bad reps. Reps that Remmick would have known about before he recruited them. Squeeze is a belligerent shit who's never worked a job for the same PMC twice; Nascar's been fired from every position he's ever had, including Academi, which used to be Blackwater."

He continued, "Frenchie stabbed a Congolese diplomat to death in a bar fight in Mogadishu; Cruz was dishonorably discharged for beating the shit out of a nineteen-year-old Ranger after a card game in Afghanistan. Put the kid in a coma for three weeks."

"What about Wolfson?"

"SEAL Team Three. Did a lot of good shit. Then one day stateside, he killed a teammate in a training exercise. His arm got bumped in a shoot house. It was an accident, but his finger was on the trigger, and his weapon was pointed at his breacher's skull, so he got bounced out of the teams. Did his last couple years in the Navy peeling potatoes or some shit. He's got PTSD and shouldn't be anywhere near a rifle, but Remmick brought him here."

"Jesus Christ," Duff muttered.

"When you got on the detail, I was like, 'Hell yeah, here's one man not on Alpha who I *know* will come through if we get in the shit.' But now I know what Remmick must have known all along. You're missing one of your legs. That's why you're here. You're damaged goods, Duff. Unemployable. Just like the rest of us."

"Why would Remmick want us to be damaged goods?"

"I don't know. Maybe he wants guys who can't quit, no matter how bad things get. Or else . . ."

"Or else, just maybe, he *wants* us to fail."

Gordon said, "He wants Bravo and Charlie to fail. His Alpha boys are top notch."

Duff got it. "He's stacked his team with winners and filled our teams with losers."

The bartender reentered the room, and Gordon waved her away angrily. She made a face but did as instructed. He then looked back at Duff. "You haven't asked me about me, and I appreciate that."

"Do I want to know?"

"I lost my gig with Triple Canopy in Asscrackistan because I ordered my team vehicle over an IED. We'd been warned it was there by the locals, but I didn't believe them and didn't check it out. I wanted to get back to our base." After a pause, he said, "It was chili dog night. You don't show up right when the mess opens, you wait in line behind seventy-five other hungry Joes and you don't get fed. The food there was shit, but their chili dogs were legit.

"Nobody died, but that wasn't exactly due to my diligent leadership. Four injured badly, the rest of us got concussions and a little PTSD out of the deal. All 'cause I wanted to be first in line for a damn chili dog. I was unemployable for a while, and then this Armored Saint gig fell into my lap. I was a fucking idiot, like the rest of us, but I took the job because I was desperate."

"Like the rest of us," Duff said softly.

"Yeah."

Duff's jaw muscles tightened. His eyes narrowed. "We're being set up for something."

"Lookin' that way, isn't it?"

"What do we do?"

Just then, Nascar's heavy Alabama accent crackled over the intrateam. "Charlie Five for Charlie One, over."

Duff could hear heavy rain over the transmission. "You don't sound like you're back in Crazy Horse."

"I am now." Duff heard the heavy steel door open, then Nascar climbing up into his seat. The door closed and the rain sound lessened. He said, "Boss . . . switch to channel eleven."

With a furrowed brow, Duff said, "Roger." He looked up to Gordon. "Switch to eleven."

Both men in the cantina adjusted the radios on their chest rigs, and then Duff said, "Go for One. What's up?"

"Hey, boss. Uh, did we get tasked for close protection on the VIPs?"

It was a weird question. "Negative. Why?"

"What about Bravo? Are they doing internal perimeter?"

"No. Bravo Actual is with me, and his other two are posted at the front door of the municipal building. Their truck is locked up. Why? What's going on?"

"Well, I was coming out of the shitter on the ground floor of the building, and I saw three Alpha guys leaving out the back door."

Duff and Gordon exchanged a bewildered look. "They . . . they left the VIPs?"

"Affirmative. Not Remmick, didn't see him, but three of his Joes sure as hell just wandered off. Figure there's still a driver and a turret gunner in the two Alpha trucks parked over there on the backside of the building. That makes seven dudes, there are eight on Alpha in total, so that means Remmick's alone up there with Herrera, Helm, and LaRue. That's kinda weird, isn't it?"

"Wait one," Duff said, and then he looked to Gordon.

Gordon said, "Shit . . . whatever Remmick's up to, it's going on right now."

Duff switched channels to the interteam net. "Charlie One for Alpha One, how copy?" There was no response. "Charlie for Alpha. You read?"

Remmick's transmission came through several seconds later.

"I read. What's up?"

"Uh . . . I'm just checking to see if you want us to stay here in front of the hotel, or do you want us to reposition?"

Duff thought he could hear the faint sound of rain in Remmick's next transmission. "Why would I want you to reposition? You have your orders. You and Bravo are to stay in your static positions on the east side of the building. Do *not* move until I tell you. How copy?"

"Solid copy on that, boss. Uh . . . what's your location at this time?"

"I'm in the hall on the second floor. The VIPs are having coffee in the reception area. Duff, why the fuck are you asking me where I am? Where are *you*?"

"Uh . . . I'm out front. Ditto Bravo. All good here. Charlie One out."

Duff looked at Gordon. "He didn't say anything about being alone up there. Where would he send his men?"

Duff turned his radio back to the intrateam channel, and as soon as he did so, his headset came alive, this time with Wolfson's voice. Whispering, the man said, "Charlie Two for Charlie One. Go to eleven."

Duff switched his radio back, then said, "Go for One."

"Uh . . . I relocated one block east. I'm on the roof of the store just south of the town hall. Right now I have eyes on the west."

Duff sighed. "Who gave you permission to move? You're supposed to be covering the east side like the rest of us."

"The BKs in the park were all staring at me. Made me jumpy. It was raining so hard for a minute, I thought I could move without being spotted. Crossed the street, shot down an alley, climbed up here. None of them know where I am."

Duff just shrugged. "Roger. Look, I'm kind of in the middle of something, so if—"

"Any clue as to why Alpha moved War Horse without telling us? It's supposed to be on the northwest corner of the block, but it's a half block back, parked right at the back door of the town hall. Break—"

Duff and Gordon shared another worried look.

"—Uh, and three Alpha guys just climbed into Show Horse. The vic is rolling at this time."

Whatever the fuck was going on, Duff knew it was bad news. "Show Horse is *leaving*?"

"Affirm."

"Where are they going?"

"Heading north, really slowly, like they don't want anybody to hear them revving off. Do you think it's weird half of Alpha would just drive away without giving us a heads-up?"

"Half of Alpha? The other half are in War Horse?"

"*Somebody's* got to be in it. The engine's running, the hatches are open, but nobody's up in the turret." Wolfson said, "Repositioning so I can get a look inside the starboard-side hatches."

"Don't go any closer to War Horse."

"Why not? I'm almost—"

"Stay back. Get off that roof and return to—"

"What the hell?" Wolfson exclaimed.

"What is it?"

"There's nobody in the front of the vic, nobody behind the wheel. I see Rodriguez inside through the rear hatch. He's tied up and gagged, not moving. I'm going to go down there and check it—"

"Negative!" Duff shouted. He didn't know what was happening, but he knew he had to get his guys out of here, and now. "Get off that roof!"

"What's going on, boss?"

"Listen to me. Move away from the—"

A penetrating noise battered Duff's and Gordon's ears. Just as they both reached to yank off their headsets, the glass windows of the cantina shattered, a boom from the street blasted them, and both men flew back against and then over the bar, stung by bits of glass along the way.

Above their prostrate bodies, billowing black smoke rolled into the room, the ceiling fell in, and the cacophonous sound, even through the men's ear protection, blotted out their hearing, replacing all sounds with the squeal of tinnitus.

CHAPTER 55

Duff ended up on his back, Gordon on top of him, both men's rifles and gear and armor between them. Plaster continued to rain down; they were both dazed, but Gordon spoke first as he rolled off and onto his back.

"Duff? You hurt?"

"I'm . . . I'm good. You?"

Gordon pushed up to a kneeling position. He looked down at Duff now. "Fuck! Your leg!"

Duff looked down and saw that both his prosthetic and his boot were missing. He looked on top of the bar and saw the lower appendage lying there, under a Pacifico Beer sign that had fallen from the wall.

"It's up there, hand it to me, will you?"

Gordon looked over his shoulder. "Oh, it's *that* leg. Shit."

Gordon handed it over; Duff lifted his wet pants and reattached it, then quickly came out of his daze.

Through a fresh coughing fit, he transmitted. "Charlie Two. You up?"

After speaking, he realized his boom mic was up over his right ear. He shifted it down, then tried again.

"Charlie One for Two, over?"

Gordon began to stand slowly, coughing uncontrollably, the gray-black haze still thick in the air and grit filling both men's noses and mouths.

More glass fell from the windows behind him, a continuous crackle.

Wolfson did not respond to Duff's call, but a few seconds later, both Duff and Gordon heard a transmission of indeterminate origin. Through his ringing ears, Duff asked for a repeat, while Gordon attempted to raise his own men.

Duff heard coughs in his headset, then, "Charlie One. Charlie Five." More coughs came, but at least Nascar was alive.

"Report status, Five."

Another cough. "Five is up. Squeeze and Gabby are with me in the vic. We're okay. Crazy Horse got rocked, took some shrapnel. Front windscreen is cracked, well, *more* cracked, but we are intact. The dust is still clearing around us, break—"

Duff climbed to his feet now, pushing off bottles and glassware and splintered wood and linoleum from the cheap bar. He looked into the kitchen of the little cantina and saw the bartender lying there, just a few feet away, clearly dead after being struck on the head by a falling wooden support beam.

Nascar shouted now. "Fuck! The town hall is . . . it's *gone*, boss! It's a big, burning pile of rubble!"

Duff triggered his transmit button again. "Wolfson? Wolfson?"

Gordon kept trying to raise his own men, who had been standing at the front of the town hall. "Bravo? Any Bravo elements? Corey? Will?"

Cruz's voice came over the net now. "This is Charlie Four. Me and Frenchie are fine. We were in the middle of the park. But be advised, both Bravo officers are KIA. Saw the building collapse on top of them before we got our asses knocked down. Can't see Wolfson, but if he was on the roof of the building next door to the hall, then he's somewhere in the middle of that smokin' pile. It's down, too."

Before Duff could acknowledge all this, Nascar spoke up. "Boss, get back in the vehicle, now! We don't know what's going on, but the Black Knights are going to be looking at us as the culprits."

"Roger that," Duff said. "Come to us. We'll meet you at the front door."

"Negative," Nascar said. "All the Black Knight pickup trucks are strewn around the street, some on top of each other. All between us and you. We can head south out of here, but we can't go north. You'll have to hoof it to us."

Gordon and Duff headed out the door of the cantina, their feet crunching on glass and wood and the wreckage of tables and chairs. Looking out the front door at an apocalyptic scene of wreckage, Gordon said, "Jesus Christ! Nobody survived that."

"We've got to check on the principals," Duff said.

Frenchie spoke up. "Three and Four are back at Crazy Horse, boss. Get in here with us!"

But Gordon had taken Duff by the shoulder now. "The principals? Where do you wanna look, man? C'mon, Duff, the three floors have caved in on themselves. It's gonna take cadaver dogs to find anybody in that shit."

Duff knew Gordon was right. He nodded distractedly and began heading for Crazy Horse, just thirty yards away in front of the park and across from the massive smoking debris pile.

They'd made it just a couple of steps when gunfire cracked on their right, in the opposite direction from Crazy Horse. Bullets zinged down the street past them.

Both men turned and retreated back into the shattered cantina.

Duff shouted into his mic. "We're taking fire!"

Squeeze spoke over the headset now. "Yo, boss! The BKs are firing up the street, in our direction. Two hundred meters. Am I engaging these motherfuckers?"

Cruz said, "Why are they shooting at us? We didn't do anything!"

Duff looked up at the damaged ceiling in frustration. "Shit!" Then he transmitted, "Charlie team, you are weapons free!"

Instantly the Mk 48 outside the cantina began pounding off bursts of rounds. The report of Frenchie's FAMAS, fired out through a gunport, came slower and more methodically.

Duff turned to Gordon. "Your truck is too far away. Make a run for Crazy Horse. I'll cover from here."

"You're bounding behind me, right?"

"Yeah." He triggered his mic. "Charlie team, Bravo One is leaving the cantina; open the belly hatch for him and provide covering fire. Lay down the hate, boys!"

Gordon burst out the damaged door, turned left, and ran along the sidewalk. Soon he climbed over the hood of a big Dodge Ram, then crawled below a pair of Silverados lying on their sides, propped up against a burning F-350.

Parts of the façade of the municipal building were in the road, as well, and he negotiated his way around piles of broken cinder block, twisted rebar, and wooden beams.

Once he made it past the obstructions, he ran low, then rolled under Crazy Horse and sat up. Squeeze and Frenchie yanked him through the hatch, then shut it behind him.

Once in, he pressed his radio. "Duff, I'm in, but sit tight. There are too many out here in the street right now. Wait for my call to exfil. Shit, man, they're everywhere."

"And they're pissed," Nascar added.

Gordon said, "We're covering the entrance to the hotel, so no-body's gonna slip in on you from there, but watch out for anybody coming in a rear door of the cantina. We can't see back there. You're on your own!"

Duff fired a few rounds out the window up the street. Peeking out the door, he could see more and more trucks rolling into view at the far edge of the town. The gunfire picked up; he heard ricochets off Crazy Horse and, behind it, Pack Horse, which was currently empty and locked up.

He saw no way to run through the street and make it to Crazy Horse now; lead zinged by at thousands of feet per second, and he was certain he was being flanked on all sides as the Black Knights closed on his position.

He reloaded his rifle, kneeling down on his knee pads near the front door of the cantina. Then he stood, ran back behind the counter, and sat down.

Reaching into his load-bearing vest, he pulled out his sat phone. Blood dripped down onto it as he dialed a few numbers with his thumb; clearly he had some sort of a cut on his face or head, though he couldn't feel the source of the injury.

After several seconds sitting there, an eye on the back door and an eye on the phone, the call was answered, and his wife's voice filled his headset.

"Josh? Josh, is that you?"

In response, Duff could only cough. The smoke seemed like it was only getting thicker, and he wondered if the cantina was on fire.

Fresh gunfire raked the wall of the cantina above his head.

"Josh? What's happening? Are you . . . are you under fire?"

His own rifle was in his lap; his hands weren't even on it.

Softly, he said, "I'm sorry, babe. I tried. I did my best."

"What's happening?"

"It's over. We're finished."

"No, no, Josh. Don't say that. You are going to—"

"I didn't know what I was getting into. We . . . we needed the money. That was all that mattered. I fucked it all up again, Nik. Tell the kids I love them. Tell them that every day, okay?"

"Josh."

"Just know that I tried. My heart was in the right place. I did what I thought was—"

"Sergeant Duffy!" she shouted back, startling him with the fast change in her tone. "Calm the *fuck* down!"

Gordon came over the headset now. "Duff! I think I saw a guy slip down the side alley. He might be coming in the back."

"Nikki. I'm so sor—"

"Shut the fuck up and listen! You are going to pick yourself the fuck up right the fuck now and do your fucking job!"

Duff shook his head. "Nikki, it was a setup! We're surrounded, there are hundreds of them coming for us."

"Are your men still alive?"

"Wolfson. Wolfson's dead."

"But the others! Goddammit, Josh, you are in charge, and you still have a heartbeat. Get off the motherfucking phone right now and get back in that fight!"

A rifle-wielding man appeared in the kitchen behind the bar. He turned Duff's way, his weapon high, but he was looking through the thick dust up at eye level. Duff was seated on the floor and therefore below his immediate line of sight.

Duff raised his rifle with one hand as the man registered the movement.

"Pendejo!" the Mexican shouted as he swung his rifle towards the American contractor.

Duff pressed the trigger; his AK blasted five rounds into the man's chest and abdomen, sending him spinning to the ground, where he fell next to the dead bartender.

"Josh!" Nichole shouted.

He shook his head to clear it, then pulled himself back up to his feet. "I'm . . . I'm up," he said, partially to Nichole, and partially to himself.

Gordon's voice came into his headset. "Charlie One, we've suppressed the majority of the close-in fire out here, but they are regrouping on the east side of the square. There's a fuck-ton of them, brother. Make a run for the belly hatch, now!"

Nichole shouted into his ear. "You back with me, Sergeant?"

"I'm back! I got this."

"Kick ass, soldier! Everyone's counting on you."

He hacked up dust as he moved for the door of the cantina. "Thanks, Nik. Gotta go."

He disconnected the phone, then triggered his mic. "Charlie Actual's comin' out!"

347

CHAPTER 56

Josh Duffy ran back into the rainfall, into the gunfire; he broke left and sprinted out into the street and through the burning obstructions so he could access the belly hatch on the port side of the vehicle, in the opposite direction of the park.

His feet splashed through puddles, close-in rifle fire snapped in his ears, and Squeeze laid down on the Mk 48 above him, raking the entire town of Cinco Lagrimas with big 7.62-by-51-millimeter rounds. Cruz opened the starboard-side door and opened up with his machine gun, as well, raking the park to keep heads down in that direction.

Duff slid on the ground, rolled on his armor and over his gun, under the chassis of the IAG Guardian, and then he felt Frenchie's and Gordon's hands on him. They yanked him up into the armored vehicle; Frenchie pushed the hatch closed and locked it, and Cruz did the same with his hatch on the starboard side.

Just then, Nascar shouted, "RPG!"

The rocket came from up the street; it slammed into the front of the vehicle, but it hit the steel grate protecting the grille, and therefore detonated inches away from the armor.

Duff unhooked his rifle from his sling and jumped over the console into the front seat, and Gabby passed the weapon back up to him. He was soaking wet, caked in grime and thick, black soot, and his face was covered in a thin sheen of blood. "Nascar!" he yelled. "Get us out of here."

"Where we goin'?"

"How about someplace where nobody's shooting at us?"

"That's gonna be Kansas, the way our luck is running."

"Then shut the fuck up and drive our asses to Wichita!"

Nascar threw the big vehicle into reverse and floored it, and they shot back through puddles and over debris from the building that had blown up on their left. He negotiated around Pack Horse One, then executed a perfect reverse one-eighty, slinging everyone around inside the truck, and he floored it again.

As soon as he straightened out, he said, "Engine timing is off, suspension is really fucking wobbly. Crazy Horse took some damage when that building blew. More from that RPG."

"Will she keep going?"

"For now, anyway."

A shout from Cruz interrupted them. "Charlie Four tallies new hostile technicals approaching from the north. Engaging!"

"Not without me, you ain't!" Squeeze called back. "We didn't start this shit, but I'm about to end it! Pulling the grenade launcher!"

Duff watched Nascar concentrate on his suicide run out of the town while he listened to the sound of Cruz's Mk 48 and Squeeze's grenade launcher engaging mobile targets behind. Rifle bullets pinged off the armor of Crazy Horse, but no more RPGs impacted, and soon they turned onto a road to the southeast. Here the gunfire stopped completely, for the time being, anyway.

Cruz and Squeeze immediately began reloading.

Duff was still out of breath; he'd yet to harness in, and he was in the process of trying to remove his dirty and cracked ballistic glasses so he could see the road ahead.

Gabby leaned up next to him with a towel and began wiping his face. "Mr. Duffy? You are bleeding. Your face is covered, just like Mr. Gordon's."

Mike Gordon said, "We're wearing the same window glass. We're okay."

"What happened?" she asked.

It was Nascar who answered. "Remmick and his Alpha men just got smoked, along with Wolfson, the VIPs, the two dudes from Bravo, and Archuleta. *That's* what happened. We're the only survivors, except for the half a million Black Knights on our asses."

Duff turned and looked back to Gordon. "Not so sure about that."

Nascar glanced Duff's way. "Huh?"

Gordon said, "Christ, Duff! What in the fuck is going on?"

"I don't know, but I'm going to find out." He flipped his radio to the interteam channel. "Charlie, for Alpha. Come back." Upon receiving no response, he said, "Charlie Actual, Alpha Actual, how copy?"

Frenchie shook his head, then spoke softly. "They're all dead, boss. Give it up."

But Duff raised his voice and tried again. "Any Alpha element. Any Alpha element, respond on this net, over."

Gabby looked around, as confused as most of the rest in the truck. "They were all killed in the explosion, yes?"

Duff waited about ten seconds, used the time to strap himself into his harness, then depressed the mic again. "Well . . . I'm guessing by the fact you boys are all playin' dead that we weren't supposed to see Alpha team parking War Horse in front of the west side of the town hall and then driving off to the north in Show Horse, were we?"

Duff waited several more seconds, then clicked in again. "I bet that throws one hell of a wrench into your plan, doesn't it, Remmick?"

"What's goin' on, boss?" Nascar all but whispered.

Duff was about to reply to him when he heard squelch on the radio. And then Remmick's voice, a dark and ominous tone. "As a matter of fact it does, Mr. Duffy."

CHAPTER 57

Heads turned throughout Crazy Horse. Squeeze buttoned up his hatch and sat down. "What's goin' on, Eleven-B?"

Frenchie just said a soft "Merde" to himself.

Before Duff could respond, Gordon keyed his mic. "Bravo One for Alpha One. You blew up the meeting? You fucking killed the delegation?"

"A bit more complicated than that, Gordon. Above your pay grade."

"Considering the fact that your plan, whatever it is, obviously involves leaving me and Duff and the rest of us to die, I'd say I'm not getting paid damn near enough."

There was another long pause. Duff got the impression Remmick was trying to figure out his next move. Finally he said, "Tell you what, fellas. Since you guys aren't going to call back to HQ and tell everybody that me and my team died as heroes, I think we better meet up and negotiate."

"You gotta be joking," Duff said. "You just murdered something like fifty people. There's gonna be five hundred Black Knights raining down on our asses in a few minutes. We're getting the hell out of here."

"You think you're going to drive out of the Sierra Madres to safety?

Over one hundred miles. One truck, a handful of guys, and a terp? How much gas you got? Pack Horse Two had all the reserves. You'll have to avoid the towns, so where you gonna fill up?"

Gordon said, "Me and Duff have sat phones, dumbass! We'll get the Mexican army up here, and we're gonna call Armored Saint and tell them you smoked the whole delegation."

"Shit, Gordo," Remmick said. "That would sure suck for me. Why don't you pull out your sat phone and make that call right now. I'll wait."

Duff and Gordon looked at each other. They snatched their phones up and looked at them.

After a few seconds Duff sighed. "You canceled the Inmarsat service to our phones."

"We planned for just about anything. Just now, the second you let slip that you knew what was up, we bricked your phones. You guys are all alone. No chance in hell of getting out of this."

Duff stuck his phone back in a pouch. "I'm guessing you've got a solution for us, don't you?"

"As a matter of fact, I do."

"And I'm supposed to trust you to let us all walk away on the other side of your plan? Why would I do that?"

"Look, I'd rather cut you boys in than spend the rest of my life getting chased down because, by some miracle, you made it out of here and talked. Believe me, when you hear my pitch, you're going to want a piece of this action."

"I'm listening."

"Negative. We'll talk in person. There's an old airstrip, twelve miles from town. Just stay on the road to the southeast; eleven miles out, you'll make a right down an old logging road. You can find the turn on your sat map. Look for the partially camouflaged aircraft. I've got a C-130 inbound, and there's room for all of us to fly out of here together."

"One big happy family."

"Not really. You boys aren't getting on board my plane till we have ourselves a little powwow. I need to be convinced that I can get you and Gordon to comply. You came down here to get paid, and I'm going to see to that if you play ball. But Flores . . . she's a true believer in all this bullshit. You better convince her quick that her only way out of here is through doing exactly what we say.

"Haul ass, Duffy, the Black Knights are gonna regroup and come looking for us. I want to be wheels up in thirty mikes. Alpha One, out."

Cruz was the first to speak up. "Yeah, *that's* not a trap."

"Totally legit," Squeeze said. "Fuck this guy, Alpha's gonna kill us! You know that, TL!"

Duff turned to Gabby. "Look. We have to play for time here, figure something out. It's possible I can make him believe that me and the boys will go along with whatever scheme he's got cooking, but there is no way in hell that he'll trust you to stay silent if we get out of here."

With a wince, he said, "He's going to put a bullet in your head, Dr. Flores."

Gabby made the sign of the cross, closed her eyes, and nodded. "I understand."

"What choice do we have, Duff?" Gordon asked. "The Black Knights just lost their leader, and they just lost their chance to keep the army out of their territory. They're gonna blame us for that. We try to drive all the way off the mountain, they're gonna catch us, and they're gonna tear us apart."

Gabby said, "Mr. Gordon is right. I do not trust Mr. Remmick, but if the Black Knights want to kill us, then there is no way off the Devil's Spine unless it is in an airplane, and an airplane that is leaving soon."

Duff looked to Gordon. "What about the SAMs?"

"Yeah . . . Why the hell would we get in an airplane knowing there are SAMs up here in the Sierras?"

Duff said, "The more important question is, why would Remmick get in an airplane knowing there are SAMs up here in the Sierras?"

Gordon thought for a moment. "Unless . . ."

"That's it! That's what this is all about! Remmick has the SAMs. He must have gotten the BKs to give them up somehow, and he's going to sell them. It's the only thing that makes any sense."

Gordon understood. "If Remmick is willing to fly out of here, then it must be safe to do so, so whether we talk our way on, beg our way on, or fight our way on, we've *got* to get on that aircraft."

Duff addressed everyone now. "He's right, guys. Nascar, take us to this airstrip. I'll check the sat map. This is some kind of a setup, no doubt about it. I have a feeling we aren't supposed to make it the next eleven miles, so everybody strap in, we're rollin' hard!"

Gordon spoke up to Charlie team. "Yeah, expect to get hit!"

Frenchie said, "I've expected to get hit for three days, and I have not been wrong once."

CHAPTER 58

Dina Latham opened her front door at five thirty in the afternoon. Nichole was right on time for the nightly drop-off before heading for her night shift, and just as always, Mandy and Harry were in tow.

"Hey, Dina," Nichole said, and then she shooed her kids into the house.

Dina called after them, "You guys want to play out back on the swing set?"

Both brother and sister squealed and ran to the sliding glass door off the den.

Dina looked back to her neighbor, and only now did she realize today was not like every other day. Normally Nichole dressed in light blue, yellow, or pink scrubs that she wore while working her janitorial job. But now she wore jeans, a U.S. Army sweatshirt, and boots. Dina didn't know Nichole all that well, but looking at her face, she realized she knew her well enough to know she was clearly agitated.

In an instant, Dina knew Nichole had somewhere to go.

"Hey, neighbor. Everything okay?"

"Not even close to okay. I'm going to need a favor. And it's a big one."

"What's up?"

"I have an emergency. I need you to keep watching the kids for a while. It's just a couple of days. I promise."

Dina took a half step back. "A couple of *days*?"

"I'll pay you back, I swear. I'll pay your rate, twenty-four hours a day, until I come home. I wouldn't ask if this wasn't so important. It's Josh. He's in a little trouble."

"I . . ."

"I *have* to go, Dina. Please."

Dina sighed a little; she was secretly happy for the money she'd make, but she wasn't going to make it too easy. "Oh . . . gosh, Nichole, you know I've got Drew, and the mornings are a little crazy with his feedings and—"

"This is life or death. Josh would do it for you or Phil, and you know that."

Dina crossed her arms. "Five bucks an hour is a steal, even for two sleeping kids. My day rate is twenty-five."

Nichole deflated right in front of her as she did the math. She expected pushback, but then her neighbor brought her shoulders back. "Fifteen, and I'll clean your house for a year."

She shook her head. "I can clean. Phil hates cutting the grass, though. His sciatica."

Nichole nodded; the matter was resolved. "Every week. Josh will be happy to." She then said, "Can I say bye to them real quick? I have a plane to catch."

"A *plane*? Where are you going?"

"Trust me on this, Dina. The less you know, the better."

CHAPTER 59

Shane Remmick sat quietly in the front passenger seat of the limo. Alpha Five drove, but there was no one else on board. Just ahead of their vehicle, three flatbed trucks bounced along the bumpy road towards the airstrip, still a mile or so away. Each flatbed had an Alpha team member driving and a second riding shotgun to protect the big crates of missiles and launchers, and all the Americans remained in radio contact, coordinating the maneuver.

The moment the IED had gone off in War Horse, Alpha team shot the Black Knights truck drivers, then pushed them out of the vehicles and assumed their positions. Alpha team was alone now, but they wouldn't be for long.

Remmick had heard from the C-130, and it was just minutes away.

But even though this part of the plan was going smoothly, Alpha One was sullen at the moment. The plan had been for Bravo and Charlie elements to survive the blast, to report back to HQ that Remmick and the rest had died in an IED explosion, and then they themselves would die, either at the hands of the Black Knights or at the hands of the Zetas.

Cardoza had built in multiple redundancies to this scheme, and Remmick had okayed everything. His seven men he'd handpicked both for their skill and for their willingness to fuck over a few has-been contractors and a bunch of drug dealers to make a couple million each, making sure everything went off without a hitch.

But Josh Duffy, Mike Gordon, the bitch from the museum, and a couple more Charlie losers were proving to be one hell of a hitch.

Turning off the men's sat phones had been a stroke of genius by Jason Vance, Alpha Two. The men would have no way to communicate until they got down off the Spine and found a phone, and Remmick had to make sure that never happened.

This was a short-term setback; he would right the ship and sail onwards, but he remained sullen because he was going to have to explain this to Oscar.

Just then his sat phone rang. He switched it through to his headset. "Yeah?"

"It's Cardoza. Where are you?"

"We're on the way to the airfield. Where are *you*?"

"I'm already here. The rain has stopped and it is clearing. Conditions are good."

"Archuleta's man. Diego. Where is he?"

"Dead in his truck. I shot him when we got here."

Remmick nodded. "We did the same to the drivers of the flatbeds. The aircraft is inbound."

Cardoza said, "The Black Knights will come this way very soon."

"The aircraft will be there on time. We'll need fifteen minutes to load and board. I'll post security. We'll be fine."

"Bueno. Then it is all going to plan."

Remmick said, "Actually, no. We hit a little snag."

"Oh?"

"My fall guys aren't falling for it."

"What does that mean?"

"Some men survived. Men who know I'm alive. They put together that we blew up the municipal building."

Cardoza was silent for a long moment. "Where are they?"

"I've got them heading towards the airstrip. They're just ten minutes or so behind us."

"Well then, they will drive right into the Zetas."

"Exactly. Call your man, tell him to let the first APC and the three flatbeds pass, and then to destroy the second APC."

"I will do that now. They will block the road right after you pass. I'll see you at the airstrip."

The phone disconnected, and Show Horse rolled on, the men alone with their thoughts, but they all revolved around one theme: the fact that, in just hours, their lives would be like something from their wildest dreams.

CHAPTER 60

Hear that, boss?"

Duff's mind had been drifting away from the ride along the road, focusing instead on the near-impossible situation they'd all find themselves in once they arrived at the airstrip.

But Nascar's question snapped him back into the moment, and immediately he understood what his driver was asking him.

"I hear it," Duff said. Crazy Horse was rattling and clanging more and more by the minute. Four days on unbelievably bad roads had done a number on the vehicle, and a pair of RPG strikes along with the fucking vehicle-borne improvised explosive device Remmick had used to kill the delegation and Archuleta certainly hadn't done a thing to improve the ride quality of Duff's APC.

But now he heard the sounds of metal on metal, of gears grinding or missing altogether, of a massive engine that sounded like it was deprived of fuel or oxygen or both.

"No chance you'll let me stop and get under the hood, see what I can see?" Nascar asked.

"No chance at all. We're five miles to the airstrip. Have a feeling, one way or the other, we're not going to need Crazy Horse anymore after we get there."

That dark comment hung in the air a moment. Gabby was praying softly, in Spanish, and the other four men sitting in the back with her just looked out their windows in silence. Gordon had taken Wolfson's starboard-side gunport, his M4 carbine poking out and his eyes in the glass. Squeeze, up in the gun turret, wiped dust from his goggles and peered ahead.

The road they were on, if one could call it that, was composed of volcanic rock. Brittle and dusty, such a dark gray that it was essentially black, the road wound north along the western side of a small valley.

A second road was below it, down a short hill. The lower track looked like it was used by donkeys worked by loggers who culled the forests for building materials and fuel. It was wide enough for a vehicle but on the sheer edge of the valley, with a sharp drop-off to more lava rock below it.

The two roads ran parallel, one some thirty feet above the other, a brush- and rock-strewn hill separating them.

Squeeze said, "The way this road is snaking around the side of this valley, it's tough to see what's ahead. Nascar, you catch anything last time we rounded a turn?"

"Sure did. I tallied mountains, pine trees, and black dust. The rocky road we're on and the dirt road below it. Same shit we've been looking at for—"

Cruz interrupted them. "Got contact, rear! Two trucks pulled out of the trees behind us and are following. Two hundred meters."

Gordon said, "Here we go."

Frenchie shouted now. "More vics on the left! Fifty meters out and above us in the trees."

The sound of gunfire came instantly. Bullets pinged off Crazy Horse's already battered armor and slapped against the cracked ballistic glass.

None of the men on board waited for the okay to engage. As far as these men were concerned, every single living thing here in the high Sierras was hostile.

Outgoing fire raged.

"Who the fuck are these guys?" Cruz asked while squeezing bursts from his 48 out the back.

Squeeze said, "Black Knights! They heard about Cinco Lagrimas and set up to wait for us."

Duff didn't have a shot to the rear or to the left; he just kept his AK ready as he evaluated the situation. He was a leader now, not just a gun monkey in the back, and he had to have a plan.

First he said, "Not the Black Knights. This is a coordinated ambush. The BKs wouldn't have had time to set this up."

Gabby said, "This is like last night."

Duff nodded. "It's *exactly* like the trap we rolled into last night. And that means it's the exact same group."

Nascar said, "Also means they're gonna have the damn road blocked ahead. Shit!"

Outgoing fire picked up even more. Cruz and Squeeze belted out round after round from their light machine guns, and nearly as much incoming fire pocked the road or the hill around them, or hit the left side or rear of the vehicle. Nascar was essentially gunning it now, the engine sounding like a wounded animal in its death throes.

They followed the upper road around a bend and immediately swung hard to the left as it turned to go back into the piney woods.

Squeeze shouted just as they lost sight of the winding road on the valley. "Roadblock. One klick ahead on this track."

"What?" Nascar said. "I didn't see it."

"Caught a glimpse before we went back around the bend."

Duff called out. "Squeeze, we're on the higher road, but there's a dirt road right below us on the right. Could you tell which road the roadblock—"

"Definitely this one, the bigger gravel road. We're heading right towards the blocking force, boss. If they've got RPGs, then we're in some serious shit. We don't have four other vics to draw fire. It's just us."

Nascar added, "And we're already shot to shit. This girl isn't gonna take too much more damage."

Gabby spoke softly, but there was a tremor in her voice. "What are we going to do?"

"We fight!" Frenchie said, and he dumped a long burst from his FAMAS at men in the trees above.

Squeeze shouted now. "Boss, just did a 360. I count twelve, say again, one-two technicals. Six o'clock, nine o'clock, and dead ahead."

"Copy," Duff said.

Now Gordon shouted. "Aircraft! One thousand feet, our four o'clock. C-130, looks like it's on final approach through the valley. Gonna land somewhere up ahead."

Duff shouted back, "That's our ticket out of here, we just have to keep these guys off our ass and punch through that block."

Cruz said, "Me and Squeeze can keep the technicals on our six back!"

Frenchie said, "I'm engaging enemy on the hillside. Gordon, shift over here and use the other gunport."

"On it!" Gordon moved behind Squeeze's legs, opened the rear port-side steel flap, and jammed his rifle out. Immediately he began firing bursts up the steep hill. The trucks up there were off-roading it—moving slowly, with men in back firing inaccurately because of the undulating surface below them. Still, there were a lot of men and a lot of guns.

"Why aren't they firing RPGs?" Squeeze asked.

"They're waiting for us to get to the roadblock," Duff replied. He looked to Nascar now. "It's up to you, man. Can you get us through?"

They turned a bend and could see the obstruction clearly now. A pair of pickups in the road, a stack of felled pine logs behind them. Men stood around, rifle and RPG barrels visible, even at this distance.

The road wound back into the trees, and their view ahead disappeared.

Nascar said, "I . . . I don't see how we can—"

Duff screamed at him. "I need a solution! We'll be around the last bend and right in front of them in sixty seconds!"

"Let me think!" Nascar said. He was driving as fast as the vehicle would go now; they were bouncing up and down and left and right every second, only their harnesses keeping them from going airborne inside the APC.

Nascar had a sudden thought. To Duff he said, "The road below us. I can't see it from over here. What's it look like?"

"It's fifteen yards down or so, about a thirty-degree angle." Duff sighed. "You can't take that hill, you'll flip us, roll us all the way over the road and off the cliff into the valley."

"Any big boulders, trees, other obstacles on the hill?"

"What does it matter?"

Nascar shouted at his team leader now. "Are there?"

Duff looked. "Uh . . . it's mostly scrub brush. Ankle high, knee high in places. Not bad. There's some loose rocks. But it doesn't matter, the angle is way too steep to—"

"*About* fifteen yards down to the road, or *exactly* fifteen yards?"

"Exactly?"

"I need to know!"

Duff looked down the hill.

"It's . . . twelve yards, give or take, depending on the bends. Yeah. Right around twelve."

"And thirty degrees down, exactly?"

"I don't have a fucking protractor!"

"I need your best guess, TL!"

Squeeze yelled behind them, his words loud in their headsets. "Thirty seconds till we're in front of that roadblock again!" He emptied his magazine shooting into the pines above. "Frenchie! Forty mike-mike!"

Frenchie passed up the six-shot grenade launcher.

Duff said, "It's about a forty degree decline here. We've got twenty seconds till we're on them, Larry. What's the plan?"

"You trust me, boss?" Nascar asked.

"Yeah, I trust you. But whatever it is, do it the fuck *now*!"

"Squeeze!" Nascar shouted into his mic. "Button up and strap in!"

Squeeze lowered the launcher and the MG and sat down in his seat, rushing to strap into the bench. "What are we doin'?"

Nascar was in charge now, not Duff. "Everybody lock tight and grab somethin'! I'm gonna flip the APC over onto its roof, then slide it down the hill, flip it back on its tires on the road down there."

"Aww, fuck *no*, you ain't!" Squeeze said.

Gordon shouted, "Whoa, wait a sec—"

But Duff silenced everyone. "Ten seconds to secure your weps and strap in!"

"This is a very bad idea," Frenchie muttered, but he slung his rifle over his shoulder and cinched it to his chest with the tabs of his sling.

Nascar turned his attention to Duffy. "Tell me when it's clear, boss. Give me the distance to the road and the angle."

The road wound back to where they could see the roadblock ahead.

"Thirty degrees down now, twelve meters, we're clear of obstructions, sort of. We're in the line of fire."

Two men in the roadblock began aiming their RPGs at the approaching APC.

"Not for long, boss."

Duff turned to Gabby. She was in the middle of the cabin but strapped into her seat. "Cover your head," he said, and she adopted a crouch like she was about to endure a plane crash.

"Here goes nothing!" Nascar shouted as he floored Crazy Horse at the roadblock.

Eighty meters ahead of them, a pair of RPGs left their launchers, streaking side by side up the road towards them ahead of gray smoke trails.

At thirty miles per hour, Nascar turned the wheel from twelve o'clock to two o'clock, and they shot off the side of the road just as the rockets streaked by on their left.

CHAPTER 61

nstantly they tipped over at speed, slammed onto their starboard side, then flipped upside down. The momentum of the vehicle plus the angle of the hill meant they slid on their roof, the turret was instantly sheared away, and loose items crashed all around the six people inside Crazy Horse.

They banged against rocks and thick roots while the undulating hillside itself threatened to spin the truck like a top, but it kept going down the hill, flipped onto its left side now, and then, just as it reached the flat dirt road, it used the last of its sideways momentum to teeter back up.

It crashed down hard on its wheels, then jolted forward; Nascar's foot was still on the gas. He had to jack the wheel to the left to keep from going off the cliff and into the valley, and fully one half of his big back right tire skittered over the edge for a moment, creating an avalanche of rock, before digging into the earth, finding purchase again, and racing back onto the road in a massive cloud of black volcanic dust.

And then, miraculously, Charlie team found themselves fully on the logging road, racing forward, in the same direction as before but just below the roadblock.

Two more RPGs raced towards them from just above, but both sailed over the damaged roof of Crazy Horse and continued down to detonate harmlessly in the valley.

Duff had caught a loose rifle magazine to the mouth during the rollover. His gums bled, but through the blood, he grinned wide. "Holy shit, Nascar! You fucking did it!"

Almost to himself, the young Alabamian muttered, "I'll be damned."

"No way that just happened," Squeeze said from the back.

"Gabby, you okay?" Duff asked.

"Yes," she said, but Duff saw a cut at her hairline that bled down her left temple.

"Frenchie, treat Dr. Flores. Everybody else good?"

Gordon said, "I threw up in my mouth, but I'm good."

"Three is up," replied Frenchie as he opened his medical bag on his chest.

"Four's up," Cruz said from the back, though he sounded like he was in pain.

"You good?" Duff asked.

"The buttstock of my MG caught me right in the nuts."

Duff smiled a bloody smile at this. "Nascar, you hurt?"

Nascar spoke louder now. "I'm up, I'm good, and I'm a fuckin' rock star, boss!"

Squeeze was last to reply. "I might have shit my pants, but Six is here. Goin' up top."

He opened the roof hatch, found that the steel turret that had been protecting him was now gone, and then immediately ducked back down. "Or not."

The truck sounded like it was about to fall apart, but Nascar kept his foot down on the pedal. Duff called to the back. "Cruz, what do you see on our six?"

"I see a bunch of dumb fuckers with their dicks in their hands. They're up on the higher road still, facing the other direction, trying to find a way to turn around on a tight bend."

Duff nodded at this, then reached for a rag to wipe blood from his lips. "Nascar bought us some time, but we have to deal with Remmick now. Everybody get to your gunports and stay vigilant."

The green C-130 idled in the middle of the bumpy grass runway, its four turboprop engines spinning and its back ramp already down. Some five hundred yards behind it, the runway sloped down to the lip of a canyon a mile and a half deep.

Cardoza stood by his Jeep close to the C-130, and Remmick could see that the mastermind of this entire scheme was on his phone, fully engrossed in a rapid-fire conversation.

The three trucks full of missiles rolled to a stop behind the aircraft, and the Alpha men on board them leapt out and began stripping the tarps off the big crates.

Remmick had his driver park Show Horse another fifty yards up the grass strip, well to the side of the runway, and then when all his men and gear were out, he grabbed a bag out of the cabin and opened it. He pulled a pair of thermite grenades from the pack, and Alpha Six reached in and did the same on the other side.

"Fire in the hole," Remmick said, and he tossed both his live grenades into the front seats. Alpha Six threw his two into the back via the port-side hatch, and the men shut the doors and began walking away.

Now there would be no real evidence that Remmick and his men made it to the airstrip. Yes, the remains of Show Horse would be found, but it would be completely destroyed, and there would be no way to prove Alpha team was with it at the end.

The thermite began cooking off inside; it would take minutes to totally involve the vehicle in flames, and more time before the gas tanks ruptured and it exploded. Remmick had ensured that it was far enough away from the aircraft to not cause any problems.

Remmick now stepped up to Cardoza by his Jeep as the Mexican slipped his phone into his pocket and looked in the American's direction. Remmick said, "My guys will start loading the SAMs from the trucks to the plane."

Instantly, however, Remmick could tell that the normally unflappable Oscar Cardoza was agitated. "What is it?"

Cardoza sighed. "I just heard from Lobo, the leader of the Zetas. The other APC broke through their blocking position two minutes ago. Six more of his men are dead or wounded. The Americans are coming this way."

"Son of a bitch!" Remmick looked back across the airstrip to the road that came out of the pines. The old cargo plane under camo netting was thirty yards to the left of it; it looked like weeds and brush were growing up around the aircraft. He said, "Are the Zetas at least in pursuit of them?"

"No. They had to leave the road and escape into the hills. The Black Knights are on the road now, up from Cinco Lagrimas. There are two hundred men coming this way."

"How long till the BKs are here?"

"Lobo says maybe twenty minutes, but we'll be gone by then. You need to worry about those security men. They will be here much sooner. What will you do about them?"

Remmick thought it over a moment. "I'm going to do just what I told them I'd do. I'm going to negotiate with them."

"Negotiate?"

"We have to protect this shipment until it's in the air. If we get into a firefight, those bastards on Charlie team have a grenade launcher. They'll target the aircraft and the SAMs and blow us all into that canyon at the end of the runway. No, I'm going to appeal to their sense of reason. I'll throw them money and a lifeline. They will be motivated to catch a ride with us."

"What if talking doesn't work?"

Remmick answered by triggering his mic. "Alpha Three. Load one of those SAM launchers, grab a scoped rifle, and get into the tree line over there on the north. You need a view to the road coming up from the south."

"Who am I shootin', boss?"

"Convert the missile to an antitank weapon and wait for my

command. I might need you to shoot some dismounts, too, so have your rifle handy."

"Charlie team?"

"Yep. They're still in the fight, but not for long. How copy?"

"Good copy, boss." Alpha Three was behind the C-130, some distance away, but Remmick watched as he pulled a crate off a truck and let it fall to the ground. He opened the lid, pulled one of the two long missiles out of its foam encasement, and then hefted the big launcher. He adjusted his rifle sling, left the other missile in the case, and began running towards the tree line to the north of the airstrip, in the opposite direction of the road that came in from the south.

"What are you doing?" Cardoza asked.

"A little insurance."

"If you can use a missile, why do you have to negotiate? Why don't you just blow up the armored truck as soon as it arrives?"

Remmick offered a rare smile. "There's an old saying: Diplomacy is the art of keeping the enemy talking until your archers are in range."

"I don't understand."

"The Igla-S is a surface-to-air missile. It's going to take my guy ten minutes to modify it to take out a ground target. No . . . those guys coming here now have a decent hand, for the time being, anyway. I'll keep them engaged."

Cardoza nodded. "It sounds like you have things under control. I'll get in the aircraft."

"No," Remmick said. "You will help my men haul crates up that ramp. Just because you're the mastermind doesn't mean you don't have to work up a sweat."

"Very well," Cardoza said, and he began jogging off towards the C-130.

CHAPTER 62

Crazy Horse was in its death throes, and everyone inside the vehicle knew it. It sputtered and coughed and jolted and rocked. Squeaks grew by the minute; a strut had been badly bent in the rollover, so Nascar had to fight the wheel to keep the nose pointed in the right direction.

Finally, he said what everyone knew. "We're about to break down, boss."

But Duff wasn't listening. Instead, he peered through the spider-webbed bulletproof glass. He said, "There's the airstrip. The C-130. A burning APC, I bet Remmick torched it."

They drove a little closer, Nascar moving the now-smoking vehicle slowly through the trees. Duff said, "I see three flatbeds. Those crates on the back are going to be the missiles. Looks like they're already loading them on board."

"How do you want to do this, Duff?" Gordon asked from behind.

"First, Nascar, pull up the road to the edge of the strip, but stay tight against the pine trees in case we need to get out and fight."

"Roger." The vehicle slowed and stopped. Duff could see through the all-but-shattered ballistic glass that the men at the plane two hundred yards away were stopping what they were doing and looking in his direction.

"I'll walk from here. Alone. I'll keep my mic transmitting so you can hear what I'm saying."

Gordon said, "You're actually going to get out of the vehicle and talk with him?"

"What choice do I have?"

"I'll go, Duff. You've got people to protect. All my men are dead. Plus, I'm the one that got you into this, and—"

"And," Duff interrupted, "I don't trust you to get me out of it."

"Well, if you're going, then I'm going, too."

The matter settled, Duff said, "All right, everybody, listen up. Frenchie is Charlie Three. He's in charge now. Gabby, you sit right there on the bench. I don't want one of Remmick's men taking a shot at you, thinking he can tie up a loose end."

"Okay."

"Squeeze," Duff continued. "You're up in the roof hatch with the M32. I want high-explosive grenades ready to blow that aircraft to hell if it comes to it."

"Not with you standing right next to it."

Darkly, he said, "Yeah, well, I might not be standing for long." To Cruz he said, "Four, stay on your MG, but get all the ammo you have strapped to your body somehow in case you have to bail to the tree line. Keep your eyes on our six. Figure either the Black Knights are on the way or the guys we just hoodwinked back on the road are coming to take another crack at us."

"Roger, TL."

"Frenchie, I want you outside your hatch, scanning the scene in your scope and listening to every word I say. You're running this show now."

"D'accord." He cracked his door, stood on the running board, and aimed his FAMAS towards the activity in the middle of the derelict airstrip. "Looking through my scope now. Range to Remmick is two hundred meters. You say the word and I'll eliminate him."

"It might come to that. Just listen to what I say and report to me what you see." He turned to Nascar. "You can fly a plane, right?"

Nascar looked at him like he was crazy. "I flew helos for Academi. I can fly fixed-wing, too, but only single-engine or light twins. I sure as hell can't fly that C-130."

Duff sighed. Looking around, he saw the aircraft under the camouflage. It was right next to the tree line, only fifty yards or so to the right of Crazy Horse. "That plane over there. It looks simple enough."

Nascar leaned over Duff to look out the passenger-side window. "Give me the binos." He took them from Duff and focused on the aircraft. "It's a beat-up old twin prop. A CASA C-212. Little cargo hauler built in Spain. Probably down here for runnin' drugs. You could pack a lot of weed in that cargo hold."

"Can you fly it?"

"You're kidding, right?"

"Right now you can assume that I'm dead serious about every word I say."

"Does it run? Does it have electric, does it have fuel? Hydraulic fluid? I mean, yeah, I could fly it if it were flyable, but it doesn't look—"

"Slip out the back of the vic, get into those trees, and go check it out. See if we can use it as a backup ride out of here if worse comes to worst."

"I can tell you from fifty yards away. It's a piece of shit."

"Do it anyway," Duff snapped.

"Sure, boss."

Now Duff made quick eye contact with Gabby. "It's going to be okay."

"The Lord is with you, Mr. Duffy."

He nodded. "Gordo. You ready?"

"Not really, but . . ."

Gordon and Duff opened their hatches simultaneously. Together they began walking towards the aircraft. Men loading missiles into the C-130 stopped what they were doing and aimed rifles their way, so both Bravo One and Charlie One unslung their own rifles and let them fall to the ground. They did not remove their handguns, but they kept their hands up as they walked across the airstrip.

CHAPTER 63

Well, I have to hand it to you boys. You both look like shit, but you made it this far."

Remmick wasn't covered in the dust and grime and blood from the IED or the near-continuous fighting of the last half hour. While Duff and Gordon looked like they'd rolled down a mountain together, hitting every rock along the way, Alpha One's Oakleys were clean and intact, his back ramrod straight, and the rifle on his chest clean, gun oil glistening.

Duff had to speak loudly because they were just twenty-five yards from the idling C-130, but also because he was transmitting for the benefit of Frenchie and the others back at the truck two hundred meters away.

He said, "The group on the road who just ambushed Crazy Horse. Those were the same guys as last night. Not BKs. It was some other group working for you, wasn't it?"

"Very good, kid. They're Zetas."

"Zetas?" He said it himself in case those in Crazy Horse couldn't pick up Remmick's words from the microphone Duff wore over his mouth. "There aren't any Zetas for hundreds of miles."

"We have . . . some . . . shared interests. They are up here supporting my mission. But I wouldn't worry too much about them. There are fifty or so left in that force, but about two hundred Black Knights are on the way here, right now. ETA, I'm told, is less than fifteen mikes."

Duff spit blood onto the grass. "These crates they're loading up the rear hatch of the C-130. These are the surface-to-air missiles the UN was after?"

"Right again."

"Your entire plan was to use the delegation as a way up here, and then to kill them. Then you guys slip away with the SAMs."

"The UN plan was to come in here, grab those MANPADS, and destroy them. Fuckin' launchers are worth one point one mil each on the black market." Remmick laughed. "You think I'd take this bullshit suicide run for seventy grand? No, boys, my cut in all this is twenty million, tax free."

Duff said, "I'm guessing the plan was for us to get wiped out on the road by the Zetas. Maybe after we called in to Armored Saint and said you guys were all killed in the attack." When Remmick neither confirmed nor denied, he said, "What's the plan now?"

"That depends on you and Gordon here, but it mostly depends on you. I like my chances with Gordon playing ball, but you're the wild card, Duffy, aren't you?"

Gordon's eyes narrowed. "What do you want from us, Remmick?"

"What do I want? I want you to be rich. Two and a half million each. Gordo, that will pay off a lot of child support, help you get retrained for some other type of work. The PMCs haven't come calling since you blew up your team on a fucking corn dog run in Afghanistan, have they?"

"Chili dog," Duff corrected, but neither of the other men acknowledged the comment.

Gordon said, "*You* came calling."

"I did, yes. And now you're here, and I'm giving you the opportunity of a lifetime." He turned to Duff now. Behind Remmick, the men were still loading crates up the rear ramp of the big green aircraft. "Duffy, two and a half mil has surely got to be enough to get the little missus to hang up her toilet plunger, don't you think? What about Mandy and Harry? What kind of Christmas did they have on a mall cop's salary last year? Tell me about their college prospects if you turn me down right now."

"Fuck you," Duff said softly.

"Okay," Remmick laughed. "You're one hard-ass hero, I get it. But what about your Joes still alive over there in Crazy Horse? I'm feeling generous. I'll give them a mil each. That and, of course, a flight off the mountain, which, considering present circumstances, is goddamned priceless. Dr. Flores will tell you that the narcos down here have a saying: 'Plomo o plata.' *Lead or silver.* You can get a bullet, or you can get rich. Well, same deal here. You can come with me and get paid, or you can stay here and face a couple hundred Black Knights, who are ten minutes out."

"And what about Flores?"

Remmick shook his head. "Non-negotiable. We leave her here for Archuleta's people. We keep our hands clean, and nature will take its course."

"They'll kill her," Duff said softly.

Remmick shrugged. "Nature's a bitch." He turned to Gordon. "Gordo, you're on board, right?"

Gordon's eyes narrowed. "What's to keep you from tossing us out of the plane once we take off?"

"Self-preservation. Do a head count. I've got two unarmed pilots, an unarmed loadmaster, and eight armed men, including myself. There are six of you boys. You all keep your personal weapons, we get on the plane and stare one another down in the cargo hold all the way to Bogotá if you want. That's a fair fight, if it comes down to it. Hell, a bullet won't blow up an Igla-S, but any grenade detonations might, so we'll all have an incentive to keep it polite and friendly while on the aircraft."

"And the money?" Gordon asked.

Duff turned and looked at him with amazement, realizing suddenly that his friend was actually considering cutting a deal.

Remmick said, "It will be wired into an account I have in the Seychelles. I'll pay everybody via wire, wherever you want, as soon as we've made the delivery to the buyers in Bogotá."

He added, "If we all keep our traps shut, nobody else has to die."

Duff said, "And you are selling the surface-to-air weapons to . . . to *who*, exactly?"

"Does it even matter?"

"Not to you, obviously."

"You're goddamned right, it doesn't matter to me. Bad guys are going to get bad-guy shit and do bad-guy shit. With or without me, it's going to happen. Might as well facilitate it a little bit and get paid in the process. And now, gents, so can you. This is a hell of a good plan. I've got everything I need to pull this off, although, I gotta say, a little more compliance out of you motherfuckers would be helpful. Better just tell me if you want me to deal you in or not." To Gordon he said, "Bravo One?"

"I . . . I don't know." He looked to Duff. "Not like we have much of a choice."

Duff stared at his old friend in disbelief. "Gordon, you can't really be considering—"

"It's this or die, man."

"What about Gabby?"

"We give her a gun, food and water, and get her into those pines. She knows this area. She'll be fine."

Duff rolled his eyes. This was fantasy. He knew Gabby wouldn't survive an hour on the Devil's Spine. Remmick knew the same thing, otherwise he would shoot her himself.

But Gordon told himself what he wanted to believe, and he looked at Remmick. "I'm in, boss."

Duff said, "Mike. No."

"Smart man, Gordon," Remmick said. "Duff? What say you? Think of that little family back home."

Duff sighed. "No. Charlie team is out."

Now Gordon tried to appeal to him. "C'mon, brother. Don't be crazy."

Remmick said, "Duff, you are *nothing*, just an Eleven Bang Bang, Army infantry. Yeah, you rolled in some hot details as a PMC, but you're not a sled driver, you're a sled *dog*. You *were* a sled dog, till you lost your leg. Now you ain't shit.

"Be a leader for once in your life. You've got men left alive in that gun truck over there. After all we've been through, are you really going to sign their death warrants?"

"Well, I sure as hell am not going to sign them up to sell surface-to-air missiles to fucking terrorists."

"So . . . you're going to just stay here while we fly away? Hug it out with the Black Knights when they show up? That's your plan?"

Duff raised his voice a little, making sure Frenchie was picking it up. "I've got four weapons trained on you and your men, including a grenade launcher ready to blow that aircraft full of missiles so high NASA's gonna be the first to call it in."

Remmick laughed again. "Nice try, kid, but a little too obvious. I saw that one coming. I've got my Alpha Three in the tree line back there behind me with an Igla-S pointed at your APC. I have an open line with him right now through my headset, and he's hearing our conversation. If I tell Ray to fire, he's going to blow Crazy Horse into oblivion."

Duff cocked his head. "You're gonna shoot a surface-to-air missile at a parked truck?"

"Ask your boy Cruz. He's former Special Forces. He knows how enemy weps operate. It's an easy mod to have an Igla-S take out a ground target like an APC.

"Yeah . . . you're playing a bad hand now, Duff. I can turn your boys and your girlfriend over there into canned soup if I want."

In his headset, Frenchie spoke. "Cruz confirms it *is* possible to convert the Igla to an antitank weapon."

Shit, Duff thought. This prospect hadn't even occurred to him. All his people were sitting in an armored car that would be no match for the warhead of an Igla-S.

The men stood in silence for a long moment, until Remmick said, "Cat got your tongue, Duff?"

Softly, Duff said, "Please."

Remmick glanced at his watch, and then looked back up at Duff. Into his mic, he said, "Alpha Three. Do it."

"No!" Duff screamed.

He saw the missile launch out of the pines behind Remmick, in front of the nose of the C-130, and just sixty or so yards away. It streaked past him, a white trail of smoke behind it, and Duff spun around to watch, praying the weapon missed its target.

But it slammed straight into the grille of Crazy Horse, detonating it utterly and completely. Steel doors shot in all directions, the roof hatch launched into the air, the ballistic glass windshield crystallized to nothing, and the boom of the explosion almost knocked Duff down where he stood two hundred yards away.

CHAPTER 64

Duff just stared, his eyes filled with tears, his heart clenched tight in his chest.

Mike Gordon put his hands on his head, his face a mask of disbelief.

Behind him, Remmick said, "Impact! Target destroyed. Less men to pay off. And one less indigenous busybody bitch to tell the world what went down."

Duff started to reach for his pistol. "Fuck! I'm going to kill you, you son of a—"

"Don't move, Duff," Remmick warned. "Now Alpha Three's got a rifle on *you*. I give the word and you catch a bullet to the grape. This is your last chance to survive to see the sunset, and that's just because I'm feeling generous."

Mike Gordon recovered from his shock, then squared off to Duff and drew his own pistol. He leveled it at his friend's head. "*Please*, Duff. I'm doing you a favor, man. You've lost enough already. You *don't* have to die today."

Josh Duffy slowly dropped into the grass onto his knee pads.

Remmick looked back over his shoulder. "My guys will finish loading here in two minutes, and then we're rolling off that cliff and out over the valley. I'll give you thirty seconds to decide."

He turned to Gordon. "Mike, I like where I *think* your head is at, but if that sidearm moves in my direction, Alpha Three is going to drop you next to your sobbing boyfriend."

Gordon nodded. "I'm solid, boss. Just trying to get me and my friend out of here."

Duff hesitated, but then he made a decision. He would stand back up, reach for his pistol, pull it on Remmick, and take the inevitable bullet to the head. All his people were dead, everyone he'd been entrusted to protect, and there was nothing left to live for. He wasn't thinking of Nichole or of Mandy or Harry. He was only thinking of the team he'd led up into the mountains to die.

His eyes narrowed and he looked up at Remmick. Just as he began to push up to his feet, however, the crack of squelch came in his ear that told him a transmission was coming through.

"Boss?" It was Frenchie. Duff dropped back to his knees, bewildered. "We're okay. I got everyone out the back of Crazy Horse just before it exploded. We're all under the netting with the old cargo prop plane. I have sights on a sniper in the trees on the other side of the C-130. Say the word and I . . ."

"Take him!" Duff said.

Remmick cocked his head. "Take who?"

A single gunshot cracked behind Duff, who was in the process of launching to his feet and drawing his pistol. Remmick reached for his rifle on his chest, and Gordon swiveled his weapon towards Remmick's movement, confused by what was happening.

Remmick shifted aim to Gordon, the more immediate threat. Gordon shot Remmick in the forearm with his pistol, but not before Remmick squeezed off a round from his carbine.

Gordon flew back to the ground, and almost simultaneously, Duff felt a powerful impact on his own torso, rocked on his heels, and fell flat onto his back, his pistol tumbling away next to Mike's still body.

Alpha Two had shot the Charlie team leader from thirty meters, just as Duff was about to fire at Remmick.

Remmick crumpled to his knees, clutching his arm and screaming in pain.

Alpha team members raced over to the scene, their rifles scanning all around.

Everyone still thought Charlie team had been blown up in the missile attack on Crazy Horse; the single round Frenchie had fired had been mistaken for Alpha Three's rifle firing, possibly hitting Gordon at the same time as Remmick shot him.

Remmick clutched his bloody arm, groaned in pain, and let his men pull him up to his feet. He looked back at Gordon and Duff. Gordon was covered in blood and drawing his last breath, and Duff was flat on his back, his arms out to his side. Remmick didn't see blood on Charlie One, but he saw blood on himself and wanted to get in the C-130 to receive treatment for the ugly wound through his arm.

The Alpha men began running back towards the airplane.

"Duffy? Duffy?" It was Frenchie's voice, and it roused the dazed man lying on his back in the grass. He opened his eyes and found himself confused to be staring at a sky that was quickly dimming as late afternoon gave way to early evening.

He lifted his head and saw the big green aircraft begin to taxi past him from right to left, away from the canyon and farther up towards the tree line to the west.

And then Duff looked down at himself. He could tell by the pain in his upper chest that someone had shot him high center mass, obviously aiming for his head but missing low because Duff had been launching to his feet when he was shot. The round caught the heavy plate of his body armor, but if it had hit him any higher at all, Duff knew he'd have a hole through the top of his rib cage near his right shoulder, and he'd be fucked.

It hurt, but it wasn't a gunshot wound, so he pulled himself up. As he did this, he spoke into his radio, "I'm okay, Frenchie."

He crawled over to Gordon now. Mike was dead; his eyes had rolled up, only the white showing through his low-hanging lids. The blood from his neck oozed, but it did not spurt.

"Shit," Duff said, and then he transmitted, "Where's Remmick?"

Frenchie responded. "He ran up the ramp as the plane started taxiing away. Too many Alpha men were in the way. I didn't have a clean shot at him and didn't want to give away our location."

Duff looked around as he spoke. "Gordon's dead. Remmick says two hundred Black Knights are a few minutes out. We need a plan."

He looked at the C-130. "The plane is heading up the airstrip, *away* from the canyon. Why are they doing that, Nascar?"

Nascar replied over the radio. "That's a big plane, and it's full of cargo. He needs every bit of this airstrip to take off. He'll turn around, apply brakes and full power, and launch into his takeoff roll. When he gets to the end of the runway, he'll have to dip down into the canyon for speed."

"Got it. Squeeze, can you nail that C-130 with your grenade launcher before he takes off?"

"I could if I hadn't left it in Crazy Horse. It only had two rounds left, and I only had time to grab the Mk 48 and the ammo. Sorry, boss."

"You made the right call. We're going to need that MG." He then looked at the airstrip where the aircraft had been parked. There was an open crate there. He stood and ran for it. As he did so he called for Cruz. "Charlie Four. You know how to fire an Igla-S?"

"That's an SA-7. A monkey could fire it."

"Well, we don't have a monkey. Can *you* do it?"

"Fuck yeah, I can."

Duff arrived at the crate, and he saw a missile, but the launcher was missing. Quickly he looked up at the tree line to the east, where the missile had come from a minute earlier.

He snagged the long missile out of the foam casing and began sprinting for the launcher in the trees. "All right," he said. "I've got a missile, I'm going to grab the launcher and haul ass over to you. Cruz, you got any reservations about taking down that aircraft and removing those SAMs from the hands of terrorists?"

"And killing a bunch of Americans?" he asked.

Squeeze jumped in. "Yeah, but they're all assholes."

"Good point." Cruz sighed. "Fuck it. I'll blow those sons of bitches out of the sky if I can. You'd better hurry, though. The C-130 is twenty seconds from turning around to position for takeoff."

"Yeah," Nascar said. "And the Black Knights can't be far now."

Duff was completely winded by the time he found the dead Alpha man lying next to the missile launcher and the sniper rifle. He picked the launcher up, loaded the missile he'd been carrying, turned, and began running back across the grass airstrip. As he ran, he panted out his plan over the radio. "Okay. I'm coming your way. The rest of you, you'd better get ready for a fight. We're going to destroy this C-130, and then we're going to turn and face the Black Knights. This was a one-way trip when we signed up for this gig, but now we know it, and we can go out on our own terms."

"Hoo-yah, Duffy," shouted Cruz.

"Hey, boss." It was Nascar. "I might have another option, but you ain't gonna love it."

"Not in love with my plan, either," he puffed. "I'm all ears."

"While you were shooting the shit with Remmick, I got in this old cargo hauler over here. The airframe looks okay. The tires are intact, though they're pretty low. I'm at the controls now. The plane is beat to shit, smells like a cat died in the cockpit."

"Probably the last pilot," Squeeze said.

Nascar ignored him. "Elevators and ailerons work. The only problem is the battery is stone-cold dead. I can't even read the fuel gauge if I don't have electrical."

"And you can't start those engines, either, can you?"

"Well, I can, but you might not like how I'll have to do it. Gabby says that canyon at the end of the runway is eight thousand feet deep. I looked at the sat image, it's straight down, no obstructions to the river."

Duff was only one hundred yards from the cargo plane now. Behind him, the C-130 began turning around to face the airstrip. Still running, he said, "What are you saying?"

"I'm saying maybe we roll this bitch down the hill next to the airstrip, pick up some speed, jump in, then shoot off the side of the canyon. Once we start diving, the props will spin, and it should give us a little electrical power. I might be able to fire the engines."

"There are a lot of 'shoulds' and 'mights' in that plan."

"True. Of course, gettin' killed by the Black Knights is a sure thing if we don't get the fuck out of here, so . . ."

Duff thought it over. "We concentrate on taking down that C-130. We might die, but we'll save thousands by getting those missiles out of the hands of terrorists."

CHAPTER 65

Oscar Cardoza stood behind the pilots, leaning into the cockpit as the C-130 turned 180 degrees to face the airstrip and the canyon beyond. Remmick stepped up next to him, clutching his now-bandaged forearm.

"All the Americans are dead?" Cardoza asked.

"At least one is left, but Charlie One and Bravo One are out of the fight. The BKs will take care of the rest."

"And we have all the Iglas loaded?"

"They are in the cargo hold. The ramp is still down because some of the crates are still on it. My guys are pulling them up the ramp and will close it before takeoff."

The pilot stepped on his brake pedals with his toes, then pushed the throttle forward. The aircraft shuddered as the engines revved, but it didn't move forward.

The pilot looked back at Remmick. "Get that ramp closed! Let's go!"

Cardoza shouted, "I'll do it," and he began running to the back.

But instead of finding the Alpha men working hard to slide the remaining two crates off the ramp so it could be closed, he saw them all talking to one another, with the last two crates still sitting on the lowered ramp.

"What's going on?"

"Alpha Three isn't on the aircraft," one said, confusion in his voice.

"Who cares?" Cardoza snapped, and he went to grab the first case. An Alpha contractor followed him down the ramp and started dragging it.

As he did so, the American said, "He has one of the launchers."

"Then we sell fifty-eight instead of fifty-nine. He doesn't get his cut, so we all earn the same."

Together they got the first case up the ramp and were pulling the second. The loadmaster stood there, ready to raise the ramp once the men and equipment were clear.

The Alpha operator looked worried to Cardoza. The Mexican wondered if Alpha Three had been a friend of his, and he didn't really give a shit, but he asked, "What's the problem?"

The crate and men were clear of the ramp. The aircraft bolted forward, knocking everyone off balance. As it rolled, bouncing over the bumpy grass strip, the loadmaster hit the button to raise the ramp, right next to Cardoza.

The Alpha man stood there next to him. He shouted to be heard. "Three fired one missile out of that launcher."

Instantly, Cardoza understood. Remmick had just told him that at least one member of Charlie team was still alive. "Are you saying there might be an enemy out there with access to an antiair launcher and an antiair missile?"

The ramp was halfway up, and the turboprop screamed down the runway towards the canyon.

"Stop the takeoff!" Cardoza shouted, but he wasn't wearing a team headset, so only the man next to him heard.

The plane continued gaining speed as it rolled down the airstrip.

Cardoza looked at the stacks of crates, of the men standing around, and he looked at the closing hatch. With only a moment's hesitation, he ran up the rising ramp and dove headfirst out of the rear of the rolling aircraft, just as the ramp shut behind him.

CHAPTER 66

Duff was still running across the strip with the big launcher, his body armor and magazine racks, his less-than-perfect cardio-vascular fitness, and his prosthetic leg all slowing him down.

As he ran for the cargo plane, Cruz came over his headset. "Boss, that C-130 has started his takeoff roll. He's going to dip into the canyon and fly off, and if he knows he left SAMs on the airstrip, he's going to fly low outta here."

"Meaning?"

"Meaning I won't have a shot at him from here."

Duff understood now. "But if we get in the air . . ."

Nascar finished the thought. "Then I can chase after Remmick. This plane isn't as fast as his, but the range on that SAM has got to be five miles."

Cruz said, "Half that, effectively, but Remmick won't know we're chasing him, so he probably won't be flying at top speed. We can do this."

"I do *not* like this plan, TL!" Squeeze chimed in. "Why don't we just shoot the C-130 with our machine guns?"

"Right now they don't know you're alive. We won't detonate the missiles with our guns, we'll just draw fire, and they'll still get out of here."

Cruz shouted now. "I've got trucks approaching on the road from the south. A lot of them!"

Duff didn't turn his head to look. "How . . . how far?"

"Six hundred meters and closing."

"That beat-up cargo plane is our only chance," Duff said.

"So move your ass, boss!" Nascar shouted.

Duff arrived at the aircraft just as the four Charlie operators had yanked off the netting.

"Damn. This piece of shit looks worse up close."

Gabby said, "Believe me, the Black Knights look worse up close, too."

Gabby climbed into the copilot's seat, and Cruz and Squeeze ripped brush away from the front of the plane so it could be moved.

Duff climbed up the small open rear ramp and put the missile under a bench that ran down the right side of the fuselage. Cruz and Squeeze began pushing the starboard wing, and Duff ran back out the rear to help Frenchie on the port side.

Nascar was pushing at the back, and he yelled to Dr. Flores in the cockpit. "Gabby, you steer with the foot pedals, we're heading for that decline. I'll tell you what to do from out here."

"We're not going down the runway?"

"Too far, we're going to go off the cliff to the side."

The five men pushed the aircraft on its soft tires. It moved slowly at first but then picked up speed as it began going down the decline towards the cliff. The airstrip was on the left, and it continued out on a spur that gave it a lot more length before dropping off over the canyon, but it was clear to Duff that Nascar was aiming for a point just a couple hundred yards away. They wouldn't have much ground to pick up speed, but Duff figured gravity would give them all the speed they needed as soon as they fell into the mile-and-a-half-deep canyon.

Just then, the zing of rifle rounds pierced the air around them.

Cruz shouted, "Contact rear! Enemy three hundred yards behind us."

Frenchie said, "Push harder, mes amis!"

More automatic gunfire whined as it raced past. The men firing in the trucks would be dealing with a lot of jolting and bouncing, and their aim would be adversely affected, but Duff knew as well as anyone that it just took one lucky round to create a very bad day.

"Don't engage!" he shouted. "Just keep pushing!"

Nascar said, "Gabby, step down on the right pedal. Not too much. Good! Okay, we're on the hill, we're picking up speed! Everybody in, now!"

"Me first!" Squeeze shouted as he ran for the open ramp.

But Nascar beat him inside. "I'm the pilot, asshole, out of my way!"

"Charlie Four is in!" Cruz shouted as he fell onto the floor of the cabin.

The aircraft's ground speed was increasing with every yard of the steep gradient.

Duff dove in right behind Cruz, climbed to his knees on the bouncing floor, and turned to look behind him. "Where's Frenchie?"

Nascar spoke into his mic. "I'm at the controls!"

"Come on, Frenchie!" Duff shouted.

The older Frenchman was ten feet behind the small open ramp now, running as fast as he could, but he looked like he was losing ground. Duff held on to the vertical gas lift bar and stepped down to the edge of the ramp. Reaching out as hard as he could, he said, "Take my hand!"

"I'm trying!"

Gunfire ripped through the air yet again; the approaching trucks were no more than one hundred yards back now. A round pierced the fuselage on Duff's right. He ducked his head, but he leaned out at full extension now, desperate to get a finger on Frenchie's hand.

"Toss your rifle!" Duff yelled, and Frenchie did so. This made him a little faster, but he still wasn't gaining on the aircraft, which itself was speeding up.

This wasn't going to work. Duff shouted. "Nascar! Slow us down!"

"I can't! We're ten seconds from going off the cliff! We need speed to—"

And then Frenchie pulled up, slowed, and stopped. Putting his hands on his knees, he panted into his microphone, then said, "I'm sorry, Duff . . . I can't make it."

"No!" Duff shouted.

Forty feet behind the open ramp, Frenchie turned around and drew his pistol, raising it at the enemy vehicles.

"No!" Duff shouted again.

Frenchie fired twice and then was cut down by merciless rifle fire.

"Frenchie is down! Charlie Three is down!"

Nascar shouted into his headset now. "Hang on to somethin', everybody! We're goin' airborne!"

Duff raced back into the cabin, ran towards the cockpit, and said, "How do I close the ramp?"

"Forget the ramp," Nascar said. "Here we go!"

The pounding, jolting, bouncing of the ground gave way to a sudden quiet, and the quiet soon gave way to the sound of wind growing in volume and intensity.

The aircraft was more or less level for a couple of seconds, and then the nose dipped forward, and it began plummeting straight towards the earth.

Nascar shouted, "Oh shit!"

CHAPTER 67

Duff looked out the windscreen at rocks and trees and, a mile and a half below, a white river that seemed to be getting larger every second. "Do you have control?"

From the pilot seat, Nascar shouted, "Does it fucking look like it?"

He wrestled the controls, the strain of the effort evident in his voice. "Have to get the nose up to get some lift! Pullin' . . . as . . . hard . . . as . . . I . . . can!"

"Start the engines!"

"Not yet. Need more . . . speed."

Squeeze shouted from the back, "We're fallin' like a rock, that's not enough speed?"

There was a loud sound; at first Duff thought it was a gunshot.

"What was that?" Gabby screamed.

"One of the control lines broke to the ailerons. It's okay, there's a backup."

"Then why the hell are we still falling?" Duff asked.

"Do you *see* me workin' on it?"

"The river down there," Gabby said. "It is getting closer."

Squeeze shouted at the top of his lungs now. "Fly this thing, you redneck piece of shit!"

"Everybody shut the fuck up!" the pilot screamed back. "Okay, firing the engines. Here goes nothin'."

The two wing engines coughed, sputtered. They both backfired, one at a time, and then the props began to turn and hum as black smoke poured out behind them.

But they were still dropping at a 60-degree angle towards the earth.

Nascar said, "Have to . . . keep . . . pulling . . . up. I need everybody to crawl to the back of the cabin."

Squeeze wasn't having it. "You mean by the wide-assed-open rear hatch?"

"It will help me get the nose up."

"Do it!" Duff shouted. "Climb up the floor. Use the legs of the bench on the side as a ladder if you can get to it. Gabby, you stay put in the copilot seat!"

The three men crawled to the back of the airplane and hung on to one another at the top of the ramp.

Squeeze looked at Duff with terrified eyes. "This was a shitty idea, Army!"

Nascar said, "Wait! I feel it! The angle's decreasing." Duff felt it, too. After a few more seconds, they were at level flight.

Cruz said, "We're flying!" Then he cocked his head. "We're flying, right, Nascar?"

"Ah yeah, baby! We're fuckin' flying!"

"Do you see Remmick's aircraft?"

"Let me bank to the north." The plane began a gentle turn. It was only a few seconds before Gabby spoke up.

"Mr. Nascar? The far side of the canyon is getting closer."

"I got it."

They missed hitting the eastern wall by no more than one hundred yards, but soon they were heading north and climbing higher in the canyon.

Duff was back looking over Nascar's shoulder into the dark canyon, early evening shadows covering everything. "Anything?"

Nascar kept looking. Finally he said, "There!" He pointed higher out of the windscreen. "He's flying low and slow in the canyon still. Probably trying to stay below radar as he heads north. About two klicks right off our nose."

Duff said, "He doesn't know we're on his ass."

Cruz said, "I'll ready the weapon."

They flew for just a few seconds more, and then Gabby spoke up. "Mr. Nascar, I am not a pilot, but does the fuel gauge look low to you?"

Nascar looked at the gauge and thumped it with a gloved finger. "Shit, shit, *shit*! Duff, fuel gauge not even registering a drop. This is gonna be a short flight!"

"Then what?" Squeeze demanded.

"Then we're goin' down."

Cruz held the launcher in his hand, and he looked back up towards the cockpit. "What, you mean, crash?"

"Dude, you think I'm gonna dead-stick us to a runway somewhere?"

But Gabby was looking on the bright side. "Well, we're a lot better off than we were a minute ago."

"Roger that, doc. For now, anyway. Might as well enjoy the ride before it all goes to shit again."

CHAPTER 68

Shane Remmick had been dividing his time the past two minutes by both watching the takeoff through the cockpit windshield behind the pilots and retightening the bloody bandage on his right forearm. Gordon's bullet had hit bone, possibly breaking it, and the pain was excruciating, but still Remmick was feeling the elation of escaping with his life along with sixty million dollars' worth of shoulder-fired missiles.

They were climbing higher, out of the canyon, when he realized his headset had been knocked off his head, and now it hung by the radio cord below his knees. He put it back on and immediately heard his men trying to raise him from the back.

Before he could respond, however, Alpha Two rushed into the cockpit, worry on his face.

Remmick reassured him. "Lost my comms for a second. It's fine." When the man didn't change his expression, Alpha One said, "What's up, Vance?"

"Ray never made it on board."

"Shit. He must have gotten sniped when it all went crazy back there."

Vance shook his head. "Ray's not the problem, though. The launcher and one missile are still back there on the deck."

Remmick knew that even though Duffy was likely dead, there was at least one member of Charlie still alive. "Shit. Where's Cardoza?"

Vance said, "As soon as I told him about the missing SAM, he jumped out of the plane."

Remmick's hand fired down to his sat phone in his cargo pocket, and he looked at it. Oscar Cardoza had called three times, all in the last ninety seconds.

Fuck.

Remmick's head spun around, away from Alpha Two and towards the pilot. Screaming into the man's ear, he said, "You got countermeasures on board?"

"Countermeasures?"

"Countermeasures!"

"We've got chaff and flares." With growing alarm, the pilot said, "Why?"

"Deploy them! There's enemy with a MANPAD back there on the airstrip."

The pilot immediately began deploying hot flares and canisters of exploding metal foil from the sides of the C-130. While he did this, he pushed his controls forward, giving them more speed and sending them back down below the lip of the canyon. "We stay below the canyon's edge and nobody can hit us from that airstrip."

Remmick wasn't convinced they were safe. "Deploy everything you got. Now!"

CHAPTER 69

I n the CASA C-212, one half mile below and now well over a mile behind the C-130, Duff looked at the launcher in Tony Cruz's hands. "We doing this thing?"

"It's ready to fire, boss."

Just then, Nascar said, "Remmick's plane is firing flares and chaff. He's dipping lower."

Duff said, "He knows we've got a launcher. I don't know if he knows we've got a plane."

Cruz shouted, "Hurry!"

Squeeze, Cruz, and Duff went to the rear of the aircraft. The port-side hatch wasn't really a hatch at all; it was just an opening with webbing buckled across it. Cruz looked around at the situation, then shouted to be heard over the roar of the propellers. "Here's how we have to do this. I don't want to hit our prop and blow us up, and I don't want the backblast from this bitch to take out everybody in the cabin. Nascar, on my mark, you need to bank to the right. I'll lean against the webbing, hold the launcher out the hatch. Once I have a clear tone on Remmick's aircraft, I'll fire, angle it to where the backblast goes out the open back ramp. Then I'm dropping the launcher and getting back inside."

Duff made certain everyone understood.

Nascar had just rogered up when he shouted, "Shit. Engine two is sputtering. Running out of fuel."

Cruz shouted, "Turn to the right!"

Duff could hear both engines coughing now. The plane banked gently to the right.

Cruz said, "You guys go up to the front!"

But Duff and Squeeze grabbed the man's load-bearing vest in case the webbing broke and he fell, doing their best to stay out from behind him as they did so.

Cruz raised the launcher and aimed it forward into the canyon, and just a little bit higher. There, in what remained of the light from the sunset above the canyon, the green C-130 banked left and right as chaff and flares ejected from its sides.

In the C-212, the engines both coughed one last time, and then the aircraft went silent as the props stopped turning.

Nascar said, "We're gliding. Altitude seven thousand, three hundred."

But Cruz wasn't paying attention. He pressed the homing trigger on the Igla-S, and there was a buzzing sound as the seeker in the warhead began looking for a target.

A second later there was a louder, higher-pitched hum.

"I've got tone! It sees the plane through the chaff! Launching."

Duff turned away and pressed his face into the wall of the fuselage, his hand still firmly on the shoulder strap of Cruz's body armor.

The missile launched; flame and smoke raced out of the back of the aircraft as it shot away, missing the port-side wing and climbing up straight towards its target.

Cruz immediately dropped the tube out the hatch and was pulled in by Squeeze and Duffy. All three men fell back to the deck.

Quickly they began crawling forward towards the cockpit, but Nascar gave them the play-by-play in their headsets.

"Missile's tracking. It's tracking! The C-130's still banking, he's evasive. Missile's ignoring the flares and chaff, it's still on him!"

Duff climbed to his feet and looked over Gabby's shoulder, and Cruz looked past Nascar just as the warhead detonated against the starboard-side wing of the big C-130. The aircraft began spiraling down in front of them, straight into the canyon, going lower and lower until it was out of view.

The sound of a massive explosion came soon after, telling everyone on board the aircraft had detonated while still in the air, its one-hundred-plus missiles blown to hell along with Remmick and the other shitheads of Alpha team.

Nascar pumped a fist in the air. "Splash one, motherfucker! I'm a goddamned fighter pilot!"

Cruz was more subdued. "Holy shit. I just blew up Shane Remmick. I'm gonna be famous."

"Only if we get out of this shit," Duff said. "Nascar! How long till we have to ditch?"

"We're at six thousand four hundred feet. I can keep us aloft for about three minutes max."

"We need as much distance from the Black Knights as we can get."

"Roger that. We'll keep gliding north through the canyon as far as we can. It's getting pretty dark; everybody help me look out to make sure I don't hit a wall."

"Oh my God," Gabby whispered to herself.

CHAPTER 70

Oscar Cardoza stood deep in the woods, enshrouded in cover and in darkness, watching the airstrip in front of him. Over two hundred sicarios stood around, looking off into the canyon, talking to one another, making satellite and radio calls. It looked like a headless creature to Cardoza; their leader had been killed, and now they were just a band of rudderless killers, with vengeance their only unifying characteristic.

Cardoza had no plans on leaving the woods until they were long gone.

He'd heard the distant muffled but unmistakable sound of the C-130 blowing to bits just a minute ago, and he knew in a heartbeat that his entire plan, his scheme to save himself and to get himself out of Mexico to safety, had gone up in smoke along with the stolen missiles. Remmick was dead, the missiles were gone, and the buyers he was to meet with in Bogotá wouldn't be paying him sixty million dollars.

All was lost. He considered walking out into the Black Knights and waiting for them to shoot him dead, but only for a moment, because Oscar Cardoza was a schemer, and his brain could not help but begin working on this puzzle, searching out a way for his fortunes to change yet again.

The biggest wild card still in play was the small group of Armored

Saint men who had thwarted his plan. He'd seen them roll off the side of the canyon in the aircraft, and though he'd neither seen nor heard the aircraft again after that, the fact that Remmick had been shot down miles to the north told him the little cargo hauler had been converted into an ersatz fighter plane, and this meant the men had survived.

These men would know everything. No, they wouldn't know about Cardoza himself, but they would know about the Zetas, they would know about Remmick's plan, and they would certainly know Remmick had had an accomplice, someone to arrange for the Zetas to attack.

Grupo de Guadalajara, the Sinaloan cartel, and even the Black Knights, led by whichever Archuleta lieutenant had survived the day: they would all put together that the consultant who had masterminded this plot was at the center of the attempted double cross with the missiles, and Cardoza's precarious predicament would only get exponentially worse.

He realized he had to find and finish those men in that old, beat-up cargo airplane before he could do anything else.

He pulled out his sat phone, placed a call, and held it close to his ear.

After several rings, it was answered.

"Bueno?"

"Lobo, it's me."

"Cardoza? Where are you?"

"I'm at the airstrip."

"With Los Caballeros Negros?"

Good, Cardoza thought. Lobo was close enough now to know the BKs were here. "No, amigo. I'm in hiding, but I can't get back to my Jeep. I need you and your men to come and get me when these pendejos leave."

"What was the explosion?"

"The explosion was an aircraft full of Americans and stolen missiles. One of the Armored Saint men tried to get away with them, and the other Americans blew him out of the sky."

Lobo processed this a moment. "So . . . so we're finished?"

"Almost. We need to find these last men. There can't be more than four or five of them, but they know enough about what happened to cause a lot of problems for us. They're in a little cargo aircraft, flying north through the canyon."

"That sounds like your problem, Cardoza."

"They're trying to get out of the Sierra Madres. They know what happened up here. They can tell the world the Zetas were here and American bodyguards staged the attack on the Black Knights. The fucking army won't invade the Devil's Spine; they'll invade *your* territory up north. The Black Knights will lick their wounds and come calling, as well. We have to destroy them."

"I don't have a fucking plane to chase them with."

Cardoza smiled. "Archuleta told me himself that plane wasn't airworthy and hadn't been flown in years. There's no way it would make it very far. Get down in that canyon and find out where they crashlanded."

Lobo didn't like being bossed around; this Cardoza knew. But he also knew Lobo would be thinking about his own leadership back in Juarez. He had to do this for them for the very survival of his organization. "Bueno. I'll have a truck come pick you up at midnight. The rest of us will head north along the Spine now, then make our way down the canyon to find the gringos."

The phone went dead. Cardoza would have to sit here in the trees for four hours, but he wouldn't be idle.

He'd be planning his next move. Sixty million dollars was up in smoke, but his dream lived on. He'd adapt and overcome.

Cardoza was a survivor.

CHAPTER 71

Nascar fought with the control column. "I thought it was hard to pilot this piece of junk *with* power. With a dead stick, it's damn near unresponsive. And there's a bend in the canyon up ahead."

"What do we do?" Gabby asked.

Nascar said, "I need everybody to move to the right side of the cabin! Help me bank this hunk of junk."

The three men in back did so, Duff, Squeeze, and Cruz pressing their bodies as tight to the starboard wall as they could. "Is that helping?" Duff called out. He could still hear all the others through his headset, but there was so little noise in the small plane they really didn't need the radios.

"Yeah!" Nascar shouted back. "Banking to the right. Okay, move back where you were."

No sooner had Duff come up behind the cockpit again than he heard Nascar curse.

"Oh shit!"

He was about to ask what the problem was now, but he looked out the windscreen into the dim evening light, and he saw the problem himself. "Shit."

In the copilot's seat, Gabby said, "Shit."

"What's wrong?" Squeeze shouted from behind.

Nascar replied. "The canyon is narrow here, and there's a bridge across it!"

Duff spoke authoritatively. "Go under it!"

"Can't go under it without nosing down into the river. We're at three thousand feet."

"Go over it, then!"

"We need to lighten the load if we're gonna get over that. We've got about ninety seconds till impact."

"How much do we lighten the load?" Duff asked, already looking around.

"Always sucked at math, boss. That's why I'm down here in Mexico flying a busted airplane."

Duff didn't stand around thinking about it. He knew they had no time. "Charlie team! Dump ruck! Everything out of the aircraft but your weapons, what's on your belts and chest rigs! All backpacks and shit in your pockets out the rear hatch!" He quickly amended himself. "Keep your med pouches on your belts, though."

The men pulled off their packs, their radios, rations, grenades, and flashlights and threw them out the side hatch or the rear hatch.

Squeeze said, "We got no food and water now!"

Duff replied, "Finding water's not gonna be a problem when we hit the river. We good, Nascar?"

"It's not enough! We're not gonna clear the top of the bridge!"

Duff shouted again. "Strip body armor! Keep your guns and ammo!"

The nearly silent gliding aircraft filled with the sounds of Velcro tabs ripping as the three men in back took off their armor plates. These were tossed out the hatch, as well.

Nascar said, "Gabby, I can't take my hands from the controls. Pull out my plates, hand them back to one of the guys."

It took her several seconds to get under Nascar's chest rack, but soon she had his front and side plates out. He leaned forward and she pulled out the rear steel rectangle and handed everything to Duff, who immediately threw it out of the aircraft.

"That's it," Duff said. "We good?"

Nascar emitted a groan like an injured animal. "No! We're gonna impact in forty-five seconds!"

Duff turned to the others. "Rifles and ammo! Get rid of them!" He reached forward, grabbed Nascar's carbine, and started to move towards the back.

Squeeze said, "Fuck that! I'm not dumping ammo!"

"The hell you aren't! Toss everything except sidearms."

Cruz turned towards the open rear cargo hatch, laid his back against the front bulkhead, and raised his Mk 48 machine gun. "Here's how a Puerto Rican dumps ammo!"

He opened fire. Fully automatic rounds sprayed out the back.

"I heard that," shouted Squeeze, and he followed suit.

Duff could barely hear anything over the gunfire, but Nascar shouted loudly enough to be heard. "Hey! Hey! That's working! It's giving us some propulsion. Duff, you shoot, too, straight out the back!"

Duff knelt down, his back against the pilot's seat, and he flipped the selector switch on Nascar's M4 to fully automatic. He sprayed a magazine out the back in under three seconds, then pulled another off Nascar's chest rig, reloaded, and fired some more.

Nascar shouted again. "Keep it up! It's working!"

Squeeze finished a reload and again pressed on his trigger. Cartridges and links from his Mk 48 sprayed all over the place, but he kept up the fire. "I'm a motherfuckin' jet engine of death, bitches!"

Cruz ran dry and quickly reloaded. "Last mag and I'm Winchester!" He again started shooting out the back.

Squeeze yelled, "My barrel is melting! Oh yeah, baby!"

And then it all went silent as the last echo of nearly nine hundred rounds bounced off the canyon walls and dissipated.

The men threw out the carbines and machine guns.

"Nascar?" Duff called out from the back.

"It's gonna be close, boss! C'mon, sweet Jesus!"

Gabby cried out, "Please, God!"

And then, seconds later, Nascar spoke again. "We did it! We're over!"

Everyone cheered, and Cruz and Squeeze high-fived each other.

It was silent for a moment, and then Nascar said, "One thousand feet and we go in the drink. We've got about a mile. I want everyone at the rear ramp, ready to jump on my command."

"What about you?" Duff asked.

"Gotta hold the controls steady. By then it will be too late for me to get out. I'll bail after hitting the water."

Duff knew there was no other option. "Don't you fuckin' die. That's an order."

"Best order ever, boss."

Duff put a gloved hand on Gabby's shoulder. "Let's go."

She put her hand on Nascar's shoulder, said a quick, silent prayer, and gave it a squeeze. Then she was heading to the back with Duff.

Squeeze and Cruz were already there, looking at the water below.

"That ain't a river," Squeeze said. "That's a fucking fire hose!"

Nascar called from the front, "Not yet. Wait for my signal. We're still too high."

Squeeze turned to Duff now. "Boss, is that peg leg of yours gonna stay on in the water?"

"It's not goin' anywhere. I've got my pants leg tied so tight in my boot I couldn't get it off if I wanted to."

Cruz called across the ramp, "Squeeze, can you swim, man?"

"Why the fuck you asking if I can swim? Because I'm black?"

"No . . . because I can't."

Squeeze cocked his head. "How the hell is it an ex–Green Beret can't swim?"

"I qualified, but that was a long time ago, and I almost fuckin' drowned. I haven't been in any water other than a hot tub in ten years. You throw my ass in *that* river and I'm as good as dead."

"No problem, brother. Hang on to me when we jump. I got you."

"Thanks, man."

Duff turned back to the cockpit. "Hey, Nascar! We're gettin' pretty low."

"Not yet. Not . . . yet. Not . . . *Now!* Go! Go! Go!"

All four of them leapt out, thirty feet above the raging river.

Ten seconds later, the old cargo plane went in and immediately flipped over as it was pulled down the rapids.

CHAPTER 72

Josh Duffy dragged his exhausted body to the shore in near darkness, coughed up cold river water, and immediately slipped on a rock covered in moss. Only his Arc'teryx knee pad kept him from cracking his patella as he went down. He pulled himself back up and found his footing; despite years of self-directed physical therapy, his balance wasn't good because of his prosthetic, so he put a hand on a high boulder before turning around and looking back at the water.

Only a little moonlight shone down into the massive canyon, its reflection sparkling off the whitewater rapids.

He had no idea how far he'd traveled downstream, but it felt like he'd been in the water a minute or more. Looking around, he saw no one else around him. He couldn't even spot the plane and wondered how far it could have possibly traveled before crashing.

He shivered with the cold, coughed to clear his throat, then shouted, "Gabby! Squeeze? Cruz?"

"I'm here," someone called from behind, and he turned to see Gabby Flores already on the shore behind him. She was lying on a rock, wearing her khakis and black Armored Saint polo, and she was shivering, as well. Her forehead was still bleeding, but the water had washed most of the blood away. "Mr. Duffy. I thought you were dead."

"Have you seen anyone else?"

"No one."

They moved downstream a little farther, then went back to the bank, calling for the missing men.

Finally Duff heard another voice coming from somewhere out in the water. He quickly identified it as Squeeze, more from the content of what he said than by the sound of his straining voice. "We're comin', boss! This is the heaviest fuckin' Mexican I've ever met."

"Puerto Rican!" Tony Cruz shouted back, and Duff knew that at least three of his people were somehow still alive.

He and Gabby found Squeeze and Cruz in the shallows a few seconds later. Squeeze was slamming his hand into the stockier man's back, trying to get him to cough up water. As Duff arrived, Charlie Four hacked up three times the amount of river that Duff had just himself puked up.

Squeeze said, "If you weren't so damn busy *drinking* the river, ya might have been able to *swim* the river, dumbass."

Gabby came out into the knee-deep water and helped Squeeze pull Cruz ashore.

"What about Nascar?" Duff said now, looking downstream.

"There!" Gabby pointed. Duff followed her hand and saw the CASA C-212 upside down, wedged in between a pair of boulders out in the rapids. It was easily 150 yards away and barely visible with a white belly surrounded by white rapids.

"Oh no." The orientation of the aircraft told Duff it was unlikely his driver/pilot had survived the crash.

Still, they all went to the shore and began hurrying along the rocky bank. Cruz was far behind the others, still recovering, but he didn't seem to have any injuries.

Cruz said, "If he's in that plane, he's dead."

To this, Squeeze replied, "That dude's too dumb to die."

As they ran, Duff said, "Nobody goes back in the water but me, understood?"

Squeeze shouted back at his TL. "You're the boss. You got to send your Six out for shit like that. Don't you know nothing about being an asshole?"

Duff said, "I'll do it."

They arrived at a cluster of smooth boulders that led almost all the way to the wreckage. Duff started to climb the first one, but he fell, slamming his chest into it and then spilling off into the water. It was still shallow here, so he pulled himself back up, but with his prosthetic, he wasn't able to feel his way with his left foot, and he got it wedged into a crack in the boulders.

"Shit!" he said.

Squeeze was right beside him. "Duff, I swim better than you, and I walk better than you. I'm Nascar's best chance."

The young man's logic was irrefutable. Duff just said, "Be careful."

Squeeze launched up on the boulder like some sort of a jungle cat, and then he made his way, carefully but quickly, out towards the middle of the river.

Duff, Cruz, and Gabby just stood in shin-deep, swiftly moving water, shivering from head to toe.

Squeeze had to climb off the last boulder before the aircraft, and he splashed down in the rapids, holding on to the trailing edge of the port-side wing to keep from washing away. He went hand over hand, his head just barely out of the white water, and then, with the three looking on from the shore, his head went under.

Gabby shouted in surprise.

Duff said, "He's gotta go in the plane to look for him."

Duff turned to Cruz. "You hurt at all?"

The bridge of the man's nose was badly cut, blood ran down his face, and Duff had noticed a little limp when they'd been heading up the bank. But the Puerto Rican ex–Special Forces soldier just shook his head. "Never better, boss."

"There!" Gabby exclaimed, pointing at the aircraft.

Duff turned and saw. Two heads bobbing in the water. Squeeze fought to get back to the boulder, dragging Nascar behind him, and then he inched his way, swimming along with a hand on the rocks, as he came closer.

Duff and Cruz went out chest deep to meet them. As he got closer, Duff realized Nascar was completely limp; Cruz had him around his neck.

"Is he breathing?" Duff asked.

Squeeze had a severe look on his face, only visible because Duff was inches from him now. "He's breathin', but somethin's wrong with him. He was in an air pocket, but as soon as I pulled on him, he started screaming. I think he passed out."

"Okay, let's get him to shore gently."

It took another minute to carefully bring Charlie Five into the shallows, and once they did, he seemed to wake a little. His eyes opened, fixed on Duff. "What . . . happened?"

Duff said, "You're a hell of a good driver, you're a pretty good pilot, but you *suck* as a sailor."

Nascar smiled a little, and then his eyes suddenly shot open and he let out a shrill scream that echoed off the canyon walls.

"What is it?" Duff said,

"My legs!"

Duff looked back and saw Cruz trying to push the man forward in the chest-high water by his feet. He stopped immediately.

Cruz said, "I think they're both broken."

"Shit," Duff said. They were a mile and a half deep in a canyon. How the hell was he going to get his people out of here with a man who couldn't walk?

They moved him the rest of the way by his shoulders; once on the rocks, he screamed some more, and when he was out of the water fully, he belted out another wail.

Duff examined his legs. "Yep. Both snapped down by the ankles."

Nascar had been in shock, but he was coming out of it enough to realize his predicament. "That's not good." He just moaned the words.

Squeeze knelt over him. "You're good, brother. I still got my med pouch. Gonna get you high as shit and then carry your ass outta here."

Nascar smiled, despite it all. "Thanks for saving me, Squeeze. Forget everything I said about you behind your back."

Squeeze patted the Alabamian on the forehead, stood, and walked a few feet away to be closer to Duff and Cruz.

To Duff, he said, "The fuck we gonna do, boss?"

Duff tried to sound resolute, although he was anything but. He was exhausted, sore, freezing cold, distraught about losing two men and an old friend, and unsure what the hell they were going to do to get out of their predicament. But he lifted his chin and answered as if the solution was obvious. "We're building a gurney for Nascar and then we're moving."

"Moving where?" Cruz asked.

"North."

"Why north?"

Gabby said, "North is the right decision. If we can get as far as Creel, the cartels don't own Creel."

"How far is Creel?"

Gabby shrugged. "It's one hundred miles."

"Jesus Christ," Cruz muttered.

But Duff was finding his backbone again. "We're going to Creel. We'll find a vehicle somewhere. Squeeze, give Nascar some morphine."

Duff went over and knelt down next to Nascar now. "Larry. We're going to take care of you, but this isn't going to be fun." He forced a smile. "We'll laugh about all this later, though."

Nascar's eyes were closed. "There ain't no later for me. I'm not going anywhere."

"We're not leaving you."

"Boss, listen to me. We may have flown seven, eight miles, tops, from the airstrip. We might have left the Black Knights behind on the Spine while they regroup, but they'll figure it out, and they'll find us. Plus, those Zetas who've been hittin' us for two days are gonna still be on our asses. Since we blew that C-130, everybody is going to know

411

exactly where we are, and they're gonna show up here at the wreckage. There's ways down into the canyon we don't even know about, and they've got all the four-wheel-drive trucks they need. Maybe not in the next thirty minutes, but inside of an hour, they'll be walking this bank. You have to get the hell out of—"

"We're not leaving you. End of discussion."

Larry sighed. "It's your funeral, but it's also the funerals of the other folks you're here to protect."

Duff rose and turned to the others. "Let's get moving."

CHAPTER 73

Gabby Flores led the way through the dark along a mostly overgrown trail that ran just off the rocky shoreline of the river. They moved north but painfully slowly. Gabby wasn't the problem; she was sure-footed and her eyesight was good. But behind her, just behind Duffy, Squeeze and Cruz struggled to carry Nascar on a litter they'd made from pine tree branches that they'd been able to break free of the trunk. They'd lashed them all together with medical tape and ACE bandages from their med kits, and though it wasn't perfect, it did hold Charlie Five's weight.

They'd splinted his legs, as well, but not until the morphine they'd dosed him with had kicked in. Still, he'd screamed in pain and passed out as soon as they wrapped the limbs against more branches.

Everyone was still wet, still cold, but the exertion would keep them alive through the night. No, the concern wasn't the elements; the concern was the group of men surely hunting them down here in the canyon.

Between the five of them, they had four Glock 17 pistols, along with three extra magazines for each weapon. Duff had relieved Nascar of his sidearm; something about morphine and handguns didn't seem to be a good fit, so now Duff carried his driver's weapon tucked into his belt.

Using the guns would be a definite last resort. The one thing they seemed to have going for them right now was that the enemy didn't know exactly where they were, but everyone in the group, Nascar included, figured it was just a matter of time before they would be located and engaged.

In the back of the line, Cruz whispered, "Boss. Boss?"

They all stopped, and Duff came back to him. "Need a break?"

"Yeah, man. Just for a minute."

"Take twenty," Duff said, and he took the makeshift handles of the makeshift stretcher, and they began walking again.

Cruz walked along with him. "We've been at this for two hours, and I bet we haven't gone more than a mile."

From the front of the gurney, Squeeze said, "Ninety-nine to go. Yay."

Nascar's slurred speech was louder than the others. He didn't have the filter to whisper with the drugs coursing through him. "You guys are . . . crazy. You gotta put me down and haul ass. You're never gonna get outta here carrying me."

"Damn," Squeeze said. "Nascar's trippin' on that morphine."

Duff said nothing. He feared Charlie Five was right. Duff's worry was overtaking his exhaustion, and his mood was much lower than he could allow himself to show to the others.

After no more than a minute, Gabby appeared in the dark in front of him and spoke softly while they continued moving forward.

"I see a trail that leads up. Probably all the way out of the canyon. But it's very steep."

"How steep?" Duff asked.

"Like a staircase in some places. There will be ledges and little plateaus on the way up, but mostly it will be like climbing a mountain."

"And *that's* a trail?"

"It's a goat and donkey trail. The locals around here bring their animals down here for water. Humans can make it." She looked at the gurney now. "If they are local goat herders and very fit."

They arrived at the trail a moment later. Duff would have walked right past it and couldn't imagine how Gabby could have noticed it in the darkness, but as he stepped up to it, he saw that it was, in fact, a steep and winding track, nearly vertical in some places that disappeared around a craggy rock a couple dozen feet above.

Instantly he knew there was no way in hell a man could be carried up that extreme an incline.

Squeeze and Duff put Nascar on the trail on the riverbank while they assessed the situation. As addled as his mind was with the narcotic pain medicine, Nascar fully recognized his own predicament. "Duff. Give me my pistol back, sit me up against a rock facing the trail. Let me take a few of these fuckers out before I go. I'll buy you guys some time."

"No," Duff said.

Nascar started to protest, but quickly Squeeze knelt over him and covered his mouth. "Everybody down!" he whispered.

Duff, Cruz, and Gabby dropped low on the trail behind boulders lining the shore.

"What is it?" Duff asked.

"I think I saw a light shining upstream."

Duff asked the group. "Anybody hear anything?"

Cruz whispered, "I haven't been able to hear shit since we popped a thousand rounds in the back of a little cargo plane. I'll scan for contact." Cruz pulled his pistol, stood up slowly, and looked over the boulder. A moment later he knelt back down and faced the others.

"Yep, one flashlight, I see a few men behind it. They've got rifles. They're on the other side of the river, but they're moving in the same direction as us. Might be an advance party."

"They look like Zetas?"

Cruz shrugged. "They look like assholes. That's all I know."

Gabby said, "Let me see." She stood and peered over the boulder, then knelt back down.

"Narcos."

Squeeze said, "Boss, we can hide Nascar in the brush by the trail head. Then we can—"

"No," Duff said flatly, but he had no viable plan of his own.

Cruz grabbed Duff by the arm. "If we engage these dudes, then the fifty behind them will rain down on us. Rifles versus pistols, you know how that'll end. There's no other way."

Duff was slow to admit his men were right, but finally he crawled over to Nascar. Squeeze removed his hand from the man's mouth.

"Larry, I need you to listen up."

But Nascar already understood. "It's all good, boss. Just give me my piece. I'll dump a mag into them. Blaze of glory and all that shit. You guys get safe."

"We *will* come back. Do you understand me?"

"Sure thing." He didn't believe it for a moment, Duff could tell. Larry knew his die was cast the moment that aircraft flipped and his legs snapped against the rudder pedals.

Now Duff looked at the other men. "As deep in the brush as we can get him. Nascar, keep your mouth shut. Even through the morphine, this shit's gonna hurt."

They lifted him by the waist and the shoulders and walked him just a few feet into thick weeds. He winced and tensed his muscles as the agony coursed through him, but he didn't make a sound. After they placed him down, his back against the canyon wall, he was under cover except from straight ahead. If someone shined a flashlight his way as they passed on the trail, they would see him, and there was nothing Charlie team could do to prevent it.

Duff knelt over him again. "Here's a morphine autoinject. You're already dosed, so if you shoot yourself up now, you'll just die. Give it at least three hours, wait till the pain is too much, then dose yourself again."

The blond man just nodded.

Duff pulled the pistol out of the small of his back. "And here's your Glock. Do *not* fire on those guys unless they see you. Just lie here quietly and maybe they will pass by and—"

"It's been an honor working with you, boss."

Duff didn't want to hear it. "My order for you to stay alive remains in effect."

The man leaning up against the rocks smiled a little. "I'll do my best."

Nascar shook everyone's hands, but no words were exchanged. Gabby then said a soft prayer and gave him a hug. When she stood back up, Nascar said, "Now get out of here."

Duff rose and whispered. "Everybody . . . We're moving. Double time up that trail. Gabby leads."

After one more glance back, Duff turned away and headed off into the dark.

Nascar looked down at his pistol, and then up at the trail ten yards in front of him.

"Come . . . to . . . Daddy . . . boys."

It was only a matter of minutes before he saw a flashlight's beam shine on the trail right in front of him. The enemy had crossed the river at some point, and they were over here now. Nascar raised the weapon out in front of him, tried to focus on the front sight through hazy eyes, and waited.

A sicario with a rifle and a flashlight passed, sweeping the beam back and forth, but he quickly continued on to the north and out of view. A second then a third sicario passed by, but they were relying on the light of the point man to guide them and not looking up into the bushes.

Three more men walked past soon after, but again, no one saw him.

Nascar lowered the Glock into his lap and shut his eyes. Softly, he said, "You jackwads got lucky."

Seconds later he fell asleep.

CHAPTER 74

Larry Nascar Evans wasn't going to win, but he damn well planned on making a good showing for himself.

He was in Lincoln, Alabama, at the Talladega Superspeedway, riding strong in the middle of the pack in the YellaWood 500, a 188-lap NASCAR Cup race. He was behind the wheel of a mustard-yellow Ford Mustang, wearing the emblem of the Atlanta Police Department, and right now he was in the thick of it. A pair of Camaros right in front of him, another Mustang on his right, and on his left, just this side of the yellow line, a Chevy SS with an M&Ms logo that had been trying to nose ahead of him for the past lap and a half.

Somehow Larry got in front of the SS on the back straightaway, boxing him out of the inside lane and forcing him back. His eyes flashed to the speedometer, and he saw he was at 204.2 miles per hour as he passed the line, completing his 153rd lap, and his Mustang would have given him more if not for the two assholes in front of him.

His crew radioed that he was in ninth place, and with thirty-five laps to go, a strong and tight car, and only one more pit stop, he felt confident a top-five finish was in his grasp.

He raced into turn one; he felt the 33-degree bank in the track and his car pulled hard to the right, almost as if it wanted to slam into the wall, but he fought it, kept it smooth as he found his line in the traffic.

He got tight behind the 18 car; its black-and-gold Armored Saint logo got closer and closer, then he made his move. The Camaro went from his windscreen to his rearview as he used the energy of its draft to shoot by, and then he turned just inside the Black Knights car, with its crossed AK-47s painted gold on a bloodred hood.

Out of turn one, it was almost clear; he headed for the straightaway with his foot stomping the pedal, scanned his rearview, then looked ahead as he neared a row of cars. He blinked hard but didn't recognize the shape of the vehicles; they sure as hell weren't stock cars, so he shook his head to clear it, as if to reset the image.

Another glance into the rearview, and his dreams of a strong finish melted away in an instant.

An oversized Camaro with a large black *Z* on the hood was drafting behind him; it tucked inside adroitly, then tapped his left rear corner panel.

Larry Evans felt his back tires leave the track at two hundred miles per hour; he corrected back to the right as he fishtailed and raced right for the wall at the top of turn two.

His Mustang slammed hard, crumpling like an empty soda can, and instantly Larry's legs jolted with pain, white-hot fireplace pokers jabbed into his shins. He kept sliding, spinning, tumbling, but somehow through it all he could still see the Z car as it passed, and just before he blacked out, he realized that no matter how strong his hopes and dreams for success, the Zetas were going to beat him.

Larry Evans closed his eyes.

Larry Evans opened his eyes.

It was pitch-black dark. He blinked, blinked again, but still could see absolutely nothing.

It all came back to him, but only because of the exquisite pain in both his legs.

He was on his back by a riverside in the bottom of a canyon in Mexico, left behind by his team, surrounded by bloodthirsty narco assassins. No food, no water, no chance.

He was a long, long way from the podium at Talladega.

He heard a noise, movement in the brush, close but not right on top of him. He started to feel around for the Glock he knew he had close by, and as he did so, he felt a presence above him.

A whispered voice came a foot away from his nose, but he saw nothing but black.

"Don't make a sound."

He started to lurch up, but multiple sets of hands held him down. Another hand covered his mouth.

The presence above came closer, whispered into his ear. "They . . . are . . . *everywhere*." It was Duff's voice. Fresh pain in Larry's legs made him want to cry out, but he fought it, nodded once.

Charlie One spoke again. "We've got a plan to get you out of here, but we have to give you morphine first. Squeeze is gonna hit your thigh with it. You understand?"

Nascar did not understand. Charlie team had left him hours ago. How the hell were they here? Why the fuck would they come back? But he nodded, at least thankful for the high the morphine would give him.

He felt the needle plunge into his leg, the quick wash of relief, and he lay there because there wasn't anything else he could do.

Duff said, "About an hour after we left you, we came across a goat herder on a plateau camped out for the night. He had a donkey, and we bought it off him. We left Gabby and came back down here. We're going to load you up, strap you on tight, and head up this mountainside. It's gonna hurt, every step of the way, but it's gonna work."

Tears formed in Evans's eyes, but he didn't know if it was from pain, from the fear of what he would have to endure, or from the gratitude he felt that he'd not been left out here alone to die.

Duff's voice remained in a whisper, but now it was less soft, more authoritative. "There are twenty-five sicarios in this canyon close enough to hear you cry out. We've seen flashlights sweeping to the north and to the south. You can't make one fucking sound, you got me?"

Nascar nodded again.

"Bite down on this."

Nascar opened his mouth and took a strip of leather, probably from the bridle of the donkey, which he could now tell was the source of the noise in the brush. Cruz grabbed him by his upper thighs, Duff grabbed him by his shoulders, and Squeeze helped him onto the animal. The donkey brayed a little, shuffled left and right, and this made some noise, but they got Nascar flat on its back, facedown, then lashed him with more leather straps, all the way up and down his body, and all the way around the beast.

Five minutes later they were a few dozen feet up, past the boulder. Cruz pulled on the donkey, Duff and Squeeze pushed from behind, and the animal reluctantly complied.

Nascar bit down so hard on the leather his jaw hurt almost as much as his legs, but as the fresh morphine kicked in, and the climbing sensation of the animal below him turned into a repetitive rhythmic pace, he somehow fell asleep again.

It was past dawn when the four surviving members of Charlie team arrived at the plateau where they'd left Gabby with the goat herder. The goats were gone; the boy had continued up ahead of the crazy gringos and the local girl who gave him a pistol and two cool wristwatches in exchange for a donkey.

Flores was lying against a tree, huddled into a ball for warmth, but she climbed back to her feet when she saw them.

She put her hand on Nascar's head; he was strapped facedown to the donkey still, but he looked up at her and gave her a drugged-out smile.

Cruz, Squeeze, and Duff all fell flat in the grass; the exhaustion they felt meant they couldn't go another step. They drank from a water bottle Gabby got from the goat herder, and then she gave some water to Larry.

Gabby asked, "Did you see the Zetas?"

"Yeah," Duff said, his eyes closed already as he lay on his back. "We left them down in the canyon. They're not from around here, so I guess that's why they didn't see this trail."

Gabby said, "They'll see plenty of trails in the daylight, and they'll leave the canyon before long." Then she smiled. "I have some good news."

Duff's eyes opened. "I'll take it."

"The Tarahumara boy told me another route out of the canyon. We can reach it from here. He said it's less steep, even some four-wheel-drive trucks have taken it."

"How much farther till we're out of the canyon?"

She shrugged. "It will take all day, into the night. But the highway is up there, maybe we can find a vehicle when we get there, head north towards Creel."

Duff nodded, still too exhausted to stand. "In thirty minutes, we're heading out."

Gabby reached down to him, pulled the pistol out of his holster.

Duff said, "What are you doing?"

"I've had my rest waiting for you. I will keep guard."

"You know how to use that?"

"Sure. I watch TV."

This didn't exactly fill Duff with confidence, but the fatigue won its battle against reason, and Josh Duffy fell asleep moments later.

CHAPTER 75

Just after ten a.m., Maxwell Henderson sat in the small office of Henderson Aviation in El Paso, Texas, his Stetson boots up on his desk and an iPad in his lap. He was in the process of getting the latest weather for today's flight, not that it really mattered much. This time of year, in both Texas and Sonora, Mexico, the weather was virtually always the same. Other than a little turbulence below ten thousand feet as he passed south of Juarez, conditions would be excellent this afternoon, of this he had no doubt.

He reached for his coffee, told himself he had to check in with maintenance about another aircraft in his fleet that was having an engine overhaul in Tucson, and then he'd grab lunch outside the airport before his two p.m. flight.

He was surprised to hear a knock at his door. His pilots were all out, the maintenance guys usually called instead of heading over from the hangar to the office, and his secretary had a sick kid home from school, so she hadn't come in.

"It's open."

The Stetsons came off the desk when the visitor entered. Henderson stood up quickly, confusion overtaking his brain.

He didn't hide his puzzlement when it made its way into his voice. "Captain?"

Nichole Duffy, née Martin, nodded back at him. "Chief."

She was older than when he last saw her, but she was just as attractive. He'd never liked her much at all, but he did have to admit she was easy on the eyes. She wore jeans and a gray T-shirt, she carried a backpack on her back like she was a college student, and her hair was in a tight bun. She wore no makeup at all, and the intense look in her eyes brought Henderson back to a night a long time ago. A night he'd been trying for seven years to forget.

He stepped around the desk. "Come on in."

She shut the door behind her, met him halfway across the room, and they shook hands.

"It's . . . it's good to see you." Quickly he added, "Sorry I haven't been back in touch. Nobody's saying much of anything. Heard any more about your husband?"

"He's gone silent."

Henderson nodded slowly. "And Armored Saint?"

"They won't speak to me. Hung up in my face last night."

"Yeah, I talked to my buddy there, he said it's gotten political down in Mexico, and Armored Saint is in cover-their-ass mode. He wouldn't give me any more intel." Henderson shrugged. "Weird he cut me off like that, but he was my only inside connection. Don't know what else I can do for you, to be honest."

"I do," she said flatly. Her eyes bored into his, and it made him uncomfortable.

He cocked his head a little. Defensively, he said, "Okay."

"I need a ride to Creel."

"*Creel?* In Chihuahua? To do what?"

She bit her lower lip; he remembered her doing this back in the army. "Josh told me the motorcade would go there at the end of their movement through the mountains. I'm going to be there when he gets there."

"You don't even know where he is now."

"If we're lucky, he'll be rolling into Creel by the time we land."

Henderson cocked his head. *"We?"*

"I don't have money for a plane ticket to Mexico. Maxed out a credit card to get this far. I need you to take me to Creel. You said you were going down today."

"To Hermosillo. I said I was going to—"

"You can change the flight plan. All I need is for you to drop me off at the airport. You can gas up and be on your way. I need this, Max."

He shook his head. "I can't smuggle someone into Mexico."

"It's not smuggling. I have a passport. Just add me to your manifest and give me something that looks like a crew ID."

Henderson sat on the edge of his desk. "I'm a little worried about what you're going to do down there."

"What I do is my business."

"I'm sorry, I just can't. You know I'd do anything for you and Josh, but—"

"I'm not asking much, Chief."

He barked out a little laugh. "You're asking a lot."

"I'm not asking much," she repeated, "in comparison to what Josh did for you."

Henderson lurched back as if hit. "C'mon, don't pull out that card."

"You know you'd be dead if it wasn't for him. And you know what I did for you after that. You could have faced a court-martial for your actions that night, and I covered for you because you were getting out of the Army in a month. I didn't have to do that, but I didn't want you to miss out on your pension."

"I appreciate everything you guys did for me then, but—"

"But *nothing*, Chief. I am going to board your aircraft and you're going to take me to Creel. Do that, and our score will be settled."

"Is that a threat? You're going to tell the Army what happened in Iraq?"

"I might."

"Like they would even give a shit. And anyway, if you admit now that you lied on your after-action report, they would—"

Nichole interrupted. "They would be angry at me. *You*, on the other hand, have government contracts. Contracts you got because of your military service, contracts you could lose if your discharge was changed to something other than honorable."

Henderson said, "I'll ask again. Is that a threat?"

"I'm giving you the opportunity to do something in return for all that was done for you seven years ago. You got your life, and you got a pension. All *I* want is a motherfucking ride to Mexico."

Henderson stared at her with malevolence, then sighed. "You were always a tough cookie, Captain."

She stared back at him. "I do believe the word you used back then was 'bitch.'"

He looked at the floor. After a time, he said, "I'll add you to the manifest, change the flight plan." He added, "This is fucking nuts."

"When do we leave?"

Henderson shrugged and looked up. "Since I've got to go to Creel first, I guess we'd better leave now."

"Excellent."

CHAPTER 76

After he got the all clear from Cruz and climbed back out of the brush, Josh Duffy realized, not for the first time, that he and the other Armored Saint men would have long been dead if not for Dr. Gabby Flores. Once again she'd detected movement on the trail, and once again she and the rest of them got off the trail and deep into the woods shortly before a patrol passed by.

She'd led them out of the canyon the night before, unquestionably saving Nascar's life in the process, and she'd used a small paper map she'd kept on her body the entire time, even in the river, to guide them on foot to the north, helping them stay off the highway and skirt any villages in the area where the Black Knights ran things.

Twice earlier today she'd sensed trouble, and twice they'd hidden in thick pine forests as trucks rolled by close.

This time it had been a foot patrol, and Gabby said she was almost certain these were Black Knights. It didn't really matter to Duff whether they were Black Knights or the Zetas—both groups wanted him and his team dead—but Gabby's expertise was certainly the only thing keeping him and his men from stumbling straight into a firefight.

Around one p.m. they came across an old wooden wagon that had been built to be pulled by a donkey, and they'd put Larry in it, giving the poor animal the respite from having a man on his back for most of a day. With this, they made better time; they were traveling almost three miles per hour now and planned on taking as few breaks as possible until darkness fell.

Everyone in the group, save for Nascar, had blistered feet. They all had sunburn even though the temperature was only in the forties. The group was hungry; they'd had nothing in the past twenty-four hours but some berries Gabby pulled from some bushes, but there were little streams and brooks, and even wet snow hanging on the pine trees, so access to water had not been a problem.

Duff knew they wouldn't last much longer unless they found a vehicle; they were still over eighty miles from safety, but Gabby insisted they couldn't move through any villages in this part of the Devil's Spine.

Simply put, there was no one here they could trust.

They'd have to just keep pushing north until, eventually, they found a way off these mountains, or these mountains found a way to kill them.

CHAPTER 77

The Cessna Grand Caravan owned by Henderson Aviation and contracted by the Drug Enforcement Agency to deliver computer hardware to the DEA foreign regional office in Hermosillo, Mexico, landed 220 miles to the southeast of its intended destination. It was late afternoon here at Aeropuerto Internacional Creel when the aircraft touched down on a runway hot from the sun, then taxied to a fixed operating base to be filled up.

A customs official met the aircraft as soon as the stairs were lowered; he checked the passports of the pilot and copilot, Maxwell Henderson and Nichole Duffy, and then stamped them. That done, the two Americans climbed down onto the tarmac.

Henderson started for the building to arrange refueling, but Nichole stood there, at the nose of the Grand Caravan, looking out over the airport.

Henderson stopped after a few feet and turned to her. "So, what's your plan?"

She didn't answer him at first; she only stared across the tarmac.

"Look. I've got some cash. I'm carrying ten thousand pesos, that's five hundred U.S. dollars' worth, and it's all yours. I'd give you a card, but I really don't want my name associated with whatever you plan on—"

He stopped talking when it was clear she wasn't listening. Two doors down from where they'd parked was a hangar and a small office building, a typical airport fixed-base operator. A sign on the building advertised air tours over the Copper Canyon, but Nichole wasn't looking at the sign; she was looking at the three helicopters sitting on a helipad there in front of the building.

A small Robinson R44 was close to her. Behind it, she recognized the silhouette of an Airbus EC-120 and, behind that, a larger Agusta-Westland AW109. There was no crew around any of the helos.

Henderson waited a moment, then said, "The pesos will cover a taxi ride to town, a hotel room, and food for a few days. You can start making some more calls to Armored Saint. I'm sure as soon as Duffy gets to town, they'll let you know."

She did not respond to what he said. Instead she asked, "Have you ever flown the EC-120?"

He was surprised by the question. "Flown it? I have one in the fleet. A 135, too." He looked out at the helicopter in the center, the one she was obviously referring to. "Mine's a little newer. Good ship."

"Seats five?"

Henderson's eyes went from the helo to the woman standing next to him. "Yeah? So?"

"What's the range?"

He staggered a half step back. "Wait. Just . . . just wait a second. If you're thinking about—"

She turned to him. "What's the fucking range, Chief?"

"Four hundred seventy-five miles. But if you—"

"Want to go on a joyride?"

He barked out an annoyed laugh. "I think I'll pass. What, you're going to fly up into those mountains and start looking around?"

"There's only one highway on the Devil's Spine. I stole a map from a library. I don't know that he's on it, but I *have* to go up there and look."

Henderson shook his head. "Five hundred bucks. I can give you that." He reached for his wallet. "Then I'm done. I'm heading to Hermosillo. Good luck to you but—"

"Josh saved your life."

He looked back at her. "Face the facts! He's dead! Armored Saint doesn't have confirmation, so they haven't notified you, but if the last time you talked to him, he said he was surrounded by hundreds of shooters, then . . . I'm sorry, but he's gone."

She stuck out her hand, he put a big wad of pesos in it, and she took it. "Thank you," she said, but she made it clear that she didn't mean it.

Henderson said, "You can't just rent a helo for ten thousand pesos. Not even in Mexico."

"I'm not going to *rent* a helo. I'm going to charter one to see the beautiful Copper Canyon."

"I don't know much about these parts, but I do know the Devil's Spine isn't in the Copper Canyon."

She shrugged, turned, and said nothing else. She just began heading for the FBO two doors down.

Max Henderson stood there, hands on his hips. Softly, he said, "Crazy bitch," and then he turned and headed for his own FBO.

Sixty minutes later, Nichole Duffy sat in the copilot's seat of the EC-120, while an affable, middle-aged, pudgy pilot named Guillermo did his final checklist before taking off. She wore a headset so she could communicate with him, and his English was good, though heavily accented.

"Okay, señorita. This will be a forty-five-minute flight into the Copper Canyon. I'll show you the rivers, the trees, the mountains. It will be a beautiful time for you."

She asked him questions about the helicopter, the controls, the amount of fuel on board. At first he thought she was just nervous, but quickly the man realized she was as interested in the helicopter itself as she was the canyon they planned on visiting.

This was unusual, as was the fact that his passenger today was a single gringa, with no husband or boyfriend or family with her. A sightseeing tour for one person was odd, but Guillermo was happy for the four thousand pesos, and he was ready to get into the air.

"Okay, señorita, shall we climb into the beautiful sky?"

Now was the moment of truth. Nichole's hasty plan was to get this far, and then, right before takeoff, to tell the poor man she had a bomb in her backpack, and if he did not get out of the aircraft, she would blow them both to pieces.

She didn't love this plan, but it was all she had.

At the point of no return, she grabbed the man by the arm. "Wait."

He turned to her. "Everything okay?"

Here we go, she said to herself.

But then she noticed Guillermo's eyes flashing away from hers, looking past her and out the copilot's side window. His brow furrowed suddenly. Nichole turned around to look herself, and then her heart sank.

Five Mexican police cars raced up the tarmac, their lights flashing. They encircled the helicopter quickly.

"Take off!" she shouted, but Guillermo just stared in confusion at the oncoming trouble.

Quickly she put one hand on the collective in front of her, the other on the cyclic between her seat and Guillermo's, and began lifting the aircraft into the air herself, but Guillermo fought her for the controls. "¿Que haces, loca?"

The helo slammed back on its skids as police with assault rifles arrived at her door, pointing their weapons in her face.

She looked past them and saw Max Henderson's Grand Caravan slowly begin taxiing away from the scene, heading out towards the runway.

Motherfucker. She mouthed the word, but he wouldn't have been able to see her.

The copilot's door opened, and she was pulled out and all but dragged away under the spinning rotor blades. A young cop shoved her up to the hood of the nearest squad car, but she fought him. He reached for her left hand to yank it behind her back, and she spun back around and decked him hard with her right.

The cop fell to the tarmac, but others were on her, shoving her to the red-hot concrete, handcuffing her, cussing and raging all the while.

A minute later she was in the back of a squad car, driving off the airport grounds.

She began to cry. Not because of her predicament but because of Josh. He was out there, somewhere, and she'd done nothing at all to help.

CHAPTER 78

Oscar Cardoza stood on the impossibly rugged dirt track, arms folded in front of him, looking out over the canyon.

He'd gotten a little sleep in a tent under an oak tree during the afternoon, but he'd been up for the past hour, mostly keeping to himself, thinking thoughts he would share with no one here.

With no one at all.

Cardoza and the Zetas were in hiding during the day just off this old dirt road because a large caravan of Black Knights had been spotted moving north on the highway above them. It was late afternoon now, Lobo was waiting for sunset, and once it came, he and his fifty-five or so sicarios, along with Cardoza, would load back into trucks and race north on the highway themselves, trying desperately to both avoid the Black Knights and to get ahead of the Armored Saint men who had crashed into the river the evening before.

Everyone assumed they were still on foot, still picking their way out of the mile-and-a-half-deep canyon, so by using the highway to get ahead of them, and by threatening every man, woman, and child they saw for information about a group of straggling gringos passing through their villa, they felt confident they could find them, and once they found them, they were more than certain they could kill them.

Cardoza turned away from the canyon, thought about who else he could call to provide him some intelligence about what was going on. He'd made a dozen of these calls already, and so far they'd borne no fruit. He'd learned that the UN mission was missing in the mountains, that the army was talking about sending a company of mechanized infantry up on the highway to search for them, but the army was still down in Aguas Calientes, and they hadn't even mustered yet for a rescue mission. He'd learned that the PMC Armored Saint was sitting in Mexico City, waiting on word, but they were keeping news of the missing delegation secret until they knew more.

He'd also learned that the United Nations themselves were keeping news of this close hold; they'd determined that once the word got out that a small group had ventured up into the Devil's Spine, any chance for that small group getting out alive would evaporate. The entire peace mission had been secret, and the absolute worst time to reveal the secret was when the peace mission was as imperiled as it now seemed to be.

But Cardoza had no one else to call. All he could do was hope that one of the people he'd reached out to earlier would learn something relevant and then get back to him.

And that call came at six p.m. Cardoza looked down at the number and cocked his head. He'd reached out to a female colleague in Mexico City early that morning; it was a low-probability chance on his part to find out information, and he hadn't actually expected to get much out of this woman.

"Cardoza," he said, his voice showing strength and authority, because that was his persona with this colleague.

The woman greeted him in English, and then she began to tell him what she knew. He looked at his watch, bored, as this seemed like it was going to be an irrelevant bit of information. But then he lowered his watch slowly, his head rose, and his eyes widened.

She talked for a full minute before he said a single word.

"Where?"

He then asked more questions, but he didn't write anything down. After a minute more, he said, "Thanks, Shelly. I really appreciate it."

He ended the call, then slipped the phone into his pocket with a quivering hand.

"Unreal," he said to himself softly, and then he began hurrying around the camp, looking for Lobo.

He found him smoking under a tree morosely while his men around him rested, cleaned guns, or pulled security, and he stepped up to the leader of this group of Zetas with both newborn confidence and a slight grin on his face.

"We are back in business, amigo. I have a plan. I need you and your ten best men to come with me in two vehicles, and I need you to put your best lieutenant in charge of the rest of the group. They can head north, as we planned; I'll give them more information soon."

"We've been through this before. You don't give me orders, and you don't give my men orders, either," Lobo said.

"Are we really going to play that game again? Let's work *together*. I know how to get to the Armored Saint survivors. Once we wipe them out, then this mission will be a complete success. There will be no one to put the blame on anyone but Los Caballeros Negros for the attack on the delegation. The army will be forced to invade, the Zetas will become stronger." Cardoza faked a smile and slapped Lobo on the shoulder. "You, mi amigo, will be a hero in your organization."

Lobo did not return the smile, but he slowly nodded. "Where are we going?"

Cardoza told him.

The Mexican from Juarez couldn't believe it. "How did you learn all this?"

The older man was proud of himself, buoyed by fresh adrenaline. "You, Lobo, you have your tactical skill and your men and your guns. I, my friend, only possess one thing." With a smile he said, "Relationships."

Lobo stood quickly and began to rally his men. They'd need to leave now, to chance the highway, and he'd need them ready for contact with the Black Knights if it came down to it.

Cardoza stood there under the tree and looked again out over the canyon. The man from Mexico City did have a plan to destroy the remaining American contractors, and it was a good one. It would almost be too easy, he told himself. But then he thought about the rest of his plan, having formulated it over the past day.

No, the rest of his scheme would not be nearly as easy as killing a couple of poorly armed Americans and a Mexican woman, but this part would restore much of the fortune he'd lost the day before. And it would take him where he needed to go: to Motu Teta, his dream island in Southeast Asia, a life without worry, days without looking over his shoulder, and nights without dreams of torture in Mexico or a supermax prison in America.

No, when this was all over, when the contractors were dead and the army had invaded, he would return to Guadalajara, he would tell El Patrón everything he had to do to get the army up onto the Spine, and he would ask for more money.

A *lot* more money.

He would make no threats, but the insinuation would be clear. Oscar Cardoza, at any time, could contact the authorities and rat him out as the orchestrator of the military invasion of the Sierra Madres.

El Patrón would know the power Oscar held, and he would be furious.

But El Patrón wouldn't kill him. This man, unlike every other cartel boss Cardoza knew, was uniquely informed enough to know that killing Oscar Cardoza would make more trouble than it would be worth.

Cardoza had connections that El Patrón knew about, and these connections would save him.

Guadalajara would pay him ten million dollars to go away and keep what he knew to himself, and Oscar Cardoza would find his way to his island. He wouldn't have twenty-five million; maybe he'd only have one girl, maybe he'd have a sailboat instead of a yacht, but he'd still have an opulent lifestyle, and he'd still have his perfect life in Motu Teta.

He dialed a number on his phone and listened to it ring, reinvigorated with his reversal of fortune and the sudden prospects of a bright future.

CHAPTER 79

I t was just before one a.m.—they only knew the time because Duff had taken Nascar's wristwatch—when Squeeze, Cruz, and Duff crawled silently over pine needles and snow, their bodies low to the ground as they neared a truck parked alongside a stream.

It was a Dodge Ram, either dark blue or black, and it was beat-up but powerful looking. They'd only found it because they had smelled the campfire from where they'd been resting for the past half hour in a copse of oak some one hundred yards from a dirt track that ran along the same shallow, rocky creek.

Leaving Gabby and the injured Nascar behind, the three men had walked to the track, then moved to the south in a crouch, following the growing scent of burning pine. When they saw light through the trees, they dropped to their hands and knees, and now they went down to their bellies as they made it to within thirty yards.

From here they could see the entire scene. Four men sat around the fire; they were awake, and it sounded to Duff from their occasional loud voices like they were probably drinking.

The three Americans were shoulder to shoulder, as low as possible, as they looked on at all the things they coveted. Warmth, food, and transportation.

Squinting into the campfire light, Duff saw something else he and his men coveted.

Guns. There were multiple AK-47s in view.

Squeeze whispered, "Those are narcos, right?"

Cruz replied, "Four dudes in a pickup. AKs. Up here on the Devil's Spine without a care in the world? Yeah, that's a pretty safe bet."

Duff didn't know if these were Sinaloa cartel, Black Knights, or Zetas, and he couldn't possibly care less. He wanted what they had, and he was prepared to take it.

Squeeze looked to Duff in the darkness now. "What's the plan?"

"We're going to kill them." The certitude in Duff's voice was no put-on. He was absolutely resolute now.

Cruz said, "We start shooting these fuckers, and hell is gonna rain down on us."

Duff just responded, "Blades."

Squeeze and Duff both pulled folding knives with four-inch blades and opened them up, careful that their locking mechanisms didn't make a sound.

Cruz had lost his knife in the river the day before, but he retrieved a multitool from a cargo pocket and opened the three-inch blade. It wasn't much of a fighting weapon, but it was better than nothing.

Cruz whispered, "Have either of you guys trained on fighting with edged weapons?"

Duff shook his head. "Not really, no."

Squeeze said, "Fixed bayonets in the Corps. Does that count?"

"Not unless you got a bayonet and a rifle." Cruz said, "Listen, Duff. In SF, I trained for years with blades. You take the guy with his back to us. Squeeze, you go around behind, not on the creek side, but on the other side. Stay away from the firelight and take the guy facing this direction. I'll sweep around along the creek, come in from behind, and do both the men there.

"Squeeze, you have the farthest to go, so when you come up behind your guy, that will be the signal for us to attack."

Duff whispered softly to Cruz, "You can kill two men with a knife?"

"We're about to find out, aren't we?" Cruz added, "Here's the ten-second lesson on how to do this. Come up from behind, cover their mouth, and go for their kidneys. Don't slash, stab. And don't just stab once. In and out, in and out, a half dozen times at least."

Squeeze muttered, "Jesus."

Duff asked, "Why not just slit their throats?"

"Because you'll cut yourself dragging the blade back towards you. Trust me, man, I know what I'm talking about. Stab away from your own body while you control theirs."

This was a savagery Duff had never even contemplated. But after a moment, he nodded. "Okay. That's the plan." He handed his bigger knife to Cruz. "You've got two targets, I'll take the multitool."

Cruz switched with him, then Squeeze said, "I got two legs, *I'll* take the multitool."

He exchanged weapons with Duff, and Duff did not protest.

The exchange made, Charlie One said, "Listen. If it *has* to go loud, then it goes loud. Pull your pistols and waste these guys. We'll hustle back and get Nascar and Gabby, and we'll floor it out of here."

The men nodded, all steeling themselves for what was to come.

Duff added, "Don't die in a knife fight, how copy?"

"Good copy," Squeeze said.

Cruz just nodded. Duff could see the man steeling himself for what he was about to do.

Squeeze put his multitool between his teeth, then crawled off to the left; the other two waited a minute, and then Cruz went to the right. Duff waited a minute more alone, then began crawling straight ahead.

The rear of the truck shielded him from the enemy by the fire at first, and Duff knew the fire itself would provide some cover, as well. Everything outside the firelight would be impenetrable blackness to the men within its flickering glow.

It took ten minutes for Squeeze to make his way ten yards behind his target, but just as the young African American was about to rise and move forward, his intended victim stood, stretched, and turned in

Squeeze's direction. He began wandering into the woods, probably to piss, and Charlie Six noticed that the man hadn't even taken his gun with him.

Squeeze did not move a muscle as the man passed ten feet from him on his right, took another step or two, and then began unbuckling his belt.

The young American rose silently, held his knife low in his right hand, and stepped up behind the man.

Grabbing his mouth, he plunged the blade hilt-deep into the right side of the man's back. Warm blood covered his hand as he yanked it out, and he stabbed in again. He struck bone; the knife didn't go hilt-deep the second time, and Squeeze felt the sting of a sliced finger. But he held the man firm, stabbed again and again.

Even though the man's mouth was covered by a glove, he squealed and thrashed, and Squeeze knew this had not gone down as silently as it needed to go.

Duff and Cruz had been waiting for Squeeze's cue, but when the man walked off into the woods, they knew they had to be ready to act.

The sound of a man crying out and thrashing instantly grabbed the attention of the three sicarios by the fire. They climbed up to their feet with varying degrees of dexterity, and all of them reached for weapons.

Josh Duffy sailed out of the darkness from behind the truck and tackled his man to the ground like a linebacker, slamming him directly into the raging campfire. The man's jacket immediately ignited; Duff had fallen to the left of the fire, but he climbed to his feet and lunged at the burning man, landing on top of him, slamming the knife into his throat as he impacted.

He rolled off, leaving the blade buried in the sicario's windpipe, and he stood up again, grabbed an AK-47, and used the buttstock as a bludgeon to bash in the dying man's face.

He then turned the rifle around, thumbed down the safety, racked a round into the weapon, and pointed it over to where he knew Cruz had been going up against two men.

But when he focused his eyes on the area, he saw Cruz standing there, a bloody knife in his bloody right hand, and two crumpled bodies at his feet.

Duff swung his weapon to go help Squeeze, but before he moved a step, he heard Charlie Six's voice. "Comin' in!"

All three Americans stood in the middle of the carnage. Squeeze had a nice cut to his pointer finger where his gloved hand had slid off the small slick hilt of his weapon, but he ignored it and let it bleed as they gathered up rifles, searched for money and car keys, and hefted backpacks and water bottles. They threw everything into the truck and started to get inside, but then Duff said, "Their clothes. Their hats. We take them."

Squeeze said, "*You* guys can play dress-up, but I ain't gonna fool nobody that I'm a—"

"Just do it."

Two minutes later the Dodge Ram turned around on the narrow track, rolling slowly, without headlights, back to Gabby and Nascar.

Nascar was loaded into the back seat with his head in Gabby's lap. Cruz crammed in next to them. Duff drove, and Squeeze sat in the front passenger seat, ready to tuck down on the floorboard and hide if they came across any traffic.

It was four in the morning when they hit the highway and began rolling north slowly, their headlights off. Squeeze took the opportunity to look through the glove compartment, and here he found paperwork showing that the owner of the car lived in Mazatlán.

Gabby gasped. "You just killed four members of the Sinaloa cartel."

Cruz quipped, "With all the hardware on them, we were pretty sure they weren't farmers."

"Including Remmick and his men," Gabby added, "this is the fourth group of enemies we have encountered this week."

Cruz said, "You're forgetting about the cops we wasted before we got into the mountains. Unreal. Five sets of assholes."

Duff drove on. "And the day is just getting started, folks."

CHAPTER 80

Nichole Duffy sat on a hard wooden chair, her upper body draped across an equally hard wooden table. Her hands were cuffed, and the restraints were themselves chained to an eye bolt in the center of the table.

Her ankles were shackled, as well, but despite all this, she had somehow managed to sleep for a few hours.

She'd not been badly treated, overall. She'd been given food and bathroom breaks. She was interrogated as soon as she arrived by a female judicial officer, a member of Mexico's state police, and although the woman had admonished the lady from the United States for punching one of her officers, she'd listened attentively when Nichole explained that her husband was up on the Devil's Spine and in desperate need of rescue.

She'd gone off to make some calls, and then when she returned, she told Nichole that she would be detained further, in this room, while they waited for someone else to come speak with her.

Nichole had no phone, no watch, and there was no clock on the wall, but considering the fact that she'd been delivered three simple meals, it felt to her like she'd been here for most of a day.

She'd not been idle in this time. Her voice was hoarse from shouting, demanding to speak with someone from the consulate, though she had no idea if there was even a U.S. consulate in this town. She further demanded that the local police send a rescue mission up the Devil's Spine, that someone from the Mexican army be brought in so she could make her case, that Armored Saint in Mexico City or in Dallas be called.

She even insisted that the young man bringing her tortillas and black beans contact the United Nations on her behalf.

The kid just shrugged. He didn't speak English and had no idea what this crazy gringa was carrying on about.

None of her efforts had amounted to any action on the part of the police, and now Nichole just lay there, draped over the table, praying for her kids back home and her husband lost up there on the mountain an hour or more to the south of her.

The door opened suddenly, and she lifted her head up, her hair falling over her eyes. If this was another meal, that would mean she'd been here a day and a half, and if that was the case, she told herself she was going to rip her hands out of the cuffs and punch somebody even if it meant breaking her wrists in the process.

But it wasn't another cop bringing another plate of food. It was a tall, good-looking man in his thirties with dark hair in a neat part, a slightly rumpled but well-made blue suit, and a regimental tie. He looked at her with curiosity, adjusted his eyeglasses, and then walked over to the table.

Behind him, a woman came through the door. She carried something under her arm, and she put it down at a smaller table in the corner, then dragged that table closer to the one where Nichole was restrained.

Looking at the device, Nichole recognized that it was a stenotype machine, used by court reporters to take dictation. The woman went back to the corner, then dragged a chair over and sat down, and the man in the suit took a seat already positioned across from Nichole.

In English, with an American accent, he said, "Mrs. Duffy. Really sorry about the delay. I know they've had you sitting here a long time." He cleared his throat and said, "Special Agent Ron Davison, FBI."

She said nothing, just looked at him through her hanging bangs.

"How are you doing?" he asked. He was polite, sympathetic-sounding even.

Nichole Duffy, however, was in no mood to be cordial. "How do I *look* like I'm doing?"

The handsome man gave her a rueful smile. "Honestly? Honestly, you look like you've had a pretty rough night. In fact, I'll go out on a limb and say you look like you got yourself arrested in Mexico and brought to this run-down jail in Chihuahua, and then you waited chained to this table for the past fifteen hours while I flew down from Phoenix."

"Is that how I look to you?"

"It is."

"Then you are extremely perceptive, Special Agent Davison."

He motioned to the woman next to him. "This is Jill. She'll be doing the transcriptions." Jill was already typing along; she didn't look up at or acknowledge Nichole.

Nichole shook her head to clear the cobwebs from sitting here alone for so long. "Look. I have to find my husband. I need the FBI to put a team together and go up to—"

"Ma'am," Davison said. "This will go much faster if you let me lead."

She stopped talking, then said, "Okay."

"You have previously told local authorities that you do not require an attorney present during an interview with them. Does that continue to be the case?"

"Why would I need an attorney? I haven't done anything."

He raised an eyebrow. "There are several witness reports stating that you assaulted a police officer."

She rolled her eyes. "That wasn't assault."

"You punched him in the face. What would *you* call that?"

She shrugged. "Poor communication skills on my part. I don't speak Spanish."

He chuckled. "Okay . . . do you assent to this interview? I'm going to need a yes or a no."

"Get on with it."

"Ma'am, that was neither a yes nor a—"

"Yes!" she yelled.

Davison sighed. "First, let me begin with my condolences regarding the death of your husband. No matter the circumstances . . . I know that this is—"

Nichole pulled on her chains as she shot up straight. "What are you talking about? He's . . . he's dead?"

Davison looked suddenly poleaxed. "Oh . . . oh my God. I only assumed they told you already. Despite your circumstances, you should have been notified first thing this morning."

She fought tears, kept her chin high though it trembled. "What? Told me *what*?"

His shoulders slumped a little. He seemed genuinely distraught. "Mexican authorities say the entire convoy of diplomats and security officers your husband was traveling with were wiped out by the Black Knights. Somewhere up in the high Sierras."

"How . . . how do they know this?"

"Armored Saint stopped hearing from the motorcade"—he looked at his watch—"forty-eight hours ago. Word filtered down from the mountain late last night, back to the army in the foothills, from locals, who said the cartel up there was involved in some sort of a battle, but the battle was over. Armored Saint says there were only twenty-two contractors on the mission in the first place, and they lost a man the first night, when they were still in the foothills. They lost four more the second night. No bodies have been recovered, except for the single contractor killed in the foothills on the first night of the mission. But the locals from the mountain said there were no survivors in the motorcade."

Nichole shook her head. "None of that proves anything. You have to go up there and look. Josh told me about the others killed, then he told me there was some sort of a setup and he was surrounded. One of his six men was dead, but the rest were still alive . . . this was Sunday afternoon."

"It's Tuesday afternoon now, ma'am, and there's been no word."

"But if you don't have his body . . . then Josh is *not* dead." Her eyes widened. "My phone. They took my phone yesterday. He would have called if he—"

"I checked your phone ten minutes ago, right before I came through that door. The only calls are from a cell phone number in Virginia belonging to Dina Alice Latham."

Nichole stopped talking. Her lips trembled. Slowly she lowered her head on the table and began to cry.

Davison gave her a long moment, then said, "Look. Mrs. Duffy. I don't think you are looking at any real time in jail down here. The federal authorities have their hands full in the area, obviously, and since you didn't actually hijack the helicopter, you are only facing a charge for the assault. I feel confident we can chalk that up to your quite reasonable emotional distress, and we can get you out of here. Probably in a couple of days, maybe tomorrow."

She didn't even acknowledge this. "What is being done to recover the bodies?"

Davison blew out a sigh. "It looks like the military will advance up to the mountain range sometime in the next three days to root out the Black Knights. They will meet resistance, for certain, but by the time they get to the high Sierras, they should have good intelligence about the location of where the motorcade was destroyed. Obviously the army's mission isn't forensic investigation; it's to win what is, essentially, a civil war, but as soon as the area is secure, I'm certain some sort of recovery operation will take place.

"These things take time, more so in the middle of a war zone, as you might imagine, so you are going to have to remain patient."

Now Nichole's head rose slowly, and she looked at Davison. "You are FBI, and you are saying I probably won't be charged by the Mexicans."

Davison cocked his head. "That's all correct."

She was still crying, but through the tears she said, "Then what are you doing here? Why didn't someone from the consulate come down?"

"I have to get a statement about everything you know about the mission. We understand from the judicial police here that your husband had been calling home every day. We'd like information about those conversations."

"Why?" she asked again.

"Ma'am. Over fifteen Americans, several other foreign nationals, two high-ranking members of the United Nations, and two Mexican diplomats have been killed, and the FBI has an interest in liaising with local officials down here to find out everything we can about the incident."

This made sense to her. Through continued sobs she said, "I'll tell you whatever you want to know."

CHAPTER 81

The truck had been a godsend for the utterly exhausted Armored Saint employees, mostly because of its comfort, allowing them to get off their aching feet, and not for the speed at which they had been traveling.

In five full hours of driving, they had covered only about thirty-five miles, a glacial pace on a blacktop highway, because they were constantly pulling the vehicle off road and into hiding places every time they saw another vehicle approaching.

They'd also actually passed oncoming vehicles, then raced off the road and taken up a defensive position in case their presence here was reported.

Each time, Duffy, Cruz, and Squeeze would get out, their stolen AK-47s at the ready, prepared to engage whoever might have seen them on the road.

Then, when it seemed the coast was clear, they would climb back into the truck, and Duff would set off again.

Still, thirty-five miles put them within forty miles or so of Creel; they were more than halfway down the mountain range now, and Gabby felt like, finally, they were in an area where the villages would be safe to pass through, unless, of course, the Zetas or the Black Knights had gotten ahead of them and were lying in wait.

They'd fed themselves with canned beans, cold tortillas, and even some hard candies they found in the bags of the sicarios, and they'd drunk bottled water. The men each chewed several individual bags of instant coffee for the caffeine, but Gabby had declined, finding the concept repulsive.

Cruz had bandaged Squeeze's finger, and Nascar was in and out of consciousness due to the effects of the morphine injections he'd been getting, but they used the last of it while they drove, so soon enough, Duff knew his Charlie Five was going to be in absolutely exquisite pain. His splints were holding his lower legs stationary, but the swelling and soft tissue damage from the breaks would be agonizing, and there wasn't a damn thing Duff could do about it except get his man some medical care.

They left the highway around nine, taking a dirt road that ran down the mountain more steeply, following a sign that announced a gas station. The Ram was on fumes, and though they didn't have any money or anything to trade other than guns, Duff was prepared to do whatever he had to do short of killing an innocent station attendant to keep this truck running.

They rounded a blind turn on the hillside and suddenly found themselves rolling through a tiny village, a few stores alongside the road, a couple dozen mudbrick houses up a hill on the left, and a forest next to a tilled field on the right.

But there were no people in sight. No vehicles. No cooking fires burning.

It was surreal, as if the entire place had been abandoned, and Gabby didn't like this one bit. "This isn't good. There should be people out during the day."

A little farther up the road, they found a gas station, and for a moment their prospects looked good, but as they rolled up into it, they saw that the pumps were turned off and the station was closed.

Duff said, "We're almost out of gas. Maybe there's a way to get the pumps working."

Gabby said, "While you do that, I will try to find a local for information."

Duff pulled around back to hide the truck. There was a small lot back here, next to the open muddy field. To Duff, the field looked like some sort of grain had been planted, and it was just sprouting up. This was a first; for the past few days all they'd seen were poppy farms.

As they sat in the truck, Duff looked around. "Gabby, I don't want you going off alone."

"Believe me, I am safer alone than I am with you."

"What about Cruz? Will you take him? He'll leave the rifle, hide his pistol under his shirt."

Cruz was dressed in a sicario's jeans, boots, and black shirt with a scorpion stitched into the back. There were cuts in the shirt at the right kidney and bloodstains, but as far as Duff was concerned, he'd fit in.

She looked over at Charlie Four. "Will you keep your mouth shut?"

Cruz said, "I barely understand the Spanish down here; I'm definitely not gonna start jawing with somebody in one of those other languages you speak."

The two of them left the gas station on foot, crossed a street, and then took a gravel path up the hill there towards a cluster of little shacks.

Duff and Squeeze broke into the gas station via a back window; Squeeze went through it and unlocked the door. They then carried Nascar and the four AKs inside and put the makeshift gurney on the floor behind the counter of the ramshackle place, and then Squeeze and Duff looked out the front window.

Squeeze said, "Pretty good concealment here, but not a lot of cover. These walls are too thin to stop incoming rounds."

"Yeah," Duff agreed. "I don't want to get into a gunfight here. I'm going to go look around to try to figure out how to work the pumps."

There was a stockroom full of boxes, and a back office not much larger than a phone booth, and Duff ducked his head in there quickly to make certain it was empty, and then he started to turn away to check the stockroom.

But he stopped, his eyes widened, and he turned back around and looked in.

There, on a messy little desk no bigger than an end table, was a telephone.

Hoping against all hope, Duff lifted the handset off the cradle and held it to his ear, and he was rewarded with the most beautiful sound he'd ever heard.

A dial tone.

"Squeeze! We've got a phone!"

"Like, a *working* phone?"

"Yeah, man. A landline."

Squeeze raced back into the office and looked at it warily. "Somebody might be tracing calls from around here. You dial for help, and we don't know who's going to come for us first, the good guys or the bad guys."

"True."

But Duff decided he had to try. He would call one number and one number only. As Squeeze went back to pull security, Duff dialed his wife. To his surprise, the international call went through, but then the phone went straight to voice mail.

"Shit," he said, and then he hung up without leaving a message. After wrestling with the decision for several minutes as to whether he should try someone else, he decided he would only trust Nikki. He didn't trust Armored Saint, he didn't trust the Mexican authorities, and he knew the more calls he made from this phone, the larger the chances that some bad actor was going to figure out where they were hiding.

With frustration anew, he went back to trying to figure out how to get some gas out of the pumps out front, telling himself he'd try Nikki again in a few minutes.

CHAPTER 82

Special Agent Ron Davison had almost wrapped up his interview by eleven a.m., which would give him just enough time to make a flight to Phoenix leaving at one thirty.

He'd yet to tell the woman across from him he'd be leaving, but he'd be sure to get her a cell with a cot and not force her to remain chained in this interrogation room another night.

U.S. Marshals would come and collect her, maybe tomorrow, maybe not, depending on how it all got worked out with the Mexican government.

Not that it looked like the woman cared anything about herself or her predicament, frankly. She only asked about her kids back home, and she only lamented the disappearance of her husband.

Davison stood up to stretch his legs and to go get Mrs. Duffy a fresh cup of coffee when he cocked his head a little. Hearing a sound outside, he walked towards the locked interrogation room door.

He turned back to Duffy and saw that she obviously heard it, too.

"It's a helicopter," he explained, assuming she wouldn't recognize the faint humming.

She just stared at him. "UH-60."

He cocked his head.

"A Blackhawk," she added, and then he nodded.

"Uh . . . if you say so. That's probably going to be Policía Judicial. State Police. Wonder if they're going to move you." He looked around. "This is a municipal holding facility, got to figure wherever the Mexican staties take you, it will be at least a little better than this. I'll discuss that with them when they get here, make sure they understand your circumstances."

A minute later the door was unlocked from the outside, and Davison, ready to do his best diplomatic moves on state cops, suddenly lurched his head back in surprise.

The new arrival was in his forties; he appeared Mexican, and he wore a suit and tie. His hair was gray at the temples, but to Nichole he looked like a formidable individual, despite his wide, toothy grin.

Nichole watched Davison as he stepped towards the new arrival. It was clear he was confused but pleased to see the man in front of him. "Oscar? Great to see you, man!"

The new arrival spoke English without any noticeable Mexican accent. "Ron! Didn't know you were up here. Good to see you. How are things in beautiful Phoenix?"

The men embraced warmly.

"All's good, man. Family's good. I haven't seen you in years."

"It *has* been too long, my friend."

Davison turned to the woman at the table and made his introduction. "Mrs. Duffy, this is my former boss in Phoenix. Supervisory Special Agent Oscar Cardoza; he got promoted several years ago, and now he runs our field office down in Mexico City."

"It's a pleasure to meet you, Mrs. Duffy."

CHAPTER 83

At eleven twenty a.m., nearly two hours after they ventured off in search of information, Tony Cruz and Gabby Flores reappeared, walking down a rough footpath across the street on their way to the gas station.

After finding the gas tanks at the station to be bone dry, Duff had been calling Nichole, getting no answer, for the past two hours, but in between these brief and futile diversions, he'd worried about his two missing teammates.

As they came through the door, he slapped Cruz on the shoulder and gave Gabby a hug that surprised her. "Shit, guys. We were worried."

Gabby just looked at him with concern, and Cruz moved quickly to an AK lying on the counter and made certain a round was chambered.

He was all business, and something was wrong.

Gabby replied, "I think you should be worried about *all* of us. The Black Knights are here."

"Here? Here, *where*?"

"I didn't think they would come this far off the Devil's Spine, but they've set a roadblock on the highway just to the north and a smaller one on this road, not far from here. All the locals have left, moved up into the hills, as far from the road as they can get."

"How did you learn all this?"

"A Tarahumara who lives higher on the hillside. He came down to ask us why we were still here. He said he heard all this from the fleeing villagers. The BKs ordered everyone into the town square at eight a.m. and asked them if they'd seen gringos. When they found out no one had, they decided they had gotten ahead of us, and they would wait here for us to arrive. They are blocking a bridge over a river less than a mile to the north."

"Son of a bitch," Duff said.

"What are we going to do, boss?" Squeeze asked.

Duff looked back to where Nascar was sleeping behind the counter. There was no way they were going to carry him up that hillside to hide in the woods, and the truck had been running on fumes already. Plus, he didn't want to leave the working telephone here at the station.

He addressed Cruz and Squeeze. "We harden this gas station. Line the front windows with boxes and crates, barricade the door. Nobody gets in unless we let them in. How copy?"

Cruz said, "We're gonna fight the Black Knights?"

Duff shook his head. "We know something they don't. The Black Knights aren't the only group looking for us."

Gabby understood suddenly. "The Zetas. The Zetas are coming, and when they get here, we won't be either group's biggest problem."

Squeeze was already pushing a display case towards the front door, and Cruz began doing the same.

Duff said, "I'm going to find something to secure the back door with. Gabby, check on Larry. While you're at it, listen for the phone."

She turned to him in surprise. "The phone? We have a *telephone*?"

CHAPTER 84

Supervisory Special Agent Oscar Cardoza stood in the interrogation room in front of Special Agent Ron Davison, but his eyes were on Nichole Duffy. She eyed him back curiously. When no one spoke for a moment, she said, "So . . . you're FBI?"

His toothy grin gleamed. "I might look like a local to you, ma'am, but I was born and bred in the great state of Texas."

Davison, Nichole realized, was still perplexed as to why the head of the FBI in the Mexican capital was way up here. "What brings you up to this little backwater? This isn't your beat."

Cardoza laughed. "Hardly. I was in the area, if you can believe it. Heard from Phoenix about your visit down here to interview the U.S. national being held in connection to that tragedy over the weekend in the mountains, and I wanted to check in and see if I could help."

"Yeah, hell of a thing," Davison said. "Mrs. Duffy's husband was one of the contractors."

"Is," Nichole said, but she was drowned out by the man from Mexico City.

"I can't imagine what you must be going through now, Mrs. Duffy. Believe me when I say we are going to do everything we can to find the missing men."

Nichole's head rose up at this, but Davison cocked his head. "*Missing* men? I'm hearing there were no survivors."

"Hey," Nichole protested.

"Sorry," Davison said. "No *known* survivors." Davison turned back to Cardoza. "Can we step outside a second?"

"Sure."

Davison looked to Nichole now. "We'll be right back."

Dryly, Nichole replied, "I'll just wait here, then."

The two men went to the door; after a knock, a judicial police officer opened it, and they stepped out into a hallway, away from others. The transcriptionist followed them out and went looking for a bathroom.

The metal door was closed and locked behind them.

When the men were alone, Davison said, "Help me understand your role in this, Oscar."

"D.C.'s got me looking into it."

"Really? I didn't get any word at all you were coming up."

"The head of the security detail who was killed in the bombing was Shane Remmick, the Navy SEAL. U.S. contractors failed to protect UN and Mexican government dignitaries. D.C. is expecting this to turn very ugly."

Davison nodded at this. "What's the thinking down in Mex City? Sinaloa cartel did it to stop the peace process?"

"No. No way. There's been no chatter that Sinaloa even knew about the peace plan. The only thing that makes sense is that the BKs lured the delegation up there, and then they attacked them."

"But . . . why would they do that?"

"They would do it as a big fuck-you to international involvement in affairs in the Sierras. Bringing law to a lawless land was an exercise in futility. The UN and the Mexican government should have known better."

Davison nodded. "Well, obviously you know more about this kind of stuff than I do." He jerked a thumb at the interrogation room. "She's insisting her husband, Josh Duffy, is still alive. Last time she talked to him on his sat phone, he was in the middle of a gunfight and was totally fucked. He admitted as much to her. The guy's obviously dead, but she won't listen to reason."

"No phone calls from down there on her cell?"

"None the last time I checked."

"When was that?"

"Before the interview." He looked at his watch. "Couple hours now. What? What are you thinking? You know something I don't?"

"Let's take another look at that phone."

Davison shrugged. "Yeah, it's locked up. I'll get the key from the jailers and double-check after I wrap up here. Trying to make a one thirty flight back home."

Cardoza said, "Actually, do you mind going to check on it now? I'd like to talk to the witness a moment."

Now the younger man cocked his head. "You want to talk to my witness?"

"I do."

"Well, Jill took a bathroom break. If you wait a few minutes, I'll let you—"

"I'd like to talk to Mrs. Duffy now, Ron."

Now Davison put his hands on his hips. "Without a transcriptionist? You ever handed over your witness in the middle of an interrogation to another agent without a transcriptionist present?"

"Can't say that I have, but a supervisory special agent, a friend, never asked me to." He let the implication hang in the air a moment before saying, "I am asking you to, Special Agent Davison."

Davison put up his hands in annoyed surrender. "All right. No need to pull rank here. It's weird, is all. It's fine. You go back in, I'll go get her phone, but I can tell you right now, hubby hasn't called because hubby is dead."

"Thanks, Ron." Oscar went back inside the room, telling the guard at the door in Spanish to keep the transcriptionist out. He stepped over to the woman at the table and sat down, facing her with a smile.

"Mrs. Duffy. I just have a few questions."

"I'm *not* starting over with another damn interrogation."

He smiled. "I checked in with the office yesterday afternoon and heard a tale about the wife of one of the security guards on the UN delegation. Seems she came down here to help her poor husband, then got picked up by the judiciales and was about to get interviewed by the FBI. I secured a helicopter this morning and came right up."

"Why?"

"If we are going to find your husband, bring him home, then we need to work together."

Her hopes rose in an instant. "You actually believe he's alive?"

"I do. In fact, I'm almost certain of it."

"Why doesn't Davison believe?"

"I know things that he does not know."

"Such as?"

"Someone killed four members of the Sinaloa cartel early this morning, stole their truck and their weapons."

"And you think it was Josh?"

"I *think*, Mrs. Duffy, that when my colleague returns with your telephone, we will have some news that we will both be pleased with. If he and his friends managed to get a truck, they could well be out of the most rugged part of the Sierras by now, which means they could have found a town with telephone coverage."

As if on cue, the door clanged open, and Davison entered with Jill.

Cardoza said, "Ah, here we are."

Davison appeared utterly astonished. "I'll be damned, Oscar. Five calls in the past two hours placed from a landline near the town of Del Cobre. I checked a map in the lobby. That's three hours' drive south of here."

"Josh called?" Nichole shrieked.

"*Somebody* called, that's all I know."

Her chains rattled as she reached out. "Give me my phone! Give me my phone!"

Cardoza said, "Calm down. We will call the number back. Together."

But Davison didn't hand it over. "Oscar . . . How did you know she'd be getting a call? Why are you here, pushing your way into my investi—"

Cardoza said, "We all three need to know what happened up there on the Devil's Spine, yes? Calling Mr. Duffy—assuming that's who we will find at the other end of the line—is in the interests of everyone in the room."

Nichole reached again. "I'll call him."

"You will call him on speaker," Cardoza said, and then he stood from the chair Davison had been using, offering it back to his junior colleague. "Ron . . . It's your case, but that would be my suggestion."

Nichole saw the older man subtly pulling rank, but her focus was on her husband.

"Yeah, okay. Sure," Davison said, and he sat down at the table and dialed the number that had been calling. While it went through, he put the phone on speaker and laid it in the center of the table.

It rang four times before it was snatched up.

The voice on the other line was scratchy, hoarse. "Nikki? Is that you?"

Nichole forced strength into her voice. "It's me, Josh. Where are you? *How* are—"

Davison leaned forward, astonishment evident on his face. "Uhh . . . Mr. Duffy, this is Special Agent Ronald Davison, FBI. It's good to hear you're alive. We just need to know where you are so we can come get you."

There was a hesitation, and then Duffy said, "A little village. I don't know the name of it. Off the Devil's Spine, halfway down the range, I guess. It's on a road a couple miles east of the highway."

Davison said, "You're calling from Del Cobre, it's right about where you specified. Does that sound right?"

"Yeah, maybe. We commandeered a truck this morning but stopped here for gas. Came across this broken-down station. There wasn't any fuel, but I found a phone."

Oscar Cardoza leaned over the table now. "Who else is with you?"

Duff hesitated a moment. "Who's speaking?"

"Supervisory Special Agent Oscar Cardoza. Also with the FBI. I am here with Davison and your wife."

With a little trepidation in his voice, Duff said, "With me is

Dr. Gabriella Flores and three of my team. The rest of the detail is dead. One of my guys, Evans, is hurt. Fractures to both legs. We've been pursued for two days overland by the Zetas. I think they're on the road just behind us. The Black Knights have a roadblock less than a kilometer to the north of us. There's going to be a big fucking battle here pretty soon, and we'd sure like to be gone when it happens."

Davison said, "One second, Duffy, I'm going to put you on hold." He looked to Cardoza. "What he said doesn't make any sense, Oscar. The Zetas are east of here. *Way* east, at the Texas border, around Nuevo Laredo."

"He's a gringo security guard. No offense to either of you. He doesn't know the difference between Los Zetas and the Sinaloa cartel and Los Caballeros Negros."

Nichole said, "If he didn't *know* they were Zetas, he wouldn't *say* they were Zetas. He told me Dr. Flores knows the area and the people, and she's right there with him."

Cardoza said, "None of this matters now. We need to get him out of that village and out of danger. We'll take the Blackhawk I arrived in, be down there in forty-five minutes."

Davison was taken aback. "We can't fly into the middle of a drug war."

"Yes, you can!" Nichole chimed in, then looked at Cardoza. "Please! You heard him, you're his only chance."

Davison said, "We've got to talk to Phoenix and D.C. and clear—"

But Cardoza tapped the mute button. "We understand, Mr. Duffy. We have a helicopter here and can be there in under an hour."

Duff was confused by this. "You're in Virginia and you can be here in under an hour?"

"No, Josh," Nichole said. "I'm down here. In Mexico."

Duffy suddenly sounded terrified. "You're here? No. No, you *can't* be. Listen to me, Nik. You can't trust *anyone*. Not even the Americans. Definitely not the Americans. We don't know who set us up. The whole thing was an attempt to steal shoulder-fired missiles and wipe out anyone who knew—"

Cardoza interrupted. "Your wife is in the hands of the FBI, Mr.

Duffy. We will take care of her and get you both back over the border. But tell me, who else have you been in contact with?"

"No one. I didn't know who might be listening in on the line. I thought I could call Nichole and she could contact the people I need to reach from up there. I didn't know she was down here."

"You've made the correct decision, sir. We think this conspiracy goes higher in the Mexican government; they could be monitoring phone calls out of the area. Stay off the phone, stay right where you are, and we will come to you."

Cardoza ended the call, but Davison was on him instantly. "*Conspiracy?* What conspiracy? What are you talking about? And what was *Duffy* talking about? Shoulder-fired missiles?"

Cardoza was official now, not collegial as he'd been before. "I'm not at liberty to explain it all to you, Ron. Not right now. We have to get the survivors out so that we have the evidence we need."

Davison reluctantly let it go. Nodding, he said, "Fine, but I'll need to coordinate with the federales to get us enough men to—"

Cardoza said, "Not necessary. I have a team with me."

"A team? A team of what?"

"Judicial police. Plainclothed. Undercover."

"But . . . why are you working with state police? Why not the federales?"

"There was no time to go through channels. Look. Duffy and his people will be overrun way before you can secure approval from Phoenix. I'm taking responsibility; your ass is covered. I'll go down with the team and extricate the four of them, be back here in an hour and a half."

Cardoza turned to Nichole now. "Your husband does not know who to trust. There are going to be multiple adversaries close by, so we need to do this quickly and cleanly. It would be very helpful, as long as you are willing, for you to come along with me to pick him up. A friendly face will reassure him."

Nichole was astonished she was being invited on the rescue mission, but she immediately said, "Of course! Of course, I'll go!"

"Excellent." Cardoza looked to Davison. "Unlock her."

But Davison did not move. "Oscar, what the *fuck* is happening here? She's *my* detainee. You can't just take her down south and put her in danger like—"

"She's a detainee of the state police of Chihuahua. She said she was willing to go. I'll have no trouble getting the cops to comply here and release her to me." Again he said, "Unlock her."

Slowly, Special Agent Davison reached for a set of keys in his pocket, but his mistrustful eyes remained on the man in front of him.

CHAPTER 85

J osh Duffy hung up the phone, stepped out of the office of the gas station, and looked through the window. The rain began falling hard and sudden, just as it had yesterday. Gazing at the storm beating down on the hillside of mud huts across the street, he watched a torrent of water race down the road like a swiftly moving stream.

Thunder cracked above them.

He told the others about his conversation with Nichole and the FBI, and the mood became ebullient, until Squeeze asked, "How are they going to land a helo in this shit?"

Duff shrugged. "I don't know. Visibility is still a couple hundred yards, more or less, though I don't know what it's like above us."

A groaning came from behind the counter, and Duff stepped around to check on the wounded man. "How you feeling, Charlie Five?"

He stopped groaning and looked up at his team leader. "Morphine helps, but I think it's wearing off."

Duff said, "We gave you the last of it. There's some Tylenol here in the gas station, we can give you that." Squeeze went to grab a box of painkillers, and Duff added, "Friendlies are inbound." He looked out the window. "Weather permitting. We'll get you to a hospital soon."

Squeeze showed up with a bottle of water and four Tylenol, then knelt down and gave them to Larry. As he did this, he looked up at Duff. "Hey, TL, you think we're gonna get into trouble breakin' into this closed-down gas station? I've been eating these Twinkie-looking things and drinking Dr Pepper."

Duff said, "You think we'll get into trouble for shooting down an airplane?"

"Yeah, well, at least that's something cool. B&E on a shitty Pemex station to steal snack cakes in a podunk corner of Ol' Méjico doesn't have the same ring to it."

Gabby watched the rain outside at the window. Duff stepped over to her now.

"I'm glad we've had you along for this, Dr. Flores. Sorry how it all turned out for your people."

"If we survive, we can tell the world what really happened."

"Yeah. Except we don't really know, do we?"

"We know Mr. Remmick was working with Los Zetas to destroy the motorcade and steal the missiles. Hopefully that's enough to save the Sierra Madres from war."

Duff squeezed the grip of the AK-47 hanging from his neck. "Hopefully."

CHAPTER 86

Nichole Duffy was led out into a light rain by Oscar Cardoza; they both now wore blue raincoats with the letters *FBI* emblazoned across the back in bright yellow. Davison wore a clear poncho he'd borrowed seconds earlier from a local cop inside the building, and he followed them out, trailing behind twenty yards or so. He wasn't going on the rescue mission; he thought Cardoza was acting like a lunatic, but still he continued behind them, all the way to the helipad, where a single Mexican judicial police Blackhawk helicopter was already spinning.

Nichole was helped inside by Cardoza, and then the Mexican himself climbed aboard.

She buckled in, then began looking around her in puzzlement.

Ron Davison arrived at the open hatch below the spinning rotor blades, and he shielded his eyes from the rain as he shouted to be heard. "You can't take off in this weather!"

Before Cardoza responded, however, Davison looked into the cabin, and he lowered his hand from his face. He was now looking at the same thing Nichole Duffy was looking at.

There were ten armed men inside the helo. The lower portions of their faces were covered with masks, like many police forces in Mexico. They carried M4 rifles, wore magazines across their chests and civilian clothing, and stared at the American man and the American woman.

Cardoza said, "The pilot tells me he can pick his way there flying below the clouds. The rain is worse over Del Cobre, but he assures me he can do it."

Davison kept staring at the masked men, who stared back at him.

Nichole spoke up now, herself yelling to be heard. "The helo is full, Cardoza. How are you going to pick up Josh and four others?"

Cardoza smiled. "A tight fit, but we'll make it work. Where we're going, we want as many men as we can take." He turned to Davison. "We'll be back."

Davison said, "And I'll be on the phone with D.C."

Cardoza shrugged. "That's fine with me. Call whoever you want."

Davison stepped closer and leaned in the side hatch, his face inches away from Cardoza's. "What the fuck are you doing, man?"

"I'm not loving your tone, Ron."

Davison shook his head, as if he'd just made a decision. "No. You aren't going anywhere. I'm going to need you to wait."

Cardoza cocked his head. "You *what*?"

"Oscar, I don't spend a lot of time down in Mexico, but I do work at the border. These guys, these aren't state police. These guys are hard-assed . . . these guys look like fucking narcos."

Cardoza showed a tired little smile. "Unfortunately, Ron, you are more perceptive than I gave you credit for."

Davison took a half step back. He turned and looked at Nichole; she looked at him with terror, and then he reached for his pistol, a SIG Sauer P226, which he carried in a shoulder holster. But the rain poncho impeded his hand getting inside his suit coat, and before he could lift the poncho and draw, Cardoza shouted a single word.

"Lobo!"

Just as Davison got his hand under the plastic covering his upper torso, one of the Mexicans next to Cardoza raised his M4 rifle and fired a burst of rounds into the special agent's chest at a range of ten feet.

Davison fell back onto wet concrete, blood spurted behind him, and the helicopter jolted into the air an instant later. It began climbing and speeding up horizontally as municipal and state police began rushing out of the detention center.

Nichole Duffy sat with her back at the rear bulkhead, facing forward, towards the cockpit. She was surrounded by armed men, and she was face-to-face with Oscar Cardoza.

He handed her a headset, which she took with trembling hands. He placed a similar set on his own head.

Once she had it on, she fought the terror she felt and spoke calmly. "You aren't FBI, are you?"

Cardoza smiled. "Oh, yes, ma'am, I am. Eighteen years, commendations to prove it. And I am a U.S. citizen. I am *also*, however, a consultant for various concerns, and I am a private businessman."

"What kind of business?"

"The kind your husband very negatively impacted two days ago. He cost me many millions of dollars, and that makes me very angry. He also killed many colleagues of mine, and that makes me angry, too." He gave a little smile. "Less angry than the money, to be honest, but still pretty angry."

"So that's why you're after him?"

"I'm after him because he has information that, if it became public, will get me killed. Plus, I will fail in my mission in the mountains, and that would get me killed, as well.

"I can allow neither of these things."

Cardoza looked out at the rain. "I've spent two days with my colleagues chasing him and his group north. Your husband and his little team stole a truck this morning, and we lost them. But I knew there was no way they could have made it all the way out of the Sierra Madres, so when I found out the wife of one of the men was here, claiming she'd been in phone contact with her husband as recently as two days ago, I had the Zetas send me a judicial police helicopter down from Nuevo Laredo to come and get you. You have changed my luck, Mrs. Duffy. I knew that if your husband was still alive up there, he would reach out to you as soon as possible." He grinned his menacing grin again. "And knowing he's contacted no one else makes for even better news.

"I'm afraid, like poor Ron back on the helipad, your husband has left me no choice. I am going to be forced to kill him."

She looked him hard in the eyes. So hard he was momentarily disquieted. She said, "No, you're not. I'm going to kill you first."

His disquiet dissipated, and he laughed now. "Tough words from a housewife."

Nichole turned away from the man in front of her and looked again into the cockpit over his left shoulder.

But Cardoza kept talking. "We will land at the gas station, and we will take him and his colleagues. We must be fast; the intelligence he provided about Los Caballeros Negros being in the area was very helpful but also very disturbing. The last thing we need is them getting involved right now, but we will use this storm to our advantage. We'll come in from the east, low, and the enemy forces a kilometer away won't even hear us until we open fire." He sniffed, looking out the open hatch at the heavy weather. "And when we open fire, we will be moments away from leaving the scene."

Nichole kept staring into the cockpit, but she said, "This had to do with missiles?"

"At one point, yes, but your husband ruined that opportunity. Now it has to do with me achieving the outcome I was hired to achieve in the Sierra Madres. Once the army invades, I will be a very rich man, and I will leave Mexico, and the United States, and never look back."

Nichole focused back on Cardoza. There was something in his tone. She said, "There's more to all this. I can hear the desperation in your voice. You *have* to leave. You are doing this out of self-preservation, aren't you?"

Cardoza regarded the woman for a long moment as the helicopter raced over the outskirts of Creel. He was clearly impressed with her powers of perception, aware he might have misjudged her as a naïve and meddling idiot for coming here in the first place.

"A few months ago the FBI opened an internal investigation into me. I wasn't supposed to know about it, but I found out. They suspect I have been working with the cartels." He waved a hand around. "Where would they get an idea like that?" After chuckling at his own joke, he said, "I've spent the last few months dreading the recall to D.C. that I was sure was coming, but then I learned of the missiles in the mountains and of the delegation being sent. And then I learned Armored Saint was coming in to protect the delegation."

He shrugged, almost apologetically. "I've used Armored Saint before for my own devices. They hire corruptible men. I met with Remmick in Dallas, we worked up a plan, and he hired his team accordingly."

When Cardoza said nothing else, Nichole asked, "And then?"

"And then, my dear Mrs. Duffy, your husband blew Remmick, one hundred sixteen missiles, and sixty million dollars out of the sky."

Now Nichole was the one to smile, but only for a second.

"That grin on your face won't last for long," the FBI man said darkly.

Cardoza looked to the man he'd called Lobo now. "Get one of your men to gag her. Tie her hands, too."

She turned away again and looked back over his shoulder, watching the pilots as they worked, until a bandanna was forced into her mouth, and another tied around it.

CHAPTER 87

Tony Cruz had found a little radio behind the counter of the gas station, and he played it softly while everyone waited. It was Bandera music, the only thing he could tune into, but it was at least a distraction from their predicament.

After a time, Squeeze said, "Hey, Gabby. You actually like this shit?"

She sat on the floor behind the counter, cradling Nascar's head in her lap. "The music? No, not really. I prefer classical. Vivaldi. Rachmaninoff."

"Then why are we listening to it?"

Nascar opened his eyes a little. "You think there's some country on there? We could crank up the Kenny Chesney."

"I'd rather listen to this," Squeeze muttered.

After a wince of pain, Nascar said, "If I could get up off this stretcher, I'd change it myself."

"If you could get up off that stretcher, I'd be back home in Philly by now."

"I told you dumbasses to leave me days ago. Don't start bitching about—"

Duff turned away from the window. "Knock it off, everybody. We've been in this together from the start. We're going to get out of it together." He stared into the rain as he said, "Except for Frenchie and Wolfson."

No one spoke for a moment, and then Cruz said, "Turn the music off."

Squeeze let out a tired chuckle. "Figured a Puerto Rican wouldn't mind a little—"

"Turn it off! I hear something!"

Duff cocked his head. "Yeah. I hear it, too."

Cruz was certain now. "Helicopter inbound. From the east."

Duff said, "They're smart to sweep around east, avoid the Black Knights to the north."

"Won't the Caballeros Negros hear the engines?" Gabby asked.

Duff looked at the storm beating down on the hillside. "Doubt it. This rain will muffle the noise at that distance, as long as they fly low."

Suddenly the sound increased; rainwater hitting the concrete in front of the gas station whipped hard against the window glass, and a large Blackhawk landed in the gravel road, some twenty yards beyond the gas pumps.

When the rotors spooled down enough for the rain against the window to lighten, Duff peered through the glass. "Gabby, what does that say?"

She stood next to him now. "Policía Judicial. State Police."

"And the emblem on the nose?"

"It's the shield of the state. I can't make it out from here."

Eight men climbed out of the open hatches of the helicopter; they wore civilian clothing and masks, and they fanned out around the aircraft in the downpour, providing security in all directions with their M4 rifles on their shoulders.

The phone in the office began ringing. Duff ran back to it.

"Yeah?"

"It's Cardoza. Come out with your people. No weapons, hands raised. We will search you for our safety and then put you on board. Standard operating procedure, I'm sure you understand."

Looking out past the counter, out the windows and into the street, he said, "You sure brought a lot of dudes with you."

He laughed a little. "Hey, man. I might have Mexican heritage, but I'm from Texas. You've spent more time in these mountains than I have. This is a scary place."

Duff nodded. "Okay. We're coming out. We'll leave our weapons here in the station. We have a man on a litter, so give us a second."

"Please hurry. The Black Knights are close."

Duff hung up. "Everybody disarm. Cruz and Squeeze, grab Nascar. I'll go out first. Gabby, you're with me. Hands raised."

Duff unslung his AK and laid it against the glass next to the door, then unholstered his Glock and put it on a cardboard display for Bimbo snack cakes. He raised both hands and pushed open the glass door with his hip, then stepped out under the awning in front of the station.

Gabby was a half step behind, and then Squeeze and Cruz, carrying Nascar, came last.

Over the sound of the rain, Squeeze said, "Those dudes are cops?"

"You know they wear masks down here," Duff said. "We're fine."

He took a few more steps; they were fifteen feet from the door to the gas station, and they were another seventy-five feet to the swirling rotors and the armed men outside the helo.

Then Gabby grabbed Duff by the shoulder.

"What is it?"

"The helicopter. I can see the emblem now. It comes from Tamaulipas State. We are a long way away from Tamaulipas."

"Well . . . maybe Cardoza flew in from there."

Behind him, Cruz said, "Nascar's getting heavy, boss."

Gabby said, "It's just that . . . Nuevo Laredo is in Tamaulipas."

"So?"

"Nuevo Laredo is the Zeta stronghold."

Duff was moving before she finished the sentence, spinning around. "Back inside!"

Duff grabbed Gabby by the arm and flung her back to the door. He got ahead of the men with the stretcher and held it open. Gabby dived in, and then gunfire erupted from back by the helicopter.

Squeeze was holding the front of the litter; he made it through the door and Larry was carried most of the way in, but then Tony Cruz lurched forward, dropped the litter, and fell down in the doorway.

He'd been shot in the back.

Duff hefted an AK, spun around towards the window, then saw that Cruz and Nascar were on the floor. Squeeze went prone as the window glass began to shatter from gunfire, and he grabbed Nascar by the arm and yanked him farther inside, away from the doorway.

Duff dropped to his knee pads, reached for Cruz, and Cruz reached out for him. Just as their hands met, a second bullet struck Charlie Four between his shoulder blades as he tried to crawl through the door. He dropped down on his face, dead in the doorway.

"No!" Duff screamed, and he rose to his feet, flipped the fire selector lever on his AK to fully automatic, and brought the iron sight to his eye. He fired a burst at the closest masked man, shooting him in the chest and sending him flying onto his back on the street.

Squeeze had a rifle now, too, and he fired bursts at men outside, as well, but so much incoming fire tore through the gas station that both men were forced back down to their knees, behind the barricades they'd built from boxes and displays.

Nascar shouted on the stretcher. "Cruz! What about—"

"He's dead!" Duff shouted, and then he slid a rifle across the floor over to Nascar on the other side of the open front door.

The man on his back took it, flicked off the safety, and aimed at the doorway.

"Shit!" Squeeze shouted. "What the *fuck* is going on?"

Gabby was down low, as well, farther back in the station, tears streaming down her face.

The gunfire stopped suddenly. Only the sound of bits of glass falling from the window to the floor was audible in their assaulted ears.

And then the telephone in the office began to ring.

CHAPTER 88

Squeeze found an opening between two stacks of boxes of motor oil so he could get eyes on the activity at the helicopter without raising his head. There was one enemy down in the street, clearly dead, and another was getting treated in the rain for a bloody wound to his hand.

Squeeze said, "I'm covering. Go for the phone, boss."

Duff crawled around the counter to the office, and he picked up the handset.

He spoke before Cardoza had a chance. "We couldn't help but notice that you just flew in from Zetaland."

There was a pause, and then, "I really can't fathom why you were working for Armored Saint. You truly are a cut above the typical security contractor type, aren't you?"

Squeeze called from his place behind the boxes. "I tally a couple of guys over by the telephone pole across the street. Can't tell what they're doing through all this rain."

Duff ignored this, and his jaw tensed. "Where is my wife?"

A low, ominous chuckle came next. "Mr. Duffy. Can you see the open hatch of the Blackhawk?"

Duff could not see from where he was, but his heart sank anyway.

And then Squeeze shouted from the front of the station again,

476

"Boss? There's a woman, hands tied and mouth gagged, in the hatch of the helo." Duff took Squeeze's tone to mean he understood this was Nichole.

"Shit!" Nascar shouted from the floor.

"Listen to me, Cardoza," Duff said as he pulled the phone out of the office, straining to see Nichole and a man holding a gun to her head, just inside the helicopter's hatch. "I don't know why you're working with the Zetas, and I don't give a shit. But if you don't release my wife, right now, I'm going to hang up the phone and start dialing numbers in the U.S. I'll put your whole damn operation on the evening news."

"I'm afraid that won't be possible," Cardoza replied confidently. "The instant this conversation ends, my men have orders to cut the phone line. This is the last call you will ever make.

"Here is what I *will* offer you, however. If you come out, along with Dr. Flores and any surviving men, you have my word that no harm will come to your lovely wife. This is checkmate, amigo. Come out now. It's the only chance she has."

Nascar spoke up from his position on the floor near the door. "Boss, if he's trying to offer us some kind of a deal, then I say we just open fire on those fuckers. He's lying, whatever he says. Your wife has a better chance in the middle of a gunfight than she does if we just drop our weps and surrender."

Duff knew Nascar was right. This man and his Zetas were going to kill every last one of them, Nichole included. But despite this, he said into the phone, "We're coming out. Give me a second to talk to my men."

"Be quick. We've made a lot of noise. Los Caballeros Negros will be interested in all the gunfire."

"I understand."

Duff hung up the phone. Waited five seconds, then lifted the handset off the cradle. As he did this, he heard gunfire outside and then an explosion.

Squeeze said, "They just shot the transformer on the phone pole."

Duff heard no dial tone. He put the phone back in the cradle.

He walked over to Gabby now. His voice bore no confidence whatsoever, but he said, "We have no choice. Me, Squeeze, and Nascar are going to shoot it out with them." He looked to the two men and said, "Don't fire in the helicopter. You might hit Nikki."

They nodded.

Back to Gabby, he said, "Get in the office. When we all go down, you just drop to your knees and put your hands in the air."

The woman shook her head. "They will torture me to death. If you all go down, I'm going to pick up a gun and use it on myself."

Duff drew his Glock pistol and handed it to her. "I'm glad to see you're thinking clearly." He looked around. "Okay . . . let's get lucky."

"Señor Duffy?" He turned back to her. She said, "We have a saying in Spanish. Creer es poder. It means . . . believing in something can make it happen."

Duff nodded. "I like that." He turned to his men. "Okay, boys. Three versus . . . nine or ten. Not the best odds, but not the worst we've faced this week. Let's start banging."

Squeeze dragged Nascar a few feet on the floor to where he could lie on his stomach, prop his AK magazine on the tile, and aim out the shattered glass front door at the men outside. Duff took the far left side of the window, and Squeeze went far to the right, and this put each man fifteen feet away from the next.

Squeeze said, "We got this."

Nascar replied, "Easy day."

"Everybody got a target?" Duff asked.

"Roger," Nascar said. "Dude to the left of the cockpit."

Squeeze said, "Guy prone in front of the tail rotor."

Duff nodded. "I'm going to drop the guy in the rear of the side hatch. Nikki looks like she's up behind the pilots."

"Count us down, boss," Squeeze said.

"Three . . . two . . ."

Suddenly the Blackhawk applied full power and lifted quickly into the air. The Zetas on the ground around it looked up at it, clearly as surprised as those in the gas station were.

It quickly began rising into the heavy rain.

There were seven men left in the street, and Duff found a new target. "Open fire!"

As the helicopter made it fifteen feet or so in altitude, Duff saw someone fall from the hatch. At first he feared it was his wife, but when the figure hit the ground and then crawled up to his knees, he realized it was the man who'd held a pistol to Nikki's head a moment before.

Cardoza had somehow fallen out of the Blackhawk.

Lobo grabbed the gringa by the back of her neck and slammed her down hard on the deck of the now-rising helicopter. He didn't know why they had launched into the air; that was a question he was going to ask the pilots in a moment. But the instant he saw the tied prisoner raise both her booted feet and kick Oscar Cardoza out the side hatch and down to the ground, he knew he had to take care of her first.

Wrestling with her, he found her to be surprisingly strong. Even though she had her hands tied in front of her, she fought viciously, until Lobo and the only other Zeta on board both slammed their rifle stocks into her head.

Below them, furious gunfire raged. The helicopter could not have been thirty feet in the air, but it banked hard to the right, throwing Lobo off balance for a moment. He righted himself, then climbed up between the pilots while his man straddled the American woman, forcing her to be still.

"What the fuck?" Lobo asked the pilots, but quickly he learned the answer. On the gravel road just in front of them, a long row of black pickup trucks raced in from the north, and men in the beds of the trucks fired, both at the helicopter and at the Zetas left below on the street.

Lobo shouted, "Los Caballeros Negros!"

The pilot turned to him. "We're getting out of here!"

"No!" Lobo shouted again, and then he put his rifle on the back of the man's head. "Not without Cardoza, and not without making sure all the gringos who can talk are all dead."

He looked outside the hatch. "Land us in that field behind the gas station. One hundred meters away."

"But Los Caballeros Negros will still destroy us."

Lobo leaned out the hatch of the helicopter and looked to the south now. "No, they won't. They have something else to worry about."

A line of pickup trucks, white and gray and silver and brown, began rounding the turn from the south, racing up towards the gas station. These were Lobo's men, and they'd arrived just in time.

CHAPTER 89

Duff fired on the Zetas in the street, but only for a second. He quickly stopped, then stared in amazement as men began falling down dead outside, more than he and his two teammates could possibly engage.

A Zeta spun to look up the road to the north, then swiveled his rifle around to fire in that direction. Instantly he was cut down where he stood.

And then Duff understood. A pair of black pickup trucks raced into view from the north; men were standing in the beds with rifles. Behind them, more trucks, and behind these, even more.

Oscar Cardoza was up on his feet, and he ran to the gas pumps. Crouching behind them, protecting himself from the north, Duff realized he had a shot at the man from his angle.

But he didn't fire. He realized that the helicopter might not come back for anyone else, but it would probably have to come back for Cardoza.

And his wife was still on that helicopter.

Gabby watched from the office as trucks appeared in front of the gas station. She took one look at them and said, "Los Caballeros Negros!"

Duff shouted now. "Where's the helo? Where's the helo?"

"It's behind us," Squeeze said. "Low still, I can hear it!"

481

Gunfire kicked up again out front. Instinctively the three men in the gas station ducked for cover, but quickly it became apparent no one was firing at them.

Duff chanced a look over a crate of Pepsi bottles and saw more trucks in the street on the left, and there were now two forces engaging each other at a range of just thirty or forty yards.

Gabby shouted over the noise. "Los Zetas!"

But Duff wasn't listening. He ran to the back of the gas station, looked out, and saw the helicopter landing in the muddy field there, roughly one hundred yards away.

They'd be after Cardoza, and Duff was going to make sure they got him.

Josh Duffy ran back towards the open front door. He shouted at Squeeze while he passed, "Get the back door open! We're gonna head that way in just a second." Without waiting for a reply, he leapt over Cruz's body in the doorway and ran forward. Staying low, using the gas pumps as a small measure of cover, he was betting on the two narco groups being so focused on each other in the road that he could reach Cardoza.

Cardoza was flat on the ground, watching the fight in the street just twenty yards away. Duff came up behind the prostrate man, kicked the pistol he held in his hand free, and grabbed him by the back of the neck. He yanked him hard back towards the gas station.

Nascar laid down suppressive fire as Duff got closer, and then Duff threw the FBI man inside, over Cruz's body and onto the floor.

Duff himself was only a step away from getting back into the station when he felt a sensation like a blow from a baseball bat to his right shoulder. He stumbled in, hit the ground next to Cardoza, and rolled in freshly spilled blood.

It was his own.

Josh Duffy knew what getting shot felt like, so he realized instantly that he'd just caught an AK round that hit the top of his shoulder and then exited.

Squeeze grabbed Cardoza by the hair and dragged him farther in, while Nascar crept to Duff. "Shit, boss, you got tagged!"

"I'm . . . I'm fine. Who's winning that fight out there?"

Nascar rolled to look out the front door, then rolled back, wincing in pain as he did so. "Nobody, from the looks of it."

"Good. We're going out the back to the helo." He then called out for Dr. Flores. "Gabby?"

Flores was there in an instant, the Glock still in her hand. "Yes?"

"You stay here with Nascar. We will secure the helicopter and then come back for you."

Nascar said, "Take her with you, I don't need her."

Duff shook his head. "We do it my way. We *will* be back."

Gabby nodded.

He pointed a finger in Nascar's face. "Don't die, that's a standing order!"

"Have I let you down yet?"

Duff took Cardoza, who was still clearly dazed from his fifteen-foot fall and his impact with the gravel road, and put his rifle in the man's back, then shoved him forward, out the back door and into the thunderstorm.

Nichole Duffy's face bled, and she felt her right eye swell, but she pulled herself up to her feet nonetheless. There were two men in the cabin of the Blackhawk with her and two pilots up front. Looking around, she saw that the one called Lobo was on his phone, his rifle held with one hand out in front of him.

She couldn't understand what he was saying, but she assumed he was communicating with his forces fighting in the street on the other side of the gas station. The other Zeta, a man no more than twenty-one years old or so, had his gun trained on a group of men who were approaching through the muddy field.

Lobo saw them, too, and he immediately put his phone down, then pushed the Zeta's gun out of the way so he wouldn't fire on them. He grabbed Nichole and pulled her out of the Blackhawk, put her on her knees, and placed the barrel of his gun to the back of her head.

CHAPTER 90

ardoza walked quickly through the muddy field with his hands up. He'd been instructed by Duffy to do both these things, and Duffy held the AK-47 in the center of his back, so he wasn't going to argue. The black man—he looked like just a kid to Cardoza—walked along with them, but his gun was high on his shoulder, already aiming at the helicopter ahead.

Cardoza saw Lobo with his rifle at the woman's head, and another Zeta foot soldier stood right next to him, in front of the Blackhawk's hatch.

As they neared the helicopter, its rotors spinning above it, Cardoza spoke to the man behind him. "That bullet wound in your back looked pretty bad, amigo."

"I've had worse."

"Really? Impressive. Well, your wife will have worse as soon as my man blows her head off."

Next to Duffy, the black man said, "I got my rifle on the dude aiming in on your old lady. Say the word and I drop that mother-fucker."

"No," Duff said, "he might still shoot her. Aim at the other man."

Squeeze kept walking forward, but his gun shifted an inch to the right. "I got him. What's the plan?"

"Creer es poder," Duff said.

Cardoza turned around and looked at him in surprise but was rewarded for it with the barrel of the AK jabbed into his stomach.

"Walk, dick."

Behind them, the constant chatter of rifle fire continued unabated. Duff knew it was just a matter of time before one force overpowered the other, and whoever won the battle would make their way over to the obvious noise of a helicopter's engine. Cardoza had allies in the street behind, but Duff himself did not, so his chances remained poor.

The three men arrived in front of the helicopter seconds later. Lobo had Nichole on her knees in the mud still, but his eyes were on Cardoza, waiting for instructions.

Squeeze said, "Well, fellas. Looks like we got ourselves a Mexican stand—"

Duff interrupted him. "Don't say it."

Squeeze fell silent.

Cardoza spoke next. "Mr. Duffy. You can't win. The Black Knights or the Zetas will be here in seconds. If it's the Black Knights, we all die. If it's the Zetas, you die. My friends here are more than able to kill both your wife, your black friend, and you before—"

Cardoza stopped talking suddenly when he noticed the two Zetas in front of him look away for an instant, back behind Duff and Squeeze and Cardoza.

Duff saw it, too, and more importantly, he saw their rifles move, rising at some new threat behind.

Duff assumed the Black Knights were coming through the field behind the gas station, and they would all be cut down in seconds, but he didn't look back to confirm this. Instead, he just shoved Cardoza out of the way, shifted his aim towards Lobo, and shouted to Squeeze. "Now!"

Both Americans fired. Duff shot Lobo through the bridge of his nose, snapping his head back and slamming him against the fuselage of the helicopter. His body dropped down by the tires.

Squeeze's round took the Zeta in the forehead; he also slammed into the side of the Blackhawk, then fell face-first into the mud.

Cardoza crawled through the rain for Lobo's rifle on the ground, just feet away from him. Duff shot him in the back of his right thigh, and then Nichole dove onto the rifle, scooped it up, and pointed it at the wounded FBI man in the mud next to her.

Only now did Duff turn around to see what had drawn the attention of the Mexicans. Assuming it to be attacking Black Knights, he instead found himself looking at Gabby Flores behind the wheel of the blue Dodge Ram they'd stolen from the Sinaloans early that morning, with Nascar sitting up in the truck bed, a rifle in his hands aiming at the helicopter.

They were halfway across the field and racing closer.

His wife's voice shouted over the gunfire. "They're taking off!"

Duff turned around to see the Blackhawk lifting into the air. Squeeze held his rifle with one hand, leapt over Cardoza and Lobo, and ran past Nichole, then vaulted into the cabin of the helicopter when it was just a couple of feet above the ground.

Duff and the others just watched from below as the aircraft rose twenty feet or so above them, and then it just hovered there for several seconds.

And then it lowered back down again.

Everyone moved back a few feet except for Cardoza, who writhed in pain in the mud. A big rear tire put down within two feet of his head.

Once the Blackhawk landed and those on the ground could view the inside of the cabin, they saw that Squeeze had a rifle to the pilot's head and a pistol to the copilot's head.

As the Dodge Ram skidded to a stop, Duff turned to help Nascar out from the back. He tried to lift him onto his back, but the bullet wound on his right shoulder made him cry out in pain.

Duff dropped to his knees in the mud, feeling the effects of blood loss now for the first time.

Nichole climbed into the helicopter, took both weapons, and told Squeeze to help her husband. She held the guns on the pilots while he leapt out and hefted Nascar onto his back, and together, with Gabby helping Duff back to his feet, all four of them moved to the helicopter.

While Nichole covered the flight crew, she glanced out the helo back towards the gas station.

"Oh, shit," she muttered softly.

A row of pickup trucks were racing across the little parking lot, all heading for the Blackhawk.

She began to yell to the others to hurry on board, but the pilot and copilot exchanged glances with each other, taking her distraction as an opportunity, and they pulled nine-millimeter pistols from their shoulder holsters and swiveled around to raise them to her.

Nichole saw the movement, spun back around, and pressed both triggers.

She shot both pilots dead as a dozen pickup trucks closed on them.

CHAPTER 91

Josh Duffy rolled onto the deck of the helo next to Nascar and Squeeze, and Gabby climbed in behind. Squeeze had already begun firing on the approaching trucks with an AK he picked up from one of the dead Zetas; the noise was incredible, and hot spent shell casings bounced all over Duff's prostrate form.

Nascar sat up and got into the fight, too, dumping a full magazine at the vehicles looming down on them.

But Duff didn't fight. He just looked around for his wife, realized she wasn't in the cabin, then looked up at the front of the helo.

From his vantage point he could see that the man in the left seat was slumped forward; blood had splattered the windscreen in front of him. He couldn't see the other seat from where he lay, but before he could shout his wife's name, gunfire began ripping into the cabin from the trucks. He looked back and saw even more black trucks passing the gas station and heading this way, and still he had no idea where his wife had gone.

Suddenly the pitch of the Blackhawk rotors changed, and it lifted into the air. He screamed, terrified Nichole was being left behind.

"Nikki! Nikki!" He didn't have the energy to stand up, so he just yelled where he lay.

Gabby Flores crawled across the deck to him. "Your wife . . . she's flying the helicopter!"

"Wha— She's *what*?"

Squeeze fired his last magazine out the side hatch as they flew off, then looked to the front of the helo. Glancing down at Duff for an instant, he said, "Tell me she knows what she's doing!"

Duff couldn't answer that question. As far as he knew, she'd never flown a Blackhawk in her life, and she hadn't flown *any* helicopter in more than five years.

But they were in the air, up in the clouds, and the gunfire that had been whipping past them in the cabin had ceased.

Squeeze found a medical kit in the judicial police helicopter, and he crawled over to Duff. "Shit, boss. Back of the shoulder. Blew out some meat. You ain't gonna be pitching for the Phillies anytime soon, but I can stop the bleeding, at least."

He wrapped the wound tight, then helped Duff to his knees. Duff began to crawl across the cabin to just behind the pilots' seats, and Squeeze helped him do this.

Duff arrived, reached out, and put his left hand on his wife's shoulder. He saw the blood on her face, and her right eye was all but swollen shut, but he also saw the steadfast determination she exhibited anytime she did anything. She was fully concentrating on her work now.

Duff had to shout to be heard. "Can you get us home?"

Still looking at instruments and the windscreen, she said, "Would you settle for 'away from back there'?"

"I would *definitely* settle for that."

"Good. Then as long as I don't hit a mountain, I won't disappoint you."

Before he asked, she said, "The whole way down here from Creel I was studying the pilot and copilot. I've got this pretty much figured out." She shrugged a little. "I think."

She quickly looked back at him. "Jesus. You've lost some blood."

"I'm fine."

"I really wish you'd stop getting shot."

"That makes two of us." Duff cocked his head suddenly. "Who's watching the kids? Please tell me they aren't down here, too."

She shook her head. "Dina has them. By the way, you're going to be cutting Phil's yard for a hundred years."

Duff laughed at this. "I'll start next Saturday."

Still concentrating on her flying, she said, "Even Phil and Dina will give you a week off with a bullet wound to your shoulder."

Duff smiled. "I love you."

Nichole smiled back, mouthing the words to him as she managed her controls.

Behind him, however, Duff heard Nascar shout from where he lay on the deck. "I love you, too, boss."

They flew on, just above treetop level, descending the hills towards the flatlands of Sonora as the rain began to slacken.

Three miles behind the fleeing helicopter, a man crawled on his hands and knees through the mud of a freshly planted wheat field, grunting and groaning with every excruciating inch. The bullet wound in his thigh was agonizing, and he had no chance of putting any weight on the leg at all, so standing up and running away was out.

He'd heard the gunfire, and he'd heard the helicopter take off, and then he'd heard the trucks pull up behind and men climbing out cursing. But he kept crawling. Twenty-five yards, fifty yards, his face and chest and arms and legs completely covered in thick viscous mud.

He was just a dozen yards or so from the wood line when he felt a sudden pressure on the back of his leg, right on top of his gunshot wound. He screamed out, both in pain and in terror, and then he looked back over his shoulder.

Five men from Los Caballeros Negros stood there. Rifles in their hands. Black silk shirts, mustaches, and sheer malevolence on their faces. They picked the older man up out of the mud and slung him into the bed of a pickup truck that had pulled up to collect him. Some of the men jumped in back with him, and as soon as the truck started rolling back towards the road, one of their number leaned down close to the wounded man's face.

"When we kill you, you'll go to hell, but you'll thank us just the same, because hell is going to be so much nicer than what we have in store, amigo."

Supervisory Special Agent Oscar Jesus Cardoza Ortega closed his eyes and tried to picture his beautiful island near Tahiti, but in his mind's eye, he could see nothing beyond the Devil's Spine.

EPILOGUE

The hot water cascaded down the man's body; soap got in his eyes briefly, but he blinked it out, let it wash down the drain.

Josh Duffy braced himself up in the shower with his left hand, stood on his right leg, and turned off the water.

Seconds later he reached out past the curtain and felt around on the vanity for his prosthetic leg and rubber sheath, but when he found nothing, he called out.

"Nikki! Where's my leg?"

"Mandy's bringing it!"

Duff wrapped himself in a towel, opened the shower curtain, and found his daughter running in from the tiny hallway, his lower limb in her hand.

"Mommy said it was stinky. We cleaned it up."

Duff grinned at his beautiful five-year-old. "You guys take such good care of me."

Mandy laughed, handed over the leg, and skipped out of the bathroom.

All alone again in the bathroom, Duff's broad smile remained.

———

Fifteen minutes later he was dressed in a coat and tie; he'd combed his hair carefully since the incision from his second shoulder surgery had not yet healed, and then he came out into the living room.

Nichole was there on the couch with the kids, all sitting in front of the TV. She saw her husband and motioned to the screen, then said, "Hurry, you're going to miss it."

It was the news, another story about the events in Mexico that Duff had been in the middle of just four weeks earlier. The stories were slowly getting more and more accurate, he'd noticed, and the less sensational of them were actually somewhat informative.

The screen cut from stock images of the rugged Sierra Madres to the United Nations building in New York City, and Duff smiled when he saw Dr. Gabriella Flores—who looked so utterly different in a blue dress, designer eyeglasses, and her hair down and coiffed—as she addressed a committee of the world body.

Duff sat down, marveling at Gabby's change in appearance, and only after several seconds did he tune into her words.

"I wish to personally thank you, from the bottom of my heart, for this opportunity to speak with you today. More importantly, I would like to express the gratitude my nation has for your approval of the peacekeeping force that will be securing the mountains. It will be a difficult challenge—I know this firsthand, of course—but the lives that will be saved with your intervention cannot possibly be counted."

Nichole reached over Harry and held Josh's hand. He squeezed it back and looked at her. The last faint graying around her right eye had cleared up, and she appeared to be one hundred percent healed.

Which was more than he could say for himself. His shoulder was stiff and sore; the two surgeries were both successful, but it would be some time before he'd be able to get back to work.

Just as he looked at his wife, she looked at him. She said, "Babe, we've got to get you a new suit before your next interview. No offense, but on CNN yesterday, you looked like a mall cop."

Duff laughed. "I hate to break it to you, but I *am* a mall cop."

She shook her head. "You were. Now you are a celebrity."

He just shook his head now, and his happy mood evaporated. Nichole saw it registered on his face. "What is it?"

Duff shrugged, but only with his left arm. "They've got me on CNN, Fox, then NBC later today. They're treating me like I'm some kind of hero."

"You *are* a hero," Mandy said.

Duff smiled at her, then looked back at his wife. "Tony Cruz. Jean François Allard. Scott Wolfson. I couldn't bring them home alive. I'm no hero."

Nichole shooed the kids into the kitchen, telling them they could have a snack. Then she moved closer to her husband. "But you made it out with three people who could not have survived without you. And you made it out with the truth, and that will save so many others."

He didn't brighten much. She kissed him, then said, "I got a text from Larry this morning."

Now Duff brightened. "How's he doing?"

"That tough son of a bitch is walking. Driving his physical therapists crazy down in Houston, but he says he'll be out of the hospital later this week."

"That's awesome. I need to reach out."

"No, you don't. He and Darnell are coming to D.C. just as soon as he's released. They're going to be deposed by prosecutors at the Justice Department."

"Who's Darnell?"

She belted out a laugh. "Darnell Brockington." She laughed again. "Squeeze."

Duff chuckled at this himself. He had no idea the Marine even had a name.

"Anyway," she continued. "Armored Saint is toast. It's a good thing we got our lawsuit filed before the government prosecutes them."

"It's funny," Duff said. "I got into this whole thing because of money, but now money is the last thing on my mind."

She nodded. "Yeah. We have each other. We have the kids. We have everything we need."

They embraced for a long moment, and then she added, "And we have eight thousand three hundred and thirty dollars."

Duff lurched back in surprise. "We do? How?"

"Armored Saint sent a check. Came today. They are paying you for five days' work." She rolled her eyes. "What a bunch of assholes."

Duff shrugged. "I'll call the other guys, make sure they got paid." He sighed a little. "The lawsuit is a long shot, babe, you have to know that. Could drag out for years."

She nodded. "Yeah, probably will."

Duff said, "I'm worried about finding work, Nik. Let's face it, one-legged bodyguards aren't exactly in high demand these days."

His wife held both his hands and faced him now. "You just worry about getting healthy again. Let me worry about everything else. The money Armored Saint paid will keep a roof over our heads and food in our family's bellies. Considering everything that's happened, I think we should be grateful for that much right now."

Duff nodded; they embraced again, then looked back to the TV screen. Gabby Flores finished her comments by thanking the six American security contractors who helped her survive the mountains so that she could tell her story to the world. She named them all, first the three who died, and then the three who survived, finishing with Josh Duffy.

Loud applause followed; she thanked the assembly again and left the dais. Glancing into a camera as she passed it, she smiled.

ACKNOWLEDGEMENTS

I would like to thank Allison Greaney, Trey Greaney, Kristin Greaney, Josh Hood (JoshuaHoodBooks.com), Rip Rawlings (RipRawlings.com), Steve Feldberg, Jack Stewart (JackStewartBooks.com), Don Bentley, (DonBentleyBooks.com), Brad Taylor (BradTaylorBooks.com), and J.T. Patten (JTPattenBooks.com). Thanks also to Dave Marris, Mike Cowan, Jon Harvey, Barbara Peters, and Mystery Mike Bursaw.

A very special thanks to James Yeager, Jay Gibson, and all the incredible staff at Tactical Response (TacticalResponse.com).

My warmest appreciation goes to my agents, Scott Miller at Trident Media and Jon Cassir at CAA; my editor, Tom Colgan; and all the other remarkable people at Penguin Random House: Sareer Khader, Jin Yu, Loren Jaggers, Bridget O'Toole, Craig Burke, Jean-Marie Hudson, Christine Ball, Claire Zion, and Ivan Held.

COMING FEBRUARY 2023

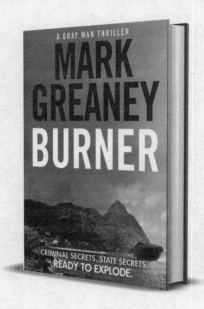

Court Gentry is caught between the
Russian mafia and the CIA in the latest novel
from the new king of the electrifying
non-stop action thriller.

*When you kick over a rock, you never know
what's going to crawl out.*

AVAILABLE TO PREORDER NOW